W9-CEI-878

BEYOND THE STARS

AN EPIC OF THE AMERICAN WEST

David William Ross

SIMON AND SCHUSTER
New York London Toronto Sydney Tokyo Singapore

Simon and Schuster
Simon & Schuster Building
1230 Avenue of the Americas
New York, New York 10020

This book is a work of fiction. Names, characters, places and incidents are either the product of the author's imagination or are used fictitiously. Any resemblance to actual events or locales or persons, living or dead, is entirely coincidental.

Designed by Levavi & Levavi
Manufactured in the United States of America

1 3 5 7 9 10 8 6 4 2

Library of Congress Cataloging in Publication data

Ross, David William, 1922–
Beyond the stars: an epic of the American West/
David William Ross.
p. cm.
1. West (U.S.)—Fiction. 2. Indians of North America—Fiction.
I. Title.
PS3568.084318B49 1990
813′.54—dc20 90-30014
CIP

ISBN 0-671-70314-5

To all those whose love for me
has made my life possible.
—D.W.R.

CONTENTS

Principal Indian Characters

PAWNEES:

- White Buffalo Horse, ancient leader no longer on tribal council
- Red Legs, one of tribe's active war leaders
- Lame Fox, a young Pawnee

CHEYENNES:

- Black Water, war chief of the Cheyennes
- White Fringe, young warrior killed on the Sweetwater

SIOUX:

- Red Moon, respected war chief of the Brules
- Strikes-His-Enemy, companion and counselor of Red Moon
- Coyote-Singing, son of Strikes-His-Enemy
- Hawkfoot, a war leader of the Brules
- Big Blood, a war leader of the Brules
- Gray Owl, chief of the Oglala
- Blue Buffalo Robe, chief of the Hunkpapas
- Stone Maker, chief of the Minneconjous
- Wandisapa, war leader of the Minneconjous
- Diving Hawk, Sioux warrior captured by the Crows

	White Man's Medicine, killed by Crow Warrior Black Shield
ARAPAHOS:	Fighting Eagle, chief of the Southern Arapahos
	Medicine Fox, adopted son of Fighting Eagle, taken from the Osage
	Blue Jacket, son of Fighting Eagle
	Little Hand, war chief of the Arapahos
	Hawk, a war leader of the Arapahos
	Bold Heart, old wise man of the Arapahos
	Yellow Tongue, a young chief of the Northern Arapahos
CROWS:	Ironfoot, warrior, now minor medicine man
	White Tail, chief of the Crows
	Big Owl, war chief of the Crows
	White Bead, Crow maiden, mate of Marcher, mother of Beaver
	Blue Lodge, Crow widow, mate of White River, mother of Chipmunk
	Spotted Horse, chief of the River Crows
	Black Feather, warrior from River Crows
BLACKFEET:	Jumping Calf, chief of all the Piegans
	Blood-on-His-Moccasin, war chief of the Piegans
	War Belt, respected warrior of the Piegans
	Long Otter, greatest scout of the Piegans
SHOSHONES:	Rising Hawk, war chief of the Shoshones
	Far-Away-Storm, young warrior of the Shoshones

Until the very twilight of their independent existence, the western Amerindians continued to kill each other more than they killed white soldiers; there was no stage of the European-Indian wars in which the whites lacked willing, bloodthirsty allies. . . . All tribes had an ethos of violence—there were no Amerindian pacifists.

Comanches: The Destruction of a People
T. R. Fehrenbach

PROLOGUE

He came along the river front with the sun over the far shore, watching the speckled bronze shaft of light it laid across the muddy water to its setting point. He was a tall man, his body gaunt, his face covered with a dark scrub of beard half hiding the lean and sharply angled jaw, making him look older than his twenty-six years. Like all hunters who worked the upper Missouri, his clothes were badly stained and frayed, his homespun pants bound with strips of buffalo hide around the lower legs to protect them from the underbrush. He wore a slouch hat tilted over the coarse black coat that hung loose enough to show a heavy gun tucked in his heavy belt. He was moving slowly now, almost hesitantly, as though unsure of his destination.

Abruptly, the river path ran out at the dock area with its rotting wharves and moss-covered pilings. Here a group of drunken river hands blocked his way, arguing abusively over a cask of whiskey stolen from a lone bateau that had just been poled up the river from St. Louis. He knew them for the human vermin they were, pirates bred by the untamed river. Two of them brawled viciously in his path. Others were moving toward them, but noticing him they suddenly halted, shifting awkwardly, a few staggering back to open a space around him. He stood motionless until the two brawlers turned and saw him too. They lurched away slurring a string of oaths. He moved on again, his deep-set hazel eyes sweeping ahead to a stretch of river bank that opened in a grassy shoal between two docks. Around some beached pirogues and light canoes squatted a line of dark ferret-eyed breeds, spawn of renegades red and white. These he looked over more carefully, these drifters who chopped off the heads and hands of their victims to destroy their identity before consigning them to the river. Noticing him standing above them, some of them shifted about. A few tried to engage his stare, but in the end it was they who looked away.

He had to wonder why he had come back—not because it was here on Whiskey Hill that he had killed three men, but because this place reminded him with renewed agony of the man whose death had brought him here only a year ago.

He turned away from the river and lifted his gaze to a row of saloons perched high on the embankment. His eyes swept their paint-chipped and sun-blistered signs, but he had no need to read their names. His destination this night was the same as before.

Only a few days ago he had escaped a Sioux ambush on a hide train he had hired aboard—one of just three of its twelve men to survive—and this morning, on a landing a few miles north of Independence, bone-weary and finding himself again down to nothing, he had struck a deal with a man who in some ways could have passed for the devil.

He started up the embankment toward the saloons. A handful of Kaw Indians, most of them torpid with drink, lay sprawled beneath their blankets in the narrow roadway before the row of bars. A few squaws, pockmarked and lice-ridden, sat dumbly beside them. Above these a sizable crowd of noisy half-drunks lined either side of the nearest saloon's entrance, some of them balancing on wooden boxes that served as seats, bracing their boots against the hitching posts. A few of them nodded as he went by, but most of them stared stonily ahead.

The saloon's swinging doors were gone, long since victims of some patron's violence, but as his tall frame rose to fill the vacant archway, the setting sun behind him thrust his lengthening shadow across the rough plank floor till it reached the feet of two clean-shaven and well-dressed men standing expectantly at the bar. Everything about them said they were Easterners, that they were waiting, were bothered, perhaps even angered by the squalid setting they found themselves in.

"Mr. Marcher?" he asked casually, using the only name he had been given.

One of them stepped forward. "Yes, I'm Marcher . . . André Marcher." The man spoke hurriedly and quickly extended a smooth but surprisingly powerful hand. He was tall, like the other, had light brown hair, blue eyes, and something both forceful and wary in his manner. He gestured to his companion. "This is my brother, Ben Amiel," he said, but his eyes stayed with the newcomer. His brother—half brother, he remembered Fess telling him—had brown eyes and dark hair streaked with gray. More relaxed, his handshake, if less powerful, was far more convincing as a greeting. They were handsome men. It was a family that clearly enjoyed strong bodies and good looks. "Quality folks," Fess had said. "One from Virginia and t'other from Washington, and both riding the best horseflesh I've seen in these parts for some spell."

He nodded at the brothers without expression. "Mr. Marcher. Mr. Amiel."

Marcher's eyes were still on him. "And what might your name be, friend?"

"White River."

Marcher was silent for a moment. "White River," he repeated slowly. There was an awkward moment of silence, then Marcher said, "Is that an Indian name?"

"It's a name."

"Perhaps Mr. River would care for a drink," said Ben Amiel, sounding more congenial.

The bartender had ambled down beside them. "Ev'ning, White River," he said, bobbing his head in a gesture that could have passed for respect.

White River nodded.

"Whiskey?"

He was still feeling the dulling aftereffects of Fess's mash. A bracer might help. He nodded again, this time to the glass.

The two brothers had taken in this exchange and now pulled back from the bar and assumed more relaxed positions.

"Mr. Fess did not inform us you were Indian," said Marcher, faintly cordial.

Downing his drink, White River snapped back, "I'm not."

Ben Amiel cleared his throat sharply, but Marcher seemed unable to stop himself. "Then you do have a proper name."

"This one suits me fine."

The older brother pointedly leaned in front of the other. "I think we should be discussing our travel plans with Mr. River. He was good enough to come here this evening. I'm sure he has some questions we can answer. Speaking for myself, I have a thing or two in mind I'd appreciate his opinion on."

White River took a quick glance around. He had noticed the strange cloud of silence hanging over the normally raucous crowd when he entered. More than one tough had been watching the well-dressed strangers over his glass. When White River appeared, their feral eyes began shifting away. Without comment he motioned to the brothers to pick up their drinks, and together they moved to a far table.

Once settled, Marcher, sitting up close to the table, was the first to speak. "Mr. Fess told us you know this country like a native and should be able to get us to that Platte island without trouble."

White River thought back to the meeting on that landing with Fess this morning, still drained from his ordeal, drinking Fess's mash whiskey and listening to him talk about easy money to be made. That was the thing about Fess . . . dressed as if for the mayor's funeral and smoking tobacco that smelled enough like perfume to make another sniff at it and feel small and deprived, while White River stood in his filthy and sodden clothes, lucky not to be in some Sioux camp watching his limbs being roasted one by one over a slow fire. The whiskey had quickly masked his exhaustion as he braced against a piling listening to Fess tell about two Easterners who had a map that led to a grave somewhere deep in Sioux territory. Apparently the grave contained something that made it worth finding again, though Fess made the whole thing sound more like two bereaved heirs searching for an old homestead. "Had two of my best men ready for a fact, all set to handle the whole thing, and then, by golly, something came up and they had to leave town and push on ahead. But they'll be waiting for you on that island up the Platte. They'll take these gents on from there and you're just naturally shut of 'em for good—and two hundred richer to boot." Two hundred gold! That hide train was gone and with it his pay, his only horse, his threadbare belongings. It galled him to admit it now, but Fess had known his man. He was down to only the grub he could shoot, and figuring as much, Fess had been waiting for him on that landing.

White River looked up at Marcher. "What else did Fess tell you?" he muttered, noticing the well-groomed clothing and soft, polished boots of the brothers and becoming conscious for the first time of his own soiled, coarse-fitting outfit. Amiel seemed indifferent to the contrast, but Marcher's eyes shifting over his crumpled coat said something else.

"We know there's been some Indian trouble lately, but Mr. Fess said it sounded more serious than it was. In any case, he felt the army should have things settled shortly."

White River half mumbled his next words, his resentment for Fess taking hold of him. "For a gent who's never been in any honest-to-God Injun trouble, Fess sure seems to shine at settin' other people straight about it."

Before Marcher could reply, Amiel said, "Mr. Fess assured us he is completely familiar with conditions in and around Sioux territory. Apparently he is privy to secret army reports."

White River couldn't help wincing at the notion of the army assisting Fess, a man half of Missouri knew had his bloodied if invisible hands behind stage ambushes, acts of violent piracy, even murder. Fess was the smooth forward paw of a corrupt band of land speculators, smugglers, and a dangerous covey of thugs. For a moment he thought of warning these two, but people who messed with Fess ended up inside Missouri catfish. Clearing his throat uneasily he said, "Seems ole Fess told you a heap of things. Did he happen to tell you that where you're going is God Almighty dangerous country?"

Marcher could no longer restrain himself. Pushing his brother aside, he snapped, "Are you telling us you're not interested in taking this job?"

White River let out a small sigh. No, that's not what he meant, not with the promise of two hundred gold when they reached the island . . . enough of a stake for a man to build himself a landing, outfit a hide train, even start a small hauling business. He'd told Fess he'd do it, but all day it had troubled him, having had to make a deal with that scum, especially tonight returning to this place and having to think back on Buzz Matlock. Buzz had always taught him a man could be read by the company he kept, often saying "Sin rubs off just like soot." Well, Fess was out of it now and White River was in it. His deal was with these two Easterners and their crazy scheme to find an unmarked grave in hostile country where a man would have trouble finding a tomb atop a butte with funeral pyres around it. And yet maybe this was his chance. Maybe he could make it to that island without crossing any Sioux. Maybe. Suddenly he felt dog tired. He wanted to get this meeting over with. "Gentlemen, about this island we're headed for up on the Platte . . ."

Marcher straightened in his seat with the trace of a smile. "Exactly, and we'd like to hear what your plans are for getting there. I assume you've brought some sort of map."

"We won't be needing any maps. Maps don't tell you where you're likely to be ambushed and murdered. Fact is, we'll have to cut our own trail. T'would be quicker along the river, but with war parties scouting the bluffs it'd be the most dangerous way to travel. I figure our best chance is to stay well south of the river, holding to ground that should be safer but sure won't be easy to cross. So we'd best try 'n fetch some help."

"Help? What kind of help?" asked Marcher.

"Injuns. Pawnees if we can get 'em."

"Mr. Fess said you knew this country like the back of your hand," declared Marcher. "Now you tell us you need help?"

Ben Amiel waved Marcher to silence. "Suppose you let Mr. River finish."

White River rubbed the stubble on his cheek as he spoke. "Mr. Marcher, one thing you oughta know here and now. When a man's trying to stay alive in Injun country he can't get enough help. Walk into any Sioux lodge and you'll see plenty of skulls of folks who could have used more help. The Pawnees have been fighting Sioux long afore white men got in their way. There's some rough and untracked country to cross. Getting you across it safely is my business, and in my business most folks allow stayin' alive helps stayin' in business."

Ben Amiel looked strangely relieved. "We're ready to follow your directions, Mr. River."

"Well, a few things better be said before we start. Fess tells me you're well armed."

"We've both brought two of the new Henry repeating rifles," said Marcher. "They're extremely effective weapons."

"Well, that can't hurt, but don't start shootin' till I tell you something needs shootin' at. Noise travels out there and most redskins like to know what's causing it. We'll carry extra water, but don't waste any. War parties worry less about how long you can fort up if they can cut you off from water. If you're bringing money, 'specially gold, don't bring more than you need till you get back. There's not much law out there, and there are whites more dangerous than Sioux when it comes to smelling gold, 'specially on that island you're headed for."

Marcher regarded White River with an uneasy frown. "And just what do you mean by that, Mr. River . . . what about that island . . . is it the men on it?"

White River shrugged. "Oh, I guess they're no worse than you're gonna find in any bunch out there. But no better either. Don't forget that island is just an island, it ain't a regular settlement. Only reason folks are a-squattin' there is to fort up with enough guns to scare off big parties of Sioux. Most of them won't pay you no heed, but there's a few that wouldn't be there if they could mosey over here without chancing a meeting with some U.S. marshal with two eyes and a passable memory."

Marcher's frown deepened as he turned to his brother, at which Amiel, clearing his throat, appeared to take over as spokesman. "We appreciate your frankness, Mr. River. You have advised us candidly on what to expect, but we've gotten the impression that your feelings about Mr. Fess are rather different from ours. Frankly, he has impressed us with his connections and considerable influence in this town. You must know . . . he must have told you . . . that once we get to that island he has two men there who are going to guide us to the completion of our journey."

White River looked down, recalling Fess's fleeting reference to two of his "best men" who had to leave town "when something came up." What "came up" was likely a sheriff with a posse. "Two men, eh? Did they happen to have names?"

"We're to meet a Captain Josh," said Amiel. "He's reputed to be very experienced and quite competent. He and his partner were up in that area when the military closed the trails and they were unable to return. Fess, by some arrangement he has with army couriers, got word to them to await us there."

Confused, White River was on the verge of asking Amiel to repeat himself, but then he knew that what he had heard was all too clear: Fess had convinced these greenhorns their guides couldn't return because the military had closed the trails, when any local could have told them the trails were closed only for wagon trains carrying families or stage coaches carrying civilians. Armed men traveling at their own risk could go anywhere they chose. There was an awkward moment as White River rubbed his forehead.

"You know this Captain Josh?" asked Marcher.

"No." He frowned, trying to shake off the effects of exhaustion, whiskey, and his loathing for Fess. "Gentlemen," he said, his voice now lower but more resolute, "I think you'd best get Fess to tell you a lot more about this Captain Josh, where he came from, and how he happens to be a guide in Sioux territory. I've been pounding horseflesh over this spread of country most of my life, riding scout for the army and huntin' every stretch of river, and I never heard tell of him."

An uncomfortable silence followed, broken only when Amiel, fixing his eyes on White River, said, "Are you telling us something is wrong?"

"I'm telling you to corral Fess and find out who this Captain Josh is and what brand he's wearing."

Again the brothers exchanged glances. Amiel brought his elbows forward on the table, moving his glass away before he spoke. "I'm afraid that's impossible, Mr. River. We received a note from Mr. Fess this afternoon saying he would be out of town for several days. He indicated that since we were now dealing with you, his presence would no longer be needed. I might say he stated again he had full confidence in your ability to guide us safely to that island."

White River almost laughed. He should have figured that swill-sucking Fess would light out as soon as he'd pulled this filthy deal together. One way or the other he was going to rob these men and now White River was part of his plot. He drew his head back and glanced around the saloon.

"You say you don't know this Captain Josh or anything about him?" demanded Marcher.

"That's right, I don't. Nary a thing."

"Then what makes you think anything is wrong? If he works for Mr. Fess, he should be reliable."

White River bit his lip in irritation. Reliable? There were gents around Fess who would kill you for practice. "Look, Mr. Marcher, I may not be able to advise you myself on what you ought to be doing before you chance traveling, but I think I know a fellow who could. There's a U.S. marshal here in Independence who might be downright anxious to chat with folks just like yourself. Could be he'd have a fair bead on this Captain Josh. I'd make his acquaintance first chance I got if I was you."

Both Amiel and Marcher shifted uneasily in their seats until Amiel replied, "I'm not sure that's a very good idea, Mr. River. You see, when we first planned this venture Andy tried to make our arrangements from Washington, only to be told the territory we're planning to enter isn't open to civilians such as ourselves. We knew there would be risks, but unfortunately we didn't know that what we were intending to do was now, because of some recent treaty, against the law. That bit of bad luck explains, as I probably needn't tell you by now, our dealings with Mr. Fess. Still, whatever he's up to, if he is scheming, it's hard to see the wisdom of drawing the law's attention to our interest in entering Sioux territory." White River could only stare blankly at the man. "You see," Amiel continued, his voice growing more diffident, "we are looking for a lost grave, and this search is neither an impulsive nor sentimental venture. We've staked a great deal on finding it."

"We'll find it!" declared Marcher, his jaw set.

A long silence hung over them before White River finally mumbled, "Then you're still set on going."

"Absolutely," said Marcher, "and I don't think we should be worrying about this Captain Josh till we meet him." He patted the side of his jacket, which rose against the bulk of a pistol. "We're not exactly helpless, you know."

White River could think of nothing more to say. He needed that two hundred dollars; it was his chance, maybe his only chance, for a rooted life. The kind of life he had only known once, with Buzz. Certainly the thing didn't make much sense. But what in life did? Just as finding that grave appeared to make a mortal difference to these brothers, getting that money now made a mortal difference to him. He drew himself up in his seat, and after taking a sharp, audible breath said, "Well, gentlemen, for a fact that island isn't getting any closer. If you're bent on going, we'd best be talking about leaving."

Amiel drew from his pocket a folded paper and spread it out in front of White River. "Here's where we're hoping to go," he said, a trifle anxiously, "and we have reason to believe this map is very accurate."

Just like Fess is to be trusted, thought White River. He looked at the well-worn paper. It was a reasonable map of the country south of the Black Hills. There were several small markings he could not decipher, but apparently they were surrounding local features that would enable a reader to pinpoint a solitary spot marked *X*. Whoever created that map had used that *X* as his starting point and had traveled east from there to strike the Niobrara, following it down to the Missouri and Independence. It was a strange route, but men working up a map in hostile country did strange things. It was clear, however, that the Platte island would be a logical first step. Once that far west, it was a straight and not very long leg north into Sioux country and to the grave site. He was glad his part in it ended at the island.

"I can see whatever you're huntin' must be mighty important, gentlemen, maybe more important than staying alive. Tracking that far into hostile country . . ."

Marcher interrupted, "We don't need any more warnings, we're through discussing whether we go or not. Our only question now is when do we start."

White River gave a deep, weary sigh and pressed his chair back. "Tomorrow morning 'bout sunup."

"What do you need?" asked Amiel.

"I need a horse."

"We'll buy one at the stable where we keep our mounts. It's the Great Western near the hotel. They seem to have several for sale."

Glancing at the door, White River noticed it was getting dark. "Reckon you'd better be getting back," he said. The river breeds squatting between the docks were astir in his mind again. Likely some of them worked for Fess. They liked to work at night. Fess knew the brothers were probably carrying cash for their trip in boot linings or money belts. "When you leave, don't go by the river," he cautioned. "Go up back and through town."

"Is there some danger?" asked Amiel.

"There's a heap less if you stay away from the river. I'll be at the stable come dawn." After the two brothers left, White River stood on the porch watching them mount fine-looking horses and ride upward toward town. He shook his head. There was no accounting for life or the folly of men.

It was almost dark now, and as he turned his gaze from where the brothers had disappeared to glance over the river, he saw the evening star glowing brightly in the western sky. It seemed to him more lonely than ever before, hanging in solitude over that great country out there, the country to which he was now returning, which held in its soil the grave of poor murdered Buzz Matlock, who would have asked no more than to become one again with the land he loved. Maybe there was a reason why he had come back to this rotten sinkhole, maybe he had been allowing its evil memories to crowd from his past its few moments of joy. Looking up again he realized that star was somewhere hanging over little Lydia, probably the woman in her by now beginning to shape her body. But in his mind he retained the image of a young, girlish figure with wide, uncomprehending eyes holding to his as the covered wagon she rode in moved away. In that moment both of them knew that the life they had lived with Buzz was gone forever and the emptiness in their hearts could only grow with the years.

PART ONE

PAWNEE

1

Eastward a haze hung over the prairie like a sheath of silk; to the south puffs of clouds sat like tulip bulbs along the horizon. The searing heat of noon was rising behind the brisk winds of morning, and now there was only a faint sighing among the higher tufts of buffalo grass. To the north and northwest the land rolled endlessly, wearying the eye with its sameness. The only relief was a river rising far to the west in towering mountains, whose snow-trimmed peaks looked at this distance like arctic islands on the low rim of the sky.

The ancient war chief of the Pawnees, White Buffalo Horse, halted his small party on the open slope of the valley. Here they commanded their best view that day of the great spread of country beyond and the low-lying saffron bluffs that marked the way of the river.

The old chief wound the single rein around the tall wooden pommel of his saddle. His old corded body, straight as a spruce, relaxed slowly, then suddenly bent in a single supple movement to a half crouch over his pony's neck. The pale squint of his eyes, all but lost behind endless webs of skin, narrowed even further as they played upon the country beyond the river, unlocking its capacity for deceit, judging its intent as a man sums up the face of a stranger by night. But as his lids finally closed, his heart was singing. Surely it would not be long now, surely death would find him here, a warrior in a warrior's grave, not a man turned squaw to be buried in cow dung under the law of the whites. There was a motion behind him and to his left. That would be Red Legs, one of those who called him "Grandfather." Ah well, am I not ancient—I, old Buffalo Horse? Am I not truly a man of the forgotten past? Have I not sung with warriors whose faces lie beneath fifty snows?

Red Legs urged his pony alongside the other, his eyes remaining fastened to a distant swell of land beyond the river. White Buffalo Horse knew Red Legs was watching three tiny brown specks that were clearly elk moving in swift, jerking motions toward the west. Even at this distance a seasoned eye knew their noses were searching the wind, their wariness apparent. The Sioux were coming.

Red Legs waited till his long staring acquired a meaning of its own, then said huskily, "Our old one has forgotten the lessons of his youth." His voice was low, edged with exasperation but held down, so that it reached their ears alone. The four young Pawnees and the three whites behind them saw only two men in an almost casual community grunting softly to each other.

"This old one has learned the ways of a warrior well enough to have counted coup on our enemies long before the snow in which Red Legs came to his father's lodge."

White Buffalo Horse's reply brought new lines to Red Legs' already tortured face. "Had he learned them better our young ones here might now live to see half as many snows as he."

Red Legs glanced about briefly in what seemed an incidental movement to relax his body. Actually it was a grim measuring of the group and their position for what his heart told him was shortly to be their plight. He had come on this brave and foolish journey only for the sake of these young ones who had slipped away to follow this old storyteller, this man who had carried a pipe in the fabled war against the Osage, so many years had he lived. But now he knew the old man wanted to die, wanted a warrior's death. His long suspicions were suddenly grim reality. These youths, seeking only a boyish adventure, were being led to their graves. Red Legs had more than a gifted eye for the signs of coming conflict. He was a renowned warrior in his own right. Had not the spotted sickness and incessant war on all sides broken the power of his people, he would have been a war leader to reckon with.

He saw the youths watching him alertly. Though inexperienced and lacking the old training, they knew only too well they were deep in enemy country and that the air between him and old Horse had grown strained and unnatural like the sky before a sudden freakish storm. He decided they would fight bravely, but surely they would die unless he could avoid what a pounding in his chest told him was fast approaching—avoid it until nightfall and then somehow under the friendly cover of darkness lead them back again to the east. Unthinkingly he stretched out a strip of rawhide holding his medicine bag about his neck and gripped it between his teeth. Again his eyes swept the terrain about them. Oh, great Tirawa, what a madness was this! And not one of these boys had felt the sun of his thirteenth summer.

Red Legs turned back to White Buffalo Horse, for too much looking about would betray his thoughts. Swiftly he brought the whites into his calculations. Unlike most Indians, Red Legs had respect for white men, particularly in a fight. One day, his heart told him, the land would be theirs from sun to sun and the Indian would stand on the prairie without a tomorrow. Two of these whites, the ones called Amiel and Marcher, waiting and wondering behind him now were clearly new to this land. Though they had come well armed, he sensed from their movements had they not been carefully guided, this vast and trailless country alone would have defeated them. If a fight could not be avoided they too would die, courageously perhaps but foolishly, like the young Pawnees. The third white somehow depressed Red Legs. He was not like the others, or for that matter like any whites he had known. He was more like a drowsy hawk whose eyes in habit combed the prairie from horizon to horizon, his mind lying adrift and seemingly lost like one who ponders a dream that will not surrender its meaning. Red Legs did not like White River. There was a thing between them, deep and inexpressible, such as exists between wild animals sensing each other's presence by night. Yet White River, for all that, had the look of a cruel and crafty fighter, a man who dealt with death as others might make idle talk. It might be he would not live to see another sun, but death would surely come slowly, even reluctantly, to this man.

Old Horse had pulled loose an unwieldy war lance that had been tied to the right scarf of his saddle. Now he braced its butt end against his right foot and straightened himself up with the air of one who rises to match some inner portrait of himself.

Suddenly a thing electric and irreversible arose between them.

"It is enough—we go no further!" snapped Red Legs.

"The voice of his medicine spirit calls White Buffalo Horse to the island in the river. The will of his spirit helper is the will of White Buffalo Horse." He glanced slowly at the faces behind him. "All go."

Red Legs reached over and grabbed the single rein. "The young men of the Sioux will dance our heads around their fires tonight. Their women will cut off our manly parts and make them playthings of the camp—to be thrown at last to the dogs. We are already like blind calves surrounded by wolves. Surely if this is the will of your spirit helper you have found a day to taste death."

"You cannot argue with the medicine spirits, Red Legs." The old man's voice rose in an icy whine and flecks of spittle frosted the rim of his lips. "You have seen these whites whom you have so taken to your heart, they do not argue with their gods."

"Our spirits are not the God of the whites!"

White Buffalo Horse paused and looked down, as though his eyes were peering through some misty veil in his mind. In the end he simply muttered, "True."

"Our spirits have not saved our people. Our hunting lands and our many sons have been taken from us."

"True."

Suddenly Red Legs' voice was seized by a haunting quality. "Old one," he said, "think upon our people. Think upon them." White Buffalo Horse's ears picked up Red Legs' strange new tone and immediately a deep and terrible communication began between them. "Where we were many now we are few—where we were once great in war now we fight like the badger from his hole. Is it not enough that death sits in every lodge, that it rides the wind and stops the hearts of our children while we dream and make the medicine offerings in vain. Is it not enough that each snow finds our people weaker, our enemies bolder—coming more and more often for our horses, our scalps. When these young men lie stripped and butchered upon the prairie, remember it will be you who placed them there, it will be White Buffalo Horse who brought the keening into the lodge of his own children, you who heaped this great new badness upon our people."

White Buffalo Horse looked long and solemnly at the distant horizon, his thumb moving slowly over a rough surface it had found on the shaft of the lance. He was suddenly very weary. Red Legs' tone had invaded him, opening up deep veins of agony, humiliation, and pain. Finally his glance fell to where his thumb continued to explore the ruptured seam of wood. "Maybe White Buffalo Horse's spirit helper is dead," he said at last, his voice spent, lifeless.

Red Legs did not answer immediately.

"White Buffalo Horse's medicine has been strong," he said finally. "He has lived for many, many snows. He has counted coup on many enemies. Our people, our young warriors, will sing his deeds. He will be spoken of in the councils as long as the sacred waters flow. But hear me now, my heart is speaking. White Buffalo Horse has grown blind to the living. His heart is in the land of the dead where his spirit helper has gone. Who follows him will not see the sun rise again. These youths must go back to their lodges. Our people need them. Red Legs will try to bring them back. We are surrounded, and only a few against many. My heart is like the winter ice when I see the sign about us, but I will try to bring them back. White Buffalo Horse no longer leads here. He is not to speak to the young ones again." Then, after a long pause, White Buffalo Horse heard in flat, lifeless words what Red Legs' peculiar tone had already told him clearly and intimately moments before. "If our grandfather does not do these things I say, Red Legs must kill him."

2

André Marcher tugged down the brim of his hat, vainly trying to increase the shield it offered from the sun. Then he looked about him quickly, tightening up his youngish face like a man bothered with thirst. Before him the terrain was blazing. Blue and yellow rocks shimmered together under boils of restive air; sunburnt grass carpeted the lowlands and cropped above the mounds.

It was a harsh land, he mused, noticing a small lizard perched motionlessly under the lip of a rock down the draw. He could feel it worrying his flesh, wearying his spirit, slowly working to grind him into its own substance.

He dug his hands into the back pockets of his jeans. Impatience and resentment were his real burdens now. He had hoped to be on that island before dawn, to find this damned Captain Josh, to be that much nearer to Paul's grave and the fulfillment of his hopes. But now it seemed that nothing was ever certain in this agonizing waste. He kicked a small stone in irritation, then pulled his hands free, using the heels of his palms to knock dust from his jeans. "If they know we're here, what the devil good is it doing us to wait?"

The question was fired at White River. White River let the remark hang in the oppressive heat until a quick-darting bird he was watching disappeared behind a pile of blue-streaked rock. Only then did he half mutter, "We ain't for certain yet where they be."

"Or *if* they be?" returned Marcher.

White River kept scanning the valley.

Ben Amiel, squinting in his usual silence, turned slowly, rubbing his legs, trying to get comfortable after the long stretch in the saddle.

"Andy," he said, looking at the Pawnees, "these people are natives of these parts." His eyes closed on Red Legs, whom the other two sensed he had grown to admire. "They don't strike me as a breed that imagine trouble 'less they see some."

Marcher grimaced and dropped slowly to the earth. He looked closely at White River, evaluating him for the hundredth time. There was something in that man's manner that tantalized and tormented him—from that first night to this very moment. "So we're holing up here looking for them, while they're out there looking for us. Is that what this hullabaloo is all about?"

White River leisurely waited again before answering. "Yep," he grunted, turning to engage Marcher's stare. "And most folks allow it makes better tellin' later when you get to see them first." He regarded Marcher easily, as though there were no issue between them.

"Why don't we try talking to them . . . making friends," Marcher said evenly. "They've got no quarrel with us. We're not going to make any trouble for them."

White River glanced back at the valley again, his sharp, unshaven face expressionless. "Sioux don't take much to squatting 'round making friends—'specially when they're riled." There was a short silence, and then, almost as an afterthought, he added with a casualness that seared Marcher's nerves, "Your just being here is reason aplenty for them to come fetching hair. Sioux reckon these diggings to be theirs, and to hear 'em tell it they've yet to see a white man that didn't mean trouble."

Marcher's eyes widened, then settled down again, but still held to the tall, hunched form of their guide. Ben noticed his brother's eyes holding that strange mixture of irritation and interest that Andy alone could manage.

"All right, then." Marcher's voice rallied against the heat, his eyes still playing on the gaunt figure as though baiting him. "You seem pretty much at home in all this—how do we get to that island?"

White River's attention had gravitated to a dust devil on a bluff to the east. "Luck, I reckon," he said, now completely distracted.

"Luck!" Marcher's eyes shot skyward for an instant. "You mean we are just going to sit in this godforsaken ditch and depend upon luck?"

Before White River could answer, Ben's hand had come down heavily on Marcher's shoulder. "Andy, be reasonable." His tone seemed to placate, but there was an unwilling whisper of authority edging his normally mild manner. "Remember, this is Indian territory. We haven't seen a soul in days and we're trespassers here by any man's reckoning. And remember, we're alone, likely outnumbered, and violating the law to boot. What do you think you can do—send a courier to Washington?"

Marcher was undaunted. "There's a fort up ahead somewhere. Can't one of us get through and bring back some troops? They can't say no to respectable citizens who need protection."

Ben pulled a crushed white handkerchief from his pocket and rubbed his face with it. "Respectable citizens—if that's what you want to call us—don't deliberately violate the law," he muttered solemnly. "Remember what we were told—if troops did show up, it would only be their duty to pack us all back east." He turned to stare down at the young Pawnees huddled together at the far end of the draw. The youths were clearly frightened, if making a brave show of it for each other. Two were dancing about quietly, the others painting each other's faces with clay. Ben glanced at Red Legs, perched between the young Pawnees and the long-chanting White Buffalo Horse. Like White River, Red Legs was staring silently into the valley before him, his eyes closing from time to time in brief rest. "Jesus, I feel sorry for that man," Ben whispered, bending over Marcher's shoulder, "trying to get these youngsters back with nothing but that antique musket to hold off trouble."

Marcher threw a quick glance down the draw. "They're running out on us, aren't they," he snapped. "And I'll wager they know what they're about. We'll be left here fighting these hostiles while they hightail it home." His tone increased its cut. "I still think we ought to keep going." He nodded abruptly at the chanting White Buffalo Horse. "If that old codger is still willing to lead, I'm willing to follow. Seems to me anything is better than sitting here."

White River turned and looked silently and intently at Marcher as a man does when he is weighing out a troublesome thought, but in the end, to Ben's relief, he said nothing. Instead he slumped back against the bank of the draw and pulled the slouch hat down over his face. Marcher waited for him for a few moments, then said briskly, "So we're not going to try for the fort, are we?"

White River's voice rose from beneath the rim of his hat. "If there be soldiers enough in that fort to scare off these Sioux, Mr. Marcher, they'd be doing it. Better get some easin' . . . could be a worrisome night."

There was silence until Marcher whipped off his hat and began to raise more dust with it from his jeans. "You think a man can sleep in this heat?"

"Didn't say sleep . . . said easin'. Eased-up men are likely to be luckier than those sitting around stewing about whiskey already down some varmint's gullet."

Marcher braced himself brusquely against a boulder protruding from the sloping bank and gazed down the valley to the west. His tongue moved futilely over his dry lips, his eyes narrowing as he fought off the glare of the sun.

"I think we're damn fools sitting in this washout, waiting for God knows what, when a child could see there is nothing between us and west of here but open country. We could easily make it along these bluffs until we spotted the military or they spotted us or something. We're paying you to get us to that island, Mr. River. Let's go!"

White River lifted his hat to stare up at Marcher. The sky arched above them and the sun beat futilely against the unfeeling earth. Unnoticed, the lizard's head had reappeared in the shadow of the rock. Now there was a new light in White River's eyes. It had Ben Amiel back on his feet again making a sideward motion to put himself between the other two. Suddenly in the quiet he realized that White Buffalo Horse was still chanting, though now with a faint hoarseness in his throat. White River's eyes settled before he spoke, and Ben Amiel released the breath he was holding. "Get that thinking out of your head, Mr. Marcher. Them soldiers, if there be sech, might just as well be in Texas for all the helping they can do us—besides, you're likely to find out before you're finished that most times hereabouts luck will fetch you further than a regiment."

Awaiting his opportunity, Ben brought Marcher further down the draw. Andy twisted with impatience, saying nothing, taking quick breaths and holding them, his face tightening in disgust.

"Leave him alone," Ben said finally. "I'll venture he knows his business better than you or I."

Marcher threw an accusing look up the draw. "Damn it, Ben, we've been holed up here for hours. We'll never get to that island if we squat down and hide every time there's a hint of trouble."

"Hint of trouble? Andy, are you insane? Look at the faces on those Pawnees, they're frightened to death. Truth is, so am I. Only a damn fool wouldn't be."

Andy swung around and stood with his back to his brother. "So now I'm a damn fool!" They stood in silence for a moment.

Ben, suppressing his own annoyance, went on. "Andy, listen to me. Whatever you think of that man, he's our only chance of getting out of here alive. Leave him alone!"

Andy turned back, his irritation suddenly igniting to anger. "Ben, if you're so damn scared of getting scalped, why in hell did you come? Why didn't you stay home, become a lay preacher like your father?"

Ben's head came up with a snap. "My father lived and died an honest man, which is a hell of a lot more than will ever be said of yours."

Andy turned away again. "All right, Ben, I'm sorry. It's just that I'm sick of watching you stand around wishing to Christ you were somewhere else. I should have done this alone."

Ben wanted to turn away himself, but he knew that this friction, already dividing them, would only grow in silence. "Andy, get a hold of yourself. We're doing this together."

"Are we?"

"Yes, but there are risks no sensible person . . ."

Andy's face was suddenly closer to his. "Ben, I came out here to see this thing through, and it's time you got through your head I intend to do just that—no matter what the risks."

Ben took a step backward, staring strangely at his brother. "Of that I have no doubt," he muttered, but then, letting his eyes fall to the reddish clay at their feet, he shrugged helplessly and turned away.

3

White River was not asleep. From time to time he arched his back and glanced furtively into the swells of heated air that rose to shimmer above the valley floor, each time feeling again that cold stiffening at the top of his spine. He knew it for what it was, had known ever since that moment they left the creek bed and stepped out onto the valley plain. His senses were picking up the subtle vibrations of death.

He knew now it had been a mistake seeking out the Pawnees, but with the military closing and patrolling the river roads and the back trails being watched, the open country posed a problem to which the Pawnees had seemed the solution. But from the beginning he knew it had not been right. The old auguries of his youth in the north country were coming back. He remembered Black Sun, the wise Arikara, telling him from his deathbed that the Pawnees, even though a kindred race, carried the taste of trouble and death in their mouths; that the sign for them was the sign of the wolf, and the eye of the vulture followed them wherever they rode.

At their village on the wide loop of the river, even after he had spoken to them in Arikara, a language akin to their own, they had treated him with a sullenness that bordered on contempt. Their chiefs stood with their big bellies and their soldier hats, mouthing broken English and giving curt answers to his many signs for help. They had no guides to lead these fools into Sioux country. The Sioux and their allies—the Cheyennes and the Blue Men, the Arapahos—were making war on the whites. The red pipe was traveling everywhere, and even the brave-talking whites were huddled in their fort at the mouth of the Laramie or on that island further down the Platte.

As their answers grew shorter and their discourtesies more pointed, Marcher, probably remembering something he had read in books about Indians, suggested they offer these stubborn faces a few knives, a hatchet, or some cloth perhaps to win them over. But White River knew better. The Pawnees, with the curious prescience of the tribal system, knew that their strength was ebbing. There was scarcely a tribe within traveling distance that could not measure in blood the unrelenting terror these warriors, so arrogant in past years, had spread in every direction from the Platte country. Some of the smaller tribes had been forced to become vassals. But now their power had been broken by the white man's fevers and the many enemies they had brought upon themselves. Had it not been for the ready guns of the whites, they would long since have been driven from their hunting grounds, their villages becoming gathering places for vultures and wolves. No, these grim faces were not anxious for the special deaths that would be meted out to the once feared Pawnees by the foraging tribes upriver. Besides, the numerous well-mounted and war-minded Sioux, who alone of their neighbors they had never decisively defeated, might at any moment sally into this very village, and every man, woman, and child would be needed to survive such a fight.

As they turned away from the village, White River quietly decided they would chance it on their own. It was a decision he should have stayed with.

Just before dawn the following morning, he had come up slowly from his blanket, his rifle on the ready, his senses telling him someone was in their camp. Through the gloom he saw a tall Indian standing beside his horse not twenty-five feet from where he lay. White River rose slowly and started toward the stranger. As he drew nearer he discovered it was an old man holding himself erect with one arm pointing westward and the other holding on to an ancient lance. They had pitched their camp only a short distance from the village, and this man was obviously a Pawnee. White River lowered his gun and made the sign for talk.

"Me take white men to island in river." The old one's voice was high-pitched and seemed to come with effort. White River knew from the rustling behind him it had awakened the others. "What is it?" Marcher called huskily.

"An old buck says he'll throw in as guide."

There was silence as each considered the matter. "What do you think?" said Marcher coming to his feet.

"Think we'll give him a twist of tobacco and send him on his way."

"Why?" Marcher was up now and hurrying to join them. "Hadn't we ought to let him try—we've got nothing to lose, have we?"

By now Ben Amiel was also up and quietly approaching. Into the silence he asked softly, "Does he know the country?"

"Me know medicine trail to island in river," said the old man vigorously pointing westward with his lance.

First light was filtering into the clearing, easing the darkness and bringing the heavy web of lines that was the old one's face into clearer view. White River peered at him quietly. "Nope, I don't think so. His senses are probably gone—'twould be too risky."

"Look," said Marcher, extending his face to bring it nearer White River's, "getting to that island is mighty important to us. Anything that's likely to help, I'm willing to try. You said yourself the Pawnees know this country better than anyone. Unless you've got better reasons than you've come up with—he goes."

White River stared back at him. From the Indian village nearby a dog began to bark. It seemed to have a strange effect upon White River. He turned his gaze to the sky as though he were evaluating the coming day. He could feel the presence of the heavy-breathing Marcher beside him, and he wondered if his long-smoldering irritation with this man was entering his decision. "Saddle up," he said abruptly and, swinging away, walked quickly to the stretch of grass where they had tethered their mounts.

Later that day and many hot and dusty miles to the west, White River had waited until they had made a sudden turning, then instantly called for a halt. The broiling sun was descending the sky, and shadows that were stunted to the north lay ready to commence their ancient inching to the east. "What's the matter?" asked Marcher, always the first to speak.

"We're being followed," said White River evenly, his eyes on the old Indian who, they had discovered after much probing, was called White Buffalo Horse.

The old one looked back indifferently, his motions indicating there could be no danger. White River pulled his rifle from his saddle and motioned for the others to do the same. Marcher's was out in a moment, but Ben Amiel moved reluctantly, his eyes questioning White River's as one who does not welcome violence. "What do you think?" he asked cautiously.

"You never can tell," responded White River, signaling them back behind a shoulder of black shale. The old Pawnee stayed in the open, simply bringing his pony about slowly and effortlessly to greet whatever came. In time the faint movement of horses could be heard, the sound growing so slowly that one might think it would never present its source. But suddenly behind the far end of the rock four young Pawnees appeared, their eyes fixed on the ground below, their gazing so intense that their surprise was almost total when their mounts suddenly bucked and began to sidestep to avoid running into White Buffalo Horse.

White River watched the young boys looking abashed at the old Indian as they strove to settle their mounts. It was clear they expected White Buffalo Horse to be very angry. But he said nothing. He only looked at them. A boy named Lame Fox spoke first. "White Buffalo Horse, we have come to go with you to the far country. You are a great warrior. We will learn many things from you. Perhaps we will take many scalps and horses back to the people. Life in the village is very dull. We wish to be warriors, warriors like the great White Buffalo Horse. Do not send us back, Grandfather."

There had been a long silence in which White Buffalo Horse regarded the youngsters vacantly almost as though he hadn't accepted their presence. Then, without a word, he turned his pony again and made the sign for going on. White River was about to hail him back to tell him there was no room for children on this journey, that there was already trouble enough, but Marcher was too quick for him.

"Good!" he almost shouted, as he saw what he knew were young Pawnees starting to follow White Buffalo Horse. "These chaps look young enough to have their senses about them. Now we're going to have a real scouting party. Hell, this will be great, nobody's going to attack children!"

White River felt rage sweeping over him. What did you say to a mouthy greenhorn who had yet to see his first half-crazed brave quartering a man with his hatchet or pushing a white-hot gun barrel into his gut? Not attack children? Did you tell him the Sioux would make kindling of Pawnee children half their age if given a chance? He tried to keep his mind on that two hundred dollars. It was all that mattered.

Marcher moved ahead immediately with the others as they started forward again, but Ben Amiel lingered behind, keeping his mount even with White River's. In time he said, "I don't get the feeling you approve of much of this." His voice was gentle, unobtrusive.

"Oh . . . calculate your friend stands a fair chance of not approvin' of what he's gettin' into," White River said, surprised at the evenness of his own voice.

"He's a little quick on some things," Ben said thoughtfully. "But he's got guts. I'm sure you can count on him if there's trouble."

"Count on him for what?"

Amiel looked startled. "For doing his share, I guess."

The following evening they were stretched around a small fire made from dry wood and buried deep in the rocks. Though sleep soon began to sweep over the weary camp, White River's rest was fitful. There was much that disturbed him, not the least of which was the fact that White Buffalo Horse was sleeping in a sitting position. The only men he'd ever known who would not lie down to sleep were those caught in a winter storm who rightly suspected that if they embraced the ground, it would embrace them for good.

Well after midnight he rose from his blanket to see if the old chief had finally gone to ground, and it was then that he saw suddenly, in the dull amber glow of moonlight, a second figure sitting next to the chief. The man was too large to be one of the young bucks, and White River instinctively brought his rifle about before he realized that to kill this intruder if he was not alone would only ensure their death. He settled back and spent the night watching these two figures sit together in eerie silence.

As the light gathered, White River could see the newcomer was a Pawnee, not a young one but a man with a sturdy body and hair roached like a warrior. He decided to rise and put his pack together, thinking it would help some when Marcher and Amiel discovered the stranger to be moving casually about himself. It did. Only the young Pawnees looked surprised and made startled sounds when they discovered this new visitor. They watched the two men smoking quietly beyond with concern, then sat together whispering in the way of boys.

The unheard conversation that started after the pipe had been passed lasted till the sun was over the horizon. Then the two warriors rose and approached the young Pawnees, the visitor speaking to them quickly and curtly, motioning them to their ponies. As they left, the newcomer turned abruptly to White Buffalo Horse, pointing as he did to the southwest. White Buffalo Horse did not answer but instead moved off slowly to his mount.

White River did not know why, but in his bones he felt things had improved. That day they shifted to a course further away from the river, and now they seemed to be holding to the low ground. The newcomer, whom White River heard the boys calling Red Legs, was looking about him sharply as though he were seeking landmarks or places where special caution was demanded. By noon White River was convinced this silent, almost morose Pawnee knew his business. The island seemed closer now, and the promise of a safe end to this idiotic trip grew.

That night Red Legs came forward to scatter the brush the young Pawnees were gathering for a fire, advising them with a few grunts that they were making cold camp and passing among them some meal and meat he had taken from his saddle. It was clear he was angry at them, but he made no words that White River could hear. The whites he completely ignored.

White River, bracing his back against a boulder, chewed on his cold jerked beef and listened to the night noises about them. They seemed normal enough. With this Red Legs around he felt he could chance a good sleep tonight. A man needed sleep. Fatigue was the father of carelessness in hostile country, and those wise to the ways of this land knew that a man who slept often enough never slept too deeply. He pulled his blanket snugly around him. Tomorrow might be a good day, he told himself comfortingly.

It was. Their last.

By the next night exhaustion and thirst had begun to play their roles. The land was running higher and drier as they pressed to the west, and outcroppings of rock began to rupture the earth on all sides.

White River finished his jerky and forced himself to stay awake, following Red Legs' figure through the faint light as he moved about their camp. Funny how an Indian could put weariness aside, seeming to have some animal reserve that white men approached only when driven by things beyond their reason, like love or hate. White River smiled when he saw Red Legs settling on a high knoll to the east. This would not only give the Pawnee a clear view on all sides but an early warning if anyone had followed their trail.

Before daylight White River was up, his sudden rising movement bringing Red Legs to one knee on the knoll. No other motion passed between them and as Red Legs' silence continued into the morning White River thought it a strange business. He knew Indians well enough to know the Pawnee resented him, but Red Legs had to know that they were the only two in this company who could sense the impending danger and now they weren't talking. Well, it was not a thing for stewing on. With Marcher along there was plenty of jawing for those needing it.

The sun that morning betrayed a heavy gray mist lying in the low spots and gathering at random stretches on the prairie. "'Twill burn off soon," said White River, motioning them to their saddles. However, as the young Pawnees left hurriedly to bring up the mounts, Red Legs grunted suddenly in muted alarm and gestured for silence. Everyone froze as he fell quickly to the earth and held his ear tightly against the ground. In time he stood up, his breath slowly filling his chest, making him seem taller as his heavy eyes looked long and gravely at White Buffalo Horse.

"The buffalo are running, Grandfather. It is time to turn back."

The old chief did not answer. He sat looking at Red Legs for what to the whites seemed an eternity. Then he stood up holding himself erect and pointing firmly to the west. "All go." His voice sounded high again after the depths of Red Legs. "White Buffalo Horse has had powerful dream. His medicine showing him safe way to island in river." He turned and stared back at the listening Pawnee in a faintly mocking way, his head arched as though lightly puzzled. "What has happened to the heart of Red Legs? The sound of running buffalo does not turn strong warriors into gophers. These buffalo do not run from our enemies." He paused and looked about him as one who easily sees the powerful spirit things and knows them as friends. "In White Buffalo Horse's dream, his spirit helper says the sound of running buffalo means island is close. Many, many whites there. Many, many guns. All safe." He turned in his stately manner and started toward his horse. "All go!"

Behind those questioning, doubt-ridden eyes White River could feel the distress that was festering in Red Legs. Among all Indians of the high plains dreams were great and sacred things, every tribe alive with its folklore of the miracles their dreams had made possible. To go against them was unheard of, for without them life was a night that could not hope for day. Many a man had willingly perished because he saw himself in a dream being called to the spirit world. Women saw birthmarks on the faces of their children while carrying them, and so they were born. Starving people had many times been saved by dreaming, sometimes in delirium, of where there was food. There was no answer to White Buffalo Horse's words, none at least to which Red Legs could give life. The only answer lay to the west.

As though these strange words had not taken place, White Buffalo Horse resumed his position at the head of the party and they started moving forward again, the young Pawnees apparently mystified by the exchange between their elders. Red Legs was the last to mount up and follow.

Within a half hour they began to enter a great din caused by aroused animals. They had been just rising from a ravine when they came upon the buffalo. The sun was well up and flooding the prairie, the mist had been nearly burned away, and about them they saw the thick dark hulks of the great animals, winded and wild-eyed on the grassy swells of the plain. Here and there the bellowing of stray calves searching for their cows signaled the disarray a sudden run had brought upon the herd. In a moment Marcher was pulling his rifle from the scabbard, shouting to White River, eager to know if he could risk a few shots. White River discouraged him with an abrupt wave of his hand, while his eyes went with the sudden rush of Red Legs who was moving up quickly alongside White Buffalo Horse, bringing him to a halt. Unable to hear anything in the din, White River managed to determine from the signs that passed between them that Red Legs was suggesting he be given time to crawl to higher ground and scout the country ahead. It did not seem to need discussing. Nothing else was sane at this moment. A buffalo hunt along this stretch of river—if that, indeed, was what it was—could mean but one thing. Yet, incredibly, White Buffalo Horse ignored this rudimentary step for survival and in the end, after taking one of his long and incomprehensible looks at the sky, raised his hand again in the familiar signal to continue ahead.

White River, masking his amazement, pulled his bay out of the procession, and moved over to the left flank. No one seemed to notice this gesture except Red Legs, who came back and moved his mount abruptly to the right. There was no denying it now, the character of matters had changed. White River did not like it. He could not explain it to himself, but they were moving now like men adrift and caught in a ruthless tide. As he wondered if he wouldn't be damning himself for a fool before the day was out, his eyes began to search the ridges about them, his instincts breeding a low fever in him, his senses alarmed by the fact that Red Legs, in spite of his granite exterior, was now clearly as edgy as antelope with fire in the wind. But even so they moved along without incident, the brittle moments beading themselves together into minutes, and the minutes into hours.

The buffalo continued to thin out, fading away until at last only an occasional lonely and outcast bull watched the procession mutely from a distance. Finally, as the prairie swells grew barren again, one of the young Pawnees, probably bored at the slow pace of things, broke the silence with the first shrieking notes of a buffalo spirit song, making Red Legs yank swiftly over and bring his quirt down savagely across the boy's back. After that the silence droned in again, fringed only as before with the evasive creak of leather and the low dusty thudding of hooves.

The sudden sight of a young buffalo cow circling near a distant hillock, head down and bawling as though wounded, made White River instinctively rein about.

As he spun toward it, he discovered Red Legs was already in action, wheeling his own mount out of the procession and quirting the pony hard in the direction of the bawling cow. He raked the mustang's flanks and followed Red Legs at a full gallop.

He finally reined up beside Red Legs, who was sitting motionless on his heaving mount not fifty feet from the bawling cow. An arrow had been lodged in its neck, but too far forward for a quick kill. The long gray shaft of the arrow stuck out boldly in the sun, one of its turkey tail feathers loose and flickering back and forth in the breeze.

With a grunt that ignored White River's presence, Red Legs pulled his horse about and, applying his quirt as vigorously as before, started back toward the others. White River studied the low-lying ridges about him cautiously before he followed. There was no need to speculate anymore. This half-crazed and weakened animal could not have traveled more than a few miles, and that arrow in its neck had come from a Cheyenne bow.

When he rode up to the others he saw Red Legs repeatedly making the three-fingered sign for the Cheyenne to the still stoic and unresponsive White Buffalo Horse, but White River was done with looking on and listening and hoping against hope. He came up to White Buffalo

Horse, the great octagonal barrel of his Smith & Wesson pistol in his hand, his eyes alive with a deep anger. "Big danger!" he spat cuttingly. "Cheyenne, maybe Sioux war party close. Now we hide." White River swept his right hand under his left in the sign for hide. "Night come, we go." He pointed the gun barrel to the west.

White Buffalo Horse watched him impassively. Whatever his thoughts, they were lost behind the dim squint of his eyes. While they waited, Red Legs pulled his mount away and sent the young Pawnees into a clump of dwarf trees a hundred yards south of the trail.

Finally the old man rose in his saddle and waved his arm slowly about him, calling out, "This land of enemies. Did white man expect to find friends here? Friends on island very close . . . half-day march . . . we go fast"—he made the sign for moving quickly—"running elk not taken by wolves."

"We hide!" repeated White River, the gun inches from the other's chest. "Go to island tonight."

The old chief regarded him again for a long moment, then rose up in his saddle and looked about him. "Where white man hide?"

White River looked about him. The plain was uneven but it was sparse of growth, and only the low places offered any hope of concealment. But low spots were suicidal against seasoned fighters, and if caught without warning they would be as good as dead. Reluctantly he knew the old man had a point. Even Red Legs seemed to sense the futility of staying where they were. Again, ignoring White River, he paused a moment beside them, telling White Buffalo Horse that he was going to scout to the northwest and that the old chief should stay with the others till his return. If he came back on the run, making the danger sign, they should start moving in the direction he was riding at once. He did not wait for any response but was off quickly, bending low over his mount, his head disappearing behind his shoulders, the stock of his old smoothbore appearing in his left hand.

Before the hour was up the Pawnee was back, his horse breathing hard and his mind seeming only half on the words he offered to White Buffalo Horse and, because he was sitting close, inadvertently to White River. It was a small hunting party. Cheyennes. Their tracks showed they had gone across the river. They had taken very little meat. Apparently they were in a hurry. They had ridden around quite a bit, though he did not have the time to follow all the tracks to see if any had crossed theirs. His eyes, however, said the risk was a real one.

"Ah, running away," said White Buffalo Horse in seeming contempt.

"Or seeking help," cautioned Red Legs quickly—too quickly for it to be a new thought. Red Legs knew something about Cheyennes. They were not to be confused with Kaws or even Arapahos. They didn't often run away. He swept the area around them with his eyes, anxiously pondering their next move.

Perhaps sensing this indecision in Red Legs, White Buffalo Horse pulled himself up in his saddle again. "We follow secret trail to island in river . . . reach island before sleep . . . many, many guns there . . . all safe."

Now Red Legs' glance fell to the ground, showing his shame at questioning the old chief in front of a white. "Is there such a trail, Grandfather?"

The old squint of eyes rose to the sky again. "Did not White Buffalo Horse dream it?"

Marcher and Amiel were suddenly beside them. "Is the old chief ready to get moving again?" Marcher demanded.

White River nodded. Peculiarly enough, movement was beginning to have its virtue. Perhaps they could make it quickly to that island. Perhaps the old Indian had a point. Perhaps the hostiles would need to cross the river and organize an attack. Perhaps the safest direction was straight ahead. Perhaps.

Red Legs must have been drawn to the same slim chance, for he had mustered the young Pawnees and was leading them silently to their place directly behind the old chief. He himself fell back a long way off to the right of the whites, riding far out, a lonely figure against the sky grappling with thoughts already raw from handling.

For a spell White River watched White Buffalo Horse move knowingly among the prairie mounds, winding from hidden ravine to hidden ravine with the certainty of one traveling a path about his own lodge. Then suddenly he turned into a dry creek bed which slowly began to arch its way off to the northwest. They were now swinging toward the river, and the land in mock preparation began to rise. The dry creek bed drew narrower and deeper, forcing them to ride in closer. On both sides there began to appear giant white boulders towering up so that only in odd and unexpected moments could they see clearly the plains about them. White River found himself beginning to study each bend in the dry creek bed more and more closely. So alert did he become that in surprise he realized he could hear his own breathing. He loosened the rifle in his scabbard without knowing he had done so.

Then without warning the creek bed wove to the west and came abruptly out onto the great open stretch of land that swept to the river and on to the bluffs beyond. The old chief raised his hand in a signal to stop, but he himself was already on the exposed rim and looking upward as though he were following a map in the sky. Suddenly White River knew what had disturbed and ravaged his mind for so many days. How had he missed it? How had he allowed this suicidal procession to continue until now the very land itself had turned against them? The old man was a fool looking for death. And he, White River, twice the fool for not sensing it sooner. Even now, had not Red Legs gone forward to restrain him, he would be moving out onto the slope of the valley, holding that ancient lance aloft as a final symbol of his insanity.

Red Legs, who had exchanged some words in a low voice with White Buffalo Horse, was now looking back at them, his eyes seeming to say, This is an interesting place and we should remember it, his glance swinging to and fro as though he wondered if they were all there, if their horses were in need of a rest, if it had not been a test of things, their coming so far. White River studied those eyes, but he did not think that was their intent at all. He saw that they struggled to mask a stark, frantic message. Their moment for survival was gone. It was too late.

4

"Now, I'll be go-to-hell, Josh, what you fixin' to do?" The little man lay on the ground with his pant leg ripped apart from boot top to thigh. An arrow protruded from his back thigh muscle, its flint tip just breaking through the fleshy inner part of the leg. The bleeding was not profuse, but blood fell in steady little drops from a tiny rivulet that had made its way down the feathered shaft of the arrow.

Josh was stooping over a fire, the bend of his body giving him the thickness of an ox. He was heavily bearded, his features coarse and worn, his eyes cradled in a perpetual frown. He seemed to be both preoccupied with the task at hand yet annoyed at the irregular circle of trappers, traders, and other trail drifters who were watching him closely as he took an ash-white knife from the fire and approached the embedded arrow.

"You be careful, y' hear, Josh. Be careful!" snapped the little man. They were situated in the center of an island which was less than a quarter of a mile long and not quite two hundred yards wide. Beyond and on both sides, the river, its surface sheen reflecting the high cobalt sky, made only a faint murmur that ran lonely against the ear. There were willow groves on either end of the island and a patch of thicket that rose in the center and spread along the south bank.

Josh settled down on his knees matter-of-factly, put the wooden handle of the knife in his mouth, and with his powerful hands broke the arrow shaft a few inches from the leg. Then he forced the little man's knee up to brace it against his chest. "Hold her there tight now, Neff," he murmured in a harsh whisper, and with a grunt he pushed the arrow head up through the broken skin.

"Jeeeeeeesus Christ!" screamed Neff. Josh paid him no heed, but instead grasped the head of the arrow and pulled the broken shaft on through the leg. Now Neff tore his hat off and stuck its soft crown into his mouth, his teeth going through it as Josh took the knife from his mouth and seared the wound on both sides with the fiercely hot blade.

The smell of burned flesh rose as Josh called at random to those watching about him. "Be there maybeso a jug of whiskey hereabouts?"

A squat trader, his face projected forward until it ended in his lips, pulled a jug covered with soiled burlap from a leather pouch slung over his shoulder. A new man to the island, he sauntered toward them tapping the side of the jug with his finger. "This here be as good as you'll git, I'm thinkin'. Tennessee brewed and hard to come by." He handed over the jug, throwing in cordially enough, "Name's Benson. Trader Benson. Always totes the best whiskey in this here whole terr'tory."

"Mighty obligin'. Name's Josh. Captain Josh." Pulling off the cork, he nodded at the little man lying grimacing with pain on the ground beside him. "This here little fellow is my partner, Neff Hammer. Got hisself shot up some."

Josh raised the jug to his lips, choked monstrously at the first swallow, then forced down another, his fist thumping desperately on his stomach, preparing it for heavy doings. "Gawd!" he bellowed at the trader.

Some of the men in the circle snickered. "That's what he's been feedin' those Sioux, Josh," one of them offered. "That's how come they're actin' so orn'ry." The others laughed, but their laughter faded swiftly.

Josh poured some of the fluid on both wounds and was swinging about to return the jug to Benson, when suddenly Neff was up and grabbing it from him, hurriedly filling his own mouth. Much of it came back through his lips, but some of it went down, bringing helpless tears to his eyes.

Josh came to his feet and stared meditatively a moment at the river. "Figure you'd better rest a mite, Neff," he said. "I'm goin' to bind her up some."

He took his knife and started back to where he had tethered the horses among the willows near the lower end of the island. He was planning to cut a strip off Neff's blanket roll. It would be all he could do for now. The wound looked clean, though, and with luck would likely heal.

With Josh gone, the trader Benson blew his nose noisily on his sleeve, then stepped out to peer down curiously at Hammer, his head cocked so he could confront Neff's upturned face. "What were you two fellows fetchin' out there anyways?"

Neff Hammer dropped his chin and disengaged his eyes. "Just doin' a mite of huntin'."

"Huntin'? Up in them foothills with Sioux raisin' hair just about everywheres?"

"Our luck run poorly. That's all."

An old trapper, his cheek puffed with a wad of tobacco, shifted it in derision and spat into a pothole a few feet in front of him. " 'Pears to me you were luckier than you was deservin'. If them Sioux and 'Shiens we helped you get shut of a while back hadn't been ridin' jaded stock, maybeso you wouldn't be here."

The others muttered as they looked speculatively at the long amber ridge where the bluffs met the sky turning smoke blue as it neared the horizon. Behind those bluffs the war party had disappeared. Most of those present were too seasoned to think the Indians had been scared off. It was the open ground and the river bed that had to be crossed before they could get to the guns of these men that discouraged the Sioux.

Benson continued shaking his head in mild astonishment. "Sure seems tarnation foolish nosin' 'round out there with sign so heavy a man couldn't hardly lower his britches without he wipe out some. How'd you come to tangle with 'em?"

Neff Hammer propped himself up on one elbow and looked about for Josh. In the distance he caught the heavy figure starting toward him again. Maybe with something tied on his leg he could get himself up. He had the horseman's inveterate dislike of the ground.

"Well," he began, "we'd just raised us a big old bear—drilled him clean through, we did. Run across't him sleepin' on a rock as big as a church, spread right out there in the sun. Could tell the way he lit out he was fair hit."

The old trapper grunted. "Bear that's fair hit don't light out."

"Well, we was gainin' fast on this big devil and would have finished him quicker than spit, but, Jesus, there was the God Almightiest parcel of Injuns you'd ever seen a-comin' straightaway at us."

"Must have heard your shots and cut across your trail," surmised Benson.

"Reckon that was the way of it," allowed the trapper. "By rights you should have been surrounded before you knew they was close. Ain't too many gets away from Sioux if they has first lick."

By now Josh was among them again, the strip of blanket trailing from his hand, his great body moving in a strange wooden motion which made Neff anxiously seek out his eyes and find them still holding to the river in a long leaden gaze.

Later Neff rolled himself some tobacco and tried to get comfortable in the saddle rest that Josh had set up for him. The two of them were alone now, the rest of the island's inhabitants having gone over to the south bank to watch a small herd of buffalo lumbering out of the breaks, moving toward the river in their strange swinging gait.

"There's buffalo meat a-comin', Josh," piped Neff, his voice high and reedy. "Reckon we ought to get some."

"Don't stew on it, Neff. We will." Josh looked painfully at the horizon to the east. "Mebbe raise us some Sioux hair too afore we get shut of these diggings."

Neff turned quickly, his hand going up to deflect the sun that flared behind Josh's shoulder. "Let's leave 'em be, Josh," he said querulously. "We didn't figure on feuding with no Injuns." He looked at his bandaged leg. "Jesus, they like to kill me!"

"If a little nick like that has got you talking rabbity, Neff, reckon you'd better not go any further. We're fixing to go into Sioux terr'tory and you knowed it from the beginning."

Hammer lifted his head again, but this time he said nothing. His eyes instead wandered out to the bluffs lying back from the river. Neff Hammer had small stomach for this country; everything about it soured his fancy. As he reckoned, bad luck had been bedeviling them for weeks, and everywhere he looked this country seemed to promise more. Besides, something was wrong with Josh, and it was not a thing a man could talk about or bring up in a question. Yet it was there, and a fellow got the feel of it more and more often.

"What if we're wrong?" he said finally.

"That don't make sense," growled Josh, settling down with a greasy rag and a short ramrod to clean his pistol. "Fess said they wuz heading for the Black Hills with a map of sorts to get their hands on something mighty, mighty important."

Neff's small eyes came back seeming smaller. "Josh, how do we know it's gold—could be a heap of things."

Josh looked down the barrel of his gun, then blew through it quickly. His tone was betraying a growing irritation with Hammer. "Those Easterners ain't traipsing all this distance to pick berries, Neff, not with what it's costing 'em, not without there being somethin' mighty handsome a-waiting." He shifted his glance to check their distance from the others on the south bank. "Maybeso you're hankering to traipse back to St. Louis and visit a mite with that marshal and his friends, 'pears to me he'd take mighty kindly to such sociableness."

Neff turned away and spat in disgust. "You knowed I wasn't studying nothing like that."

Josh was up now and going through his pockets. Neff's smoking had put him in mind of the makings. He remained silent until he had lit up. "Neff, we got to get heavy enough staked so we can cut trail to Californy. The law hereabouts ain't as poor on memory as my choosing, and besides, Cousin Fess is getting mighty toothy about that little sum of money we owe him."

"A fellow as will take money for hiding his own kin ain't very tall in my reckoning."

"Now, Neff," Josh said deprecatingly, "Cousin Fess looked tolerably good when we was only a whoop and a holler ahead of that marshal and his friends. Fess is only asking his due."

Neff grimaced at this, the dark lines of his face deepening. His hand rubbed the back of his neck for a moment. "Can't either of us read for all git out, damn it!" he snapped. "How do we know what was in that letter from that Marcher feller?"

Irritation was edging Josh's voice again. "Fess has no call to be fawfawing us. This gent and his brother wants someone to guide them into Sioux country. 'Pears they has a notion where they want to go but don't want to chance it alone. For a little company they're obliging to pay three hundred dollars." Josh threw a dull wink at his companion in an open effort at encouragement that was wasted on Hammer. "Must be mighty important they get there."

"That was three hundred dollars from Independence," insisted Neff, his mouth taut now like a man sensing in himself some hitherto unknown pocket of fear. "How's they supposed to git up here from

Independence? You can see for yourself the river's alive with Injuns and that damn blue-bellied cavalry—one will raise their hair, t'other will turn them back."

Josh puffed his cigarette and turned to view the plain to the south where the buffalo were still lumbering toward the river. Here and there one would stop and lift its nose warily to the wind. But the wind was out of the southwest and strong enough to keep the warning scent away. In another ten minutes they would be close enough to shoot into, and the men on the island would be chewing thick pieces of hump steak before dark. Perhaps he'd better get his rifle and get behind the thicket with the others. He wanted to claim at least one cow so they would have meat to carry a ways up north where the shooting was mighty risky, as their recent bout with that grizzly had proved.

"Neff," he said, his tone a cold mixture of resignation and disgust, "Fess has reason aplenty to make sure them gents get here. Best quit a-stewing over it. This damn uprising ain't real handy, but men with such important business to do ought to be able to find their way around a handful of Injuns that can't shoot for shoutin' and green cavalry that ain't allowed out after dark. And best you stop bitchin' about Cousin Fess. He's better-looking than a rope. Likely you 'pear to forget we two are in powerful demand, and if they once catch us they ain't planning to saddle up for that chore again."

Josh had his rifle in his hand now and was getting ready to go down and join the others behind the thicket. He pressed out the rolled tobacco with his boot. "You wait here, Neff, I'm going to shoot us a little grub. It will look powerful good if we have a supply of meat on hand when them fellows and their poke, which Fess says is mostly carrying gold pieces, throw in here. Shows we've been working."

Nehemiah Hammer watched the thick figure of Captain Josh make its way toward the thicket, walking again with that strange wooden gait. Then he picked up a willow twig and scratched the dirt beside him thoughtfully.

Josh settled a little to one side of a cluster of men peering through the thicket at the herd now approaching the south bank of the river. He wondered, now that he was alone, why his mind was drifting so much. He kept having to go back and recall things he knew he had been thinking about, but they had gotten away from him. It seemed to him his mind ran on like that river, changing every moment and swirling into patterns that seemed thrust upon it by some obscure pressure from beneath. He tried to keep his thinking on some of the things Cousin Fess had said, but they kept getting away from him. Things like the money they would make from these brothers, how half of it was rightly Fess's, although Josh suddenly couldn't remember why. Something was subtly shifting the sands of his sanity, and he fought hard against his fear that it had to do with the dark secret that crept about the far reaches of his mind like an evil rodent.

It came as it always did, that gaily decked steamboat making its turn on the river, the one he was to have taken in St. Louis on Easter morning, taken to New Orleans, to Vera Cruz, to maybe even . . . but the broad, chuckling Creole face rose against the steamboat, and he swore as he remembered how he had gotten himself that whore, gotten himself drunk, robbed, diseased. At first it had just filled him with a white hate that uncoiled from time to time, but then that sore appeared on his member, and the fellow that Cousin Fess sent him to told him it was whores' rot and just to pour some whiskey on it and forget about it since there was no curing. He kept whiskey on it aplenty and it finally went away, but somehow he knew the rot was still in him gnawing slyly at his mind and body.

He thought about Neff and how that little yellow-bellied bastard had squealed and broken wind like a pig pinned with a pitchfork when the Sioux jumped them. Josh couldn't remember Hammer getting off a single shot during the run for the island, but then, with his mind shifting, he wasn't sure. Leastwise he managed to calculate that Neff wouldn't amount to much if it came to any tolerable fighting. Too bad he hadn't ended up with a fast and ready gun for a partner. As he watched the water, Josh glanced in memory over the years, muddling over how he had fetched and carried for Fess, remembering the barge he had taken down to New Orleans loaded with the stolen pelts Fess had come by one way or the other. How Fess had told him he could call himself Captain after that and gave him fifty dollars and a quart of whiskey for that God Almighty risk he had taken. Fess had always told him he'd be sitting high and mighty one day, though Fess never quite got around to adding how this pleasurable state of affairs was going to come about. He looked up at the herd again. They were very close now. As he raised his rifle, he could see Fess smoking his expensive cigars behind his barrels of cheap whiskey in St. Louis or Independence and making like this Dakota country was safer than church. Well, Fess could jaw all he wanted about what lay in the making, but Josh couldn't get over the feeling that the eyes of something evil were finally upon him and they were watching him with a peculiar grin.

5

Red Legs, his eyes warily on guard for the slightest incongruity in the landscape, raised a tiny pebble to his mouth, an old way of keeping the mouth moist, the mind away from water.

Beyond White Buffalo Horse sprawled the three whites. To Red Legs they seemed peculiarly quiet and unconcerned. Even when he told them he was going back, even when he made the hopeless sign for going on, indicating the land was alive with Sioux, even then they had not grown angry. The older one, this Ben Amiel, seeming to understand that the young Pawnees had to be saved, had nodded knowingly and offered Red Legs some tobacco, obviously wishing him well. The younger one called Marcher simply stared at him as though he knew his thoughts would not please the Pawnee and had best not be said. Only the one called White River had spoken, watching the horizon over the edge of the draw, saying, without looking at Red Legs, "Likely to be as many behind us now as ahead . . . Sioux have toted the war pipe a few times before . . . they're bound to calculate that a bunch holing up here as long as we have is studying turning back." Red Legs had no answer for this frightening logic. He knew only what he had to do. "Is better to die going home," he said, turning away and feeling empty, no longer hating this one whose words seemed so much stronger than his.

There was water, but very little, and some of that precious little had to be used to quiet the horses who sensed the river and had to be taken back to the creek bed where there were still thin stalls of shade. The guns, bandoliers, and canteens, the meager margin of survival, were brought forward and lay in disorder along the bank of the gully, the several repeating rifles with the silver nameplates of the whites looking formidable alongside the single muzzle-loader carried by Red Legs. The young bucks clung to their bows and arrows, and White Buffalo Horse held silently to his ancient lance. There was something awkward yet dreamlike in the way they moved about, the tall whites drifting slowly down the draw, the young and shorter Pawnees scurrying about, their eyes searching the rims to the north, their excitement suddenly infused with a curious and anxious restiveness.

Throughout the day Red Legs had watched the whites out of the corner of his eye, half expecting to see them making the medicine words to their Great Spirit in the sky, but they seemed only to mumble to each other and try to sleep. For a moment he envied them. The whites were surely a strange people. The Sioux might kill these three, perhaps three hundred more before the tomahawk was broken, but death would not discourage the whites, they would be back before the victory dances were over to fight again.

Red Legs glanced to where White Buffalo Horse was chanting to himself. Now the old one was propped against a rock, his eyes closed though his head remained poised as if he were looking out into a far, far distance—an old man peering backward through his misty memories toward some past horizon, his lost years stretching out before him until in some faint distance he glimpsed again the summer of his life.

Red Legs listened to him only idly. His chant at first told of ancient times. Ah, Tirawa, were not the Pawnees one with greatness then, had not their many enemies lived in terror of them, had not their hunting parties foraged along this river at will, their women and children coming along in laughter and in play, so safe was it behind the wall of Pawnee braves. Red Legs had not listened since leading the young Pawnees to the far side of the gully where they could not follow the old man's endless lament. It was only now when Red Legs heard White Buffalo Horse start to sing of Storm Walker, that almost mythical medicine man of the Pawnees, whose gigantic figure and black headdress were some of Red Legs' first memories of life, that he quietly shifted the pebble in his mouth and began again to follow the strange chant.

It was a thing too strong to turn from. No one in the history of the tribe had ever had medicine as powerful as Storm Walker's. It was known that his medicine had once saved Red Legs' entire village. When Red Legs was only a stripling of a boy, most of the warriors of his village had left to follow a powerful Sioux war party which, surprising them at dawn, had taken many of their horses and some of their young women. A terrible storm struck the village, lightning and hail plummeting down from the sky like an avalanche. The people had hugged their robes within the lodges and sung the many medicine songs, for it was feared it was a bad omen. It was. As the ravaging storm subsided, Storm Walker came down from a nearby hill where he frequently went during the heart of a storm, as it was his medicine, to tell them he could see from that height that they would soon be surrounded by a great force of Blue Men, the Arapahos, that was coming against them. The icy fear that spread in the hearts of the people deepened when they heard that with the Arapahos was a band of Comanches. Oh, the Comanches, the hated ones, a vicious, arrogant people, nomads who lived by plunder, born predators who preyed upon men and were recognized throughout their wide domain as savage fighters.

Red Legs remembered how, on that distant morn and on the brink of extinction, the old ones of his village tried to deal with their fears, realizing there was little time to waste.

The few warriors left in the village, their numbers desperately swelled by old men and boys, began to paint themselves, bring up their best ponies and sing their war songs. Women shrieked from their lodges as men raced past, pleading with them to be brave, to fight for their breasts, their thighs, and the other good things of their bodies. Other women cried to their children. Still others ran to throw wet logs on the great fires in the center of the camp in hopes the heavy columns of smoke would be seen by their warriors to the north—an ancient signal of distress in those times. Little boys like Red Legs slipped from behind their mothers' blankets to scamper to the west slope of the camp and watch White Buffalo Horse, already a warrior of many coups who had not gone with the others because of a wound received in a raid but a short while before, giving directions to the gathering braves and leading them to where they could make their best stand.

It was a day a child could not forget. The wind that followed the storm over the prairie carried with it war cries that would echo down the years and remind the man of those many-feathered faces of death. The enemy struck with a fury that showed they knew a great victory was almost in their grasp. Brave and determined as the Pawnees were, the Comanches broke through their lines time after time, and it was only with costly, far too costly, fighting that they were finally pressed back. It seemed that the next charge must be the one that could not be withstood, when suddenly a second storm struck and both sides drew back. It was an even larger storm than the first, yet so great had been the Pawnee losses that the keening from the women could be heard rising above the tumult.

Suddenly Storm Walker, who had worked his way through the enemy lines during the storm to climb his hill, appeared before the warriors telling them he had just had a great vision that must give them hope. He had seen a great scarlet mountain surrounded by a deep, grassy plain. At the top of the mountain was a great bird, the Sun Bird. It could not be seen, but its light made the top of the mountain radiant. As it rose before his eyes, his medicine had whispered to him that all the Pawnee braves who died defending the people on this day would be mounted on magnificent horses which would carry them up this mountain, there to sit in a sacred lodge where there would be laughter and much happiness in this land of eternal light where the Sun Bird dwelled.

This he told them twice, for at first they could not believe his words. But then the warriors started to sing together, for their hearts had been down and not one expected to survive the day. To have a vision like this from such a strong and wise one as Storm Walker made it a different thing to die.

The enemy was back, the Comanche chief leading the way, his great buffalo-horn headdress shaking in the wind, his lance now draped with Pawnee scalps freshly taken.

The Arapahos were pressing closer too, ready and anxious for the many coups that would soon be possible in this helpless village. As their lines drew closer, the Comanche chief laid his quirt on his horse and struck toward them, outrunning his braves. He was the first into the Pawnee lines, and as he swept through them White Buffalo Horse, though wounded a second time in this fight, lunged under the Comanche's pony and drove his war club against the oncoming mount with such fury that the animal hurled itself sideways and threw the Comanche chief to the ground. The Pawnees were hot for death now, and the Comanche chief managed only to get one knee under him before a tomahawk opened his skull and brought dullness to his fierce eyes. He died in that position, his scalp being ripped from him as his warriors came up to rescue him. But the Pawnees were throwing themselves upon their attackers now like men gone mad. Old ones, anxious to die, stood in the path of certain death to get their lances into one of the enemy, some of them receiving two arrows in their bodies before they could strike back. The Comanches, furious and howling at the death of their chief, came on like demons, some of them dismounting to join in hand-to-hand combat. But after a brave beginning the Arapahos started to hang back, one of their chiefs trying to rally them with a great war cry until a Pawnee arrow pierced his eyeball and he fell over backward from his horse. After some hard fighting, the Comanches recaptured their chief's body but then decided to withdraw—to turn their anger against the Arapahos, it was discovered later.

The Pawnee losses by then were such that any renewal of the attack would have put the village and all in it beyond hope. Yet those who were left were almost jubilant. Clearly the enemy had lost confidence in himself, had begun to doubt his own medicine, and that, as every Indian knew, was usually a sign he would not return.

That night the Comanches and the Arapahos built fires just out of view of the village, but Pawnee scouts could hear their council talk and it made their hearts sing, for their enemies were arguing. The Comanches, bitter at the loss of their chief and resentful that their allies did not fight harder, were showing their characteristic contempt for any allies they outfought. One Comanche warrior, apparently a brother of the dead chief, struck an Arapaho across the face with his bow and made the coward sign. Luckily for that Arapaho, a great clap of thunder shook the sky at that moment and a third storm began.

When it had cleared just before dawn, the Pawnees found the fires beyond the ridge were out and the enemy gone. The Pawnees stood in the dark hearing gratefully the return of all the normal noises that should fill the night. Then they gave a great whoop. That day, it was decided, should be left for keening for the dead, but the next night the warriors, even those that were wounded, said there would be a victory dance. There was much to be sung of and many offerings to be made to Storm Walker for his powerful medicine. But Storm Walker was nowhere to be found.

As dawn broke, some of the warriors, White Buffalo Horse among them, started up the nearby hill, many of them feeling that Storm Walker had returned there during the stormy night, as was his strange way. But as the light increased they realized uneasily that they were on the trail of a wounded man. The trail ended with Storm Walker's great body braced against a giant stump of tree that had been struck and shattered by lightning in the years before. A Comanche arrow was in his side, his lifeless hand upon it. But he was looking up, his eyes open and trained upon a mighty towering cloud which suddenly rose in this awesome dawning, as he had told of in his vision, like a scarlet mountain beyond which everyone sensed must dwell that great bird of eternal light.

Hoofprints of a very large horse were found beside Storm Walker's body, even though those who returned said they could not find such hoofprints either ascending or descending the hill. Some of the older men sat in council on this strange thing, and it was decided to leave Storm Walker where he was and to consider that hill sacred. And so they left the council lodge, each with his eyes to the ground, none daring to look at the sky, so awed were they by the strength of this man's medicine.

No Pawnee had ever climbed that hill since.

Red Legs shifted the pebble in his mouth again. Truly the spirits were one with his people then. He wondered if such strong medicine would ever be given to the Pawnee again.

Suddenly his eyes caught a wolf that stopped and abruptly changed course far down the river. He took some vermilion from his belt pack and drew two lines across his face. He checked the load in his smoothbore rifle and, drawing his knife, he began to work one side of the blade against a stone.

6

As darkness fell, the distant chirping of a sage hen, the sharp bark of a fox, and the lonely call of a curlew passed unnoticed by the whites, but to Red Legs they were a wall of death. The Sioux were ready and he knew it. He knew also that an experienced warrior should never have allowed this trap to be sprung, and though he tried to steel himself against it during the long, agonizing hours of what he sensed was his final day, he had found himself succumbing time after time to the womanish weakness of wishing for what now was impossible. If only he had spoken sooner. If only he had forced them further south where they would have had more water, had not allowed themselves to be caught here baked out like buffalo chips after a rainless spring, only a mile or two from water they could not reach. If only they had more horses and fresh ones, more guns, repeating ones like those carried by the whites, more seasoned warriors, more time. He picked up a handful of parched clay, watching it crumble between his fingers.

The horses had been brought forward, their muzzles held closely to keep them from neighing. They were listless and moved reluctantly. Red Legs signaled the young Pawnees to gather about him. His words were few. They would leave on foot, saving their ponies and waiting until they had reached some soft place to mount up. One coyote yip would mean to mount and follow him, two to take cover, and three to mount and ride in different directions, each attempting to reach safety as best he could. Only young Lame Fox had answered, "Uncle, can we not go first to the river for water? It is dark and our ears are good."

Red Legs stared at him for a moment. In his youth such a remark was unheard of at a time like this, but then, had not the times changed? "The river is like a bright piece of cloth, my son," he said tightly, "put in a high place to make the foolish reach for it and become an easy mark for the arrow." Lame Fox's eyes shifted slowly to the valley where the cool river ran, but he said no more.

Red Legs went haltingly toward White Buffalo Horse, his heart growing ever heavier. "Old one, will you not come back to your people?" White Buffalo Horse did not answer. His eyes remained closed, but Red Legs knew he was awake. "We must leave. It is time. It is a thing that must be done," muttered Red Legs.

White Buffalo Horse slowly released his eyes. They did not turn to Red Legs, but after long moments the ancient mouth moved. "It is bad, my son, they are many."

"I know," sighed Red Legs. Nothing more was said, both knowing that nothing now could be made better with words.

A figure suddenly appearing beside them brought Red Legs up erect. It was Ben Amiel. "You're going now?" he asked. At first Red Legs only noticed that Amiel held one of the new repeating rifles in his hands, held it in a strange way, not the way a man should carry such a weapon while he shared the darkness with the Sioux.

"We go," said Red Legs finally, his voice a mutter, his eyes still on the strong thing in the white man's hands.

Amiel turned the rifle over and held it up before him. "You know how to use such a gun?" Red Legs looked at him with puzzled eyes. Was the white man jesting at such a time? There were three such guns already in the Pawnee village, gifts from the whiskey traders to "helpers." Red Legs grunted that he could use the weapon but wondered if this white man was foolish enough to be talking of trading when everything the Pawnees carried with them could not begin to be enough for such a gun. "Good," said Ben. "Take it." He put the rifle in Red Legs' hands and began pulling cartridges from his belt. Red Legs stood in blank amazement. White men did not give away such weapons for nothing, even when they had two, especially when their own lives might well hang in the balance. Surely at least they did not give them to Indians. Amiel nodded at the young Pawnees waiting anxiously beside their horses. "Get them back safely," he said simply and turned away.

Red Legs watched him go, realizing that this white man with one great gesture had turned Red Legs into three warriors instead of one. If he lived he would see that this debt, which the other appeared to wear so lightly, would be repaid. In spite of a strange lingering wolf call that warily probed the night to the east, for the first time hope began to breathe faintly across Red Legs' heart.

In Red Legs' other hand the heavy smoothbore which he had kept carefully loaded all day seemed suddenly an encumbrance. Beside him still sat the crouching figure of White Buffalo Horse, who now had only a useless lance with which to face death. It was fitting that a Pawnee war chief who had brought many honors to his people should be better armed. It was a thing the people would want to hear. It was a thing they would ask Red Legs about if and when he returned. He placed the smoothbore across White Buffalo Horse's arms and, having no words strong enough for what he felt, moved away.

The young Pawnees murmured in surprise as they saw the repeating rifle in Red Legs' hands. It was powerful medicine, surely more powerful than anything carried by the Sioux. Red Legs ignored their whisperings and motioned for silence. Within moments they were hurrying back down the creek bed, each leading his horse, each with his eyes prying into the night, his ears picking up the pounding of his own heart.

Marcher's eyes were alive in the darkness. "You idiot, you mean to say you gave away one of our rifles! Where do you suppose we're going to get another?"

"Keep your voice down," hissed White River.

"A man does what he wants with his own property," said Ben evenly. "I seem to remember I paid for it, just as you paid for yours."

"Maybe you'll pay for it with your life before this is over."

"It's *my* life, Andy. Reckon I'm the judge of what it's worth. Besides," he said with a deepened voice, "I'd take it kindly if you kept a civil tongue in your head."

The horses stood beside them in the gully, listless, their heads hanging; a tail swished from time to time; or a horse idly stamped a hoof.

Marcher was standing with a repeating rifle in each hand, tense, irritated. Was there no one else who ever thought of getting on with matters? He saw White River standing in the darkness, apparently listening to a dim cacophony of sounds emanating from the vamp of the valley below. In his hands White River held the single-shot breechloader Marcher had watched him clean thoroughly and silently just before dark.

Marcher approached him, holding out one of the repeaters. "Do you want to use one of these?"

White River shook his head. "Feel t'home with this one. There be times when a man's better stickin' to what he's used to."

"Well, whatever you say. . . . When do we leave?"

"Depends."

"On what?"

"Put one of them guns back in the saddle, Mr. Marcher. You can't shoot both of them t'once."

Ben Amiel came toward them, stepping lightly. "I seem to remember reading somewhere how Indians don't like fighting in the dark."

White River looked at him patiently. "They'd druther come at dawn, but they'll kill you any time you're handy."

"Maybe if we fire a few rounds over their heads it might scare them off."

White River turned into the darkness, his face tightening like a man tasting a sour stomach. "Just keep off'n that trigger till you see something to shoot at." His voice struggled to stay a half whisper. "Then make certain you hit it plumb. Burning powder don't rattle Indians . . . 'spect they will be burning plenty themselves. But straight shooting, now that gets 'em to thinking every time."

Beyond them in the gully a strange, ghostlike silhouette appeared, barely discernible against the dark sky. It was White Buffalo Horse already astride his mount and poised at the creek-bed opening. The pony's head hung down as though the reins were loose, and it was only after long staring that they made out the thin line of his lance poised upright in one hand and Red Legs' muzzle-loader in the other.

"What's he up to?" muttered Marcher.

"More 'n likely got his own notions," said White River.

"If he's going out there alone, hadn't we ought to try and stop him?" Ben urged with concern.

White River merely shook his head. Even if he had been good with words, there was no way he could make them understand. Having been partly raised by Indians, he shared something of the peculiar logic of their ways. Somehow the totality of the Indian's life could be traced to that now pathetic figure of old White Buffalo Horse mounted beyond. A minute scene in a nameless drama that had stricken a race.

Even in his short span, White River could remember when the tribes of the south and southwest held the lower Missouri, the plains of Kansas, eastern Nebraska and . . . oh, a body could hardly remember, if he had a mind to, the immensity of what had gone under the white man's way. And of a certainty, the many tribes familiar to his youth were going under with it. Whether they fought this swift erosion of their being or served it made little difference. The wild free life, the only life in which they could remain themselves, was passing, and wherever and whenever it passed from a hillock, a valley, a tree or a stone, it was gone forever. Somehow Indians didn't put the stake in life that white men did. A few had tried the plowed side of the road, but most of them by far shared a mute agreement that the change demanded of them was too great. It was too far from the old ways, too devoid of the old passions, the old longings—better to join the past.

It was not a thing that could be worked into words.

And then it began. From the dark vamp of the valley the Sioux put a fire arrow into the air; as it fell, shots sounded, lost almost immediately in a chorus of wolf calls that changed suddenly to war whoops that were themselves lost in a great cry that rose beside them as White Buffalo Horse raked his pony's flanks and charged forward into the night. From the valley before them and along the bluffs to their east, where Red Legs had led the frightened youths, crazed screams ravaged the dark, so much so that the hoofbeats of the old chief's horse were gone almost at once, though his great crying could still be heard.

Marcher and Ben Amiel stood in dread fascination. So engulfed were they in the sounds of the melee that when White Buffalo Horse's muzzle-loader went off, its orange tongue darting against the sooty sky, they had to be jolted vigorously by White River as he hurriedly pulled the reins of his horse and ran up the narrow gully to the west, his long body bent over, his every motion demanding speed. When they reached the off-slope of the bluff, White River mounted quickly, signaling them to do the same. Then he shot off into the night, Marcher and Ben behind him, their horses, partly spooked by the outcry, running willingly away from a moon that edged up over the horizontal haze to lighten the eastern mantle of night.

The gully was suddenly empty, returned to time. In one of its crevices the lizard lay curled up, its eyes behind its scaly lids, patient in its primitive knowledge that there would be another sun.

A hard light opened a thin wedge in the eastern skies—light as hard as the edge of the storm clouds it had forced itself between, as hard as the light in White River's eyes as he viewed it, his thoughts his own, not to be shared by those with whom he rode. It had been a moonlit night, but the moon had grown dusky in its final hours, and the clouds had slowly stalled against the wind and gathered darkly over the land.

They had swung south, sweeping behind the bluffs in the early night, but had turned north finally to work their way westward and breach the valley where the island could be seen. They were almost at the river now, and in the dim light they could see figures on the island watching them approach, motioning to each other and then signaling them in with waving hats when it was clear that they were whites.

White River stopped at the river's edge and allowed his mount to drink. That night, in some part of his mind, he had heard a repeating rifle emptied twice and then no more, though it was clear the fighting was far from over. He wondered what a man would find if he wandered back there now. His heart told him he would never know.

Ben Amiel was alongside him, his face showing the strain of the exhausting night, his eyes weary and dull like a man who has ceased caring. Marcher was but a few feet beyond him, silent and watchful as though he could not believe the island was finally theirs.

"That's what you've been sweatin' to reach," said White River tightly, nodding ahead. It was clear he wanted no answer.

Ben looked at the island, then turned to gaze listlessly toward the east. Whatever his thoughts, he willed them finally into harmless words. "Hope luck was with those poor devils."

White River sucked in his bottom lip, but his face did not soften. Marcher threw a quick glance at the seam of light, now menaced by dark rolling clouds, and let out a gruff breath of air. "Can't say I'm fretting too much. Don't forget, they were supposed to help us get to this island."

White River pulled his mount up abruptly and prodded it into the stream. His eyes, as he looked back at Marcher, appeared to Amiel like the eyes of an angry and vengeful pharaoh. "They did," he said evenly, and pressed on.

7

The fire crackled as melting fat dripped from the barbecuing buffalo ribs, and repeatedly a quick sudden light was thrown into the eyes of four men, two on each side of the fire, one regarding the other with growing irritation. Marcher and Amiel had slept most of the day but with the coming of evening had roused themselves to devour the meat prepared for them by Josh and Neff.

Ben Amiel had not slept well, and the scruff of beard on his face could not conceal the strain carried over from the night before. The saddlebags he always slept on had felt hard as stone. Disgruntled and depressed, he only picked at the meat sizzling before him, and his speech came with effort. "There are some questions to be answered, gentlemen." He turned to Marcher, "Go ahead, Andy."

Marcher scowled, rubbing grease from the edge of his mouth as he chewed. He had been studying Josh and Neff across the fire. In addition to their ignorant manner and shady appearance, their far too hearty greetings that morning had left him irked. His voice betrayed his pique. "How long have you two worked for Mr. Fess?"

Josh kneaded his massive chest with one hand, his eyes first closing on, then finally slipping away from Marcher's. "Shoot! Must be a heap of time." His expression lightened as though he had suddenly spotted a trump point. "Fess, I'm bound to tell you, is muh cousin."

Marcher continued to study them, his rising skepticism pulling his face to a grimace that hinted at disgust. "Cousins, eh? What kind of work have you been doing for him?"

Josh threw an uneasy glance at Neff. "Scoutin', mostly." He paused, as though unsure where that remark might lead. "As you likely know, Cousin Fess has a heap of jobs a-going. But like I say, with us it's been mostly scoutin'."

"Yep, mostly scoutin'," echoed Neff, nervously scratching his stiffened leg under the strip of blanket. "Fact is, only yesterday we scouted up a parcel of them Sioux and damn if they didn't nick me." Neff lifted his leg with one hand, his eyes seeking sympathy.

Marcher regarded him with contempt. "Have either of you 'scouts' ever been in this country before?"

"Well, after a fashion," Josh allowed dismissively, as though the point lacked significance. "Now looky here, Mr. Marcher, there's no need for you to get to worrying. We got us a deal to get you two where you're going, and we're bound to keep our word."

The brothers looked at each other. Finally abandoning his attempt to eat, Ben sat back and said quietly, "We'd counted on your meeting us in Independence. It's only by the grace of God—no thanks to you—that we're here."

"That's right." Marcher's gaze was leveled across the fire. "And it's time we heard just why you two left Independence without us, and in such a hurry."

Josh pulled open his collar and began to rub his face in confusion. "Now Cousin Fess rightly agreed he'd explain. . . ."

"We heard his explanation. We don't like it. We're waiting to hear yours."

Josh turned away from the brothers and threw a desperate look at Neff, covering this move by clawing awkwardly at his pockets for tobacco. Neff, still holding his leg, pulled himself up and started to speak in a strained voice close to a whine. "Well, we just naturally . . . well, with Fess saying he was a-gonna fetch you up here safe and all, we just figured it'd be best to scout on ahead, set up camp, do a little scoutin' "—he gestured weakly at the smoking fire—"lay up some fresh grub. For a fact, Mr. Marcher, we was readying up so we could leave straightaway for that place you're headed, quick as you appeared."

The brothers exchanged glances again, each thinking back to that morning and their first sight of Josh and Neff. Both had recalled their conversation with White River in Independence and rankled at the danger and deception they sensed in this riffraff. Yet they also knew that unless they could recruit some help on this island of grim, violent-looking men, they would have to face the hostile Sioux country alone.

Marcher fixed each of them in turn with eyes almost shut in pained surmise. "I can't say I'm impressed with either of you gents, or for that matter with your story, which I'll generously call farfetched. Our correspondence specified experienced and competent people. That's what we agreed to pay for. Now we get here to find out not only are you unreliable, but on what should have been a simple scout you get yourself shot up."

"Now hold on there, Mr. Marcher, likely you know this is mighty hostile country." Josh was shifting his bulk about, trying to look more formidable. "Three hundred ain't a heap of money when it comes to risking a man's hair."

Marcher snorted disdainfully and swallowed the meat he'd been chewing. "What three hundred? It cost us two hundred to get here." He looked at them in open suspicion, sarcasm burdening his voice. "I'm sure you've already heard all this from your boss . . . Cousin Fess."

Josh and Neff looked at each other quickly. "Ditheration," wheezed Neff, his voice almost inaudible.

Marcher smiled bitterly, more to himself than to the others. "You better start thinking about being unemployed, gentlemen." He glanced at Amiel. "We'll decide what we're going to do in the morning."

Amiel studied the fire and shook his head.

Josh and Neff both had stopped eating—clearly their appetites had vanished. They looked sullenly across at the brothers, and in the silence that followed the air around the fire filled with resentment and distrust.

• • •

They had reached the island shortly after dawn, and with only a cursory exchange with Josh and Neff they had spread their gear and slumped down to sleep off their exhaustion. White River was up by late afternoon, moving the horses to fresh grass and sizing up the island's inhabitants. It was then he was hailed by Benson, the trader, and Teel, the trapper, whom he had known from many seasons in the Missouri country.

"Couldn't have been more surprised if my own grandaddy had ridden up when I first laid eyes to you," said Benson. "Nigh on a year, ain't it, since you tangled with Kane, and we ain't seen nary a Gray Man hereabouts since."

White River nodded silently. He was not anxious to be reminded of the Gray Men, renegade whites dressed and painted like Indians, who attacked and looted small wagon trains, using their hatchets to mutilate dead bodies, making it look like the work of savages.

Teel laid a gnarled hand on his arm. "Got myself drunk as all git out the night I heard you gunned that varmint down. Orn'ry son-of-a-bitch needed killing." He sent a spray of tobacco juice behind him. "Reckon you had some luck gettin' here. Sioux been doing some mighty serious crawling up and down these parts lately."

"We ran across't 'em," said White River, glancing toward the nearby camp where Marcher and Amiel were still asleep beside the huddled figures of Josh and Neff. "Wonder would you fellas mind if I throw in with you. 'Bout finished with them gents yonder."

"Why, you betcha," said Benson. "Glad for such pleasurable company. Just fetch your gear and come on over." He pointed to a clear spot fifty yards away. "After you settle in us can visit for a spell."

White River nodded his gratitude and turned away. Mention of the Gray Men had awakened in him the great empty feeling Buzz's death at their hands had left him with, and that name Chicasaw Kane still made him clamp his jaws in suppressed fury.

Somehow it didn't seem years since that cavalry man rode up to the ranch with word of Buzz's death. It was a hard story to relate, or even for him to believe.

Buzz had been leading a detail of young soldiers who had trapped some Gray Men near the Platte Fork and forced them to surrender. It was the notorious Asa Kane gang, and Asa was coming forward with his hands in the air, the rest of the gang following behind. No one seemed to know what happened, but suddenly shots broke out and Buzz dropped to the ground. Panic seized the young troopers, and as a shooting melee began the Gray Men made their escape. Only Buzz, apparently as he was dying, got off any shots, for they found Asa's body and a trail of heavy bloodstains that had come from one of the escaping riders. It was two months before anyone knew that the fleeing outlaw Buzz had wounded was Asa's cousin, Chicasaw Kane, who showed up in southern Missouri with a deep crimson scar slashed like a hatchet blow across the left side of his face.

For three lonely years as an army scout, White River listened to reports that Chicasaw Kane was somewhere in the south leading a band of ex-Quantrills, one-time southern guerrillas still living by the gun. Chicasaw was easy to spot because of his scar and the horse pistol he wore in front of him. But scouting could be wearisome work, and White River was growing itchy. One day he made up his mind to leave the army, and that was the day he met Pat Sloan in Independence. Sloan was grinning that day with welcome news. Chicasaw had been arrested near Baton Rouge and was coming to trial. It raised strange emotions in White River, but he concluded it was the law's job to deal with the lawless. Maybe now Buzz's many friends could breathe easy. It didn't seem possible Chicasaw could escape the rope.

He'd headed back to Fort Laramie to collect his pay and resign his job, wondering what he could do next, although already he realized what he deeply craved was roots. Something that would give him back the life he had known with Buzz and little Lydia.

It was at Laramie he met a soldier who had been on that fatal detail when Buzz was killed. Sensing that this man might be his last chance to learn just how Buzz died, he sat patiently in the sutler's store and bought them drinks, plying the trooper with questions about that sorry day. He followed the man's words several times and from different starting points—how the gang was cornered and already surrendering, Asa Kane coming forward, his hands raised, behind him Chicasaw and the others. They were all moving toward Buzz, who was standing with his gun leveled at them. Then a shot rang out and Buzz was down firing from the ground. Apparently all hell broke loose, outlaws and soldiers shouting and firing wildly.

The poor fellow winced as though this truth had burdened him for some time. "Remember we were green recruits, most of us under fire for the first time. Those bastards were seasoned gunmen. We found out later a lot of them had served in Confederate cavalry, some even with Jeb Stuart, by God!" The trooper looked at White River, obviously regretting he couldn't offer a more comforting story. "It ain't nothing to brag on, fellow, but truth is before we knew it we were standing watching their dust with nothing but three badly wounded recruits and Buzz and Asa dead on the ground."

White River left Laramie knowing at last how Buzz died and who killed him.

Back in Independence he was greeted by a disgusted and dispirited Pat Sloan, who told him Chicasaw Kane was on the loose again. Incredibly, the court had found him innocent on all charges.

White River stared back at him in disbelief.

"The law can only punish what it can prove, friend," said Sloan resignedly. "Seems he found himself a real reb court, packed with armed troublemakers like himself. Bastard had the nerve to get himself charged with every crime in the book. Don't need to tell you that come the trial not a witness against him showed up. And, hell, the prosecutor was too drunk to find the jury box. Kane's as free as a wild mustang now, and I understand he's been lettin' on as to how the law can't touch him."

White River spent the rest of that day sitting on a bank overlooking the Missouri, watching the river and remembering how as a child in the Arikara village he had witnessed the "death walks" of proud, fierce warriors bent on vengeance for the killing of near ones. Among the Missouri tribes a warrior who was committed by oath to the death walk before the fires of his warrior society could not return until released by a death—his or the killer's. Many, even from among the strongest, never returned. By evening he knew in his heart that this land was not ready for the cumbersome and impersonal laws of civilization. Chicasaw Kane had nothing to fear from laws rising from legislation. His kind needed laws that rose in the hearts of men.

As the evening star appeared in the west he stood and faced the horizon beyond which lay Buzz Matlock's grave, and there he chanted the Arikara warrior's oath to take the death walk, aware now that he carried a sacred burden which only a death could remove.

It was not a thing to be talked about. He said nothing to Pat Sloan, checked his gear and left quietly for Baton Rouge. But the first night he ran into Benson camping on the river on his annual trek north. Here over a mug of Benson's brew he learned that Chicasaw was around Joplin and headed for Independence.

The next day a worried Pat Sloan stopped him in town to report Chicasaw was expected by nightfall. Then, probably noticing the curious look in White River's eyes, he put his hands on his shoulders, adding weight to his words. "Don't do anything foolish, son, he's a dangerous man." White River's expression remained steady, making Sloan's face stiffen with suspicion. "Might be best you leave Independence for a spell. Believe me, Kane and his kind will get to hell fast enough on their own."

White River shrugged and pulled away.

He could smell the river in the darkness. It was rank from the decaying refuse its dropping water level always deposited in foul heaps upon the sand bars and the brush-clogged banks. It seemed to smell of evil, but he knew it was only his senses telling him he was close. He could see the lamps that hung before the saloons, looking in the distance like yellow blobs that could not penetrate the night. Chicasaw Kane was coming, that much he knew. The blacksmith pounding with his hammer and shoeing his horse made a joke of it. "Yep, he's a-comin' all right. Suppose to meet up with the Devil on Whiskey Hill tonight. Can't hardly see how a man can meet up with he'self, can you?"

"Not rightly," answered White River.

Whiskey Hill was three saloons high up on the embankment in the most dangerous part of town. He moved up toward them not knowing which one to enter first. He had passed the notorious "Hill" for years but had never stopped there. He decided on the one to the left. As he reached its entrance he saw a rough-looking sign that read "The Kicking Steer."

Inside there was a low rumble, the tables partially filled by card players and half-drunk river men. Along the bar there were clumps of men smoking heavily and joking rudely with a few painted whores or arguing with that drumlike persistence that comes with drunkenness. At the far end a handful of river breeds whispered together furtively and passed a bottle, their eyes moving restlessly over the crowd till one by one they settled on White River. He found an open space at the bar and ordered a whiskey. He was looking for a man with a hatchet scar on his left cheek, and while many faces around him showed the imprints of knives or guns, it was clear Kane wasn't there.

Then he heard an almost indiscernible murmur coming through the room, and in the large mirror behind the bar he saw Pat Sloan moving slowly across the floor and deliberately stopping behind him.

"This ain't the way," the sheriff said calmly.

White River turned and studied him silently for a moment. "A man's way is his own choosing."

Sloan shook his head. He had watched men gunning for each other for half a lifetime. Talk was worse than useless. He moved to the bar and signaled for a drink. Downing it, he turned, his face tense but resigned. "He's next door, son. He's not alone. He's with Tice, a Texas killer as dangerous as they come. They're both talking to a gent named Beck, a German from St. Louis who buys stolen goods. There may be others, and unless you have eyes in the back of your head, you had better call him out and make sure you see who moves when he does."

White River looked at him long and hard. Pat was a good man. In his younger days he would unhesitatingly have thrown Kane out of town, but now White River could see the years in his face and the first hint of retreat in his eyes. "Thanks," he said, and meant it, and started to move away.

"Remember, son, he and that Tice were both Quantrills and know every dirty trick in the books."

Sloan, left alone, turned again to the bar, one hand covering his eyes.

Next door was the Black Wharf saloon. It was noisier than The Kicking Steer, if only because a fiddle was scratching out a tune at the back end and two drunken teamsters were doing a buck-and-wing to the crude hallooing of their friends.

White River needed no help. The big man with the vicious scar on his cheek was having a drink poured for him and his squat companion at the top of the bar by a strange-looking character wearing a yellow ascot tie.

The suddenness of the moment almost robbed it of its reality. There at last, before his eyes, stood the slayer of Buzz Matlock, Chicasaw Kane. He was a heavy man with puffy lips and narrow-set eyes. He was carrying a large horse pistol, holstered almost in front of him, and his voice was as coarse as trap rock moving through a shuttle. White River's first impulse was to kill him before he drew another breath, but that was not the code Buzz had died for, the code Buzz had taught him was what separated men from craven animals who only thought they were men. He knew the squat man with silver dangles on his jacket would be Tice, and the one with the yellow ascot tie was obviously Beck, the German.

No one seemed to notice him, but he knew it was suicidal to wait. Every second from now on counted.

"Chicasaw Kane!" he called out loud enough to be heard throughout the saloon. A silence quickly rose and smothered the roaring discord, sweeping it in broken steps toward the rear. There were several heartbeats before the big man with the scar turned and said, "Me?"

"You!"

Kane tried to smile, but his harsh voice was tight and scratchy as he said, "What do you want with me?"

"Buzz Matlock is waiting to tell you. I'm calling you out."

The noise level in the saloon began to rise again. Whisperings filled the large room.

White River noticed Kane and Tice were mumbling to each other and quietly moving apart. "Start moving, Kane!" he commanded.

"Take it easy, partner, I was just enjoying a drink with my friends here. You don't . . ."

White River took a step back. His instincts told him he was giving Kane too much time. "Finish your drink," he shouted. "You won't be coming back!"

There was a quick mutter from Kane, and Beck, the German, started moving forward. "Vait, vait! Shentlemen, shentlemen, ve talk dis over, yah? Maybe ve haff a drink together, yah." Beck was raising his hands in a placating gesture as he advanced, and a cold blade of recognition shot through White River. It was happening again, just like it had happened to Buzz. Beck was coming forward with his hands high in the air, like Asa Kane coming to surrender. But Chicasaw, finding Asa between him and Buzz and Asa distracting Buzz with his raised hands, had deliberately fired through his own cousin with his horse pistol to kill Buzz.

Had he waited a split second he would have been dead, but in one movement he fired through Beck at Kane and dropped to his knees as their bullets, tearing through Beck's body, missed his head like shrieking hornets. With Beck's body crumbling he pumped his second and third rounds into Kane and Tice at the bar, then he was up and coming toward them. Tice was down choking on vomits of blood, his face lying in the contents of an overturned spittoon, but Kane was still bracing himself against the bar trying to hold the heavy horse pistol level and focus his eyes. But now White River was closing on him, rocking him back with another slug at every step until finally, his gun empty, he stood and watched the eyes of Chicasaw Kane, the murdering Gray Man, the killer of Buzz Matlock, turn to glass.

His death walk was over.

But the painful void in his life went on.

• • •

As White River stowed his gear down near Benson's fire, he noticed that he and Teel had been joined by a third man, an odd-looking figure with dull eyes and a small, hard head atop hunched shoulders. His name was Sam Gome.

White River nodded casually as he settled in an empty space beside Benson. "Still trading?" he asked.

"The same," Benson replied, helping Teel throw more wood on the fire.

"Doing respectable like?"

"Been slow—what with this uprising and Injuns cutting up and everything—figure it will shine some when things quiet down."

"How's freighting?"

"Been middling but fixing to improve right smartly." Benson's thick bottom lip came up as an expression of interest invaded his face. "What you studying, White River? 'Tain't like you to be chawing over hauling molasses and the likes."

"Got me a notion I'll set up an outfit and try a hand at it."

Benson clapped his thigh and yowled raucously. "Gosh damn, White River, I figured you for hunting, riding stage or mebbe just plain rambling—but taking to freighting!" Lines of disbelief creased his brow. "Hear'd tell freighting is a parcel of work."

"I reckoned on it."

"Gonna take hard cash to fit a proper team and wagon—ain't much round that the army ain't requisitioned and ruined. Doubt if there be enough hard money hereabouts to outfit up."

"Would two hundred gold put a wheel or two to rolling?"

"Two hundred gold?"

Sam Gome's eyes shifted to White River's feet.

"That much ought to fetch you a piece of railroad," said Benson. "Howsomever, I doubt if there be that much gold left from here to the fort. It's been swapping mostly with trade goods hereabouts for quite a spell now. Most bank notes ain't worth nothing, and even Union certificates ain't popular out at the fort, where it takes from hell to Sunday to turn them into cash."

"Well, I got it," said White River without emphasis.

"For a fact?"

"For a fact—it's pay for fetching them two gents out here."

Benson sat back, his eyes suddenly warmer with a new turn of interest. White River was serious. He was going to turn his hand at a hauling enterprise and actually had hard cash enough to try. The germ of a new idea quickened in Benson's mind. With that much hard cash his thoughts ran to the great Shuttler or Espenshied wagons that could be purchased in the wagon yards to the east. With White River as a partner he would have a man who had guts and savvy enough to get a wagon through this forbidden country. The profits made on the Denver run before the gold ran out and the war broke drifted through his mind.

"That's mighty fair pay," said Gome slowly, inquiringly, "for just a mite of scouting."

White River looked as though he wouldn't bother to answer, then said slowly, "Came close enough to not collecting it to make it fitting enough for me."

"What you suppose those two slick-eared brothers figure on doin' out here—taking in some fresh air mebbe?" Gome was looking over at the other fire and the four men grouped sullenly around it.

"They sure enough got themselves a couple of muleheads, if they're counting on them two buzzards to take 'em a piece further," said Benson, happy with his new thoughts.

"Figure one's got the guts of a treed chipmunk whilst t'other seems a mite tetched in the head," said Teel, contemplating the scene in the nearby camp. "If they ain't bait for trouble in these diggings I'm a whore from Santa Fe." He spit easily into a pothole beside him.

Gome was talking again as he deftly rolled some tobacco on a brown strip. "Likely they're getting pay aplenty if they be fetching those gents further on. Seems them fellows are right free with hard coin."

Teel threw Gome a long, curious look, but all he said was, "Likely."

In a few moments Gome sauntered over to a nearby abandoned fire, one closer to Marcher's and Amiel's. There he stood looking into the night. White River studied his movements quietly. "Now who might that gent be?" His words were rolled softly to Benson.

"Don't rightly know," muttered Benson, " . . . showed up a couple of days ago . . . didn't say what his line was, but he sure don't move about like no preacher."

Teel turned toward them with a knowing look. "A handy gun, I'm thinking. Up from Pecos country from the cut of his palaver. Ain't much on talk but he sure peppered the air with lead when those redskins came by a while back."

The conversation went back to wagon talk, Benson taking the lead now, subtly stringing together his thoughts on freighting and its high promise, particularly when two men threw in together, one handling the freighting and the other the business end. White River listened quietly, knowing Benson's drift and finding it somehow to his liking. He didn't care much for dickering about hauling rates, and his reading and counting weren't of a sort he expected business demanded, but

Benson had the quick-mindedness and inexhaustible smile of the trader.

Suddenly Gome was back, his face half twisted in a grin. "Whatever them four are up to over there they sure got a heap of good grub going to waste on that fire. What say we wander over and help 'em out?"

White River, Benson's words having focused his mind on the two hundred pay he had coming, decided there was more than food waiting for him beyond. "Let's go," he said, rising with the others.

PART TWO

IRONFOOT

8

"Be seated . . . join us, gentlemen," said Ben Amiel, his eyes running from White River to Benson to Teel to Gome. Benson and Teel smiled back at him in the firelight.

"Thank yuh kindly," said Benson, squatting by the fire and examining the cuts of meat sizzling over it. The others followed suit, with White River dropping down where he could face Marcher over the rich red coal bed.

"Rested up some?" he asked matter-of-factly.

"Some," said Marcher, but there was no give in his voice.

Ben Amiel looked searchingly at White River. "What are your plans now, White River?"

"That would take a heap of telling," said White River deliberately, his eyes avoiding Ben's.

"He's fixing to go into freighting with me," yelped Benson. "Lordy, we'll be bucking money back and forth like a bull rutting in a bank come a year or two."

"Takes time," said Teel philosophically, deciding on a well-done piece low in the fire. "Calculate you'll find money comes last."

"Speaking of money, it pleasures me to know we have some a-comin' right now." Benson was looking at Marcher, the question in his eyes.

Marcher uncharacteristically delayed answering, carefully swallowing the meat he was chewing before he said to Benson, "You collecting it?"

"I am," said White River, aware of an unaccountable tension spreading from those they had joined at the fire.

"Could be possible you'd like to make some more?" Marcher asked evenly.

"More?" White River's eyes met his, and Marcher knew he had failed.

"Yes. We have a piece to go yet, and . . . well, our plans might have to change." He threw a glance of disgust at Josh and Hammer.

"No plans of yours figure to fit any plans of mine, Mr. Marcher. We'd best settle up."

"Wasn't planning to cheat you out of it, you know," snapped Marcher, irritably reaching back for the brown saddlebag he had used as a pillow during the afternoon. "All I was suggesting was another . . ."

A tremendous howl broke through the camp from a sentry who had been sitting, seemingly half asleep, on the south side of the island not a hundred feet from their fire. "Injuns!" he bellowed, and with a sharper second call he fired his rifle into the air. White River, Benson, Teel, and Gome threw themselves from the fire while the brothers jumped to their feet.

White River rolled well into the darkness, then came up in a hunched-over run, making his way to the sentry's position. Teel was hard behind him. Others in the camp were moving toward the sentry's post like filings drawn to a magnet. White River was there first. The sentry was down behind a rock reloading his rifle. "Careful," he shouted at White River. "He's out there just beyond midstream." White River peered into the darkness and in time his eyes ferreted out the shape of a single Indian sitting astride his mount, looking quietly toward the island. After a moment the Indian raised his hand in the ancient signal of peace. "Absarokee," he called, "friend me."

Men crowded around White River, some raising their rifles. "Hold!" shouted White River. "He's a Crow, wants to palaver."

"Only jawin' we got for redskins is lead in one hell of a hurry," said a voice gruffly.

"It's talk like that that keeps a man's hair loose in this country," said Teel, spitting behind him. "Crows is good people. Wintered with 'em my own self more 'n once."

"How d' you know he's a Crow?" said a bewhiskered man standing behind Teel.

Teel called out something in a half-guttural singsong language, to which the Indian immediately replied.

"He's a Crow," said Teel.

White River stepped forward and waved him in. In a moment the Indian started toward them slowly, cautiously.

As the mount stopped beside them, the Indian raised his hand again. "Me, Ironfoot, friend of whites . . . many many snows." He spoke the broken English many Crows seeking friendship with the whites had mastered.

"I'm White River. Are you alone?"

"Ironfoot alone."

"Ironfoot—now I mind who he is," said Teel, looking at the man more closely. "A medicine man, and a gutsy one for a fact. Beats all what he's doin' down here by his lonesome—we're a fair piece from Wind River country."

"Come over to the fire," White River said casually, aware that the men around him were edgy with the whites' fear of Plains Indians. He noticed Teel moved with him.

The crowd watched with uncertainty. "Keep him over by your fire, by God, and keep an eye to him," said the bewhiskered man menacingly. "The closer he gits to me the closer he's gonna be to his great granddaddy." White River, Teel, and Ironfoot moved away, running into Marcher, Ben, Josh, and Hammer by the time they were halfway back to the fire.

Marcher asked, with what seemed only half a breath, "What the devil is this all about?"

"We're just fixin' to squat down and find out." White River was leading Teel and Ironfoot through the center of the group and back to the fireside, Ironfoot bringing his mount behind him. He dropped the rein in a patch of grass a few feet from the fire. The trail-weary pony lowered its head almost immediately and began to munch. Over the fire stood Gome, watching their return quietly, his boot toe gently urging some unburned ends of wood into the failing blaze.

White River motioned Ironfoot to the ground, making sure to settle him between Teel and himself. Then he offered the Crow some food.

"Givin' that redskin our grub?" growled Josh.

White River and Teel looked over at Josh. "They git hungry just like you," Teel snapped, and turned to spit behind him, but finding Gome settling at his back thought better of it.

"He's quite welcome," said Ben Amiel, smiling awkwardly at Ironfoot. But the Indian looked ahead stoically and made the refusal sign.

After a long silence Ironfoot took a small pipe from his waistband, packed it with tobacco from a deerskin pouch hanging about his neck, and having first offered the pipe to the spirits about him, he lifted a burning twig from the fire and lit the bowl. The others watched in silence, White River noticing the powerful build of the Indian and the many scars that told of the Crow nation's struggle to hold its lands against the Sioux, Cheyenne, Arapaho, Blackfoot, even the Nez Percé. Tall, like most Crows, Ironfoot had the broad dark face and lonely eyes of a man used to hardship and demanding little from life. He was dressed mostly in deerskin with only a touch of beadwork across his chest, and his long black hair fell down across his shoulders, its coating of grease making it shine like ebony against his dark skin. White River, noticing remnants of black paint on his face, sensed he was in mourning.

In time Ironfoot offered his pipe to White River and to Teel. Both took it but did not pass it on. For one to have refused the pipe would have been an insult to Ironfoot, and there were too many in that circle ignorant of the force of such a discourtesy.

Finally Teel said a few words in the Crow tongue, then changed to English. "What brings Ironfoot to the hunting grounds of his enemies?"

Ironfoot looked coldly ahead, his eyes searching the night sky to the north. His words when they came seemed to rise from a heart that fought for dignity despite its despair. "Ironfoot come to land of Sioux to bring the bones of his son Black Shield back to his people."

Teel and White River exchanged glances.

White River's voice softened in respect. "Where in the land of the Sioux sleeps the son of Ironfoot?"

The Indian looked again into the night sky, his eyes reflecting the dance of light from the fire, then he gave a great sigh and said something quickly in Crow.

Teel stopped chewing the plug of tobacco he had kept in his mouth even during the smoke and slowly repeated Ironfoot's words. Ironfoot nodded, then Teel turned toward White River and Benson, who had moved closer to hear the Crow. He started chewing again before he said uncomfortably, "That be clear up on the Belle Fourche."

Benson snorted and ran his hand across his face. "Man would need more luck than old Lucifer allows to get up thataway and back without he lose some hair."

"It's a fair piece," agreed Teel, "and nigh on to twenty Sioux to the square foot in some stretches." He turned to spit, remembering only as the tobacco spewed forth that Gome was behind him. He had the word "sorry" on his tongue when suddenly he saw that Gome was gone. Teel peered over his shoulder into the darkness above the south bank of the river, then turned slowly back to the fire, his eyes set strangely like a man trying to put a handle on a thought.

"What led the brave Black Shield so far from the land of his people?" asked White River.

Ironfoot looked into the fire, saying nothing, and for a while White River thought that the red man's known reluctance to mention his dead was keeping Ironfoot silent. But in time the Indian began, his voice breaking occasionally, his face showing how hollow and alone he felt. "My people have fought the Sioux after each snow as far back as our old ones remember, but the Sioux are many as the blades of grass—Absarokee arrows cannot kill them all."

White River nodded knowingly. Ironfoot told an ancient story. A murder raid and then retribution, with the young men restless for revenge. Ironfoot's son had been a great lover of horses and had stolen them so successfully from their many enemies that his herd had become the largest in the village. But it had been a glory that lasted but a day. The way of the warrior was harsh, Ironfoot was saying. He held his death song in his mouth at every turning and knew that the moccasin that fell upon the warpath too often left no returning tracks.

As Ironfoot finished, White River lowered his head in sympathy. Teel was about to speak, but his words stayed on his lips as he heard pebbles lightly crunching behind him and realized Gome was back. White River finally lifted his head to the Indian and spoke.

"The brave one of the Absarokees has traveled far. He should rest now. Sleep will be good for the sick heart of Ironfoot." White River stood and pointed to a place downstream from the sentry. "Ironfoot will spread his robe there. White River will be his shield till next sun."

Ironfoot drew himself up silently, grunted his gratitude to White River and Teel, and wearily led his pony off into the darkness.

"Poor doin's, I'm thinkin'," said Teel meditatively, watching the Indian go.

"Could be Ironfoot calculates that way too," allowed White River.

"He'll lose his hair sure 'nough," said Benson with a yawn. "Hope he takes a few Sioux with him." He slapped dust from his thighs as he got up. "Time I was beddin' down myself." He looked speculatively at White River. "Mebbe we ought to finish up our business."

"Mebbe," said White River.

Gome was on his feet. "Time I be fetchin' a mite of shuteye myself. Been a wearisome day." He moved around to the other side of the fire, his gait unhurried. "Rightly obliged for the grub, gents." He ambled off into the darkness.

White River swung around to Marcher and Ben Amiel. The brothers seemed to have been put into some mysterious spell by Ironfoot's story. "Reckon we'd best settle up, Mr. Marcher, then there be no need to trouble you come mornin'."

"If that's the way you want it," Marcher muttered, coming alive and reaching back for the brown saddlebag.

"A man's got a right to make his own decisions, I guess," said Ben to no one in particular, then to White River and Teel, "You treated that Indian very decently. I'm glad you did. Respect you for it."

"'Tweren't much a man could do when you figure . . ." White River got no further.

"What in hell's name!" exclaimed Marcher. He was shaking the saddlebag, his right hand thrust within.

"What is it?" asked Ben evenly. "What's the matter?"

"It's gone, God damn it! The poke's gone! That's what's the matter!" Marcher shouted.

"Gone? The gold?" Ben was getting up.

"The gold's gone?" clamored Josh, his gravelly voice cracking.

"Couldn't you have put it somewhere else?" asked Ben, taking the saddlebag from Marcher.

"Somewhere else? Where in Christ's name *would* I put it?"

Suddenly everyone was silent. Then Teel turned slowly and spit.

White River's voice came up steady and metallic, his eyes fixed on Marcher's. "Gold ain't hardly likely to leave by itself, Mr. Marcher."

"Meaning what?"

Josh was finally coming out of his rude shock. "Son-of-a-bitch. If some varmint lit off with that gold I'll wring his neck my own self."

"Christ A'mighty, Josh," whined Neff, "we jest got to fetch it back!"

"When did you last judge it was there?" Ben asked patiently.

"It was there when we awoke, by God, and no one's been near this fire since." Marcher's eyes, inflamed now with anger and anxiety, sought out Josh and Neff. "There weren't but a few who knew we were carrying gold . . . seems pretty plain to me. . . ."

"Hol' on there, Mr. Marcher," cried Josh, "you ain't got no call laying blame on Neff and me."

"Ditheration no," Neff added hurriedly. "If you think we got yer poke, search us."

"Mebbe you cached it a'ready," muttered Benson.

"Likely they'd do better to study you a mite," said Josh with a touch of fury. "You ain't done nothing but bleat about gittin' gold since you come by."

Benson dropped a hand to his pistol. "How and when you're wishin' to die, Josh, don't make no never mind to me. Jest keep talkin' thataway and I'll know you're ready."

Ben Amiel raised his voice. "Please, gentlemen, we can get to the bottom of this. Andy, did you leave that saddlebag at any time?"

Marcher screwed up his face in growing fury. "Come to think of it, I did leave it for a moment or two when that Indian hit camp."

"A moment or two?" Ben repeated.

"Rightly 'nough time for a gent that thinks ahead," cut in Benson, still eyeing Josh.

"Was anybody here when you left?" Ben went on evenly.

Marcher ran his hand through his hair. "Don't recall exactly." His eyes narrowed a trifle. "Got the damnedest feeling there was, though."

Teel spit in his quiet, measured way. "Friend Gome, mebbe?"

"My God, I believe it was!" Marcher exclaimed.

Neff came alive with something close to a scream. "Sure 'nough, he was here by the fire when we come back!"

"Gome's the varmint!" roared Josh.

"Hold on a minute," said Ben. "You can't accuse a man of stealing property just because you left him standing by your fire. The law would never hold for that."

Both Benson and Josh got in an oath before White River could say, "This isn't law-bidin' country, Mr. Amiel. You kinda make it up here as you go along. Now if Gome's got your poke, you'd best git to him before he caches it."

"Figure it's a'ready been cached," threw in Teel.

White River turned to the trapper. "How d' you reckon that?"

Teel told about Gome leaving and going to the river bank while Ironfoot related his tale. He told about Gome moving up and down as though he were seeking something. Ben Amiel's was the only face that still retained doubt.

"How did you happen to be looking behind you, Mr. Teel?"

Teel smiled amiably. "Old habit, Mr. Amiel, learned it from Big Sam Turner. Whilst talking with Injuns, friendly or hunting hair, keep a-looking behind you. Poor old Sam plumb forgot his own advice on the Musselshell one day and ain't hardly had need of it since."

"You said he was gone all the while Ironfoot was talking?" asked White River.

"For a fact."

"Let's rope him and thrash it out of him," snorted Josh.

"It's my money, maybe I should . . ." began Marcher.

"Mr. Marcher," White River cut in, "best leave this play to them as held a hand or two before. Rules run funny hereabouts, leastwise till you git the hang of 'em."

"Let's quit this yapping and get a-going," demanded Josh.

White River looked into the darkness in the direction in which Gome had disappeared. He could see indistinguishable figures huddled about distant fires. A strange silence lay like an evil curtain over the dusky scene. "Druther have him back here," he said evenly. "Hard debating what's staked out yonder."

"That sets up right smart, I'm thinkin'," muttered Teel.

"Want I should fetch him?" Benson asked cautiously.

White River nodded.

"Reckon I'll mosey with you," muttered Teel, rubbing his sides slowly, then shifting the latch on his gun.

"Just git him back here," bawled Josh. "I want that critter to myself."

Teel looked at him as though he found something humorous in that remark, something he had the wisdom not to mention.

9

Sam Gome came out of the darkness, his eyes, counterfeiting sleep, the color of dull slate. A half smile shifted the lines of his face as he came to a stop.

White River regarded him lightly across the fire, as though his presence was incidental to other matters.

"Gome, we got some questioning for you," growled Josh.

"Questioning?" said Gome, his lightly furrowed brow suggesting only mild interest. "What questions was you intending?"

"Questions about a pokey of gold," declared Josh.

"Pokey of gold?" Gome's chin lifted a trifle. "What pokey of gold are you jawing on, partner?"

"God damn it! The one that's a-missin'—that's which one!" roared

Josh. "We figured you could likely fetch it back faster than most!"

Gome turned his wiry body slightly to the right, thereby moving his holster to the dark side away from the fire. "Not a very neighborly way to be putting things, I'm thinking."

"No, 'taint," said White River flatly.

Gome's face was drawn up in the beginnings of a sneer. " 'Pears to me I ain't hearing rightly. Gold?" He said the word as though he had never heard it before. "A poke of gold? Can't say I mind seeing one."

Josh moved a step closer. "Where was you whenever that Injun hit camp and caused that ruckus?"

"Likely I was milling round here—same as anybody else."

"Milling round? . . . Milling round where?"

Gome's narrow face tightened. "For a fact, I don't rightly take to this kind of treating." As he spoke he dropped back a few inches to better his view of the group.

"You sure as hell got another kind of treatment coming, Gome, lessen you get right handy at some answering." Josh had taken another full stride toward Gome. White River's voice kept him from taking a third.

"It 'pears you were seen down at the water bending over as though mebbe you were cachin' something." White River's words fell easily, his tone belying their gravity.

"Couldn't have been me," Gome drawled, rubbing his chin with his left hand in a move that strove to be casual. "Was hugging the fire all the while lazy-like."

"All the while?" queried White River. "You were no ways near that water?"

"Not in my recollect. Couldn't have been me."

"Couldn't have been anybody else," bawled Josh. "We was all here parlaying with that Injun."

Gome looked like a man about to take a stand on something, but his eyes went momentarily to White River's and he appeared to change his mind. "Likely you just didn't heed me, with hell a-busting loose and all. Nevertoless I was a-squatting here listening at that jaybird all the while."

"You're a liar!" snarled Josh. White River's eyes narrowed.

Gome quickly took another step backward, his right shoulder dipping almost imperceptibly as his hand closed on the bone grip of his pistol now completely out of sight on the dark side of his thigh. His voice was suddenly like the whine of a bullet. "You fellows figuring to rile me up so you can gun me down. I've been dealt a coffin hand before and there be dead men aplenty to prove it. I never see'd no gold. And just like I was a-sayin', I was listening at that redskin's palaver and the next gent disputing it better shoot straighter than he talks."

White River moved around to where he could see Gome clearly, his eyes settling on the man as though taking him physically in their grasp. "Gome, you say you was here all the time that Crow was talking?"

"The same . . ."

White River was circling slowly to the left. "Well . . . what did he have to say?"

"Who?" Gome realized White River's leftward motion was to encumber the draw of his right-hand gun. His face tightened about his eyes.

"That Injun."

Gome swallowed slowly and visibly. "That Injun? . . . Oh, the usual . . . trying to scare up some buff . . . hoping mebbe to scoop up a Sioux scalp . . . never was minded to pay redskin palaver much heed."

"Did he mention a son?"

Gome's head hooked forward, trying to peer into White River's cryptic face. "Like I told you, par'ner, Injun talk don't hold much with Sam Gome. 'Taint stuff for a man to turn his thinking on."

White River's form was fringed now by jumping shadows. "You're running out of rope, Gome. What did he say about a young buck with a hankering for horses?"

Gome took in the circle about him with the eyes of an animal looking for a death grip on a more powerful prey. He swallowed and his mouth tightened.

"Well, 'bout that buck . . . ?" said White River, his voice now rising from deep within him.

Gome's last words were to live in every memory present but his own: "I disremember."

It lashed forth far too quickly for those whose decisions were not already made. André Marcher and Ben Amiel went to ground much too late for real cover, and Josh and Neff were left firing wildly into the dead air above Gome's body. Benson and the old trapper were barely down in time before the bullets that tore around and through White River's frame came to whine above them like so many maddened bees. Then as suddenly it was over. White River was down on one knee and Josh was kicking Gome's corpse viciously, uttering an oath as he stooped to snatch up the other's gun.

"Good Christ, he's dead!" gasped Marcher, staring at the inert form at Josh's feet.

"Needed killin'," muttered Josh, looking over at White River queerly. He was aware, now that he had Gome's gun, that Gome had gotten off three shots before White River downed him with one through the heart—and before either he or Neff could even clear leather. Vaguely he was realizing what a narrow call he had had, yet something in his mind was not ready to accept it. "God damn! Yuh shouldn't have gutted him like that, White River, leastways not till we rightly beat that gold from his mangy hide. Now how we goin' to git it?"

White River was crouching down on one knee, blood seeping between the fingers of his left hand held high on his chest. Benson and the trapper were over him now, trying to get him to lie down. He motioned them off. "Looks a mite high for trouble," muttered the trapper, "but 'taint lackin' much."

Benson offered White River his jug. White River looked at it for a moment, then replaced his gun with his right hand and raised the jug to his lips. From around them the sound of running feet began to mount. Faces appeared in the dark, taking in the situation and asking uneasy questions. A hoarse whispering swelled, and Neff Hammer began to throw more wood on the fire.

Josh, finally finished with his search of Gome's body, stood looking grimly at Neff, watching him over the rising fire. Marcher and Amiel came to stand near White River, who was taking his second swig at the jug and ignoring them both. "Something we can do?" asked Marcher, his voice devoid of its usual arrogance.

White River simply shook his head.

"Bullet went clean through," allowed Teel, bending over and studying the blood running down White River's back. "I'd bind myself up some was I you."

Benson shrugged at Teel when White River didn't answer. " 'Taint a-gonna hurt none to pour a little spirits on them wounds—leastways I hear tell."

White River handed back the jug and looked straight ahead, as though he understood his problem and could deal with it on his own. The others turned gradually to talking among themselves, or to strangers still coming up to join them. Amid a great deal of noisy confusion, Teel and Benson were doing their best to explain. Only Ben Amiel could not take his eyes off White River. White River was watching something, something that was coming toward them from the south side of the island. It was a strange form that Ben only recognized as something darkly alive, growing bigger as it moved into the pool of light being thrown by the fire. It made him gasp a little and step back, finally feeling the total exhaustion of this unbelievable night, for the form leaving the darkness and moving steadily toward them was the black-streaked body of the lonely Crow, Ironfoot.

10

Two days later White River sat outside the little shelter he and Ironfoot had thrown together with raw buffalo hides spread against a small tree on the lower end of the island. He felt better today. Ironfoot had twice cleaned and dressed his wounds, and now the sudden fever he had run the day before was gone. It reminded him how, as a young boy, he had watched the Arikara care for their wounded and how often their strange poultices helped stricken warriors recover.

The morning sun had pulled the dampness from the earth and a light breeze rippled through the grass. Settling back, he watched Ben Amiel coming slowly toward him. Amiel had been by several times the day before, but his coming had always been clearly explained by his concern for White River. Now, however, he looked different—preoccupied, depressed. White River hoped it would be over quickly.

"Feeling better?" said Amiel.

"Middlin'," allowed White River, motioning him down.

Ben settled wearily. His eyes told of little sleep these past two days. He picked up a stick and started to poke at the ground with it. "It's just that I've been wondering what your plans might be," he said.

"Can't rightly say—'cepting mebbe they've changed some."

"So I understand. I'm sorry."

"'Tweren't your doing."

Both men looked along the south bank, recalling the increasingly painful, meticulous search from dawn to sundown the day before, a search that finally ended in defeat. Both avoided looking at the little mound of rocks beyond the rushes where the corpse of Gome mocked them.

"Don't know what to make of it myself, Mr. River," Ben began hesitantly, "but Andy—well, he's bent on our going on."

White River grunted.

Ben licked his lips. "Maybe if I were to explain some things all this would make more sense. Andy isn't easy to deal with, I know, but he's been that way from the start—stubborn, headstrong, used to having his own way. This past year he's had a few shocks that might have knocked some sense into him, but I'm afraid they've made him worse." White River sat back staring quietly at Amiel. He was still hoping for solitude, but sensing the other's urgent need to talk, he listened in silence. "Trouble is, his father and he had a falling out. I guess it was for the best, but it's left Andy penniless. Worse than that, he's in serious debt. That's really why we're here."

"His pa as orn'ry as he is?"

Amiel smiled sadly. "I'm afraid my stepfather's sins are far more serious. He's a crude politician—successful, yes, but with only a road agent's interest in the public. It's not only his shameful corruption, which has brought him money and power, but he's been a terrible example for Andy."

White River stretched out slowly and squirmed himself into a more comfortable position. "Something I can help with, Mr. Amiel?"

Ben heard the other's oblique request for privacy. "I know I'm intruding, White River, but I just wanted to tell you the map we're carrying has been in the family for years. We're not on a fool's errand, Andy and I. It sounds incredible, I know, but an uncle of ours discovered gold out here many years ago, west of the Black Hills, and even though he was killed and never returned, we think we can find the spot where he made his find."

White River's eyes widened a fraction. "With that map?"

"Oh no, that map is only to take us to his grave. Paul was with a friend who buried him after he died. That map was given my family to mark the makeshift grave where he lies."

White River lowered his head and shook it, his hands coming up to cover his eyes. "Mr. Amiel, you should have told me this sooner, might have saved yourself a mess of trouble. Makeshift graves round here last about as long as it takes varmints to sniff the wind. How long since your uncle went under?"

"Twelve years ago, I believe. But let me explain, it's not as hopeless as it seems. My uncle Paul and his friend were trained navigators and both of them had studied mining engineering. When Paul discovered the gold, he made a map of the local area to be able to find it again. The map was drawn on deerskin, not paper, which he was afraid the dampness would rot."

"And you got that deerskin now?"

"No . . . Paul kept it in a silver crucifix he wore around his neck. On their way back—they had been traveling southeast for two days—they were attacked by savages. Paul was killed. His friend, after he came out of hiding, seeing wolves and coyotes gathering, hastily covered Paul's body with rocks, but in his desperation to be gone he forgot to take the crucifix from Paul's neck. However, being a trained navigator, he instinctively impressed on his mind as many landmarks as he could around the grave site. They're on the map we showed you in Independence. We're also hoping that pile of rocks will still be there; it should help mark where the crucifix lies. There's supposed to be a large nugget attached to the crucifix, proving his find."

"And this all happened, this business with your uncle, twelve years ago." White River shook his head. "How come you and Mr. Marcher got yourselves out here only now?"

"Well, this has been largely Andy's idea . . . though I have an interest in it too . . . and Andy was very young and living in Washington when Paul's friend returned to Virginia. So it wasn't until Andy . . . until Andy left Washington last year . . . came to stay with me . . . that it all came up again between us."

White River pulled himself up to a sitting position. "Mr. Amiel, for a fact you came here with some reason for telling me all this. Maybe you should get to it."

"To be truthful, I was hoping to change your mind, to get you to help us find Paul's grave. Somehow we'll see you get paid for it, and if we happen to find that gold, you could be in the freighting business in style."

White River hesitated a moment. "Mr. Amiel," he began, with a faint smile.

"Ben, please."

"All right, Ben. I've got to tell you that looking for gold in the middle of Sioux country is too hammerheaded a notion for a man with wits to conjure on. Just mosey out to that stream bed there and tuck your head under water, and whenever you have to raise up again you'll more than likely have a fair notion of jest how long you'd last."

"But the mine may not be in Sioux country. Paul and his friend had been traveling southeast for two days."

White River sank back against the earth and let out a deep breath. "You can only do so many foolish things in this country and stay alive, Ben. Reckon I've run out of my share. Soon as I'm fit, I'm heading back east. Might be some work around, still a piece of huntin' season left."

Ben looked down, trying hard to conceal his dejection. "I guess I understand." But then he looked up, turned and braced himself against the ground with one hand. "You're sure you won't reconsider?"

"Not a chance."

Ben started up, faltered for a moment, then rose slowly to his feet. "I guess it's unfair to expect it of you. You've hardly fared well with us," he said tonelessly.

White River thought Ben was leaving, but instead the man reached into his pocket and drew out a single sheet of yellow paper. "I have a little money of my own back east," he said with affected casualness. "I've drawn up a note against it for the balance of your fee. Any reliable bank will surely honor it." He handed the paper to White River. "Lots of luck in the freighting business."

White River simultaneously took the paper and rose slowly to his feet. He shoved his hat back and stared at Ben. "Considerin' the way things have come about, this ain't hardly necessary."

"We made an agreement with you, Mr. River. You met your end of the bargain."

"I don't rightly feel . . ." White River struggled for words.

"Nothing more to say," Ben offered quickly, his long figure bending as seemed to be his habit with farewells. "I'll be going along now. Take care of that wound." He gestured amiably to Ironfoot and turned away.

On the rocky spine of the island, André Marcher stopped to feel the soreness in his biceps then swung one arm in a circular motion to loosen it up. He had been turning and lifting rocks for hours, and his muscles were spent and aching. His face, grown tanner and leaner in the past few days, scowled at the sun as his lips came together in a thin line of disgust. "Damn it! It's got to be somewhere!"

"Damn if it don't," agreed Josh angrily, "but we can't dig up this whole son-of-a-bitchin' island, for a fact."

"I'm all tuckered out . . . what with my wound and all," added Neff. "Mebbe a touch of spirits would ease up the pain some."

Marcher ignored him. "Now if he started this way . . ."

"Christ A'mighty," cried Josh, "how many times you fixin' to try and smell out that bastard's tracks?"

"One more time," sighed Marcher almost to himself.

"I'm plumb beat," Josh said with a yawn, his barrel chest seeming to collapse.

"Likewise," threw in Neff, his voice coming in high and unsubstantial.

"Come on, both of you," Marcher declared, moving once again toward the stream.

• • •

Once in the stream, Neff sagged over on his side. "Josh," he gasped, "when we do this critter in let's make it real slow—Comanche style."

"Shut up," muttered Josh.

Neff ran his tongue around his mouth, then with one hand threw some water onto his face. "If this ain't the sorriest deal a man can recollect. After this I don't figure to frighten much in hell."

"Quit the palaver and heave some rocks," warned Josh.

"What for? That poke ain't here and you know'd it from the start."

"Got to stay with this gent. First things first. When we 'uns are settin' astraddle that mine of his, I aim to show this hog-headed slicker just how handy old Josh can be with a rock or two."

"You forgettin' we got to shank up into Sioux country and run down that map." Neff drew himself back on the bank. "Calculate all the bucks a-headin' for hell will be aswarmin' around the bush up there, just a-waitin' to carve hair."

"Shoot, ain't no handful of Indians goin' to ruffle us none."

"Handful? Hear tell they so thick a man can't hardly piss without gettin' an arrow through his pridesome."

Marcher was shouting to them as he pointed to two blue rocks downstream.

"Jesus!" swore Neff. "I'd like to die was I to touch another rock!"

Josh looked up, his eyes settling on Marcher beyond. At first it appeared he would say something, but then he simply settled back in the water and looked wearily up, as though his mind were groping for balance.

"Well, come on!" roared Marcher from the distance, irritation threading through his voice.

Josh shook his head slowly from side to side and raised his hand, shaking that too in mild rejection of Marcher's call.

"Damn him!" said Neff under his breath. "That Gome bastard is bound for quick company if he don't let up."

Marcher came sloshing toward them, motioning them to move over to the blue rocks.

Josh waited till he was much closer before he said, calling out to him, "Mr. Marcher, if my own heart was a-beatin' under one of them there rocks, reckon I couldn't lift it."

Marcher hesitated. "One last stab," he said, "then we chuck it." His voice had suddenly lost its edge. He was exhausted himself, his fatigue till now held in check by anxiety and anger.

Josh straightened up, his heavy features straining to smile. "Don't fret no more 'bout your poke, Mr. Marcher, there'll be a heap of full pokes directly we get us a bushel or two of that shiny stuff."

Marcher turned and trudged his way up the bank, a nagging uneasiness playing around the fringes of his mind. He pressed it back though and turned his gaze down the stream to the spot where he had seen the blue rocks. Well, what was the use, he knew he was beat. The poke was gone and Sam Gome had won. If Gome couldn't have it, they were not to have it either. He looked to the ridges that swept ominously across the sky to the north, his back and arms telling him the sun was laying its noon weight across the land.

Some wolves had run an old buffalo bull out of the breaks to the south. He could see it stumbling along, head down, strangely silent, occasionally swinging its head in a feeble effort to ward off the death-bearing wolves tearing in to hamstring the helpless beast. What a land, he thought. He saw the buffalo stumble while a wolf behind it rolled and thrashed in pain. It was a land for those willing to kill to survive, but it was a land without pretense.

He moved to a ledge of rock and viewed his now dark, disheveled figure in a pool of quiet water. For a moment he was startled. Was that hollow-eyed, sweat-streaked face his? He steadied himself and bent closer to the water. Could that really be his reflection, or had the terror and exhaustion of these past days distorted his senses? He looked about him as though the island or even the river itself were to blame. No, it was only fatigue. Underneath he was still the same André Marcher he had been a short time before, a charming, debonair young man, swaggering through Washington's boudoirs and gambling dens. One day he would be back there, he vowed solemnly to himself. Grimacing, he looked away from the scruffy, malevolent face staring up at him from the smooth surface of the river.

But the disturbing image below had turned his mind to another reflection, the one in Margo's ornate bedroom mirror, where he loved to stand tall and naked, her own gorgeous body poised beside his on her bed. They would admire their nakedness and then laugh and fall to fondling each other again, their lust seemingly insatiable. He glanced at the sun-bleached sky, his mouth suddenly tight, bitter. Who was sharing that seductively soft bed and even softer body now? This stab of pain called up yet another reflection, but it was one he had to turn away from.

He kicked angrily at the rock beneath him. Damn it! Why hadn't he listened to Margo? Why had he allowed his monstrous gambling debts to get so out of hand? Above all, why hadn't he foreseen his bastard of a father would leave him to grovel before those bloodsucking creditors, hoping to control him as he did so many others?

In the distance he could see Ben leaving White River's lean-to and moving slowly in his direction. He found himself hoping Ben would stop at their campsite. He wanted to be alone. Or did he? Could he deal again with those agonizing moments that pursued him even here?

He could see, standing here now, how far back it went. Even as a lonely child being dragged through an endless procession of private schools, he had always come home to an even greater loneliness—to a father who regarded him barely as an afterthought and a mother who seemed endlesssly preoccupied with her debt to his father. He had married her, then a widow with a child—his older brother, Ben—and saved the Amiel farm and homestead from vanishing under an avalanche of debt.

Marcher did not understand, though his mother had made hurried attempts to explain, why she was always at his father's beck and call and why his older half brother, Ben, whom he liked, chose to stay with the farm in Virginia while he was being raised in the rich, fast life of Washington. He heard many things in his childhood that only became clear a decade or more later. But he grew up to be a restless, moody youth, plagued by spells of anger and perverse mischief, his long adolescence remembered now only for the pain of puberty and the sexual arousal he felt for young servant girls, some shamefully coerced to his bed by money or the threat of dismissal. Yet through it all, it had never been his distant father or the nubile bodies of girls he longed for, but his achingly beautiful mother who more and more often seemed missing from his life. Even on rare occasions when she stayed with him she did not seem to be there, to be his.

Before him a screeching bird landed on the water, starting ripples that spread slowly and broke the sheen of the surface. Looking up he noticed Ben again now clearly coming toward him. Well, why was he standing there reminiscing? The past had nothing to offer but these agonizing memories.

It was at college that the traumatic truth thundered into his consciousness, for his peers, sons of well-to-do Washingtonians, were too sophisticated and far too worldly not to perceive that his father's unlikely political success was due to his mother's beauty, a beauty that had been shamelessly bartered for political favors in the demi-monde of influence peddling. Their sly, often lewd, remarks left him stunned, and for a time he resisted whatever companionship was offered him. But now it was impossible to ignore the many evenings she had left, escorted to late dinner parties by powerful and prominent men whose veneer of manners could scarcely conceal their expectations. It was a reality he'd had to purge from his mind, but that suppression had left him with a tension increased even at the sight of her cleavage in an endless array of bold evening gowns.

Time finally released him from the shadow of his parents' lives, though being without independent means, he was never far from his father's reach. Ironically he was grateful that, like his older half brother, he had inherited his mother's fine features. He was handsome, endowed with a powerful and graceful body, and his long-smoldering anger surfaced as only the defiant charm of a reckless young man. He became a daring, flamboyant gambler and quickly discovered that even the most fashionable women responded readily to his glances. He had come a long way from the shy, lonely boy of his childhood, and his rising self-confidence soared when he captured the favor of Margo Ramsey, the wealthy and influential widow whose ample charms had been sweeping through the sexual fantasies of half the men in Washington since the untimely passing of her husband, the esteemed Senator Ramsey. He could not believe his good fortune, even when he became aware she was not exclusively his. There were bankers and other men of prominence in her life, but there could be no doubt he was her favorite. Their lovemaking became a drug to which both were equally addicted. Yet there was a subtle imbalance in this relationship, a wisp of indulgence he occasionally caught in her eyes, even when he posed before her mirror. Margo knew his father—"only too well," she had said more than once—and would smile at Andy's petulant complaints about money. A few times she had turned more serious, warning him, her mouth set firmly, to get away from "that dreadful man." But in reality, Margo was discretion itself. She never mentioned his mother, though he was aware she knew virtually every secret of the Washington society in whose dangerous waters she had more than held her own, when strong and even brilliant men had gone under. He began to realize in time that she knew him better than he knew himself. Yet when she warned him that his increasingly reckless gambling would bring his newfound world down in flames, he would not listen. A man, he told himself proudly, does not permit his mistress to run his life.

What an incredible fool!

He sighed deeply. Did every man look back and see a point in his life after which there was really no choosing? Does life become for all of us a rising tide of events that flows ever fuller and finally knows no turning? He shook his head and glanced at the sky. That strange early life of his, all that had gone before, now seemed like a distant land where one had traveled in his youth but could no longer find on the maps of the world. His mind had long since shunted aside all but his final day in that alien world, but that day had been stamped on his memory forever.

It began the morning he awoke and was seized immediately by the dread realization that his horrendous losses at the gambling tables the night before were unpayable. His head ached and his whole body shook with tremors from the heavy drinking he had turned to during the long, disastrous night. The noon post arrived with letters from three previous creditors, all advising him they were turning to the law. His father listened to his pleas with a demeanor which suggested he understood Andy's predicament, perhaps even anticipated it. Surely he had given this eventuality some thought, for he had little trouble in hitting upon an ingenious solution. Charlotte Wells, a spindly but pleasant enough young lady, had been openly smitten for some time with Andy's charms. An offer of marriage to her would without doubt be joyously, even ecstatically, accepted. Inasmuch as her father was slated to be the next Attorney General, such a prudent and sensible move on Andy's part could well encourage his father to take responsibility for his very considerable debts. "Even a fool like you can see how both of us would find that arrangement uncommonly handy." Thus did his father define the price of his deliverance.

For a moment he was so desperate and shaken he nearly conceded, but instinct told him the real price was Margo, and her body was a narcotic he could not surrender. In the end he could only feign indignation. "That's disgraceful," he managed to blurt out, "marrying a girl just to use her family's influence."

His father snorted. "If that's virtue you're preaching, save it for that Ramsey bitch. She's given you everything else, maybe she'll accommodate your creditors so you can go on warming her bed."

Trembling with suppressed rage, he left without answering. But in a daylong walk along the Potomac he finally grasped the tragic truth that in his father's last vicious remark lay his only hope.

• • •

It was dusk when he knocked on her door. He understood the craven role he was playing, yet he waited till they were in bed and her breathing had quieted after the sensual moaning that always marked her coming climax and its release. Nothing in their long relationship could have prepared him for her response when finally, steeling himself, he made his muted request. She moved out of his arms and stared at him in disbelief. "Andy . . . Andy, are you asking *me* to pay your debts?"

Shame tripped his voice. "Margo . . . you're wealthy . . . you have rich friends."

Her face flushed, then paled. Then he heard her laughter beginning softly, rolling deep in her as though she were uncertain whether or not to share it with him.

"Margo, I'm serious!"

"I know you are, you idiot."

"I'm in trouble . . . I . . ."

"The trouble you're in, Andy, isn't the kind money is going to help. You're not an unlucky gambler, Andy. You're an arrogant young man who's allowed his vanity and buried hatred to ruin his life."

He pulled her roughly to him. "What the hell are you talking about?"

She recoiled slightly, sensing the rising of a rage in him she had never seen before. "Andy, you'd better go. Leave! I can't suffer fools, particularly in my bedroom. Go back to your father. I'm sure he can arrange something."

He turned to the edge of the bed and buried his face in his hands. "Yes, yes, he can arrange something all right. He wants me to marry Charlotte Wells."

"Ha! I wonder why?"

"You know damn well why."

"Andy, you came here for money. I'll give you something far more important—advice! I've tried before, God knows, but maybe this time you'll listen. Get away from that man before you become just like him. And you could, very easily. Marrying Charlotte would simply be the first step."

"Then"—his desperation started to gag him—"then you're saying you won't help me?"

With visible effort she smiled. "Andy, giving you money would simply postpone the day of reckoning. Your only salvation is to leave! Leave Washington! Leave him! Leave me!"

"Leave Washington?"

"Yes, this is no place for you, dear boy. You don't have the wiles for it. You could survive in a jungle, perhaps even on the Barbary Coast, but not here. Here, Andy, only the very clever and the very rich survive. You are neither." She jumped out of bed, ignoring her nakedness, and came around to stand before him. "Believe me, you must go away. You must get away from that man. He was born in the dark of the moon without the grace of God in his heart. He will not hesitate to make a bond servant out of you just as he never hesitated to make a whore out of your mother."

Something snapped inside him and his hands came up as though reaching for her breasts, but they closed around her throat and she was suddenly pulling them away, a look of terror in her eyes.

And then they were standing there, before that mirror, their reflections strangely mocking in the darkened room.

He stood there a long moment before realizing she had fled.

His mind was a turmoil, his emotions challenging his sanity, as he slipped into the house and hurriedly packed a bag. He was hoping to disappear unseen, but his father was sitting like a sentinel in the front parlor, obviously alert to his soft tread.

"Ha! Sneaking away, eh! Your bitch turned you down, so now you're crawling off."

He swung around and moved toward his father till he towered over him. "I'll be back, you bastard, mark my word, I'll be back!"

"Not here, by God. Sneak off like some sniveling swindler defaulting on his debts and you'll never set foot in this house again!"

"You know I haven't the money, and I'll be damned if I'll marry Charlotte Wells or anybody else to help your filthy grubbing for power."

"You'll regret this!"

"The only thing I'll regret is not leaving sooner. You've got a lot of enemies, Father, you'll make a lot more—one day you'll make one too many."

"You dare talk to me like that? You dare threaten me?"

"Be careful, Father. I could dare do a lot more to the man who forced my mother to offer her body to half the lecherous politicians in Washington!"

He should have known their shouting would bring her from her room, he should have heard her footsteps in the hall, but in his fury he heard nothing but his own voice. Had his eyes not caught a swirl of skirt in the parlor mirror, he would not have known she was standing there, her face stricken white, her features seeming to dissolve behind her hands as she raised them to obliterate her shame. Had he known he would have left and not have had to watch his mother in that mirror, sinking in disgrace, knowing that the lust of too many men had driven that grateful warmth reserved for a mother from her son's eyes forever.

Two mirrors—one for himself and Margo, a reflection of vain and sensual pleasure, the other for his mother, a reflection of appalled horror—they both joined in a glass fresco that marked the end of his youth.

It took several moments for him to realize that Ben was standing close behind him and speaking. "I'm afraid it's hopeless," Ben was concluding in a tone of despair. "I spoke to White River. Nothing will induce him to go. Why don't we give this whole mad business up?"

Marcher rubbed his face hard with both hands, then looked along the bank a hundred feet where Josh and Neff were sprawled. Now that Ben had appeared they were both sitting up, watching. "I've come too far to quit, Ben. If that mine is there, I'll find it."

Amiel followed his gaze to the two figures watching beyond. "With them?"

"They're as anxious to stay alive as I am. Besides, I wouldn't be worth killing unless I found that mine, would I?" He smiled coldly at his brother.

Ben studied him curiously for a moment. "Give me that map," he said.

"It's in the saddlebags. Make sure it gets back there."

Ben grunted softly and turned away, not wishing to be there when Josh and Neff came up.

Josh had moved around to the rocky bank, his left leg braced against the incline, his hat off, his great body sagging forward. "When you minded to get a-goin', Mr. Marcher?"

Marcher straightened up and kicked irritably at a finger-shaped stone beneath him. It broke and part of it went skipping into the water. Beyond he saw the buffalo had finally been brought down, the voracious wolves upon it, looking in the distance like pigs suckling a sleeping sow. "Tomorrow at sunup, damn it!" he said. "Better be ready."

He moved away, his mouth set, as was his mind, hard against this land that seemed to offer even to its own nothing but death. But it would not defeat him. There would be no turning back. That gold was his weapon of vengeance, and no real or imagined terrors of this land would keep him from it. Suddenly he stiffened. A muscle spasm in his back made him jerk about. As he whirled he caught sight of White River on the other end of the island sitting before his shelter. In spite of his pain he witnessed once again the quick, efficient slaughter of Sam Gome. Once again he saw the mute indifference White River displayed toward his almost mortal wound. He breathed heavily for a moment, his teeth clenched against a second spasm as he started toward their campsite. There was a code, by God, he could take to heart.

11

White River lay back against the earth. It took him a long while to find a position of comfort, but then no position would last long. He would have to move again, and each time he would switch Ben Amiel's paper from one hand to the other, as though its disposition were as important as his own.

He had been feeling strangely out of sorts since Ben left. Somehow the paper didn't fit into his reckoning of how things were meant to go. Maybe he was thinking like an idiot. Maybe he should be taking his pay and heading back east.

Ironfoot knelt down beside him, placing the clay bowl of broth at his hand. "White River eat, make plenty strong again."

White River smiled at him.

"Spirit of rabbit make you run swift, White River." Ironfoot's mood had lifted a trifle in the last day or two, but his eyes were still lonely, and White River knew he would not delay much longer before resuming his heartbreaking journey.

White River raised the bowl to his lips, sipping its hot contents cautiously. "Ironfoot will soon leave his friend, White River?" he asked in the low, courteous tones of regret.

"White River goes toward the rising sun," the Indian said without looking up.

"That's my thinking," said White River, suddenly uncomfortable that his words carried so little conviction.

Ironfoot nodded.

White River scanned the south rim of the island where he could see Marcher and Josh and Hammer working on their horses and packs, preparing for departure. He sipped some more of the broth, his eyes sweeping the remainder of the valley. Across the shallow channel of the stream he could see four mounted men talking and pointing west. Men were moving on, their restlessness after a few days of quiet beyond containing, their thoughts suddenly skewed with what lay beyond some distant bend in the river, or over the crest of some far-off mountains. He was one of them, a wanderer without a resting place. Had it not been for old Buzz he never would have known what a home was, for it was Buzz, an aging army scout, who found him along the river after the Sioux destroyed the Arikara village.

It saddened him to remember the little ranch a few miles from Laramie where he had grown to manhood, often leaving with Buzz on his scouting trips, learning about the far-reaching buffalo country and the bloody Indian wars being fought to control it. Few whites knew about these wars. And there were deeper lessons taught by Buzz, and Lydia too, after she had joined their life. Maybe that was the most amazing part of those good years. Eight years younger than he and he found himself learning from her.

It all started the day Buzz came home with a little girl, an army blanket wrapped around her soiled and torn clothes. She was all that was left of a wagon train massacred on the Platte. Only eight years old but after a year or two she changed their pine-planked shack into a home. With the help of a neighboring widow, Lydia began to cook and clean when town girls her age were playing with dolls. In another year or two she was scolding her menfolk for not eating properly or putting muddy boots on the few sticks of old furniture they had hammered together. Often he and Buzz looked at each other, startled and smiling. Sometimes they laughed outright, but underneath they began to love it. For years they had given each other companionship, but Lydia had brought with her a childish and caring voice, the comforting warmth of a hearth and a home. As she grew he began to wonder if there was a name for that liquid grace with which she moved her slim, delicate body, but in the end he sensed it was nameless, like the mystery that lives in many women's beauty.

Then suddenly it ended. That army messenger rode up to the ranch with his news of death, and both Buzz and the world he had made possible for them was gone.

He knew there would be missionaries coming out from the fort—remembering the Kleinhorsts who had brought him as a baby to the Arikara village, raising him amid their prayers for salvation until cholera carried them off, allowing the poor Arikara to put aside that invisible devil the Kleinhorsts warned about and concentrate on the very visible onslaughts of the Sioux. The missionaries were kind people; they prayed and accepted those of Buzz's things they felt the needy of their missions could use, but what they had really come to say was that a nine-year-old girl did not belong alone in a house with an eighteen-year-old unrelated and unmarried male like himself, whose only means of support would now be military scouting, a job for which Buzz had carefully trained him but which would keep him absent for weeks. He knew they were right, for by the next year marauding Sioux had burned the ranch house to the ground. But something in him had died when Lydia left, adopted by a family going west, folks who seemed clean and kindly enough and, as the missionaries had insisted, devoted Christians.

For the next few years and again recently, more than ever, he dreamed of someday having that life back again. Lydia was out there somewhere, he knew. But there could be no seeking her till he had a home, a place in a community, the things they both lost when Buzz died. He wondered if she thought of him. Maybe not. Maybe she was growing up, putting the past behind her.

The sound of Ironfoot moving around pulled him back to the present. He looked out on the valley, not ready to move, sleepily wondering at this land with its sweeps of space and its high free winds that Buzz loved so much. He guessed he loved it too.

He turned to Ironfoot. "Some of these men plan to head north," he said softly, nodding to the distant figures along the stream bank. "Ain't preaching it, but maybeso you might want to team up with them for a ways."

Ironfoot looked at him guardedly, his dark penetrating eyes shining from underneath his brows. "Why white men go north?"

"Nothing that makes much sense, I'm thinking. 'Pears they're huntin' a map . . . suppose to show them where big riches hide in the ground."

Ironfoot grunted and looked away. It was the Indian way of saying a conversation was over. White River smiled grimly and looked down again at the piece of paper he still held awkwardly to his chest. As he stared at it, he heard Ironfoot rise to his feet and almost instantly begin speaking in the Absarokee tongue. White River looked up to find Teel was almost upon them, having approached through the heavy thicket on their right. The old trapper was holding a neatly folded paper in his left hand as he came forward, answering the Indian in the curious rolling words of the Crow tongue.

"Sorry to spook yuh," he said casually to White River, laying the rifle hanging from his right hand against a rock. "Just thought there'd be fewer to jaw about it if I came thisaway." He winked slyly before he spat and settled himself on the ground.

"Been thinkin' on leaving, I reckon," queried White River.

"After a spell, I suspect." Teel opened the paper, holding it away from him as he examined it. "Got this off that Amiel fellow."

White River looked pointedly up the stream and gazed for a moment at the tall, lean figure of Marcher, who was now alone and settled down looking at the river. He was reluctant to utter the words, but finally he said, "More 'n likely that's Marcher's map, Teel."

Teel turned and spat. "More 'n likely 'tis."

White River grunted knowingly. "Can't give you any help if that's what you're wantin'. I've already looked at it but don't fairly know that country. It's been off limits for a long time."

"What country?" Teel's deadpan face looked ludicrous as he rolled the wad of tobacco inside his cheek.

"That country that coot Marcher thinks he's headin' into."

Teel ran a stained buckskinned sleeve across his mouth. "'Tweren't visiting on you, White River. Came by to powwow some with Ironfoot here." He said a few words to Ironfoot in Crow, making the Indian look up cautiously, his face fixed, expressionless.

"No offense," said White River indifferently, "just don't see how that buzzard has kept from gettin' himself killed. Trouble is he's likely to get some others killed while he's workin' at it."

"A mean critter, for a fact," allowed Teel, turning again to spit, "but got this map from t'other fellow, Amiel. Now he ain't a bad sort."

"No, he sure shines aplenty next to t'other." White River offered the sheet of paper Amiel had given him to Teel. Teel took it haltingly, his features as he shifted it before him tightening in a grimace of regret. "Now dang if'n I didn't read slicker 'n a schoolmarm once't, even scripture and sech, but ever since them flesh-chewing Tonkawas corralled me down to Brazos country . . . scared the livin' lights out of me . . . had me salted up for stewing by the Jesus afore some one-eyed squaw took a shine to me and I got clean away . . . but hellfire," he handed the paper back, "just naturally ain't been able to read a gospel word since."

" 'Taint important," White River said easily. "Just says that gent Amiel is putting up whole wages for me on some stake money he's got back east."

Teel stopped chewing. "Now, by Lucifer, if that don't make him a decent bugger! Looky here, Horse, 'pears now you can set yourself up right smart with them wagons."

"Could be so, I reckon."

"Great sassafras!—ain't that a-gonna make Benson wish he hadn't sloshed up a bearskinful of that mule piss of his. Reckon he had nigh on to two jugs downed when last I winded him. Wagh!"

White River drew his mouth together tightly as he stared down at the sheet of paper now flapping lightly in his hand. In another minute he finished off the cooled broth with a single gulp and pulled himself up to a straight position. He nodded to the north. "How far you reckon this Marcher's going to get if his stick floats thataway?"

"Don't pay him no heed, White River, he's a buzzard whose tail feathers are gonna git twisted one way or t'other."

"He's sure had those two river fleas a-hopping," muttered White River, again seeing Marcher in his mind ranting at the slow-moving figures of Josh and Neff. "Reckon now they got the scent of gold in their snoot they'll be hunchin' up to him like two suckling pigs workin' one teat."

"Reckon," answered Teel, anxious to start with Ironfoot.

"Likely they figure they can work his mine for him, whilst hanging him on a tree somewheres handy to watch."

"Don't rightly know," Teel said a little uneasily. "He's got a temper like a bull backed into cactus. Could be he just won't hang so easy."

As Teel began to speak quietly in the Crow tongue to Ironfoot and the two of them leaned together over the open map, White River settled back to rest, casually watching some clouds gathering to the southeast, their ramparts curving away at the will of some contrary wind. Could be a mite of rain, he thought idly, knowing the chances would be slim in this droughty season.

12

Ben Amiel stared down at the series of small markings on the map. They had been put there by Benson with a long sawblade hunting knife as Teel, following his own and Ironfoot's vague recollections and using cuss words enough to insure damnation, directed him.

Common sense dictated it had to be shown to someone who knew the country to see if it had any geographical validity at all, however farfetched. Now he had just been told it had, "after a fashion." Teel had carefully studied the map and had taken the precaution of consulting the Crow, Ironfoot. There could well be such an area in the Black Hills near a mountain whose name was scratched on the map, though it bordered on being illegible.

"Wonder, would you consider coming along, Mr. Teel—as a guide, I mean. I think you know we'd be willing to pay you later any amount you considered fair."

Teel shook his head slowly, his worn features dusky now in the growing gloom. "Mr. Amiel, I've already told you as how a rattlesnake with God on his side would have trouble getting through that country up there without he risk some hair. I've been hunted by Sioux twice in my remembering—by rights I should have gone under with Jake Tooley and old Samuels, good men both, but if a fellow messes with Sioux long enough, sooner or later he just ain't naturally going to be good enough. Take an old nigger's advice. Head back east and don't do no thinking on things till you be leastways to Independence." Ben raised his arms in a helpless gesture. It was not meant to be a dissatisfied response, but Teel chose to take it so. "Know'd you come a long ways to be put down, Mr. Amiel, and reckon it don't pleasure you none, but it beats having a Sioux buck stirring your gut up with your own gun barrel, fresh from out the fire."

Amiel folded the map as he checked a sudden shiver. "So you don't feel there's much chance, eh?" He spoke knowing how unnecessary these words were.

Teel answered idly and out of sheer courtesy. "Every gopher that takes on a coyote, Mr. Amiel, has a chance."

Later, alone by the fire, Ben Amiel turned his increasingly disastrous predicament over in his mind. The enormity of his mistake in coming at all was beginning to appall him, anger him, force him to face how much tragedy had stalked his days since Andy's maddening obsession with Paul's mine broke upon his life.

Restless and wanting to move about, he started to gather wood for the fire while across the water a snarling ruckus arose as wolves and coyotes came up to fight over the remains of the butchered buffaloes.

He looked again at the map, knowing it had brought them to this godforsaken island. In his heart he was sure it would take them to their deaths. For a moment he wished he had the guts to stuff it in the fire, but he quailed at the thought of Andy's wrath. Suddenly on the opposite shore a chorus of coyotes, probably being forced away from the carrion by wolves, yelled dismally. Something in their high lament made him shiver. Jesus, he was lonely. Was there really much left in his life? Andy was becoming a stranger, with his growing anger and almost frenzied obsession. He wondered what his mother would say if she knew that when she deeded her half of the farm to Andy, she had opened the door to this perilous venture. Suddenly with Andy and his mother joined in his mind, the leaping fire before him reminded him of the large hearth that had warmed their cozy home in Virginia. Would he ever stand again under the towering pines of Cherokee Ridge in the high, clear silence of morning, feeling a strange communion with his dead father and his young wife, Melody, lost in childbirth? Melody had only been dead a month when Andy arrived from Washington in an alarming fit of violent resentment. He was near incoherent when imparting that he had broken with his parents, and during those first nights he had sat before that fireplace till all hours, drinking and ranting to himself. Ben, patient, tactful, concealing his worry, tried to gain some understanding of what lay behind this seething rage, but all he could fathom was that Andy had left behind him some large gambling debts and saw no way he could bring his life and pride back together again, for he could see no way he could earn even moderate amounts of money.

Then one night, in a burst of excitement, Andy remembered Paul's map. It had lain for years buried and near forgotten with other family papers under a layer of attic clutter. At first the notion of using it to find Paul's grave seemed preposterous, but the more Andy studied it and talked about it the more promise it seemed to have. Even Ben stopped denying it might be a worthy enterprise, but he stubbornly pointed out that such a venture required money, money that he, a simple farmer, did not have.

Andy began to press for mortgaging the farm, but Ben adamantly refused to even think of it. He would not risk his beautiful home and fertile spread of land to traipse off looking for gold in the wilderness. But Andy's eagerness to track down Paul's mine was taking on desperate tones. One night they fought.

Then that letter arrived.

He often thought about that letter. His mother's writing, usually so perfect, seemed uneven, confused. That she had brought herself to deed her half of the farm, the only inheritance left to her by his father, who had lost his life refusing to use guns putting down a slave rebellion, to Andy without consulting himself he took to be a grave sign of how upset and distracted she must have been.

He had long ago stopped thinking about his mother's life in Washington, a city he detested as much as he did his stepfather. He was overjoyed when they allowed him to stay on the farm, where he could see little Melody, his childhood sweetheart, almost every day. But over the years he gathered that young Andy was not getting the devoted mothering—or fathering—he himself remembered. Over the years he began to sense the evil loneliness that lay like a shadow above that sumptuous house in Washington. Over the years he sensed other things, some too shocking to express. And now with Andy, bitter beyond belief and desperately seeking money, this letter arrived with its smell of atonement.

He knew then there would be no stopping Andy; any attempt would have meant a final breach between them. After a day of pondering all the disturbing possibilities, he decided to try and make a virtue out of necessity. They would mortgage the farm and both of them would go, though he left enough money banked to start his life again as a farmer, should they fail. Andy was too elated to quibble. He was already making preparations, buying and studying maps of the western trails, writing to the Bureau of Indian Affairs in Washington. Ben was never sure whether Andy wanted him to come or not, but he himself was subtly getting caught up in the wishful thinking that invaded their conversation every evening. Suppose they did find that mine? He could lift the mortgage on the farm, buy more property, start a new life—but it was hard to think of starting a new life without Melody.

Now he was sitting by this lonely fire realizing what a mistake he had made. Well, he would try once again when Andy returned. It sickened him to think of the alternatives he was forced to face. Either he left with Andy, chancing if not deliberately inviting death, or he abandoned his brother and returned to the loneliness of that heavily indebted farm, where lay the graves of his father and his young wife. As the night grew colder, he pulled his coat about him and listened to the fierce, snarling battle for food and survival that continued to rage on that shadowy shore beyond. In the distance he suddenly saw a small fire before White River's shelter flaring up to glow brightly. He wondered if it had any meaning.

They were coming toward him through the darkness. In the distant play of the firelight, Andy's tall figure rose above the other two, his arms hanging loosely by his side, like a man begrudging effort.

"Andy," said Ben tautly. Josh and Hammer held up unsteadily for a moment, then, sensing Amiel's interest in Marcher alone, resumed their shuffling stride toward the fire.

"Yes, Ben," said Marcher, an impatient weariness in his voice. His unshaven face hung dark and unreadable in the feeble light.

"They tell me around here a man's dying is his own business."

Marcher looked at him steadily. "Sounds fair enough. Go on, Ben."

"Andy, there isn't a gospel chance of this thing succeeding. It's time you saw it for what it is."

"I've been looking."

"Andy, it's a ridiculous gamble."

"Is there more, Ben?"

"You're playing with death, Andy."

"You just said it was a man's own business."

Ben threw back his head like one gasping for air. "Andy, what is it? It isn't just the gold."

"Does it matter?"

"When a man plays for these stakes, it should be for something that matters."

Marcher shrugged and looked at the ground. "I'm going, Ben. Leaving in the morning. That's an end to it." He looked up at his brother. "Where's the map, Ben?"

Ben pulled it slowly from his pocket and extended it, his mouth set hard. "You'll find some markings on it. They're supposed to help."

Marcher put the map carelessly in his pocket. There was a slackness in his motions that betrayed an indifference to what lay ahead. He looked past Ben to the fire, clearly about to move toward it.

"Andy."

"Yes, I know," said the now vacant voice.

"Even a man without a reason to live should at least have a reason to die."

"Should he?"

"Most men would need one—and a better one than gold."

"Nobody's holding you to anything, Ben."

His brother reached out and took him by the arm. "Get some decent rest tonight, Andy—you've hardly had any these past nights—then try to see it more clearly in the morning. You owe yourself at least that much. A lot has happened around here—enough to throw a man's reasoning off."

Marcher stepped from his grasp and started toward the fire. "Ben, I've thought about little else, and I'm tired of it now. Going back means there's something to go back to." His head dropped and his voice changed for a moment. "You go back, Ben. I guess there are some things a man just does alone."

13

White River drew his hand over his now heavily bearded face and raised himself up. His afternoon sleep had refreshed him enough to feel he could go down to the stream and wash and perhaps bring back some water to heat over the fire for a shave. He found Ironfoot sitting motionless at the other end of the shelter, looking quietly at the pebbled ground before him. Beyond, the distant voices of men gathering about their fires signaled the end of day.

White River did not speak until he had unrolled his pack and had drawn out an old razor, which he looked at, then left on a stone beside the fire with a well-used piece of soap. "Anything happen while I slept?"

Ironfoot did not answer at once, and when he did it was clear his mind had been far-wandering. "White River strong again."

"Rightly enough, I reckon," said White River, knowing somehow that Ironfoot had decided to leave.

"Ironfoot will think much of White River."

White River decided to cut off their talk and make his way to the water. Indians weren't much on goodbyes. He sensed Ironfoot's real desire was to be alone with his thinking and whatever spirits he wanted to make quiet prayers to.

Yet he found he was wrong. As he started away Ironfoot lifted a hand lightly and said in soft, even tones, "Much badness here."

White River stopped to turn slowly toward him. "Here?"

Ironfoot's eyes lifted to squint meditatively in the direction of Amiel's and Marcher's campsite. It suddenly reminded White River that Teel had been there with Marcher's map. "Oh," he said as though he understood and agreed. "No helping it though, I'm thinking."

"Many will die," said Ironfoot, his eyes still squinting, his great face lifting a fraction.

"Well, nobody's forcing them to go."

"Old one good man."

White River rubbed the back of his neck wondering if Ironfoot meant Teel or Amiel. Didn't matter, both fitted his description.

"White River say to friend not go to land of Lakota."

" 'Twouldn't do any good."

Ironfoot stopped squinting and looked at White River long and hard, his great dark eyes seeming immense in the dusk. They disturbed White River. He felt accused.

White River irritably switched the piece of soap from one hand to the other. "Seems to me you're going thataway yourself." White River drew off, aware of a dim feeling of shame. Ironfoot did not deserve curt answers. He found this feeling hard to shake even when the wetness of the stream felt good against his skin and his body was relieved to be rid of the stinking clothes. It was still with him when he dipped the little iron pot in the water for his shaving, and when he flexed his shoulders and knew the worst of his wound was over. He had not allowed himself to think of the ugly hole until then, but now he accepted the fact that he had been more than a little lucky. Gome had been good, born to the trigger and with a natural timing uncomplicated by conscience. He had had much on his side and had he not tried to do too many things at once. . . .

Strangely his mind drifted to the repeating rifle Amiel had given to Red Legs. It sent an empty feeling through his stomach as he heard it again, snapping in the distant darkness like the sonic convulsions of a whip, then its frightening silence made more frightening by the occasional report of a single shot that whispered who prevailed.

Somehow the rifle and the yellow paper Amiel had offered him were bound together in his mind. For surely Amiel was a feeling and unselfish man, but White River, walking back slowly, wondered if like many selfless givers he was unaware of the deceptive fortune that often lay seeded in the most unselfish of gifts.

At the shelter Ironfoot had started a small fire between two rocks. He was sitting back from it now looking at the pebbled ground, his face lit faintly by the flames. White River knew at a glance that the fire was built to heat his shaving water, but he did not comment on it. Instead he said, "Ironfoot is good friend."

Ironfoot kept his eyes upon the pebbled earth.

White River set the pot above the fire and lifted his razor, feeling its edge idly as he looked off into the darkness. "Reckon I'll talk to those fellows after all—don't seem hardly right giving them Sioux anything to shout about."

Ironfoot looked up, his eyes softer and lightly inquiring in the firelight. White River noticed he had put fresh black paint on his face and his braids were newly tied. An elk-tooth necklace White River had not seen before appeared white about the Crow's neck. "When the sun stands upon the prairie again, White River's heart will be good."

White River put his hand up to his face to test the growth, then squatted to watch the water in the pot. "Where did that map say they were headed?"

Ironfoot looked down again, his gaze intent upon the pebbles. "To little running water through land where Sioux ponies stand like clouds upon the hills."

"Damn fools," said White River without rancor. Then, after a moment, "What's the name of this running water?"

Ironfoot peered more intently at the dark pebbles. "Sioux call mountain beside little running water Innyan Kara."

White River looked over at him in resignation. "Sounds like a good place to stay away from."

Ironfoot, looking at the pebbles, did not answer.

14

Mahogany was the word Ben Amiel was trying to think of, a word to describe the color of their weathered faces bathed by firelight, each attached to a dark body that lay sprawled, devoid of contours against the darkness behind. Ben had quietly withdrawn within himself. He was weary beyond the will to talk, his senses fenced in by fatigue. Sitting back, he dimly knew something was happening about him, something important. Just what, he could not reason out. Teel had said nothing when Marcher and Josh and Hammer had slumped down beside the fire, and then few words came from among those three, each one seemingly preoccupied and bent on getting sleep.

Benson had left earlier in a sudden burst of joviality, ignited by word of White River's reborn promise of a freighting business. But now he was back, and White River with him, and Benson's face now appeared withdrawn and sober.

No one spoke at first as the newcomers filled the circle, but White River was clearly weighing the words that lay behind his visit. Marcher watched him, his eyes half closed, his body on the ground, his torso supported lightly on one elbow.

White River's words finally came as a relief. A lonely coyote yip pierced the distant night just as he spoke.

"Mr. Marcher, what you're aiming to do can't be done." Marcher broke a twig between his fingers and continued to stare at White River. "It ain't fitting for someone whose advice ain't been asked to be saying it, but for a fact, Mr. Marcher, getting in and out of that country up there calls for a heap more savvy than you and these new friends of yours are likely to come by for a spell. Man to man, if I'd knowed this fix was coming I wouldn't have brought you this far."

"Well, I'll be damned to hell," roared Josh. "Listen at that squaw man make like he's almighty something." He leaned forward. "By Lucifer, if I don't have me half a mind to . . ."

White River had not brought his gun. Squelching a flash of fury at himself, he slipped out his hunting knife and cradled it quickly in his hand.

"Look out, Josh!" screamed Neff.

White River had turned to Josh almost indifferently, but Josh had seen that faraway look before. He squirmed around awkwardly, groping for his gun like a man half wanting to bolt.

"Leave it be!" warned White River. Josh settled back slowly, his eyes blunted, subdued. White River's words were frighteningly casual. "Josh, that's twice I've seen you come no more than a coon's whisker of being dead. Next time I speculate you're fixing to make it."

Marcher had pulled himself up with an anger fused into energy. "Hold on, White River! We want no trouble with you. No one asked you to come here."

"Oh, to hell with 'em!" shouted Benson. "To hell with the whole lot of 'em. Come on, White River, if these soft-headed buzzards want to get themselves killed, let 'em!"

"Could be you're right," White River muttered, returning the knife slowly under his heavy shirt.

"Don't fret yourselves. We'll be all right. We've got everything carefully planned. We're leaving at sunup." Marcher threw the twig ends in his hand roughly into the fire.

White River's mouth settled quietly. "At sunup?"

"That's right, sunup it is."

White River rubbed his stomach as though half expecting a pain there. He turned about to find Teel looking at him knowingly and shaking his head just perceptibly from side to side. "Sunup," repeated White River. He looked back at Marcher, his clean-shaven face seeming to lengthen as he spoke. "And these two critters here are letting you?"

"You betcha," said Neff in a thin, nervous tone. "We're bound on getting an early start."

White River looked around awkwardly, searching. He had business to finish, he wanted to leave. Then, with open relief, he spotted Ben Amiel.

"What's wrong with leaving at sunup?' said Marcher, his eyes clear now but fixed on White River and curiously alive.

"What's wrong with it," mused White River as he probed through his pockets.

Teel spit out his worn plug and drew a fresh dark roll from his pocket. Before he bit into it he said, "You're a-going into hostile country, Mr. Marcher. . . ."

"Well, certainly, we're aware of that!"

Teel bit the black roll in disgust. "Well, since you're sort of handy with words and such . . . mebbe you oughta send them Sioux bucks a letter written proper and all . . . let 'em know you're coming."

"Oh, go to hell!" cried Josh, rising to his feet. "God A'mighty, those damn Injuns don't figure to scare us none. We know what we're doing."

White River rubbed his sides slowly like a man wanting to finish. "If you're set on going, get out of here just after dark," he said in a manner that demanded no attention. "Travel as much as you can by night, take enough food along, 'count of hunting will be dangerous. Stay on high ground and leave as few trails as possible. Make sure somebody who knows what to look for stays awake while you sleep, and don't hole up in any spot you can't run from. Indians are better 'n most at that waiting game."

"A tall order when you consider everything," said Teel, looking seriously at Marcher and Josh and Neff.

"You talk like we ain't tot'n any shooting irons," said Josh, heaving his rifle to readiness and patting it as though such a point could be overlooked.

Benson laughed in spite of himself. "Kee-rist! All the lead the lot of you could tote up there wouldn't do more than stir 'em up."

Marcher's face, which had been shifting visibly, settled now in a determined frown.

"Don't pay these meddlesome polecats no heed, Mr. Marcher," mumbled Josh, glowering mainly at Benson.

"Shut up!" snapped Marcher. "I've got my own opinion of this bunch and their interest in our well-being, so don't take me for a fool."

Ben Amiel was coming alive now. It had gotten through to him that Andy was beginning to question what everyone else had been questioning from the beginning. Ben had known that White River's voice was the only one that could stay Andy, and now it had happened—something had moved White River to come here, to state the case, to put behind it his intimacy with this land.

But then suddenly a yellow paper intruded upon his thinking like a large moth settling before him in the darkness. White River was handing it to him, saying, "Thought this over, Mr. Amiel, reckon it don't belong to me after all, thank ye kindly."

"Jumping Jehosophat!" groaned Benson, repeatedly slapping his stomach.

Ben looked up awkwardly. "But I don't agree."

"It's done," said White River.

"It isn't right. . . ."

"Right is what a man reckons it to be."

" 'Taint no other way, I suspect," said Teel, spitting into the fire. "Besides, hear tell freightin' is bad for a man's liver."

Marcher's darkly bearded face, in spite of its fatigue, had taken on a new strength even as it cast off its boyish sheen. Sprawled in the dim wash of the fire he seemed, as he regarded White River, a little closer to this land. "Out of the freighting business again, eh?"

"Never was in it, for a fact," replied White River.

"Well, just as well, I suspect." Marcher's words trailed off in the random way of a mind relinquishing an issue.

Benson snorted, his thick lips whitened by endless irritations. "It's a caution how some varmints can't keep their yaps shut . . . so folks would think they only look simple."

Marcher's figure tightened and swung on Benson, his face taking on a violent, almost predatory cast, but White River was suddenly around the fire, engaging him. "You got a piece needs sayin' mebbe, Marcher?" Only Teel noticed it was the first time White River failed to say "Mister."

Marcher rose on one knee. "And if I have, by God, I'll get to it, but when I'm damn good and ready!"

Teel's voice was low in pursuit of Marcher's, but it was burdened with warning. "Some things set better fer thinkin' than for sayin', Mr. Marcher."

"Hell yes! And don't think I don't know it! The way the lot of you have been squatting around here thinking I'm an idiot for wanting to go north!" He laughed in a way that made the air brittle.

Teel spat stiffly. "An idiot's an idiot, I reckon, no matter what direction he's headed in."

"Amen! And a man crawling back east again could be an idiot too, couldn't he?"

Teel waved his hand deprecatingly, as though he wanted to shed the issue. "Ain't debatin' it."

Marcher pursed up his lips. Ignoring White River standing over him, he mused into the fire. "And if he's crawling back to drift around and see what pushes him which way next, if he ends up settling for a few drunks or pipe dreams about what he hasn't got the guts to grab—he could be the God-damnedest fool of all! Couldn't he?"

A strange pall fell over the group, and at its center was the long, shadowed face of White River. Marcher pulled the map slowly from his pocket and held it before him, his eyes as he was facing the fire taking on a strange suggestion of intoxication. He could have been a shaman looking at an amulet that brings him secret strength. "Well, God damn it, I'm going! Everybody is an idiot about something, but an idiot that knows where he's going has got a hell of a lot better reason for being alive than one that doesn't."

White River's voice when it came was almost a whisper. "You done?"

Marcher appeared to be scanning his map, raising it higher in the light, examining it as though drawn to some new detail. "I am if you are," he said matter-of-factly.

Every part of White River's mind but one demanded that he leave. Marcher was starting something here, something that had already penetrated and shaken White River in a dim recess of his being, and its unaccountability gave him a vague feeling of helplessness. Search as he would, no ready reasoning rose to rescue him. He knew men well enough to know that Marcher was gifted with great guile, but here was a guile—if that in fact was what it was—which enjoyed some dark treaty with truth. What was actual and what was artificial in those last few moments he could not determine, but Marcher had just awakened something in him, that much he knew, even though its significance was as yet unclear. He found himself unable to resist a question.

"You said I couldn't start up with a freightin' business—how'd that notion get into your craw?"

Marcher's manner gave the matter little weight. "Oh, I guess it was just a thought . . . but I'll wager you wouldn't fit." He looked at White River as though measuring him. "Business is short on marksmanship and moody types that think they're misunderstood—it's long on little graces."

Benson broke in again. "Not around here, by God! Nothing but raw guts and savvy counts. What the hell is ailing you, Marcher, you been getting too much sun! You seen enough to know this fellow could get a wagon load of missionaries in and out of hell without the devil himself ever once knowing kinfolk had been by!"

Marcher's dark face curved into a quick, strained indulgence. "Wasn't talking about that."

"Blast you! What in tarnation are you jawing on, then?"

Marcher drew himself up as though he wanted to be on his feet if Benson spoke in that manner again. The play of his moods was becoming more unsettling than his words, and no one was ready when he said, almost as though it didn't matter, "Maybe White River knows."

White River felt a strange stiffening at the back of his neck. In some distant part of his mind he was glad he did not have his gun.

"All right, then," he said with a try at arrogance he did not feel. "I don't set up with no freightin' business. Reckon I'll manage anyway."

Marcher seemed drawn to his map again. "Oh." He looked up congenially, his over innocent eyes playing upon the other. But his only remark was, "How?"

"Just moseyin' around, I suspect."

Marcher nodded agreeably. "Forever?"

"It's a habit a fellow can get to like."

"You don't."

White River felt the thing in his mind moving again, but he nodded disparagingly at the map and snapped, "Beats dying."

"Does it?" Marcher's head was up fully now, his eyes wide open and inquiring. "Really doesn't matter a damn, you know. After all, a man ought to have what he wants—or thinks he wants." Marcher hesitated, looked down, and kicked at the fire. "There's little enough even at that in life."

White River hung forward for a moment as though the flint edge of some truth had wedged itself into his mind. Could Marcher know? Could he know it was not the hardships of a freighting trail that gnawed against a man's hope, it was this other thing that he told himself Benson could protect him from, but in the end no one could? The catering to strangers, settling of small, nasty accounts at the far reaches of a line, maybe the taking of anger from shallow, squint-eyed men when shipments were unavoidably and unexplainably late; and being tied to a moving machine that went where it was told, and above all the fabricated optimism and sham shaking of every hand and staying away from thoughts and feelings that might cause a customer to close his purse.

What he needed was a drink, a long, heavy drink to dampen the fire of anxiety that was spreading in him. Yet to have asked for whiskey now would have carried away the last shred of pretense that he had any mastery over things. He shook his head like a man clearing his vision and then watched Marcher with an air of routine reaching for more wood and throwing it leisurely over the fire. Marcher kept his eyes off him and seemed to be concerned with matters alien to the moment and only of his own interest. It was several minutes before he said, "Friend Benson has departed—noticed he gets a little dry this time of evening." White River watched the flames mounting into the new wood, afraid to contemplate that Marcher's quick remarks about Benson were his way of saying he knew White River's mind was on whiskey.

"Reckon I'll join him," said Teel, lifelessly hauling himself up, his eyes peculiar as they took in White River. "Maybeso old Benson is in a buying mood."

White River watched him go. The others appeared to be asleep, Josh and Neff dark heaps emitting uneven and muffled snores, and Ben Amiel over on his side, his head away from the fire. Only Marcher seemed awake and alert, almost eager to continue some chance remarks he was now making about the weather, their well-rested mounts, the fact that the danger at least hereabouts must have lessened since the island's inhabitants were moving on. In time his congeniality flowered into a confession that he needed a touch of brandy and would White River do him the great personal favor of joining him.

White River's answer was a grunt, but Marcher heard it as an affirmative one.

Brandy. He watched its amber glint as it came in a willing tongue from the flask. Marcher watched it too with the curious eyes of a man who loves something he knows better than to trust or respect. White River took the cup and felt the quick bite of the fluid as it trickled within him. The brandy seemed to fill the air about him with a quiet aroma of things beyond his narrow knowing, of things garnished with their own familiar past, roots that could recollect to a man where a century or more had gone, age-scented Bibles laden with kinfolk bound forever by banns and bloodlines.

André Marcher sat back savoring his drink. There was some rare grace about him now that even his new and gruff appearance could not quite wipe away. He exuded camaraderie in a way too total to defend against, and White River found himself watching him quietly, wondering at his strange feelings about him, looking for what made it possible for Marcher to relax and reign so easily on this harrowing and inhospitable night. He was clear finally on one thing—the man had a fearlessness about him. But it is in the way of things that there is always as good a reason for fearlessness as there is for fear and what lay behind Marcher's fearlessness he did not know.

"Not much choosing between those two when you think of it," Marcher said not unkindly, even half smiling at the prostrate forms of Josh and Neff. "I can't make up my mind whether these two rascals are running from something or hoping they soon will be."

White River tried some more of the brandy. "It's a country easy enough to get lost in."

"Um." Marcher looked at him much as a host might a guest he had overlooked. "Something got you thinking, White River?"

White River sat back and looked at Marcher for a moment. The brandy was swiftly warming his stomach and he was glad to hear an easy crest of confidence alive in his voice again. "You made a remark tonight, Marcher, I didn't rightly care much for."

"Didn't mean to offend."

"It's the way I heard it."

"How was that?"

"You said I couldn't turn a hand at freighting—meaning maybe I couldn't turn a hand at anything."

Marcher waved the suggestion away. "What does it matter what I think? All I was giving you was one man's opinion. But, mind you, I had only freighting in mind—that's a job for peasants at best. However, there are some things you do better than any man I've ever known."

White River swirled the remaining brandy in his cup and looked warily into the fire. His head came up as though he was about to say something, then elected not to, and his face settled as he bolted down the last of the amber fluid instead.

Marcher came forward to look at him in what appeared to be earnest inquiry. "You don't believe me, eh?"

"Nope!"

Marcher was suddenly filling the cups again. White River watched him pour. It mattered little whether he himself drank more or not, liquor enough to float a fort could not make him drunk this night.

Marcher's voice returned high and fixed as though holding fast to their thread of conversation. "Well, it struck me you knew what you were doing here the other night."

White River's eyes were suddenly questioning. There was no need for words.

"Yes, I mean our late friend Sam Gome—I doubt if there was a man on the island who could have dealt with him but you."

"Don't waste your while believing that."

"Ah, but I do."

White River smiled quietly, almost internally, like a man who knows better. "I suspect if you took a notion to inquire you'd find there were some mighty fast guns on the loose around here the night that fix came up."

"That has nothing to do with it. Teel said Gome was faster than you."

"He was," agreed White River simply.

"Most men would have been afraid of him."

"He was a man deservin' to be feared."

"Were you afraid of him?"

"Yes—I believe I was."

"But he's dead. Benson tells me there was a decidedly unpleasant character in these parts named Chicasaw Kane. Seems he was a murderous pig with an uncanny streak of luck—that is until you called him out. By all accounts you were outgunned, but in the end it was he and his cronies who got carried out."

"Marcher, if you got a point—get to it."

"Exactly. My point is you were convinced Gome, like this Kane, needed killing. After that nothing could save him. I suspect he knew it too."

White River looked at him steadily for a moment, then looked away and rose up like a man too long in contact with the ground. "Gettin' late, for a fact. Time I was bedded down." He took a step or two around the dying fire. "Much obliged for the spirits."

"Not at all," said Marcher evenly.

White River hesitated. "If I don't see you come morning, wish you a freight wagon full of luck."

"I think we'll be here."

White River fixed him with a new glance, doubt and almost misgivings in his eyes. "But you was bound on going."

"I am."

"Then . . . ?"

"When I'm convinced I've got the man to get me where I want to go."

White River studied him in silence for a moment, his long, lean features tilted off center, as though he were standing on one leg. Whatever his thoughts they were never worked into words, for he turned into the darkness and left.

Some time later, with the fire almost out and Marcher lying on his back, his eyes thin slits gazing at the stars, Ben Amiel drew his head out of the darkness and turned his body to settle down beside his brother. Neither spoke at first. Many minutes went by before Ben finally muttered, "You know you're a sinful man, Andy."

Marcher did not answer.

Long moments passed and a slight wind arose to sigh across the treetops, vague as their swaying in the night. Ben's final words betrayed that sleep was almost upon him for they were in a half whisper. "I think your father's met his match at seducing people."

Again it appeared Marcher wouldn't answer, but as he turned away from Ben he closed his eyes as one who still sees a sight on which he has long dwelled and said in a frozen voice that promised no thaw, "My father was an amateur."

15

The wind was rampaging in from the plains. It beat furiously over the valley, sweeping birds in the air and howling over the tumbleweed that spun about in a frantic effort to serve its will. Weather was making up to the southwest where the sky was the color of Aztec gold, but to the north lay a long, low cloud. It bridged the open land peacefully like a great white canopy that stretched farther than a man could see.

White River led his mount up to the knoll and left it to graze. He had ridden beyond the bluffs, moving cautiously through the brakes and watching the blades of yellow grass being tormented by the wind. Nothing but the grass moved. The game had disappeared and the damp, cold scent of far-off mountains came in unexpected moments. He moved up to the skull of the knoll and let his gaze drift across the high plains beyond. A huge loneliness seemed to lie upon the whole of things. He wondered where in that vastness Ironfoot could be holing up, alone with his thoughts, culling his many memories. White River stood for far longer than he realized.

When White River returned during the night, it was clear Ironfoot had left. But it was only this morning that he felt the peculiar gnawing that a man knows when he feels his life is lessened in some way he had not expected or prepared for. He had slept little and left the island early, scouting the land to the north. He found it barren, with no sign fresh enough to force concern. He was delaying now, hoping to find a trace of Ironfoot's pony tracks or some broken strand of grass which would suggest in which direction the Crow had gone, but he found none. Yet he looked on, knowing strangely that he would only have sat wondering if he had come across anything betraying the way taken.

Just before noon he retraced his steps to the east brake and struck the river below the island. As his mount drank in the near shallows, he eyed speculatively some dirty, ragged clouds in the south curling up like uncertain flights of locust. A strange premonition came over him that he was being watched and he froze in the way of a man alerted too late to a predicament that has been slowly engulfing him. It flashed over him that the next second could bring death in the whine of a slug running well ahead of the report of any gun that dispatched it, or the sickening thud of an arrow plowing its way through the muscles of his back to lodge in his vitals. His head motionless, his eyes darted along the stream's edge hoping for some reflection in the water, but the ravaging winds were whipping the surface into one crazy pattern after the other.

The moments ticked away. Could he have been wrong? Slowly he moved his bay about as though he were still idling, his movements undecided. When he had the mount standing alongside the bank, he dropped off quickly on the stream side and pulled his rifle from its scabbard. Nothing moved. Up from the bank, a clump of brush looked menacing, but when it waved in a sudden wash of wind it clearly covered nothing. Beyond, a few cottonwoods rose before a swale of low ground, ideal for an ambush. Reason demanded he look there for danger. He watched for a time, then, moving his mount in an awkward sidestepping motion, he finally commanded a run of cover that enabled him to see into the swale. It was empty. He lifted his gaze to the ridges beyond. Whatever they might conceal, they gave up nothing but the sough of the wind.

Leading his horse, he moved slowly toward them, something inside of him reasoning he should be mounted and lathering his horse in a dead run for the island. But cautious stalking revealed nothing. Now, with his nerves taut, he climbed slowly on the bay and looked about him, pulling his hat down against the wind that seemed to whisper in a thousand tones "Where?"

He did not laugh at his own foolishness. A new and firmer feeling rose in him. Whatever was with him was either friendly or too weak to attack. Without knowing exactly why, he started back again into the brake, retracing his steps a second time. He did not move in a straight line but meandered about in a way that made ambush a hard and even hazardous task. Twice he turned his mount completely about and went another way from the one he seemed committed to. In time he was once again on the high plain that ran in endless undulations to the north, and again he saw only the lonely sweeps of earth.

Having found nothing, he decided he would look again from the knoll before he started back. He would leave to the west this time and reach the river above the island. White River had no reason for this but instinct. The ground to the east was already familiar to someone or something, and this was a dangerous if not deadly advantage.

He left the bay again and went cautiously up the knoll, realizing that while he could see better, he could also be seen. He held the rifle easily in his hand, muzzle up by instinct: sighting a gun barrel coming down on a target is easier than hefting it up. As he neared the top of the knoll he slipped to his knees in order to peer slowly over the flat face of its rock summit.

When he saw it, a cold feeling washed through him. He held himself motionless, gazing at it as though it were a thing alive, his eyes fixing its identity, some understanding trying to work forward in his mind. He knew it was Ironfoot's elk-tooth necklace, laid out like a bow with one thread folded over and running straight in the way of an arrow. But how did it get there? What did it mean? He looked about him. There was nothing but the great emptiness, quieter now and darker as the wind died and roiling gray clouds swollen with imminent storm covered the skies.

He settled down beside it, trying to let the thing rest easier in his mind and meaning began to replace some of its mystery. Ironfoot had not left, he had watched the island, silently wanting something, wanting to know the turn of these troublesome things he could have left behind him. He knew the others had not left at dawn and he had seen White River scouting the plain in that direction and had watched him deep in his own troubled thinking upon that knoll, guessing his intent in the end. Now he had done something, something only one close to the Indian heart could understand. Ironfoot could not start off on such a journey without first offering prayers for help from his secret medicine spirit and making pledges, some involving severe self-torture, to be scrupulously fulfilled if his journey succeeded. This gave a brave on a perilous journey no small assistance, and White River knew it had great substance, for a man who feels that mysterious and invisible powers are with him thinks differently, more confidently, and is less given to fear or foolishness when encountering danger or even death. However, here, as with all favors from what man finds sacred, there were inexplicable laws demanding compliance if the spell were not to be broken. These laws, rigid and relentless, and personally enforced beyond any power of men to legislate, were known as taboos.

In some way Ironfoot had found himself troubled with a taboo. White River could not guess what it was, but it could well have been that Ironfoot had had some sign from his medicine that he was not to travel with others on another mission until his own mission was complete. Yet it must have been more complicated than that, for Ironfoot had let his medicine decide.

He had left the necklace there knowing that if White River found it, his medicine was signaling consent. Consent to what? White River studied the necklace, then settled down beside it. In a few moments he drew back from it and sighted along the arrow, following its aim over the wide sea of land. It pointed slightly northeast; unquestionably it was pointing to something. But what? White River peered into the distance, but the storm was breaking over the prairie and the long, dusky swells of land were disappearing from view. For a moment he thought he saw a black dot, but it vanished immediately and the first pelts of rain came hard against his face.

Well, he would have to return here again. In the clear air after the storm he would have no trouble reading its message. He marked the front and rear end of the thread representing the arrow to sight across and put the necklace into his pocket. Ironfoot was somewhere hereabouts. It had been he watching White River at the stream, wondering if his medicine would lead White River back to the telltale necklace. White River smiled. In spite of his knowledge of what lay ahead, in spite of the storm that broke viciously against him and his mount, in some peculiar way he was happy.

The storm had lashed itself to a frenzy by the time he reached the river, but he worked his way against it oblivious to the soaking he was getting, caught now in an awareness of the subtle decisions that cut the trail of a man's destiny, each impulsive step like a blade in time shearing away all others. Calm rose in him, balancing the storm without, for he knew now a man's way was never really lost. Life and even death would sooner or later find their way to where he wanted them to be.

PART THREE

ARAPAHOS

16

The Arapahos were in a bad mood.

They had killed only a young antelope after a long hunt and now they were seated about Little Hand, their war leader, intent upon their scant meal, none even asking the question that made the heart pound a little heavier and thickened the food in the mouth.

Where was Medicine Fox?

Little Hand sat with his back to the sun, where their great village lay, the one which would surely greet him with the disgrace ever in readiness for those whose medicine failed. Out of the corner of his eye he watched the shadow of a lone upright rock slowly lengthening to the east. Ah, the day was aging. Come back, Medicine Fox! The braves stared down at their food, none raising his eyes to see the torment in those of Little Hand. Little Hand's thoughts were returning to the chain of events that led them there.

When word had come to their great camp on the Republican that the whites were running from the Lakota as rabbits before the shadow of a hawk, their young men had risen and demanded that the red tomahawk be carried north to join the Sioux. There was at once much shouting and dancing and making of medicine, but there was some secret wrangling too, many of the older ones sitting moodily in their lodges, recalling the past arrogance of the Sioux, particularly in victory, but speaking mainly of the foolishness of fighting the whites. Had not the Arapahos come south to find peace? Had not some of their own chiefs, indeed Fighting Eagle himself, they said sullenly, smoked twice with the Blue Coats that very season and given the hand in the white man's way for peace?

But the young men brushed this aside and called for their headmen to lead them north, and when none of their famous war leaders stepped forth they began to meet in secret, a dangerous sign, as all the old ones knew. But it was not to be easily stopped.

Too much of the past oppressed the present. Marriage came late to an Arapaho. It required honors and property, things many of these young men did not have, things they would never have except through war. The previous month some of their young braves had captured two Pawnee maidens, had raped them until the younger one died, then three of them experimented with the other till she seized a knife and plunged it into her breast. But such moments were not enough, the loins still quivered, the mind still hungered for the firm bodies of the quiet Arapaho girls who watched these doings from afar, pensively thinking perhaps that the Pawnee men would not forget.

Finally there was no other way, so the crier came through the village and the chiefs met in council. The day was overwarm and the council lodge, surrounded by young braves already weary of words and openly testing the fit of their weapons, was heavy with the scent of bodies. Fighting Eagle, their great chief, rose first and spoke of the bravery of their people, but said also that they were people of honor and could not violate a peace made with the whites almost before the Blue Coats who came to make it were over the nearest hill.

He said also that their refusal of the red pipe the Sioux had sent them when the snow first thawed was a matter that would not go unnoticed. In respect for Fighting Eagle, the braves said nothing as he finished and settled on the earth, yet neither did they shout approval of his wisdom, for they saw it only as more of the reasoning, so typical of the aged, that tied a man's hands and brought neither meat to his belly nor honors to his lodge.

Little Hand, honest but angry and impulsive, and nursing a long and justified hatred of the Blue Coats, was next to his feet. He cried out that the whites paid no attention to their own treaties, that they were without honor and deserved nothing from the Arapaho. Their presents, he said, were made with bad hearts, meant only to keep one tribe quiet while they destroyed another. In the end they would destroy them all. Little Hand's fury spoke to the hot and impatient hearts of the braves. He shouted, in a trembling rage, of massacres well within the memory of many men there, of whole villages gone, of treacheries too terrible for recounting, his voice lowering only as he turned, his tortured face sobered and bitter, now showing the multitude of well-known scars that marked his body, traces of wounds gotten while he stood defenseless under the Blue Coats' own white flag of truce.

And yet the cutting truth in Little Hand's reasoning only served to conceal a final truth that old Bold Heart and even Fighting Eagle had long since come upon. The threat of the whites could not be dispelled by war. Was it not known that they were so numerous that their losses in battle were as a stray leaf from a forest of oaks? Yet it was not in their numbers but in their character that the death knell of the Indian lay. And even here, where was the truth? Who could really say? They came with much talk of freedom but their acquisitiveness bound everything under their sway. They spoke of justice but their justice was self-serving and more dangerous for the Indians at times than their treachery. Peace, not war, was the Indian's salvation, if indeed he had one at all—peace and time to understand this world of whites and, if possible, to barter to stand in some small corner of it. Such counsel however was wasted on the young. Little Hand sat down to long choruses of Arapaho war whoops. The braves were on their feet brandishing their tomahawks, some raising and waving their bows and spears and, a few lucky ones, their rifles in the air.

"Little Hand will lead us?" Blue Jacket called from a seat near the inner council. It was a strange thing to do, surprising many, for Hawk, their war chief with the largest following among the braves, had not yet spoken, and he was a man who dwelt much on the honors which went with his rank. It was a thing few would have dared to do and one Hawk would not forget. Yet Blue Jacket, though unambitious and given to much joking, was a son of Fighting Eagle and rarely said a thing that did not sooner or later seem right.

Fighting Eagle lumbered to his feet again, his eyes showing the strain of his thoughts. His gaze reached out and clung to Bold Heart. "Does our wise one wish to speak?" Old Bold Heart looked solemnly over the choppy sea of angry, impatient faces. He knew the hearts of his people too well to hold much hope for mere words. He did not even bother to rise.

"On this day to be weary of war is to seem to be weary of life. When we are fewer we will talk." His voice was low and unalive, only a few sitting nearest heard him, but the rumble of inquiring whispers that ran through the outer group was soon lost in a great shouting now that Hawk, who had motioned quickly to Fighting Eagle, was rising to his feet.

Hawk was not only their most prominent war leader, he was also a man sly in the ways of council and willing to wait for the foolishness of others to provide him with the growing power that Fighting Eagle had secretly come to fear.

"Little Hand has spoken well," he began. "The Arapaho must fight and remind our enemies that we are great in war—we must show those who do bad things to us and try to take our lands that they will be punished. Our brothers, the Cheyennes, say the Sioux have driven the whites into holes in the ground where they disappear like gophers, unwilling to fight. Even their wagons have disappeared from the prairie and the buffalo can feed in peace again as the Great Spirit meant him to. But let us think ahead. If we raise the tomahawk against the whites, they may come against us when the snow is on the ground and our old ones and little ones will need the cover of the lodge. Therefore we must be sure we have help. But who will help us? The Cheyennes? Yes, they have been our brothers since before the oldest one here was born. But the Cheyennes have many enemies of their own and their warriors are needed to hold their hunting grounds from the whites. Who then? I say the Sioux! If we help the Sioux now they must help us if the long knives come against us. They have many warriors. Their hunting grounds hold few tracks of the whites, their enemies are weak with many troubles of their own."

The great camp was silent. Hawk was talking hard sense; even Fighting Eagle began to hope that wisdom was replacing ambition in that strange and clever mind. Only Bold Heart closed his eyes to mere slits and waited. "Therefore I say," continued Hawk, "that with the war party Little Hand leads to the Sioux should go a man wise in the ways of council. One to ask the Sioux to promise to help us if we are attacked."

Not only Fighting Eagle but others in the inner circle, old heads wise in the vacantness and sudden littleness of life, flicked their eyes toward Blue Jacket, for surely he for his earlier slight was to have the task of dealing with the surly Sioux. It was an honor that, if extended, he could not easily decline. Only Bold Heart held completely still, as though he were keeping himself in readiness for what was to come. He alone was sure Hawk would not waste this moment on revenge, a thing that could await any empty moment in any empty day ahead, at least not if a move for greater power were possible. Hawk did not disappoint him. "I say that man is Medicine Fox! He will carry us back many good pledges from the heart of the Sioux."

The long series of war whoops and thumping of bows that seemed to shake the hot air as Hawk sat down did not come from the inner circle. Here there was a curiously depressing quiet that Fighting Eagle knew could only be broken by himself. Medicine Fox? Fighting Eagle looked at his folded hands. Hawk was surely an evil man. Fighting Eagle decided as he sat there that now he must kill him. Medicine Fox, his adopted son, was the pride of their village. Taken as a child from the Osage, he had been raised by the Arapaho as one of their own, and so great and yet so generous a man was he in all things that Fighting Eagle had adopted him as his son, a move which gave him great honor and no small amount of power. It was clear to Fighting Eagle that Medicine Fox had the wisdom to lead, more so than his own natural sons who, if not indolent like Blue Jacket, were too thirsty for war or would not talk on tribal matters even when the snow lay heavily on their lodge.

The old women gossiped that the people would look upon Medicine Fox as their leader when Fighting Eagle went beyond the stars. The whole tribe knew he was a warrior beyond doubt. The Shoshones meeting him in battle over and over again in that endless enmity so cruelly pursued between the two tribes called him Bad Medicine, and his flowing red-and-black headpiece trailing within a war party was often enough to scatter an enemy village. That he had wisdom was long known, for no party where he led the scouts had ever been taken by surprise. And the old ones noticed he would encourage no attack, however opportune, if the weak and the young in the camp were to be exposed to danger.

Hawk had shown little interest in Medicine Fox's rise in importance. They had fought well together, and though they were not close, each knew the other to be a man of courage. When Medicine Fox married Swan Caller the picture changed. Swan Caller was the granddaughter of Bold Heart, and the niece of Little Hand, two important men in the tribe. Hawk looked thoughtfully at his own wife, one he had married when he was young. Her family did not have the power of Swan Caller's, but it had power enough. She could not be shunted aside by a more important second wife; he had the wisdom not to try.

Eyeing the only door left open now to the council lodge, Hawk spent months upon the warpath, bringing back scalps and horses and endless tales of coups taken in the heat of battle. The warriors, eager for loot and honor, flocked to his heels until his following exceeded all others'. This gave him the ancient right to speak in council and he showed a skill that escaped only those innocent of the lust for power that can lie hidden in a man's tongue.

Until now he had avoided any move against Medicine Fox, but there were those who expected it as they expected the clap of thunder that comes after a fork of lightning knifes into the summer earth. And now it was here! With everyone thinking it was the lazy and laconic Blue Jacket that Hawk would fall upon, Medicine Fox's turn had come.

Little Hand, with a sudden sickening sense that he had failed again in council, was suddenly on his feet attempting to undo the harm his hatred of the whites had heedlessly wrought. He was devoted to Medicine Fox. He must now do all in his power to protect him. "Our brother Hawk has spoken well," he began, "he has shown great wisdom about many things. No one knows more about war and the face of our enemies than he. Now hear what I say. I, Little Hand, though I have led many war parties against many of our foes, I am not the greatest war leader of the people. Our greatest war leader is clearly Hawk. I say he should lead our young men on this great mission. He should carry the red tomahawk to our brothers the Sioux."

The braves shouted approval of this switch to a man they had long followed and whose medicine in war they knew to be strong. But for some the shouts were short, their attention catching on a quality in Little Hand they had not noticed before. War leaders do not give up important honors easily, let alone say in council that another is more worthy. Fighting Eagle came to his feet, alive to the moment. " 'Tis well—Little Hand has raised our hearts. It is Hawk who shall lead our young men north!"

"Then *he* can make us a good treaty with the Sioux," said Blue Jacket, smiling quietly into his upturned hands.

Hawk, without waiting, took to his feet again, looking about the council like a mother grouse examining her brood. There was no hint of alarm in his movement, only a slow general steadying as one about to share with others some all too obvious common sense. "Little Hand gives great honor to his brother, Hawk, but the warrior must place the need of his people before his own pride. Yes, we must send our young men to help the Sioux, but I, Hawk, say we should not leave our village defenseless in the season of war. To make new enemies does not sweep old ones from the prairie. The Pawnee have waited long to find our village without braves or seasoned war leaders to fight for it. They remember their own death was almost upon them when we once caught them so. The treacherous Kiowas have smoked with the Comanches to the south and their hearts are bad against us. The Utes will not sleep until they have avenged the two chiefs we killed when the melting snows first filled the streams. No, let others have their chance at honor. I have been upon the warpath many, many times. I will now give the coups and the victory dancing to others. I will stay here and protect the people so that those who go can fight with free hearts knowing that their old ones and weak ones are safe here in our village."

Murmurs of assent rose on all sides as Hawk drew himself up as though he were finished—but he was not. He looked at the air before him carefully, then said, as though he himself were puzzled by matters about him, "Hear me now, I will not speak again. If Medicine Fox does not wish to go, someone who can speak well in council must. Only if Medicine Fox does not go will Hawk lead our warriors to the Sioux." He sat down as though all the cares of the camp and the weight of many seasons were rightfully on his brow.

Fighting Eagle did not need to be told that behind him the almost golden form of Medicine Fox was rising in that modest but manly way of his, ready to do the thing that even silent children standing far in the rear knew that one soon to be chief had to do. Neither did Fighting Eagle have to be told that Hawk had won. His promise to himself stirred in his mind once more.

"The Arapaho must move as a great people move," said Medicine Fox, his strong features clear even in the shade of the lodge, "with each doing what is best for all. Hawk is a great warrior, he will stay to protect the people. I, Medicine Fox, have spoken before to our Sioux brothers. It is I who will go with Little Hand to their council fires."

Roars of approval rang from the crush of warriors, many of whom were surging to their feet. The great medicine drum in the heart of the village began to vibrate. The council was over. The chiefs began to sing their brave heart songs, and here and there a brave began to stamp the ground.

The dance of war, a ritual as old as man's ability to hate, had begun.

Medicine Fox had seated himself again behind his father, and the two of them sat together in silence until the lodge was empty. "Be wary in the land of the Lakota, my son. I saw a star fall to the north last night."

"There are many, many stars, my father—even more than there are Arapahos."

"Yes, my son, but a fallen one is gone forever."

17

White River moved through the faint light of dawn. He was sure he was almost there, but the matter called for certainty and so he pressed his mount forward, anxiously husbanding the night that was fast slipping from him. And now he knew he was there. Above him the great outcropping of rock he had seen from far to the west the morning before, and had waited until nightfall to achieve, hung like a wall of dim ash in the meager light. He turned and whistled quietly into the gray gloom he had just traversed. In time the sound of muffled hoofbeats brought two horsemen riding forward in single file, but breaking their order to gather round White River as they reached him.

"This it?" said the one who had ridden in front. It was Marcher.

"This is it," responded White River, his voice low and without body. It was meant as a guide to the others.

They took it.

"Any more signs?" said Amiel in a thin, high whisper.

"Too dark to see yet—I'd say 'tisn't likely."

"Now that we are here, do you think we can dismount?" said Amiel.

"Might as well." White River paused. "One of you'd better take these horses along the south rim of the rock and find a place to picket them. Don't get lost and don't shoot less'n you know what you're shooting at—just worrying about Injuns can make a bolting jackrabbit sound like a canyon full of Sioux."

"I'll go," said Amiel.

After telling Amiel where to look for them, White River led Marcher into one of the great clearings in the rock formation that was beginning to show its form as light gathered in the east. Something told him to seek cover at as high an elevation as possible and so he worked his way steadily upward until he reached an overhanging ledge that jutted forth just shy of the summit. Here he settled to study the land to the north and behind them to the west. There was little chance of any danger being about, but dawn was the time for serious doings in an Indian's mind—getting used to this helped a man grow old.

He had had to wait until the day following the storm before he could get a clear fix on Ironfoot's sighting, but finally he knew it pointed to a jagged piece of rock topping a hill almost at the horizon. He spent that morning hunting to the south, bringing in fresh meat which he kept the others busy drying and salting. Each man was told to carry only one canteen. There was plenty of water where they were going but stealth and shooting up the range for a man's dinner didn't mix. Before they left, they tied pieces of burlap around the horses' hooves, muffling them, making their tracks seem dimmer and older.

That evening White River led them to the knoll and watched the darkness settle over the land to the east. A few stars blinked forth in time and he studied them for a long moment before he said, "All right, we'll get going now. Best ride in single file. Don't talk unless you have to—talking keeps the hearing down."

By morning they were at the peak. White River half expected to find Ironfoot there, but instead he found the scraped image of another bow and arrow on a flat boulder near the summit, its position clearly marked by a small conical pile of stones. The arrow again pointed to the east, and White River, sighting across it, finally decided it must be aimed at a second distant outcropping of rocks.

It was a curious day they spent in the shadows of these rocks. There was no sense of sharing. One by one they slept, rose for their grub, and mouthed it quietly as they squinted across the bright sweeps of space about them. There was little talking in the heat of the day, and what remarks arose were touched with acrimony.

"We've damn little to be proud of, haven't we," muttered Amiel, glancing at Marcher and shaking his head.

"Stop yelping about those bastards!" snapped Marcher. "Did you want them following us?"

Josh and Neff had been ordered away at gunpoint, Marcher threatening to kill them if he saw them again. Amiel had said nothing, for White River agreed they'd be a hazard in hostile country, but Marcher's manner still grated on him. "Just wondering what you were figuring on doing if they showed up?"

Marcher grinned. It wasn't a pleasant sight. He tapped the stock of a heavy rifle with his toe. "Guess."

At nightfall, Marcher was anxious to move on, but White River, unable to read the night noises in the high wind, waited. An hour later the wind had died down and a great stillness came like sleep across the land. They listened together and heard nothing. "Let's go," said Marcher jumping up. White River nodded and led his mount onto the slope to the east.

Now they were at the second great outcropping of rock. The night had been uneventful, but White River, scouting the upper reaches of this formation and finding no further signs, felt that Ironfoot could not be far off. He rested near the summit, for a moment, watching a small cloud to the east come alive and blush as the first rays of sunlight began to level toward the earth. A chorus of birds, as though signaled by its high scarlet hue, broke loose upon the plain and in the swales beneath him, beginning again that cycle of life which is the only real unit of time. White River dreamed on this for a moment, when suddenly a little pebble struck the back of his neck. Had he been lower on the rock formation, he would have thought it had fallen from above. But he was too high for that. There was nothing above him but sky and so in the end he had to smile. This was not the act of an enemy. He played his instincts. "Ironfoot has been long in coming to his brother White River."

There was a silence and then Ironfoot's voice rose. "My brother should not rest his eyes upon the sky while he has enemies on the prairie."

White River turned, and without thinking they grabbed and held each other for a moment. Then White River drew back and followed Ironfoot's example of squatting down to leave less of their figures to stand against the sky. "Why has Ironfoot led us so far toward the rising sun?"

Ironfoot explained that they would have their best chance by working east of the main Sioux trails running up from the butte country to the south. He claimed the land had been quiet and he had found no sign, so they could leave that very night.

With daylight all around them now, White River suddenly decided he should get back to the others and explain how matters were. He motioned for Ironfoot to come with him, but Ironfoot simply nodded at the high, rocky nobs around him. "Tallest Indian see wolf's ears first." They both smiled at this old Indian proverb.

When he had descended, White River found Marcher and Amiel standing together in apparent discomfort, his opening remark about Ironfoot only slightly relieving the tightness of their expressions. There was bad blood between these two. White River could sense it. He wanted to talk it over with them, relieve the strain, but who could say what he might provoke? He hitched up his gun belt and stared around him as though balancing the many unsaid things in his mind. He spent the day in snatches of sleep, but by evening he was up studying the ledges near the summit. "All right," he muttered finally, noticing Ironfoot signaling from above, "Better start saddling up."

High above, Ironfoot had come slowly to one knee, his lips still aquiver as he finished some secret medicine song; then lifting his troubled eyes from below, he took a last long, wary look toward the north.

• • •

An hour before the first hint of dawning, they stopped in a small wooded area lying like a saddle of ground formed by two hills. Ironfoot waited until White River came up before he spoke. Marcher stood close by, his interest intense, his silence suggesting he was learning to listen; but in truth he was listening only to learn.

Ironfoot's words were brief and White River's agreement immediate. They would stay in this cover even though beyond lay a larger one with water and a better view to the northwest. But that one because of its water might attract Indians traveling through the section and presented in the Crow's mind by far the greater risk. Ironfoot said he would take the horses up and water them before daylight, then they could be picketed in the swale just below their cover where they would be handy if needed in a hurry. "Leave your canteens on your saddlehorn," said White River, slipping off his bay. "Bed down somewhere here but don't sleep until daylight comes and you're sure you're under cover. I'm going up with Ironfoot to fetch water. If you hear two quick hoots of an owl or shots being fired don't waste time wishing you were somewhere else—fort up."

When daylight came, it seemed only to expose to Amiel the foolishness of their plight. How the mind of man stands one idiotic notion on top of the other to make his fantasies seem achievable had often amazed Amiel and now he thought of how many ridiculous rungs had been needed in the ladder of wishful thinking to reach this bizarre and scarcely credible scene.

Marcher, he saw, was as wide awake as a child on Christmas morn as he sat questioning White River and Ironfoot, not in his normal insistent way, but as though his interest in things had become suddenly insatiable and he could not wait to learn more. White River and Ironfoot answered him sparingly, not a little because many of his questions were unanswerable. What do you expect will happen now? How far do you think we are from the hostiles? Is this place able to withstand attack? Where do you expect to be tomorrow?

White River and Ironfoot, in spite of Marcher's interruptions, were concentrating on some lines they were laying out carefully, marking each with a stick upon the ground. Ironfoot grunted in approval when White River drew a wavy line about the rest and then cut an *X* across it. After a long pause, White River scratched another line to the left and drew a circle in which he placed another cross. Ironfoot looked at this primitive map long and hard before finally grunting a second time, though Amiel felt there was a thing deep and disquieting faintly alive in his voice now. White River studied the whole sketch for a moment, then, handing his stick to Ironfoot, made the sign for the next sleep. Ironfoot squinted down uncertainly at the rude markings, then scratched a strange image above the triangle that marked their present site and pushed the stick into it. The stick swayed back and forth, looking peculiarly restless. White River nodded quietly, then, reaching for the stick again, said without raising his eyes, "Do these diggins happen to have a name?"

Ironfoot stepped back slowly and shifted his eyes to the horizon, gazing into the far distance like a man who has learned to feel what lies beyond his sight. A faint chime of warning rang through his words as he said, "Absarokees know this land only in war—we go now toward great medicine stone Sioux call Rock-That-Stands-Like-a-Bear."

18

The great Sioux encampment lay close under the buttes, the tipis scattered like white-and-dun-streaked cones along the tiny stream working its way to the east. To the north between the two nearest buttes lay a maze of wickiups showing that many warriors were there without their squaws. A few cooking fires, smoldering under large community pots, were sending up wisps of smoke at the east rim of the camp, but they were almost unattended now, for the headmen of the Lakota were meeting in a grove to the west.

Runners had gone out from other camps to summon the Oglala, Brules, Minneconjous, Hunkpapas, Two Kettles, and the Blackfoot Sioux, and word had been sent far to the east to the Yanktonais and Yanktons. The Teton Sioux knew that their last great bastion against the whites could be held only with sufficient numbers and only if their headmen thought as one. It was a brave undertaking, for the red men had always prized their individual freedom of thought and action far more than the whites ever had.

Many important war leaders were away with war parties and had to be sought in the south, where they were raiding along the river trails and harassing whites. One such was Red Moon, who brought with his large band of Brules many Cheyennes under Black Water, a chief with relations to visit among the Lakota—although some said he was delaying his return to his own village because his heart was heavy at the loss of his only son, the youthful White Fringe.

This party told a strange story of three whites being guided up the Platte by Pawnees. The whites had escaped, but the Pawnees' scalps were hanging from their belts, one an old chief's whose head was carried on an ancient war lance that was sticking up behind the camp looking dark under its mantle of flies. This great war party had gone south to capture some many-shots guns from the whites, but the soldiers' supply train they attacked on the Sweetwater had had only the single-shot guns and in a bad fight some braves were lost, including the young Cheyenne, the graceful White Fringe on his first and last warpath. They returned with only one of the many-shots guns, now carried by Coyote-Singing, the second son of Strikes-His-Enemy, who had taken it from the body of a dead Pawnee brave who died trying to save four youths. The half-breed LeGros, who traded stolen gunpowder for their best robes, said it was a very fine gun with a name, Benjamin Amiel, stamped in silver on its stock. Without that gun the Pawnee might have escaped, for he had had courage and was making his way through their trap, but once the Sioux heard the repeater firing they swarmed after him like maddened hornets. That gun sentenced him to death. Coyote-Singing carried the rifle proudly but did not, as so becomes a warrior, boastingly demonstrate its magic powers, for few needed to be told how very few shells were left.

In spite of the great strength present, a feeling of anger hung like a heavy robe in this hot season over the camp. Victories were reported but defeats too, and few could agree where the great arm of the united Lakota people should thrust its fist. Blue Buffalo Robe, speaking for the Hunkpapas, called upon the others to save their strength until the enemy came to them. "Here on our own hunting grounds where the land is our friend we will wear him down as the cunning wolves exhaust and kill the bear."

"*Hou!*" answered old Gray Owl of the Oglalas. "Let our brave brother remember the buffalo who keep the fighting bulls to the outside of their herd where the wolves are met and kept away from the calves and weak ones in the middle."

Everyone knew the Hunkpapas were well to the north, while the Oglalas sat on the southern and exposed rim of Lakota land.

Wandisapa, the Minneconjou, came to the troublesome point that smarted like a painful chip of bone grating in the chest of all there. "We have met the whites in battle many times and have defeated them," he cried, "but each victory becomes more difficult with more and more braves dying and more keening in the lodges, and why? Because our old enemies the Crows, Shoshone, Pawnees, and"—here

Wandisapa spit at the red clay beneath his feet in rage—"even some cowardly Lakotas, their bellies filled with the white man's whiskey and his sweet things, their stinking hearts filled with his false promises, have helped the whites, showing them our secret hiding places, acting as scouts in the land that was their mother so that our young men cannot surprise them. I say it is against them we should make war. Any tribe making peace with the whites is the enemy of the Lakota, any Lakota who raises his tomahawk against his own people should have his eyes torn out and be staked on the prairie where the squaws can teach him the many-fingers-of-fire death. I, Wandisapa, have spoken!"

Grunts of approval filled the crowded grove and became war whoops as the warriors massed about gave vent to a long-smoldering anger.

Red Moon sat quietly, Black Water, the Cheyenne, beside him as his guest, while Big Blood, Hawk Foot, and Strikes-His-Enemy sat slightly behind him waiting for him to speak. In time he turned to whisper to Strikes-His-Enemy, then, seeming settled in his thoughts, rose and looked about him. "I, Red Moon, say the land of the Lakota was given to us by the Great Spirit. He meant for us to have it, for he helped us in war when we took it from others. But the Great Spirit does not give things forever. He gives us life but we do not live forever. So it is with our land. He gives it to us for as long as we wish to keep it. It is not only our own people whose hearts have turned against us that will make our hunting grounds hard to hold. It is not only enemy tribes who know these lands as we have come to know theirs that blacken the sky for the brave Lakota. No, it is the weapons of the whites, weapons that make weak men more dangerous than grizzlies." He turned about and seeing Coyote-Singing sitting nearby motioned for the repeating rifle. Raising it in his hand he spoke on, their eyes catching the silver plate on the stock, engraved with the white man's strange word signs. "Here is the secret to the strength of the whites. Here is the hope of the Lakota. We must pray that Wakan Tonka, the Great Spirit, sends us many such weapons, for Wakan Tonka has meant these lands to go to the ones who hold the many-shots guns in their hands."

There was much interest and concern on the faces of the chiefs as Red Moon sat down, and Stone Maker, chief of the Minneconjous and brother of their violent war leader, Wandisapa, was standing with Gray Owl, both seeking to question the Brule further, when suddenly a flashing light from the farthest butte brought a murmur over the camp. Someone was coming. The braves turned restless and fingered their bows. As the mirror flashed on, a tall Oglala said it was only a Lakota wolf coming in with a message. But that was enough to turn the minds of the chiefs. Any message in the season of war could be the first rising breeze to be felt from a storm that still lay many sleeps away.

Little Hand, Medicine Fox, and Blue Jacket watched the haughty Sioux warrior as he pointed toward the buttes and told them to ride to the left of the butte from which a mirror flashed several times in quick succession. They had seen a Sioux wolf, a scout wearing a cape of wolfskin, ride off hurriedly as soon as they were sighted, but it was all unnecessary. Had they not come making the friendship sign, and had not Little Hand said in almost perfect Sioux that the Arapaho warriors were as brothers to the Lakota, that they had come to help them in their fight against the whites? The Sioux brave listened indifferently, his horse's rump marked with a red hand to show he had killed a man in hand-to-hand combat, and then with the flashing light he pointed toward the buttes. "The ears of our chiefs will hear your words."

"*Hou kola,*" said Medicine Fox, who spoke Sioux as well as Little Hand, but then he moved in such a way as to urge the others on.

"A wolf's heart is never made warmer by the sight of his brothers," said Blue Jacket, eyeing the seeming quiet of the buttes before him.

"You were one who did not have to come," said Little Hand testily, but he watched carefully as the thirty warriors behind him passed the silent Sioux, mumbling to each other that he made no returning sign at their greetings.

"Hush," said Medicine Fox. "Are we women that we look for soft words from men at war?"

They rode silently until they rounded the last butte on the left and then suddenly they were in the Sioux camp. Some of the chiefs were there to meet them, a courtesy always extended, and Blue Buffalo Robe, standing in full regalia, told them where they could picket their horses and rest. Little Hand gave a short talk he had prepared before he dismounted, and then the long ceremony of the guests-in-camp began.

First they rested. Then they were invited to eat around the great pots stirred into life by a multitude of haggard-looking but fleet-footed old squaws who ran hither and yon, shouting to each other and hastily putting fresh dog flesh into each pot. The warriors ate in a great circle where silence was almost total, and except for the friendly signs made between Medicine Fox and Black Water, the Cheyenne, there was little warmth being put on this mask of welcome.

When the pipe was finally lighted and passed, evening was upon them and the chiefs waited until the great fires were burning before Gray Owl, the Oglala, came to his feet. The Arapahos, even the young ones who had been raised largely in the south and knew but little Sioux, bent to hear his words. "The Lakota are great warriors," he called across the fire to them, "but they are also great men with good hearts. We have always welcomed those who came in peace or those who came as our brothers in war. We would hear you speak. What brings the Arapaho to the land of the Lakota when our tomahawks are red and our horses weary from chasing our enemies?"

Little Hand would have liked Medicine Fox or even Blue Jacket to speak for him, but as headman it was his duty, though some would think only his honor, to speak first. "Oh hear me, my brothers, the Lakota. Word of your victories against the whites have gladdened our ears. We too have fought many times against the white thieves who come with bad hearts and split tongues. Many of their scalps decorate our lodges. We have come to fight beside you and drive the whites from our hunting grounds. We have left our lodges and children to join you, the great Lakota, in war!"

The Arapaho warriors filled the air with the war whoops answered by the Cheyennes sitting opposite them behind Black Water. Some of the Sioux warriors took the opportunity to break their long silence and the night was suddenly ruptured with fierce yells and whoops that the scouts could hear from their distant knolls and wonder at.

Blue Buffalo Robe rose majestically, his headdress of blue-stained feathers trailing over his back to the level of his knees, his broad shoulders throwing a heavy shadow upon the group of Hunkpapas gathered behind him. "Blue Buffalo Robe welcomes the Arapaho who have come to fight with us. It is good to see our neighbors stand with us against the whites. But the time of war is passing. Why did not our friends, the Arapaho, come sooner, why do they wait for word of our victories before they reach for their tomahawks and run to our side?" This was a bad turn. Blue Jacket groaned to himself and Little Hand looked pleadingly at Medicine Fox.

Blue Buffalo Robe was settling himself on the ground again, leaving behind him a silence that sent the eyes of many to the ground. The taunt had been given, it must be answered. Medicine Fox came forward, his strong golden body seeming to shine as he stood tall in the glow of the great fire. "I, Medicine Fox, son of Fighting Eagle, speak to the chiefs of the Lakota as one warrior speaks to a brother warrior. In the land of the Arapaho the whites are like grasshoppers when the grass is dry. They have many forts where their fighting men stand in great numbers behind guns that live in wagons and speak like thunder. Truly, my brothers, we are surrounded by whites."

"With so many at the fringes of your lodge why does Medicine Fox come so far to kill them?" shouted Wandisapa who was seated beside Stone Maker with his gray, darkly lined face.

Ah, the wild Minneconjous! Blue Jacket knew at a glance that there was more than mischief here.

Medicine Fox faced Wandisapa squarely. "Do the Lakota not want the hand of the Arapaho in war?"

Black Water of the Cheyennes came quickly to his feet. This alone, as Blue Jacket knew, told how serious a turn things had taken. Black Water should have waited until Red Moon spoke and honored his presence, but Red Moon sat in silence, knowing how it was with Black Water—knowing how it was with men caught up in a rising tornado of tactless and foolish words.

"Hear me, oh my brothers, the Lakota," Black Water began, looking straight at Wandisapa and Stone Maker. Medicine Fox should have sat down but he stayed firmly on his feet. He was not a man to hide behind the good will or courage of another. He had asked a question, he would have an answer. "The Cheyennes have long been as one with the Lakota. Many Cheyennes and Lakotas have relations in each other's tribe. We are as one lodge, but the Cheyenne are also brothers to the Arapaho. We have long been friends. Not even our oldest ones can remember when the two tribes fought."

The Sioux listened glumly. The Cheyennes were great fighters, their bravery in battle amounting in the minds of some whites to a sickness. Even their women, tall-walking and proud and honored for their virtue, rode beside their brothers and husbands in war and carried out breathtaking acts of courage. The Sioux regarded them as valuable allies, and they were—just as for other tribes, before their numbers waned, they were terrible enemies. But the Arapaho had a far less formidable record and the Sioux in their rising wrath were collecting the only coin that counted on the high plains this season—courage. The Cheyennes had accepted the war pipe and had come with the first grass needed to keep their ponies strong. Now here the Arapaho were standing, shouting of war, when the war parties were returning, the fighting done. But Black Water was one who could talk and when he turned to Gray Owl to finish with "When the *veho,*" the spider, their term for the whites, "comes, all Indians are as one," a rash of approving grunts broke through the group.

Gray Owl came to his feet and said slowly, "The Lakota take the hand of the Arapaho in war."

Medicine Fox would have liked to sit down, to have said "It is good! You will know us for the fighters we are before long!" But that was impossible. Now Hawk's evil work, sown so carefully so many days before, was about to bear fruit. Medicine Fox had come with a tribal duty. He must extract a promise from the Sioux to help the Arapaho against the reprisals of the whites. He did not need the still surly looks of Wandisapa and Stone Maker to tell him how unpromising were his prospects. As some braves came forward to throw more wood on the fires, Blue Jacket looked up with eyes of warning. "We have traveled far today, Medicine Fox. Sleep will lighten our bodies and bring freshness to our minds."

Medicine Fox, who was still on his feet, as a signal to the Sioux that he was not finished, shook his head slowly and drew himself up as a man does knowing he is coming to a great and difficult test.

Blue Jacket dropped his eyes, thinking as he did when Medicine Fox turned on Wandisapa, *Be not too proud, Medicine Fox, remember the craft that brought you here, the craft that awaits you across the fire.*

"Hear me, Lakotas," said Medicine Fox, his voice firm and caught with the determined will that lay behind it. "I have told our brothers of the many whites that infest our land. These whites will remember that the Arapaho raised their tomahawk with the Lakota. They will come as they have before when the snow is hard upon the ground and the ponies are weak from the lack of grass. They will come to burn our lodges and kill our weak ones. They will come with men who have no lodge of their own and take the white man's paper money to kill our people. We have come to fight with you, to ride beside you in battle. We do this knowing the great Lakota will help us if we ourselves must fight against the whites. Let the Lakotas speak. Let them say that they will ride beside us when the white soldiers come to our lodges and our hearts will sing as we go with you on the warpath."

A great hush fell upon the startled gathering as Medicine Fox sat down. Who was to answer him was not clear. The faces of the Sioux chiefs, losing their proud, stony quality for a moment, were withdrawn in disbelief. Wandisapa and Stone Maker were the first to recover.

"Hou!" said Stone Maker in open derision. "Does the rabbit ask

to help the bear against the fox so that the bear will help him against the wolf?"

Medicine Fox was back on his feet.

Wandisapa was shouting. "Do the enemies that the Arapahos kill in the summer come back to fight them again in the winter?"

"The whites are many," said Medicine Fox stoutly. "Many more than even the Lakota."

Gray Owl's expression had gone from concern to cold amusement. "We do not need allies who come because they need allies more than we."

There was coarse laughter among the Sioux braves, and Little Hand got to his feet to join Medicine Fox. But Medicine Fox motioned for him not to speak. The quick anger of Little Hand was a menace this moment could ill afford.

Blue Buffalo Robe stood up, his long, narrow face as composed as a man contemplating sleep. He folded his arms before him and looked almost patiently at Medicine Fox and Little Hand. It was clear he felt the courtesy of the camp had been compromised by these needless insults and now dignity should be recalled. "Hear me, Arapahos. For many seasons the Lakota have fought and made many treaties with the whites. We have smoked with them with peace in our hearts, and when their hearts and tongues have proven false we have reddened our tomahawks in their blood. But always the Lakota have told them that we would be at peace with them if they did not come into our lands and disturb our buffalo or attack our villages. This we have always said and this we will do. One day the whites will understand that the Lakota want only peace, that we wish only to be left alone, and they will go away. But if we leave our lands and go to fight them in another place, they will think that the Lakota want to make war and will never give them peace. The brave Arapahos should know these things, then they will know how our hearts must hear their words. I, Blue Buffalo Robe, have spoken."

It was the kind of gesture that was not wasted on many. Blue Buffalo Robe had given the Arapahos an answer which left them their pride even with the refusal of their request. Yet it could be no other way. Even Red Moon, looking down to avoid the embarrassed and painful eyes of Black Water, knew that thirty Arapaho braves appearing at a time when all the fighting worth talking about might well be done were not worth a promise to send perhaps two hundred mounted Sioux warriors to fight well-armed soldiers on the flat, exposed Cheyenne plain in the dead of winter.

Medicine Fox nodded in seeming understanding at the settling Blue Buffalo Robe, but Little Hand, still on his feet, said quickly, "Does the heart of the Lakota tell them that the white man will ever give them peace?"

Ah, such foolish words, thought Blue Jacket, gripping his ankles tightly and holding his breath. And now, now, here, when they had almost slipped through Hawk's net.

Gray Owl did not bother to rise, but his angry eyes threw back the light of the fire and his voice slashed the issue to the bone. "The heart of the Lakotas tells them many things, Little Hand—some perhaps that would fall like thunder on the ears of the Arapahos."

Tension gripped the camp again, many knowing that the badness was now beyond even Blue Buffalo Robe's way with words.

Medicine Fox motioned for Little Hand to sit down, but Little Hand's anger was upon him and he cared little for their predicament. "We Arapahos are great in war," he shouted, "we have fought alone before—let the Lakota stay in their lodges—we will fight alone again!"

Black Water tried in a halfhearted attempt to make a hand signal to Medicine Fox, but seeing it was useless, he drew himself up silently and left the circle.

The Arapaho braves, including those that were tense and smoldering under the half insults that filled the air about them, watched him depart, knowing now that the night was to be a dark one. But the Sioux warriors, angered at Little Hand's words, were beginning to openly shout threats that soon dignity would demand be answered. It came to a head as one young Minneconjou jumped to his feet and, ripping off his loincloth, shook his member at the Arapahos in the greatest insult known to the Sioux.

Little Hand reached for his knife, but Medicine Fox, seeing the foolishness of giving in to the taunts of young braves when they had come on a mission that could only be served by words between chiefs, said calmly, "We have come to fight with the Lakota, not against them. When we come in war we do not sit by the enemy's fire and eat his food or smoke with him."

"Hou! Hou!" cried the rising Strikes-His-Enemy, disturbed at the unspeakable discourtesy this treatment of guests in camp involved, and secretly angered at the sight of his own young men enjoying a false bravery in the heart of their own camp. "Let the Lakota remember that they are great men—let them not talk as though the scoldings of squaws were courage."

It looked as if the worst were over, that the issue would be left unresolved, but at least left. But it was not. Stone Maker was coming to his feet, his great weathered face firm and dark in a judgment already passed. "Ah, do the Arapaho come to talk to us of war? Do they come with hearts of grizzlies ready to drive our enemies from our lands? No, I, Stone Maker, say they come to ask us to fight against the same whites which their own chiefs make peace talk with—yes, the Blue Coats, and this they have done behind the Lakotas' backs." All eyes flicked to Stone Maker, then in a strange, uneven movement back to Medicine Fox. "Yes, my tongue speaks true," roared Stone Maker, his dark face growing lighter at the edges of his mouth and along his nostrils. "This very season our own cowards with the everlasting talk of treaties in their mouths, told us that Fighting Eagle, the Arapaho, had smoked with the Blue Coats and put the mark of his hand to the peace paper."

Now a far more ominous roar began to rise among the Sioux braves, and Wandisapa rose to join Stone Maker in a sudden turn of things dangerous beyond description. Only Blue Jacket, waving his arms in the firelight, shouting to the Arapahos, who were now openly preparing to defend themselves, seemed able to demand reason from his mind in this moment. "My brothers! My brothers!" he shouted in Sioux and Arapaho both. "If you hate the whites do not give them easy victories—do not let them see our people killing each other."

Blue Jacket could not have stopped it alone, but Red Moon and Blue Buffalo Robe were both demanding silence, and even Gray Owl raised his hand impatiently to his rising Oglalas. In the end, after much sputtering, this almost fatal fire of passion was stopped—and just short of dry grass. But Stone Maker and Wandisapa, their Minneconjou hard behind them, were still standing forward, fury and outrage still the masters of their faces, their charge against the Arapahos still hanging like foul smoke in the air.

"Do the Arapahos wish to speak?" said Red Moon, hoping they would not.

Medicine Fox could not give the lie to Stone Maker and yet he could not malign his own father. He stood hesitant for a second, and then Blue Jacket, seeing how it was with him and forgetting his was the same predicament, began to speak.

"We Arapahos have looked upon the Lakota for many years as brothers. We have sat with them in council and have fought with them against the Crow and the Pawnee. We ask them now to listen to our hearts. There are some among the Arapaho who want peace, just as there are some among the Lakota, but to live near the whites is to hear talk of peace with every pipe lit . . . to hear it till the warrior thinks of it as he does the sound of crickets by night. He does not know where it comes from, but it all sounds the same. If the Arapaho had talked peace to the whites with their hearts, they would not be here, they would not talk of pony soldiers coming in the snow to burn their lodges. They would sit in their village and let those who wished to hold their hunting grounds fight. Fighting Eagle is a great warrior. He has seen much of war. His body is scarred like the old buffalo that has long fought for the herd. He is not a young warrior who cares only for himself, his horses, and his many coups. He is a mighty chief who must worry about many old and weak ones in his village. He must think of the helpless ones running before the white paid killers and wagon guns that can lift a strong man and his horse in the air and destroy them. He must stand in the warmth of the summer sun and think of the snow that will come one day from the mountains and how it will be with the weak ones then. If he makes peace with the whites, it is not his heart that makes peace. It is his memories of what the white soldier chiefs do when an Indian is slow to his pipe."

Blue Jacket spoke not only with words but with many engaging gestures and with the raising and lowering of his voice that brought meaning beyond the measure of his words. As he finished, Blue Buffalo Robe, quick to acknowledge a good speaker, grunted agreeably. Even Gray Owl, who knew more about the whites and the punishments they balanced their promises with than he cared to reveal, set his mouth as though he knew he had listened to the truth.

Red Moon, his eyes playing upon the dark faces of Wandisapa and Stone Maker, said simply, "You have spoken well, Blue Jacket, your words are good. Many moons ago Fighting Eagle's moccasins wore the warpath smooth—now he sees the people need one strong in council as well as warriors."

"What of this treaty the brave Arapahos bring with them?" snorted Wandisapa. "Do we go to fight the pony soldiers when the ice giant silences the rivers and the face of the land is like a skull?"

Red Moon did not look down. He knew the trap Wandisapa was setting for him. Strikes-His-Enemy's low clucking to the rear was unnecessary. Red Moon knew that no one chief could speak for the Lakota and that is what Wandisapa would have him do. Even if he had been in favor of this ridiculous treaty, and surely he was not, he could only have spoken for the Brules and then only for those among his tribe who were willing to follow him. War in winter was never popular. War without means of waging it and without hope of plunder was unheard of. "Red Moon speaks only for his own warriors," he said evenly. "The Brules heard well the words of their brother, Blue

Buffalo Robe, the brave Hunkpapa. The Lakota must stay close to their own land and fight the whites in their own way. If we go south to fight for the Arapaho, we may defeat the whites there for a little time, but when we take the trail back to our lodges the whites will know and they will send the soldier chiefs with bad hearts and many will suffer. Let the Arapaho deal with the whites as their headmen see fit and if they can bring us the many-shots guns, we will pay them well. But the Lakota braves are needed here in our own land. I, Red Moon, say the night is weary of our talk. Let us sleep. Tomorrow we shall talk some more."

"It is well," said Blue Buffalo Robe rising with Gray Owl.

"Tomorrow the Minneconjou will have words for your ears," said Stone Maker getting up and without a word to or a look at the Arapahos, he and Wandisapa turned away into the darkness.

"The Arapahos now have their answer," said Blue Jacket almost to himself as he looked at the fringe of darkness where Stone Maker and Wandisapa had disappeared. "Now who here chooses to sleep?"

The night began like an uneven dream where the parts do not match, where the mind is weary of discord. Little Hand had the braves sleep behind the wickiups, where they would be free under the stars and where quick escape was possible. But the braves went to earth uneasily. They had come for revenge, loot, and honor, and now they had only the sight of their leaders being rebuffed and humiliated by the Sioux. Some mumbled recklessly of Minneconjou scalps, but the wiser among them called for silence, knowing ears were important in the dark and the slightest warning might save all.

Little Hand and Medicine Fox both declared they would stay awake, that they did not need rest, one telling the other to sleep and to find strong medicine in a dream. Blue Jacket finally motioned them to silence. He did not think the night would pass quietly, but neither was he expecting an attack while they were guests in the camp. Such a thing was almost unknown. More likely the risk would lie in escape, and yet his heart told him no talk with the coming of the sun could right things now. Their presence could only keep the breach between the Sioux chiefs festering until the stale, overpolite words were withdrawn and replaced by the tomahawk. Ah, now did he not need wisdom!

A movement in the darkness at the south end of the wickiups caught the attention of all at once. Someone was coming, someone who walked evenly and made no use of the shield of night. In a moment they saw it was Black Water, his buffalo headdress missing, but his robe wrapped about him and his eyes marking his face in the dark.

For a time the four of them stood in silence, the three Arapahos waiting patiently for the Cheyenne to speak. After sensing rather than seeing the braves asleep on the ground behind the wickiups instead of within them, Black Water raised his hand, pointing to the south. "My brothers, the Arapahos, must return to their village. The hearts of the Sioux are bad this season."

"Must the Arapaho run like the chipmunk who sees the shadow of a crow and thinks it is the shadow of a hawk?" said Medicine Fox, an unnatural trace of bitter anger in his voice.

"The Lakota would not lose their honor by attacking guests in their own camp," said Little Hand—but there was that in his tone that made the statement a question.

"The Hunkpapas speak of leaving after the next sun. The Brules are anxious to return to their lodges." Black Water looked about him as though he were weighing something in his mind. "After that . . . who is to say whose arrow first left the bow?"

"We are not afraid," said Little Hand, drawing himself up in what seemed to Blue Jacket mock support of his words.

Blue Jacket looked intently at Black Water. "Our brother carries a heavy thing in his heart—is it for the Arapaho to know?"

"There is no time for the many words of council. The brave Arapahos should leave tonight. Do not go back the way you came, but stay far to the east and away from the trails that the Sioux use in their journeys south. It will be many sleeps longer for you and you will have to leave to the north to escape their wolves, but there is little wisdom in waiting in these wickiups. Stone Maker has this moon closed his lodge against his own son who went to make the whiskey peace with the whites, and his thoughts are those of a wounded grizzly whose anger has blinded him even to death."

The Arapahos were silent for a moment. "If the Sioux dare to follow us we will trap them," snapped Little Hand defiantly, not knowing his words said they would leave in secret.

"Do not waste your young men on war with the Lakota," cautioned Black Water. "It is for the chiefs to see that the warriors do not die foolishly. A brave is not made while the sun crosses the sky. We can no longer fight as the Indian fought before the white man came. Now a new spirit watches us from the mountains—he measures war not in honor but in deaths. Kill as many whites as you can, but treasure your life as the wounded warrior treasures water in the desert. As long as you live you can kill the *veho*."

"I will whisper to the braves that we must leave," said Blue Jacket, coming closer to Black Water. "You are our brother. Can we use our brother's eyes?"

Black Water nodded. "Go tonight and travel even when the sun rises till you come to the Rock-That-Stands-Like-a-Bear. There you will hide. If no one comes at the setting of the next sun, you may ride across the prairies to your lodges."

"Who will come?" asked Little Hand, confused.

Black Water looked at him as he turned to go. "If the Sioux leave camp with their wolves running over your trail, I will send a Cheyenne brave." He paused, turning again. "Listen to the words he carries in his mouth. They will be mine."

And so it was. The next day they led their horses down a deep ravine to the south, and then lay among the crumbling brown rocks to watch the towering stone that threw from the evening sun the shadow of a standing bear. Hardly a brave moved till the weary eye of heaven withdrew its swollen crimson disk from the sky. As night came and captured the nearby rolling hills to the east, Blue Jacket stood up. "It is well," he said with a sigh, "we have not been followed."

"Better had they come," said Little Hand, anger and pride stubbornly staying with him. "The warriors of my youth did not crawl off in the night like thieves stealing meat from the racks of an old squaw."

"We should have stolen some meat," answered Blue Jacket laconically. "My stomach grumbles like an old man in a bad dream, and it is many sleeps to the cooking fires of our village."

"Enough!" said Medicine Fox. "Tomorrow we will hunt. Now we must remember the words of Black Water."

That night they traveled south again, and as the moon began to rise an hour before dawn, they stopped and rested. The braves left their horses, climbing into the high, rocky places to steal quick, anxious glances behind them as daylight flowed onto the prairie. But all was still and the eye found nothing to trigger the heart as far as the tall Medicine Fox could see.

"Come," said Blue Jacket, "let us hunt. Meat will improve our spirits. There is much courage in the taste of buffalo ribs." There were many idle words among the warriors as they made ready for the hunt, light banter to cover the foreboding many found so increasingly hard to bear. Though there was no game in sight, a few said that surely there was some behind the rolling hills or rising from sleep in the hidden swales to feed on the heavier grass lying there.

Little Hand spread his arms like the wings of an eagle and then brought them together before him. They were to fan out, raking the uneven terrain, and where the game could not be stalked it would be flushed before them. Running as it does in large circles it would turn in time into the bows of warriors on either side. Little Hand pointed to a distant knoll to the south and, asking Medicine Fox to take the left tip of the sweep and Blue Jacket the right, said, "We will meet there when the sun stands straight above."

"It is well," said Medicine Fox, moving his pony in a sharp turn to the east.

"Let the eye of the eagle and the strength of the grizzly be with the Arapaho," said Little Hand, tying a secret hunting medicine bundle into his horse's mane. The braves, grunting with pleasure at the prospect of meat, nodded to him and filed away in either direction.

And so they left, spreading across the prairie like two coils of a many-colored snake unwinding slowly from its morbid middle as with new life.

19

Ironfoot watched the purple wedge intrude itself into the dark sky, becoming finally a soft pennant of light. Immediately it began to lengthen and probe toward the west. Others appeared from the east and joined it and together they quietly shredded the dark bark from the lodge of night. He was lying hard against the earth, his senses struggling to finger into the darkness, his heart telling him that this darkness, which was denying him its secret, was also his only friend and now it was clearly ready to depart. He turned about and motioned to White River, who was behind him, to start working backward and then began to withdraw himself. There was no time to cover tracks. They scurried up to the others, and seizing their own mounts, hurried the party along to the southeast. Ironfoot, stoically leading the way, kept looking at the sky and then at the horizon. Visibility was swiftly on the increase, they would soon have to take cover. Far ahead in the thinning gloom he could see the tree line of a wooded place etched against the eastern sky, a tree line that seemed to dip as though it were falling into a swale. They would make for that. To attempt more without knowing whom they had encountered would be at least foolish and possibly fatal.

They plunged hurriedly into the swale, and even as Ironfoot and White River jumped from their mounts to squirm up through the foliage on the western fringe, the range of hills on the far horizon was just coming into view.

"We might wished we'd kept riding by sunup," said White River in a half whisper. "Don't like this for a fact."

Ironfoot's strong face remained expressionless. Only his eyes seemed alive and they held to the plain before them as though it were swarming with life instead of being the fawn and bluish-gray emptiness it was.

"How many do you figure?" inquired White River.

"Many," said Ironfoot without shifting his eyes.

"If they pick up those tracks, we'd best start hunting higher ground." Neither needed to be told that the Sioux, once discovering that they had an adversary seriously outnumbered, would muster their ponies and charge them en masse. Forcing them to do it uphill took away some of their confidence and allowed more time for narrowing a man's sights.

Ironfoot kept his gaze on the rock formations now a mile or two to the northwest. Only a little more than an hour before, they had been approaching these rocks hoping to bring this quiet night of travel to an end, but Ironfoot suddenly realized from the way his horse began to move and whinny that the scent of other horses was coming downwind. The wind was almost directly out of the north and only slightly out of the west, and so reason rendered further progress in that direction too foolhardy to contemplate. Yet the answer might be a harmless band of wild horses, or a stray or two moving before the wind and following an instinct to drift in this season toward the south. Ironfoot would see. He dropped off his mount as White River came up. "Trouble?" whispered White River. Ironfoot made the silence sign and White River came even closer. Neither spoke. White River handed over the reins of both their horses to the others and indicated they were to wait where they were until he and Ironfoot returned. White River followed Ironfoot's dark figure as it glided over the ground, crouching as it did and finally coming to all fours as the Crow began to come upon some muffled sounds ahead. They were still a hundred feet away when Ironfoot dropped completely to the ground. The Crow lay for a long time, obviously listening for a sign or a movement that would betray those who held the horses, for they were not picketed, they were being held together. Nothing stirred. The land was motionless, but the sky began to come to life and a thin purple light began feeding in from the east. Day and the danger of discovery were knocking. Ironfoot gambled a few last moments, each one of which could have decided his death, to glimpse what lay ahead and lost. They fell back without discovering the identity of the invisible riders, but they were surely Indian ponies and circumstances demanded the assumption they were Sioux.

Back at the swale, Marcher was breaking through the foliage to join them, field glasses in hand. "See anything?"

"Get down!"

Marcher squatted beside them and following Ironfoot's stare toward the distant rocks raised the glasses. After a moment he said, "Nobody out there."

Ironfoot and White River remained silent. Light was flooding the landscape now and the high lavender of the sky was drifting swiftly to pink. Finally Ironfoot grunted low and White River, stiffening slightly, put a hand toward Marcher. It was for the glasses, and Marcher, understanding, handed them over without comment.

"Yep—there's two near the top . . . looks like a parcel of 'em around those horses."

"Think we're in for trouble?" said Marcher with a rising excitement in his voice. The knowledge that he might be in for his first Indian scrape sent a strange not unpleasant sensation through his body.

"Don't know. Doubt if they've got the wind of us yet—'pear to be looking t'other way."

White River soon passed the glasses over to Ironfoot, who hesitated before taking them. He knew about these strong seeing eyes of the whites, but to him such medicine was incomprehensible. He had never looked through them before. Now he held them up slowly to his eyes, uncertain as to what to expect, then was finally amazed as the mighty hand of this magic reached out and drew the rock formation, lying far away on the plain beyond, toward him. He grunted, for he could plainly see the dusky figures moving down the rock ledges and gathering about the horse herd.

"Sioux, I reckon," said White River, watching him intently.

It was not always easy to tell Plains Indians apart at a distance, but Ironfoot knew, after long staring, that these were not Sioux. Who then? It was a war party, but there were too many warbonnets and feathers for them to be Cheyennes, and then suddenly he knew they were Arapahos and he put down the glasses.

"Well?" queried White River.

"Arapahos," said Ironfoot quietly, a new puzzlement stirring in his voice.

"Arapahos," echoed White River. "Could still be there's Sioux hereabouts."

Ironfoot did not answer. There was something furtive about that war party, for he had seen many of them looking long toward the north and northwest. The Arapaho were frequent allies of the Sioux, and some of their chiefs had smoked the Sioux war pipe that very spring. But what were these hiding from here deep in Sioux territory? It was not a thing he understood. He motioned the others back into cover. Great danger was still with them, perhaps greater now than ever before, for the eyes of a wary war party are sharp.

When the sun had climbed to where it placed the first thin edge of heat upon the day, Ironfoot hooted once quickly from his perch in the low limbs of a cottonwood and, as White River looked up, made the sign for moving. White River looked at the others and decided they were in as good order as any if it came to a run. Their mounts were further below them, munching grass but saddled up and ready. Ironfoot seemed to be studying something out on the plain and when he finally dropped down it was clear he had something to relate. White River watched him take a stick and draw with it on the ground. The Arapahos had started a hunt. They were fanning out with their left wing working toward this concealed spot. Whatever they were waiting for must not have come, for surely they would not start to hunt if there were any danger close. Besides, they were heading south and perhaps going home. White River asked if they had crossed the tracks made earlier by their own mounts. Ironfoot indicated that they had not but they surely would before long. "Well, we can run or we can hole up here and trust to luck."

"I'm for staying," said Marcher quickly.

"How many are there?" asked Amiel.

"Thirty to forty," said White River after exchanging signs with Ironfoot. "But spread out like that it should take them a stretch to get started. If they see us we have to turn back. Maybe we should turn back anyway. The only chance we ever had was to stay out of sight."

"But if we run now they've got to see us," said Marcher, still speaking quickly.

White River looked at Marcher before he turned again to Amiel.

"That's about the way it sets up." He didn't care for Marcher's expression. What was that weird one thinking anyway?

"You're telling me we have to stay, then," said Amiel, betraying his lack of conviction.

"No, I'm allowing our only chance of going further is holding here. If they pick up our tracks, we've got to light out anyway."

"You're sure they'll follow us?"

"Fresh tracks of four jaded mounts, most of 'em shod, is likely to interest forty braves sporting war paint more times 'n not."

Ironfoot had slipped back up to his perch, his gaze now fixed on the expanding line of warriors lengthening across the plain. The brave on the left flank seemed to be moving more south than east now and a hope that he would miss the little swale entirely began to kindle. But the tracks were still a problem that promised calamity, and as the line neared where Ironfoot knew they lay, his eyes hardened upon them. Whether it was wind disturbing the grass or the fact that their eyes were not on the ground but on the little gentle slopes where they sought for game, Ironfoot did not know, but miraculously one brave after the other appeared to cross their tracks without a halt. Then suddenly his heart stopped. One brave halted his pony and reached downward.

Ironfoot readied himself to drop to the ground and lead the others hurriedly to their mounts. But then the brave seemed to be rubbing his pony's forelock as he looked down again at the leg, clearly testing something. Then, with one or two turns, he seemed satisfied and, swinging his pony about, he moved up quickly again to take his place in the long and now uneven line. Ironfoot let his breath out. Their tracks had not been detected. Someone in the party below him he thought must have powerful medicine, or was it just that there was something wrong with these braves? They did not sit proudly on their ponies like warriors made up for war, their head regalia seemed droopy, themselves dejected. Ah, this was surely a strange sight. He wished he had the many braves of his village behind him. His people had many scores to settle with the Arapaho. The Absarokees had suffered much from attacks by the combined forces of Sioux, Cheyenne, and Arapaho. They had lost many good men; whole villages had been annihilated, women and children being cut down with war clubs, some scalped alive. The Sioux and the Cheyennes would often come alone, but never the Arapahos. He looked at the line of horses straggling across the plain, and his restless hand closed upon his knife.

The warrior on the left flank was close now, but if he continued on his present heading he would miss the fringe of the swale by a good arrow's flight. Ironfoot began to hope. Ah-badt-deadt-deah watch your children well today. This warrior, taller than the others and wearing a black and red headdress, was clearly intent upon something to the south. Soon he would be past them and the danger over. The wind from the west picked up again and now it brought a long soothing moan from the trees bottoming the swale. He could see the brightness of the feathers in the approaching headdress and the gleam of a great silver-studded belt. Clearly this man was a high-ranking warrior, whose pony's feathered mane was being swept by the wind. It occurred to Ironfoot that the scent of horses coming downwind might cause their own mounts to whinny and grow restless. His eyes flashed down. The others were already with the horses, White River having sensed this threat and moved against it. Then the warrior passed. Ironfoot saw him moving away to the south. It was good. The sun was getting higher in the sky and the wind pressed against his face as though his secret medicine was calling to him. He looked up at the sun. It was good. He turned, preparing to jump down from his perch, when suddenly his eyes caught the tall headdress of the warrior. It had stopped. Ironfoot drew himself up, a cold feeling forming strangely in his stomach. The warrior was looking at the south tip of the swale, studying it as though his interest was mounting by the moment. What had he seen? Had he seen their tracks entering the swale and only now realized after he had passed what he had been looking at? Ironfoot strove to see the south end of the swale. The Arapaho was well below where they had hidden their horses. Surely he could not see them, but why was he delaying? Ironfoot, clinging to the north side of the trunk, shinnied up several more feet into the tree. The wind was coming in, tossing the tree tops back and making them quiver as they rebounded into it again.

Ah, suddenly he saw, glimpsed rather, the answer, for the swinging trees quickly covered it again. A deer had wandered out from the south tip of the swale. It was a young doe startled possibly by the wind or the quick movement of the others toward the horses. But now he saw it standing, saw it poised for only a fleet second, and he knew the warrior was waiting for it to move, hoping perhaps for a clearer shot. Ironfoot backed down and moved quickly to the others, motioning them to silence and moving behind them until he could see through to the south end of the swale. White River and Amiel were watching him closely, but Marcher had worked himself up into the thinning foliage at the dangerous end of the swale. It was he who flushed the doe.

The deer turned hesitantly to the southeast, grazing a moment here and there, but lifted its head repeatedly in answer to an instinct that marked the drift of danger. Ironfoot searched cautiously for the Arapaho, finding him as he half expected dismounted and preparing to stalk the deer. But the Arapaho did not come forward at once. Instead, he fell back to a roll in the plain that formed a little hill and seemed to be signaling someone far beyond, probably the next warrior in the line, who would wonder what had happened to the point rider on his left flank. Then the Arapaho came forward again, moving closer to the ground now, his bow before him at the ready. Ironfoot held close to his cover, turning and motioning White River and Amiel to earth, but Marcher was still slipping forward, crawling into the low brush.

The deer's head was up now, motionless but on the edge of flight. The warrior being upwind from the deer, which must have taken his scent, knew that the moment must decide. He tried a long, difficult shot and the arrow went home into the deer's beautifully arched neck. The animal bounded a few steps, then reversed itself, pawing the earth as blood appeared in its mouth and nostrils. It was lying on the ground kicking as the warrior approached it and bent over it with his knife. He removed the arrow, wiped it on the animal's shiny coat and tied the deer's legs together with leather thongs to make the carcass easier to carry.

Having done that he stood up, obviously about to return for his pony. But then, strangely, he stopped and looked curiously at the thinner growth covering the south end of the swale. For long moments he stood there. Clearly a thought was in his mind. Ironfoot watched him breathlessly. *Why hadn't Marcher held back?!* Had the warrior seen something? Perhaps a flash of color that did not belong or a movement in the low-hanging boughs that did not serve the wind, or perhaps he sensed the presence of something or felt the mysterious message that lies in too much silence.

Marcher, hugging the ground mutely, was cursing the deer he knew now had drawn the Indian toward the shallow fringe of the swale. Something cold in his gut told him this warrior had seen him, was pretending not to have, and was moving off to alert his war party. But the Indian went stoically to his horse, returning with it walking on the far side. He placed the deer across the primitive saddle, tying another leather thong from the animal's legs to the large wooden horn. Then, taking a long last look toward the swale, he started off leading his pony out on the plain.

As the Arapaho moved away what thoughts were in his mind would never be known, for the unbelievable happened. A shot rang out from the low thicket and a lead ball blew the back of his skull off, pitching him to the prairie as deep in death as his deer.

Shock and incomprehension paralyzed the group peering from the deep cover of the swale. The eerie moment following the roar of gunshot became a nightmare as the air was split with a loud "Got the bastard." It was Marcher. He was rising from the fringe of the swale, nodding to the others. White River came to life first, bounding toward him from the break like a flushed stag, his total being focused on one thought. Lunging at Marcher, he knocked him to the earth, then, stunning him with a wicked blow, dragged him out of sight.

Almost as White River broke forth, Ironfoot ducked under a limb on his left and sped out toward the fallen Arapaho. As the growth gave out he halted by instinct to glimpse quickly over the plain. There was nothing in sight and the wind was holding strong and firm from the west. Within moments he was over the dead man gathering the reins still clutched in the dead hand and grunting softly to the horse that began to shy as it smelled blood about it and the strange figure of Ironfoot coming up.

First he led the pony quickly back into the swale and looped the rein around a cottonwood limb, then he returned to the body, turning it over, pulling the headdress away from the face. His heart skipped a beat as he saw the blue-stained fox canine teeth hanging from the lobe of the left ear—it was Medicine Fox! Once again he looked across the plain, knowing now it would not be long before the Arapahos were back.

Before him stretched all the things that weary years of war, blood-stained beyond any people's mortal power for sacrifice and prayer, told him now had to be. The Arapahos must come back for Medicine Fox. There was not another such as he in their tribe. They would find or they would not find his body, it mattered little. They would read what happened here, there was too much sign to cover that. They would search the swale, they would pick up tracks of this alien party, and they would follow them until exhaustion drained them, made their limbs too leaden to lift.

White River was beside him now, his face gray with fury. Ironfoot met his eyes, knowing they matched the furor in his own heart. In them was a hatred of the terrible turnings of life mixed with the secret knowledge of the calamity that was upon them, a calamity born of too many stupidities for a man to believe possible. White River threw a quick look back at Marcher's body. In his heart he wished that the brainless idiot were dead.

They both squatted down beside Medicine Fox's body. White River looked out over the plain. "Think that shot carried?"

Ironfoot turned his face into the wind and his eyes scanned the land to the southwest. Then he shook his head in conclusion. "Arapaho not hear." White River, feeling the strength of the wind as though it had just come upon him, studied for a few moments this quiet plain to the southwest, then tightened his mouth and nodded in agreement.

Behind them Amiel was approaching cautiously, but he stopped several yards away, squatting down, his rifle held nervously in both hands, his eyes on the blood spreading over the ground from Medicine Fox.

White River hissed hurriedly to Ironfoot. "Think they figure to work back for this one?"

"Arapaho come back."

"Maybe so—but if they're in a hurry . . ."

Ironfoot put up his right hand. With his left he cupped the blue teeth hanging from the dead brave's ear. "This Medicine Fox, son of Fighting Eagle. Arapahos look upon him as a warrior does his shield." His eyes shifted to the southwest. "Arapahos come back . .. soon."

Now Marcher stood up and came toward them. "What the hell was I supposed to do?" he said lamely. Even in this fateful moment his arrogance remained. "God damn it! I was sure the bastard saw me!" Wincing, he rubbed his jaw. "Christ Almighty, you didn't have to . . ."

It seemed pointless to tell Marcher that if the Arapaho had seen him he would never have turned his back and walked away from a hidden enemy. "Ain't no way to put it to make it sound pretty," muttered White River.

"Meaning what?" said Marcher somewhat hoarsely, his rising anger showing in his voice.

"We're out of the gold-hunting business, Mr. Marcher. You just played our last card."

Marcher's tension now ignited his resentment at being knocked almost senseless. "Good Christ, man! It's only a God-damn Indian . . . I don't see any others."

"Andy!" said Amiel turning on him with fury. "Killing this man will probably get us all massacred."

"Best let that go," snapped White River. "Our troubles are just startin'. Give Ironfoot a hand with this dead buck. Hide him as best you can—they'll find him no matter what, but it may slow them up a bit." White River acted as though Marcher wasn't there.

Marcher, feeling the exclusion, brought his face up to White River's, his bearded cheeks and lengthening hair giving him a faintly leonine look. There was a wildness in his eyes now that gave some warning of his words. "We can't quit now, just because of a dead Indian!"

"Ain't no choice," said White River evenly. "This buck was big medicine among the Arapahos—if they run us down, make sure you ain't taken alive."

White River tried not to look at Marcher. He was feeling a viciousness in this man he had not noticed before. Something was taking hold of Marcher, and the seriousness of their situation did not subdue the thought that was now jolted loose in White River's mind. He decided to press it back for the moment, though he knew it would not really leave him for hours to come. "Get to your horses and make sure they're under cover—it's almost noon and they might be starting to drift for water," he said, hardly hearing his own words.

Marcher shuffled his feet, starting to turn away. White River, seeing him go, called after him, "Fetch your glasses, Marcher. We'd best start lookin' about . . . see what's maybe already lookin' for us."

Ironfoot took his knife and, grabbing Medicine Fox's left ear, sliced it from his head. He held it up and saw the blue-stained fox teeth dangling from it. This had been strong medicine; he would keep it. He would show it to his people if he returned. It would make their hearts sing. In truth he had counted coup on the dead brave, for though he had not shot Medicine Fox, he was the first to touch his body. It was a big coup. He put the ear in the parfleche hanging from his saddle. Amiel, looking on in disgust, made a wry face.

After looking about, Ironfoot turned and finished tying the body of Medicine Fox over his own pony. He had removed the deer, skinned and cut away some choice parts, and left the rest. He had worked fast once he knew there was no place in the swale that could hide the body long enough to count. But he had another plan, and as White River came up, looking darkly quizzical at the Arapaho tied across the mount, he explained it to him quickly. White River nodded in sudden sharp movements, readily agreeing. If they kept the body, the Arapaho would have to consider the possibility that Medicine Fox was still alive and hence would have to pursue more cautiously to prevent his captors from killing him in anticipation of an attack. Ironfoot's plan for disposing of the body was an old but good one, and White River cut off their talk with a motion back to their earlier perch at the northern point of their cover.

Here he gave Ironfoot Marcher's field glasses and instructed him to search the land about them, reporting any movement at all. Marcher and Amiel watched the Indian climb the tree, Marcher mumbling, "I thought we were in a rush to get out of here?"

"We are," said White River.

"Perhaps we should get going, then," Amiel suggested nervously.

White River fixed his eyes on Ironfoot above him. "When a man moves in broad daylight around here, he just can't know too much about who's movin' around too. Remember this is Sioux territory—those bucks that passed were Arapaho headin' south. They must have run into something or maybe just powwowing with somebody up here backaways."

"We're not short on trouble, are we?" mumbled Amiel.

"Not hardly." White River's eyes were squinting up at Ironfoot. "See anything at all?"

Ironfoot froze with the glasses for a moment, then, taking them from his eyes, came swiftly down from the perch. Quick signs filled in his halting speech. It was the Arapahos, they were gathered together and just visible at the foot of a whitish mound almost on the rim of the land. They were either in council or eating. Ironfoot could not tell, but they were there. White River took the glasses and climbed to the perch. He moved the glasses in a small arc for a moment, then steadied them. After a long concentration on the mound a tiny speck of what seemed off-colored fuzz at this distance became a group of red and white headdresses sewn together and as unsubstantial as a spore adrift in space.

He studied them for some minutes before he put down the glasses and seemed lost in thought. The ones below waited for him patiently to join them, but before he came down he made another full circle with the glasses, concentrating for the most part to the north, then in the end took a final look to the south. On the ground his old distant mood and manner seemed in part returned. "Reckon they be four miles or thereabouts from here. Could be better than we counted. If they hold up for a while—suspect we'd better too." He handed the glasses back to Ironfoot. "Keep an eye to them—whenever they move, well, we mosey too."

The day that had been so tense but a short time before seemed suddenly to drag. Marcher sat looking at White River, who seemed too preoccupied to bother looking back. Amiel stared at the ground, his thoughts his own. Occasionally White River would look up at Ironfoot and occasionally he would take a stick and draw lines and X's on the ground. Given every luck, they should be able to strike east and circle back to the river. The Arapahos might follow, but the day was waning and hoof tracks would be harder to follow by night. It bothered him that Ironfoot would continue on, for though the easiest route would have been north and then west to Innyan Kara and then north again to the source of the Belle Fourche, Ironfoot, against all common sense, had wanted to go to the Belle Fourche first to find Black Shield's grave, and then to double back south in a move that seemed suicidal. Well, it did not matter now, for Ironfoot would go as he chose and perhaps he was right. For all the madness the practical eyes of the whites found in it, behind the Indians' way often lay some primitive and impenetrable sense of the will of things that cannot be controlled and the course of an enemy no previous surveillance, however persistent, could predict.

"God damn it. I can't get over the feeling we should be doing something!" It was Marcher standing above him now.

"We are." White River did not bother to look up.

"What?"

"Stayin' alive mebbe."

"Hell—if trouble was coming it would have been here long ago!"

"Mebbeso."

"Why don't we push on while our luck's holding?"

White River came slowly erect. "Around here a fellow learns not to push his luck." He looked determinedly at the other. "We're goin' back, Mr. Marcher."

"You mean you are."

White River looked up at Ironfoot. "Any way you want it. Don't pay to waste rope on a critter already gone loco."

Marcher looked at him peculiarly, then with a hurried glance about he narrowed the range of his voice and said in quiet but almost frantic words, "Look, White River, we can make it together. We'll travel fast . . . be there and on our way in no time. It's gold, White River, I know it. Come on, we'll be partners. You said you wanted to start a freighting business . . . God, man, surely you want more than that! Property, power, the means to fill life with things that count. A man with a gold mine doesn't worry about what's lying around the next bend, friend. He doesn't wait for life to come to him. He maps it out to his liking. We don't agree on everything, but you've got guts and I respect you for it. Come on, just say you'll give it a try."

White River stared at him, the vacuous light that springs from an overtired and overtaxed mind now faint and dim in his eyes. But still he had heard the whispered siren song in Marcher's words. It had touched that vision that hung in the deep of him, that gracious home a man could feel proud of, that endless freedom and the means to find

Lydia again. Above all, that right to ask her to return with her softness and childlike beauty to restore the life that still glowed for him beyond these painful years he had endured since she left. But he knew that Marcher's mind was thrashing about like some desperate grizzly's that will not accept the relentless teeth of the trap, and he had to tell him calmly, curtly, but finally—because even that would be a form of kindness—that talking on this thing was useless, that too much was wrong to chase the matter further with words; that a man owed it to himself to stop wanting after what was already beyond reach. But he was never to communicate this to Marcher, for at that moment Ironfoot gave out with a low singing "Hiyee!"

White River's eyes turned up and immediately a cold rivulet of apprehension curved through his breast. Ironfoot was looking east!

"What is it?"

Ironfoot waited for a moment, then took the glasses from his eyes. Still he did not look down. "Lakota wolf—making scout."

"Sioux! Which direction is he headed?"

Ironfoot concentrated through the glasses for a moment, then held them away again. "Scout stay on high ridge."

White River immediately pulled himself up beside Ironfoot. "What do you make of it?"

Ironfoot's face could not hide his concern. "War party come soon."

White River took the glasses. He leveled them at the far ridge Ironfoot indicated, but try as he would he could pick out no movement or form that suggested a human scout. "Are you certain?" he muttered. Ironfoot grunted in a way that dealt roundly with doubt.

White River let his breath out in an audible whistle as he dropped down from the perch. "God A'mighty," he said half to himself, thinking if they had left earlier, at the death of Medicine Fox, and gone east, they would have run head on into those Sioux. But there was little to rejoice at. Where would they head now? If the Arapahos flushed them out they could only go northward or west. West meant across the nearby open plain where they would be visible for miles, and north was taking them further from safety, putting them deeper into a trap that was now all but shut. He told Marcher and Amiel to bring the horses up. They did. He planned to tell them what the risks were, to let them have a say-so if they wanted one. The odds were so high now a man had a right to declare his thinking.

They faced him seriously. The sun had dropped to where its rays were invading their cover in long amber shafts from the southwest. The sky to the east had lost its luminosity and its blue was molting at the horizon into the gray of a kitten's fur.

" 'Pears the Sioux have finally showed. They're comin' through the hills to the east so we can't count on gettin' out thataway. We're goin' to try to the west and circle these Arapahos. The Sioux will have trouble seein' us with the sun in their eyes and we'll try to keep high ground to the south. I can't promise anything—if it comes to a fight, we'll try to do it on the run. If anyone loses his horse, he's on his own—likely he'd be best to hunt cover and lie still. Don't pin any hopes on gettin' any pity and you won't be disappointed. Now has anyone got some thinkin' that needs talkin'?"

"Why don't we go north?" said Marcher plaintively.

"A man in his right mind would be hankering to go t'other way," announced White River. "But I reckon a man right in the head wouldn't be here to start with."

"We'll all go with you," said Amiel with a strained hint of authority. "I'm sure you know best."

White River set about telling them in which order to ride, how he would signal for dismounting, the need to keep up close after dark, the . . . His breath was halted in his throat as Ironfoot gave three quick yips and slipped down from the perch. He pointed to the south as he spoke. The Arapahos were coming! He had lost them for a few minutes and assumed they had gone south together as a party, but they had not. By accident he found them again. They had fanned out in a single line and were coming on foot directly toward the cover. They were approaching the high ground to the west and were moving behind every boulder and rise in the earth they could, as though they knew they were closing in on a quarry. White River grabbed the glasses and swung up to the perch. It took him a moment or two to find them, but he did. The picture could not have been more threatening. They had lost their chance to cross the plain to the west and the Arapahos, if they continued on, would be beneath this very perch in less than a quarter of an hour.

He came down in one bound, thrusting the glasses back at Marcher. "Mount up!" he said hurriedly. "If you're a prayin' man, get 'em in while you can." Ironfoot was already mounted and holding a rope on Medicine Fox's horse which moved nervously now under the rigid body. At a signal from White River, he dug his heels into his pony's flanks and led the way out of the cover. White River waved the others on behind Ironfoot and, swinging onto his horse, wheeled about and, heading north, left the cover last.

The horses' hooves thudded over the coarse earth, and the sun hovered like an immense orange eye above the horizon. Ironfoot held to the low ground as best he could, trying to make cover from the sparse line of trees that strung out and dissipated in a patch of stunted growth, the last dwarfed pine bending over completely, pointing perhaps to some underground spring.

White River watched the Crow press forward, knowing somehow he could do no better, but wishing foolishly he could. Yet how little difference it made. Their fresh tracks would lie behind them like a trail of fire. Luckily their horses were freshened by the day's rest. If they could clear the next rise, the reckoning could well be delayed until morning. But something told him it would be a new world by morning, and that things would never be the same again. He looked at the figures clinging to their horses before him. He wondered what thoughts they held, what they thought as they struggled to stay together not knowing when death would announce itself and perhaps call upon them to spend eternity together. He did not know. He dug into his horse and urged it forward.

And so they went, their faces down. Each one intent upon his own progress, each grim with his own dread guessing—that is, all but one. One held his horse on loose rein and bounded along, his face locked in the tight clutch of an emotion that rose and was petrified in a grin. It was Marcher. He was going north.

20

The Arapahos had been squatting behind the knoll chewing grimly and swallowing with effort the antelope Blue Jacket had killed in a herd he struck far to the west. But Medicine Fox, who had swept to the east, had not turned inward with the others. The brave closest to him had said he noticed Medicine Fox had vanished during the hunt, but when he went to search for him he saw Medicine Fox standing on a far hill, motioning him on. Thinking Medicine Fox wished to delay for game he was stalking, game that the approach of another might well scare off, the brave hurried forward knowing that he had become the new tip of the wing and must move faster than the others and with the readiest bow.

Yet several hours had passed. The antelope had been cooked and eaten, the amber of afternoon was rising like a harvest across the land, the lull that is the edge of evening was weighing on the lowering wind—and still Medicine Fox had not come in.

Blue Jacket, who was serving as scout on a low-lying ridge to the north, was the most unsettled of all. His sore eyes picked desperately at the terrain, his stomach seeming to sit high in his body feeling full, though he had eaten nothing of his food. Over and over again he relived that final scene with his father, Fighting Eagle. Each time it tightened the net his own words had woven. He had come to his father's lodge in secret while the war party prepared to leave, wanting to say he had the mind of a squaw to have spoken so in council, to have allowed Hawk to make use of his words as an arrow for the bow of Little Hand's anger, an arrow Hawk had long intended for Medicine Fox. This Blue Jacket had told Fighting Eagle, and lowered his eyes.

At first his father had been silent, a sign of displeasure, but at last he had said, "What would my son do now?"

"I will go with them," said Blue Jacket.

"Medicine Fox is strong in council, both he and Little Hand in war. Is there not bravery and wisdom enough for this thing?"

"Perhaps," Blue Jacket muttered lamely. "What would Fighting Eagle have me do?"

There was a long silence, then finally the old man said, "What does the eagle do when the snake leaves its own egg in the eagle's nest that it may strike at the brood when all are born?"

Blue Jacket, eyes down, did not answer at once. He knew his father well, knew of his growing old and uncertain so that this thing with Hawk troubled him more than it should a great chief. His first feeling was impatience. There were ways of dealing with those itching for power, wanting to wear it in their headdress as though they had struck coup upon the people. But he said simply at last, "The eagle has talons, let him destroy the serpent's egg."

"And if the eagle does not know which egg is the serpent's?" Blue Jacket knew his father's way of talking, of always putting the young where they must think again on the power of wisdom, of making them see the tragic turn that can lie in an action too quickly taken. Blue Jacket knew better than Fighting Eagle that this was why his brothers seldom came to sit at the council fire of their father, for rarely could their passion for heated action—so like a drug to the young these days—find favor here. Well, Fighting Eagle was an old chief and one fearing his failing power. Now that his will for war was seriously spent, he was an easier mark each passing day for those who played on the silly pride and the dangerous passions of an angry and deposed people. Today there was Hawk, tomorrow there would be others.

Blue Jacket decided to help his father. He did not want power himself, he saw nothing in being chief of a dying people. He would follow his medicine dream, which had said he would not fight with the strength of a grizzly but with the slyness of a fox who heard and smelled danger from afar. His strongest secret medicine was the dried and ground ears of a fox which he kept wrapped in a beaver skin and sewn inside his quilted jacket. He would tell his father in his own way that he understood the difficult things that lay before them.

"The eagle would know that the last egg to appear would be the serpent's egg, my father, for the serpent would have to find the eggs of the eagle before he left his own."

A faint smile loosened the corners of Fighting Eagle's mouth. Ah, was not this son—this child of Fire Woman—a strange one, with an old man's sensing into the way of things behind his laughingly sad eyes.

"Father," said Blue Jacket, knowing they could not talk alone much longer, "does the mountain lion push the night-crawling rat from his lair or does he leave such matters to the cubs?"

His father's old eyes looked quietly at him. "The cubs that must grow to be lions are leaving the lair. The old one must keep it clean for their return."

Blue Jacket knew that his father was speaking of him and Medicine Fox only out of courtesy to himself. His father's mind was on Medicine Fox. Blue Jacket was too strong to need to think of it as otherwise. He said simply, "He will return."

Fighting Eagle sat silently looking at the eagle fan in his hand. Blue Jacket pushed himself to the point. It was not the rule for a young man to talk so much in the lodge of his father. "A chief must think of the many, the old, the weak. If there is killing to be done, leave it to those who will not divide a tribe." Fighting Eagle knew Blue Jacket was thinking of the large following Hawk had and saw in his words the terrible truth that few whites knew the Indian lived with. There was no legislative loyalty to a single chief. The braves were free to take their ponies and their lodge poles and follow the trail that went another way. Hardly was there a tribe on the plains that could not point to another village and say there was a time when we were one. Blue Jacket looked through the flap blown open by the wind. "Medicine Fox is close to the hearts of our people. He has stood tall in council. His name will be ready on their tongues. His many deeds will come to their lips quickly. He will lead well. He will be their chief."

"If he returns," muttered Fighting Eagle.

"He will return—Blue Jacket has promised his father this thing."

Fighting Eagle's heavy face hung in the dim light of the lodge, his eyes were almost closed, but the lids quivered from time to time to show that his mind was still turning restlessly in thought. So many times had he heard the promises of warriors left empty by battle. Even great chiefs, strong in council, possessing great medicine, left nothing but squaws keening in the darkness, and perhaps here and there a wise one to remark that oratory could not change the omens sent by the Great Spirit. How was he to say this to Blue Jacket? How was he to say if Medicine Fox died his need would be even greater? Ah, but he did not need to speak. Blue Jacket could read his heart. It was in the eyes of this strange son of Fire Woman, a squaw with white blood in her, as he rose. "Let Fighting Eagle draw his robe about him in peace. I will bring him back."

Fighting Eagle's breathing hesitated for a moment. Did Blue Jacket really understand? But then the other turned to him at the lodge entrance, and now Fighting Eagle knew he did. "I, Blue Jacket, will bring Medicine Fox back, father—or I will bring my knife." If Hawk's ambitions ever filled his heart, they would be joined there with a knife.

And now it was clear the hours of final and foolish hopes had wasted away. Medicine Fox knew too well the cruelty of their circumstances to place upon them the burden of this long absence. The decision could not be delayed. Blue Jacket turned about to signal Little Hand, but the other was already coming toward him, the braves trailing after him. It was not a matter for words. The two stared for a moment toward the northeast, then Little Hand called to the warriors to leave their horses with two guards behind the knoll and to move forward like wolves, staying close to the ground and using every inch of cover. Blue Jacket moved off to his right, glancing apprehensively at the sky. Evening was forming. Why had they not moved sooner? Why had they delayed so long? He struck his bow viciously across his thigh. Here they had been idling like empty-headed squaws coming to relieve themselves in the bushes while Medicine Fox hunted alone in the country of the crafty Sioux. Why had they put Medicine Fox on the point of that wing, even though his rank entitled him to this honor? Why had not Little Hand placed him in the middle where he would not have had to meet trouble alone? These and other angry and foolish questions rankled Blue Jacket as he sped over the ground watching the ragged line of braves moving on his left. They were the questions of a man wrestling with pain that tells him he is powerless before the implacable maw of life. He tried to press it from him. A brave with anger in his throat is a careless one with two enemies. As though to compensate for his tormented mind, Blue Jacket worked closer to the earth, moving with great stealth around boulders and lying as one with the grass at each rise in the plain. None but a seasoned scout could have detected him and then only if that one was on the alert. But all of this did the heart of Blue Jacket little good, for however faintly visible he was as he moved across the plain, the eyes of Fighting Eagle were on him at every turn.

The Arapahos came into the swale slowly, their arrows on the ready, their hands tense upon their war clubs. They had already read the message written on the face of the earth beyond the swale. They had seen where Medicine Fox's body had lain, seen the bloodstains dark against the coarse grass. The tracks of whites were everywhere, but they were few and they had no friend but the darkness. The Arapahos began to move about a little more quickly. There seemed no life anywhere as they worked into the cover of the trees, so they continuously quickened their pace till in the end they were running everywhere, calling to each other, following the departing horse tracks out to where they stretched away to the north.

"They just rode off at a run," said Blue Jacket, bending over the tracks. "They cannot be far."

"Signal our horses to be brought up quickly," shouted Little Hand to a brave. He came very close, his eyes questioning Blue Jacket's.

"They have taken Medicine Fox with them," said Blue Jacket, his voice helpless to conceal his thoughts.

"We will catch them and Medicine Fox will help us carry their scalps back to our village." Then, unaccountably, Little Hand threw his tomahawk into the ground in anger. "Ho! Why did we wait so long?"

Blue Jacket did not answer. The imprint of marks where Medicine Fox's body had lain on the ground was still before him. If he had read it correctly, the blood had come from the head. Medicine Fox had not walked away. A pony had been brought up and a heavy thing placed upon it. That pony had left the cover not being ridden, but being led beside another. His heart had no words to carry his thoughts.

The horses were being brought up quickly. They could be seen coming across the plain, their tenders moving them along at a gallop. The immense sun had set now, leaving behind it a wide wedge of high wine in the heavy horizontal haze that strung out like the shadow of a serpent crouched on the western rim of earth. The Arapahos stood silent for a moment, their dark mysticism seeming to demand they pause and call upon their spirits to remove the premonition that arose from the signs many had read upon the ground.

Just what had happened no one was sure, but a brave who heard a coyote worrying the remains of the deer Ironfoot had hurriedly thrown into the eastern growth of the swale, and thinking quietly to himself it might be the remains of poor Medicine Fox, crept toward the sound, then, lifting himself into a tree, suddenly discovered a lone horseman, the one Ironfoot had taken for a Sioux scout, coming toward them with great speed from the east.

Instinctively he gave the quick uneven warning call that was their daytime signal for danger, and at once the many Arapahos who were standing impatiently about, fidgeting at the irksome wait and their own bad wondering, disappeared in the long shadowed grass and the tall covering foliage of the swale. One on the south fringe gave a long, quivering wolf call, and the horses, close now, could be seen being turned into some low ground and made to circle till they were still. It proved to be in vain. The rider had seen them and came determinedly forward, his pony as he approached showing the wide eyes and frothing mouth of an animal that has given up the energy needed for life.

He waved his bow over his head as he swept to the edge of the swale and dropped from his mount. The single white strip of paint about his chest and his long black hair tied to hang over one shoulder announced who he was: the Cheyenne brave—and everything about him said he had come from Black Water in a desperate hurry.

"Ho! Our brother the Cheyenne!" said Little Hand going forward.

The Cheyenne raised his hand in greeting, but his face was dark, drawn. He drew no pipes for smoking. Instead he struck his bow against his chest. "Should not my brothers the Arapahos be one sleep closer to their village?"

"We had to delay," said Little Hand firmly. "Medicine Fox was lost to some enemies during a hunt. They have taken him north. We must follow."

The Cheyenne looked to the north, and his eyes were the eyes of one who has lost understanding. Blue Jacket motioned him over toward the tracks still faintly visible in the fading light. The Cheyenne looked at them long and hard. They could not know his heart was telling him he had seen those tracks before across the river where they had killed the Pawnees guiding the whites.

"They are whites—but they are not many," said Blue Jacket trying to jolt the grim-looking Cheyenne into talk. Whether the Cheyenne had noticed the two unshod Indian ponies riding almost side by side, as though one were leading the other, Blue Jacket did not know, but the Cheyenne muttered meaningfully, "Does your brave-hearted Medicine Fox allow himself to be taken like a squaw?"

"He was wounded," said Little Hand, but his heart was not in his words.

The Cheyenne snorted and turned to the Arapahos gathering about the horses coming up now, trying to work away from their tenders to feed on the lush grass of the swale.

"Hear me, then. I, Two Horns, speak. Black Water has sent me to tell his brothers, the Arapahos, that they must go at once from this land. Stone Maker and Wandisapa are coming. They did not leave yesterday when your leaving was known, but their wolves found your trail and last night they rode from the great camp. I have killed my good war pony riding all night and all day, finding them, and then finding you. You will have to give me another. Mine is dying. You should also give me a good war-horse for what I have done for you. The Minneconjous are angry, their hearts are bad and their ponies are but a short run from here. These whites are riding right into them. Go now or you will never see your village again."

Little Hand drew himself up in half anger, half despair. "We cannot go back without Medicine Fox!"

The Cheyenne looked at him coldly. "Medicine Fox is on his long journey over the stars. The Lakota will soon send these bad whites to follow him." His eyes narrowed, growing even colder as though covering an edge of contempt. "Where were the brave Arapahos when Medicine Fox fought and died alone?"

Blue Jacket saw the futility of explaining this painful point and was about to offer the Cheyenne his own good black-and-white stallion, but Little Hand was trapped by the cut of the Cheyenne.

"We could not know," he shouted. "He was late returning from our hunt. It is a thing that happens often." Many of the Arapahos grunted and called their approval of Little Hand's words, but Blue Jacket, who could only look down, knew they had finally accepted Medicine Fox's death.

"You will take my war-horse," he said to the Cheyenne, without looking up. "The children of Fighting Eagle will long look upon you as their brother."

Little Hand started to speak again, but Blue Jacket put his hand on his shoulder. "Come—the Great Spirit is not with us on this day. It is not a time for more fighting."

"Are you afraid to die?" shouted Little Hand bitterly. "Even now, when the Arapahos stand in disgrace! Are you afraid to kill our enemies?"

"I am not afraid," said Blue Jacket, turning away.

Little Hand was almost in tears with rage. As a warrior he was ready for death. "What enemies can you kill sitting like a squaw at our village fires?" he called in scathing tones at the retreating Blue Jacket.

Blue Jacket stopped for a long, searching look into an inky sky to the south, then turned wearily to Little Hand. Few knew his mind was on Hawk. "I will kill one more," he said.

PART FOUR

SIOUX

21

As they came to the rim of the gorge, Ironfoot reached over, pulling Medicine Fox's body from the pony and hurling it to the rocky floor below, yet keeping the ponies moving until he was several hundred yards further on. Then he motioned to White River to hold up there while he leaped upon a boulder and began to make his way back, being careful to stay on the great rocks that lay in almost continual procession along the slope of the gorge. When he reached Medicine Fox's body, he pulled it into a crevice and hurriedly covered it with small rocks. Satisfied, he turned again and retraced his steps. It was already too dark for the others to follow his movements and when he returned they were startled and turned toward him sharply, watching him rise up and swing quickly onto his mount.

"Could be time to circle back," said White River, reacting first.

Ironfoot looked about him in the dark but did not answer.

"I'm for going ahead," said Marcher quickly.

Three quick—too quick—yelps of a wolf knifing into the night made Ironfoot dart one hand upward for silence while the others took their mounts up quickly. The wolf calls had come from directly before them and they were answered almost immediately by a single yelp to the west. *"Ah-yee,"* said Ironfoot in a dread whisper to himself. He slipped off his mount again, the others one by one in some sudden understanding following suit. Ironfoot started pulling his pony along at a half run. He moved forward on the dropping rim of the gorge and, coming to a washout, turned into it quickly. Within moments they were moving between the high boulders that guarded the north and lower basin of the depression. Here he brought them to a halt in a pocket surrounded by a mass of rock.

"Reckon we're in for it now," said White River in a tone that reached Amiel's ears as deadly earnest. "Fort up behind these rocks and don't move less'n you have to."

"They going to attack? Now?" said Amiel working his rifle from his saddle.

"Don't know," said White River tersely, "pretty dark—can't see us no better than we can see them."

Ironfoot had climbed the first ledge and worked his way between two mammoth rocks and now had disappeared. White River stood looking after him, Marcher, his repeating rifle on the ready, coming up behind.

"Maybe it's a good thing we've run into them in the dark. Now maybe we can slip by them before daylight."

White River's tall form stood mute and motionless in the darkness, his head pitched slightly forward as he listened like a man whose mind is on other matters.

Marcher waited for a few moments, then said pointlessly, "We've managed to get ourselves into a pretty bad fix, haven't we?"

"I can recollect better," allowed White River.

"Look, I think this has been pretty much my doing. I think I'll take my horse and make a run to the north. They'll come after me and the rest of you can circle back."

White River looked at him in the darkness. " 'Twouldn't work."

"Why not?"

"These Injuns have heard horses running before. They can tell the difference between one and four."

"Then you think they've seen us."

White River turned slowly, like a man sensing something in the dark. "Don't know . . . for sure."

"Then why don't we give it a try?"

Had not Marcher moved closer to White River as he spoke, the war club spinning out of the night would have killed him. As it was it glanced off his head and struck his shoulder, making him tumble to his left, his right hand going out to White River as he fell.

"Ai! . . . Ai! . . . Yeeeeee!" The war cry split the night, and White River had just time to face a gray figure rushing out of the darkness, coming upon him with one arm raised in an arc above its head. Sheer instinct made him bring the stock of his rifle around like a club, yet even this would not have saved him had not the onrushing figure tripped over the sprawling form of Marcher. White River went down with the lunging body, bringing up his knee to kick the figure in the stomach, his hand going for the flailing arm striving to deliver what could only be the blade of a knife. There was no sense to it. Death groped about, awkwardly clawing for a chance. The greasy, rank body in his hands doubled back and forth as desperately as his own. The attacker had no air. It had been driven out of him by White River's knee. But he grunted hoarsely like a hog and pulled his arm free as White River, his rifle knocked from him in the initial blow, looped his free arm around the other in a headlock. Then suddenly it was over. White River felt something sweep downward, bruising his face, and then the other's body lumped forward and went limp. White River, knowing it might have been a trick, kicked the body from him and staggered back. He pulled his pistol from his belt, half expecting to be set upon again. But there was nothing now but the gasping of the others beside him and the labored breathing, matching his own, of Marcher standing with his back against the great slab of rock, the war club in his right hand. This had been the weapon Marcher used to crush the Indian's skull as White River held him in a headlock.

"Quick," said White River with his first breath. "That war whoop will bring others. Get down, spread out. Somebody get to those horses!"

Marcher took a step forward, but seemed wobbly.

"Bad?" said White River still without full breath.

"My left shoulder . . . left arm is numb . . . coming back some . . . where . . . where in Christ's name did he come from?"

"Don't know . . . but be expectin' more."

Amiel had gone to hold the horses. If they were stampeded it could doom them all.

White River, studying the height of the pocket and hearing a loud, weird cry from somewhere beyond the dark slab of rock, motioned

Amiel to bring their horses forward and steady them. At the wall-like facing of the rock he found Marcher looking up, his rifle propped forward in his right arm.

"Hear it?" whispered Marcher.

White River responded with an affirmative grunt, then boosted himself up the rock to make his way to the crevice through which Ironfoot had disappeared, his tight quick movements prodded by fear. Where was Ironfoot, and who else would cry out in the night like that at this time, in this place? On the other face of the rock he found a drop too steep for easy or quiet descent. He crouched down trying to peer into the darkness. The heavy stillness of the night seemed alive, taut with a threat that hovered over the basin floor.

Then he sensed a form was coming toward him, but it was moving slowly, so slowly at times it seemed not to move at all. It was long moments before he could make out its awkward shape, before he could determine at last it was a man, but a man who moved with an inhuman motion as though his limbs were not coordinated. He seized his knife and flattened himself against the facing of the rock. He would not move, he would let this figure move upon him. It came closer and closer. In a moment it would be on top of him. The rough knife handle felt hard in his hand. He was not aware of the desperate grasp he had upon it. His other hand tightened, ready to dart out and pull this form into position for the thrust. But at the last instant—the last instant it could have happened—the weird cry broke out again, this time right beside him and from this figure beside him. Recognition froze him—it was Ironfoot. He knew it was Ironfoot just as he now knew that what he had been watching was Ironfoot not coming toward him but backing toward him, bent over in a crouch and watching something beyond. The moment contained an incredible danger. They were so close together that any move or whisper from him might bring Ironfoot's knife in a reflex action that permitted no thought. Ironfoot could not know he was there. He was too intent upon what lay beyond. There were only inches between them now. White River pressed against the rock and whispered as though they had been talking for an hour, "Me."

Ironfoot's head ducked low and his hands went back, but he was erect again in a moment, gripping White River and drawing him back into the crevice between the rocks. Ironfoot's hands were damp and unnatural and White River felt the strange stickiness of blood upon his arm. Ironfoot did not seem wounded, yet in the iron of his grasp lay a desperation White River sensed he had no way to utter.

Once in the crevice, Ironfoot pressed him forward saying with his hands he wanted White River to return to the others. White River backed away, not knowing any longer where sanity lay. After a few steps he fell to one knee. He could not leave Ironfoot here to face the Sioux alone and everything shouted they were hard upon him. Through the sooty darkness he began to perceive the thin wedge that was the crevice between the rocks, perceive it and then perceive an immense form rising up to fill it. The knife handle again felt like granite in his hand. Where was Ironfoot? The form suddenly entered into and became one with the mass of rock that lined the crevice. Did Ironfoot see? "Ugh." The sound flooded toward him and was followed by a sickening whine that reminded him of an animal with its tongue cut out being bludgeoned to death.

He went forward to find Ironfoot backing into him again. Ironfoot turned and pushed him roughly toward the cover. This time White River went, seeing without seeing a large Sioux warrior wedged in the crevice and almost certainly disemboweled from the amount of blood covering Ironfoot. As he reached the ledge and dropped over, the weird cry sounded again.

He fell almost into the arms of Marcher and Amiel, their hands failing to release him as the cry rang out above, instead holding him even tighter, their hoarse whisperings coming together in the darkness. "Christ! What is it? What's happening?"

He seized them back, his grip demanding silence, and pressed them away from the steep wall side of the boulder just in time to keep Ironfoot from plunging down on top of them.

The three were over the Crow as he braced his back to come to his feet, Amiel almost immediately recoiling and repressing an audible groan at the sickening stench arising from Ironfoot.

"Horses—quick," rasped Ironfoot as though his breath had run out and he was struggling to will it back.

"Stay together," rasped White River, pulling his mount away quickly to stay with Ironfoot. He knew if anything happened to the Crow, the dice of decision would be his alone. If Ironfoot had a plan, he wanted to hear it. He had none of his own. They had to wait at the break from the cover for the others to come up. Marcher, following Amiel, was awkwardly holding both reins and gun in his right hand betraying that his left arm had not recovered from the blow.

"Are we in for a fight?" demanded Marcher abruptly.

White River's hand came up in a signal for silence, but his taut mind shouted back—in for a fight . . . Christ Almighty, we've *been* in a fight!

As they huddled together, White River swung about and took Ironfoot by the shoulder. He pressed hard to drive home his meaning. "Does the heart of Ironfoot speak to him?"

Ironfoot looked about him furtively then made a sign for the rising of the sun, whispering. "Great danger then. Ironfoot try ghost medicine. Now we go. Pray much to Great Spirit."

"What does all that mean?" said Amiel, speaking to White River but looking at Ironfoot.

White River waited a moment before he answered. This was no place for long talking. "He's been tryin' to spook 'em. Likely that's our only chance. Now stay together."

"Spook them?" repeated Marcher.

"You heard right—Injuns are funny. Now don't let anyone straggle. We're likely to lose you if it comes to a run." He pushed Ironfoot forward and shortening the hold he had on his own rein started running after him.

The darkness seemed to have lifted slightly. White River remembered the moon would rise well before dawn and would raise the already oppressive odds against them a trifle more. He tried to think ahead. In all the casting about of his mind, he found but one comfort. Ironfoot was right, this was their only chance, and he himself would not have thought of it. Daybreak would surely bring death in one form or another to all of them. And it would be the death he had thought of so often. Death taking taste from a man's mouth, light from his eyes, hope from his secret heart. Surprising himself, he decided he did not want to die, he did not want to die at all. This mission, crazy as it was, might still serve his purpose.

Ducking along behind Ironfoot, he tried to reason out their predicament. Indians fought at night when they had to, but the salvation of a warrior's spirit required daylight, and this superstition ran particularly high when a brave's medicine was uncertain or weak. What they had fought back there were a few scouts with their hearts in their mouths, trying to pick up a quick coup before the surround and general slaughter that must come at dawn. Ironfoot, knowing this, had tried the ghost medicine, ever a difficult thing to do, which even when done well did not always work.

White River started to piece together what he could. The weird cry that sounded like no other cry, animal or human, in this land. That must have been the start of it or perhaps Ironfoot killed a Sioux first. Then the moving backward in that strange motion to make tracks that appeared to be going the other way, making it seem he killed those he approached rather than those following him. Then the great amount of blood that could only have come from opening the stomach and abdomen with a knife and then tearing the walls of flesh as wide as possible with the hands to make it appear that it had been done by claws. And who was to say what else? He thought of the Sioux coming on this scene in the morning—matters would be decided then.

So rapt was he in his own thinking he failed to remark their direction, but now he knew they were going north again. Surely Ironfoot would turn in time. Surely he was doing this to bluff the Sioux. But the night wore on and the stars denied his prediction. Finally Ironfoot stopped and mounted his pony. White River suddenly drew up beside him. "Figurin' on goin' east now, I reckon." Ironfoot turned and looked long and curiously toward the east, where the coming moon had already lightened the oppressive mantle of night with its feeble outer aura of pale light. "The heart of Ironfoot does not lie there," he said as though in simple explanation.

White River felt a faint sensation of shock. For a moment he had forgotten there was not a single command or warning he could give to Ironfoot. This Crow was not interested in living. He stayed alive only to reach Black Shield's grave and would probably stay alive after that only if the grave or lack of it gave him a reason to. His suggestion that they try for safety now had only momentarily confused the Crow.

"My brother goes toward the rising sun," Ironfoot said looking at the star to the north. "May the Great Spirit be with him."

Marcher and Amiel had come up. Marcher, seeing Ironfoot already upon his pony, climbed with effort upon his own mount. "Time we did some riding." Weariness and irritation were struggling for command of his voice.

Amiel's first words raised the problem. "I think we'd better stop for a bit—Andy is awfully weak."

"I'm fine," said Marcher.

"What are your plans? Or do we have any?" said Amiel ignoring Marcher.

White River looked about him in the dark. He would have liked to say, Any man's plan is a gamble now—if you're feeling lucky, make your own. But he felt the wind slowly breezing up, bringing against his face from somewhere far off the bite of high mountain air, and behind him the coming moon was feeding enough light now to ease the darkness and betray the great openness that stretched about them. In the end he said, "We can't stay here."

"Where then?" Amiel's voice promised to pursue the point.

"Ironfoot's goin' north. The rest of us can swing east and try for the river again. We won't get far. We have mebbe an hour or so left before daylight, but then again, lots of folks would allow as how we have a parcel of nerve even bein' alive."

"If Ironfoot's going north, I'm going with him," declared Marcher.

"You sure we'll be followed?" continued Amiel as though Marcher hadn't spoken.

"Can't rightly say." White River looked about him again in a way that said he was beginning to grow uneasy.

Amiel drew his hand across his face. "We all need rest . . . sleep."

"What the hell do you want to do, Ben, out with it!" Marcher's voice crackled with the strain of his own desperation.

"I want to stop this insane suicidal business from going any further! I don't know what's happened to you, Andy, and now, by Jesus, I don't give a damn, but there isn't one of us fit to travel and we're at least two days hard riding from safety—four lives are at stake here and all you can think about is that blasted mine!"

"If that's what's got you bleating like a whipped pup—go to hell back. I'm not afraid of going it alone!"

"Mount up—we've got to get out of here," commanded White River. Instinct told him to look for cover. It might be more important now than distance. They could not get far enough with what was left of the night to make a difference, and if they were not followed, cover from the eyes of stray hunters or runners might be their salvation in the end.

Amiel was still on the ground looking up. "We can't go much further now." His voice was void of compromise.

White River swung his mount around. "We'll hunt cover and see if mebbe . . ."

"Hoot! Hoot!" Ironfoot's call hammered silence into the party with the abruptness of a sledge. Everyone stood as though paralyzed. White River tilted his chin a fraction in the air. The wind had shifted. It was coming now directly from the north. Out of the corner of his eye he tried to trace Ironfoot's form in the darkness, but could not make him out. How long they stood there would have been hard to say, but after long, long moments White River was aware that Ironfoot was motioning him forward in the dark. He urged the bay cautiously with his knees and came up.

At Ironfoot's side he could see Ironfoot sniffing the air. Without a word he did the same, then looked at the Crow. "What is it?"

Ironfoot made some sign that was surely part of his secret medicine prayer before he said, "Buffalo."

Buffalo! White River smelled again and, now alerted for it, he caught the faintest trace of a high, gamey scent that was wafting thin as a spirit through the wind. By God, it was buffalo.

"Where do you reckon they be?" If anyone had asked White River this question he would have thought it was a damn foolish one. But Ironfoot put his face into the wind again and seemed to be calling upon senses that ignored the darkness and easily transformed a dim knowledge, hanging only on a thread of odor in the wind, into an understanding that rose without any reasoning to its own dawning.

"Buffalo come here," said Ironfoot at last. The scent had strengthened now and White River knew the herd had turned with the wind, following an instinct conceived in some remote crevice of another epoch when the deadly winds of the north herded some puzzled forebear toward the south. Ironfoot was making motions with his hands in the air again. "Heap good medicine!"

"How do you figure?"

Ironfoot raised his hand without looking back. "Come . . . we go . . . quick."

Hearing their words, Marcher and Amiel had come up. "What now?" said Amiel, expectancy edging his voice.

"Buffalo," said White River abruptly. "Mount and follow close up." There was some relieved excitement in his voice. Within minutes Marcher and Amiel had worked their way to either side of him. Even they could now smell the gamey musk of the herd.

"We going to hunt?" called Marcher, his tone telling of his confusion.

White River was riding with his face into the north wind, his eyes trying to ferret out in the light of a now visible half-moon the forward drift of the herd. Ironfoot must have found it already for he was moving to the left and turning in his saddle to look beyond them into the direction in which they had come. It was clear now what Ironfoot was going to try.

"Well?" shouted Marcher again.

The lowing of the herd was audible now. White River reckoned it to be a big one. "No . . . no huntin'," he finally threw at Marcher. Now the forward drifts of the animals were visible and Ironfoot was riding right toward them. There was little danger of disturbing the beasts at this point, for they were coming straight downwind and the buffalo's sight is one of the poorest on the plains. Almost at the rim of the herd, which was coming slowly toward them, Ironfoot dismounted. The others coming up followed suit. The roar of the herd had increased now to where hearing each other was becoming a problem and the horses were getting rank.

Ironfoot spoke to White River for a moment. Then White River signaled for Marcher and Amiel to come together. "There's a heap of rock about five hundred yards inside this herd—we're headin' for it. Now hold tight to your horses. They can smell buffalo but the buffalo can't smell them. If the herd spooks, don't go with it—burn leather for those rocks."

The lead animals were upon them now and Ironfoot was moving determinedly between two bulls, courageously weaving his way into the thick, dark herd. They followed close behind, hearing apprehensively the quick rise in the bellowing about them. But the herd did not change its pace. Several animals lifted their heads and stood motionless, a few looking at them, some almost close enough to touch. One bull turned meaningfully for a moment, then pushed his way into the herd and disappeared.

But their scent was being picked up behind them, and now a regular din was beginning to laden the air. Ironfoot quickened his pace, for they had come upon an opening in the herd caused by the rocks standing clearly in the moonlight ahead. As he came up to them he slipped from his saddle and pulled it from the pony, releasing a thin, worn blanket damp with sweat. This he took with him to the top of one of the rocks and opened it in the wind.

He was standing looking south at the moon-bathed plain, as White River, Marcher, and Amiel joined him. Seeing the dark herd all about them gave each some unaccountable sense of security. "God—this is a big herd!" gasped Amiel.

"Can't be big enough," White River almost shouted. The din to the south was still increasing. Ironfoot pointed below them out near the rim of the herd. White River, studying the point, saw finally a big black hulk that must have been a master bull swinging in front of the herd and moving over to where the roaring was beginning to shake the air. Here he hesitated for a moment, raising his great head into the night. He was reading their scent.

The great bull pawed the ground for a moment, then, shaking his immense horned head, turned about and bellowed deep and sonorously as he started a new swinging gait to the south and away from the scent. The herd began to lumber behind him, the new, quicker movement rippling through the dark sea of humped backs on every side. Soon, a sound like low thunder replaced the bellowing and the land about them seemed to be flowing forward as far as the eye could see. The lead bull was lost from sight, but the great herd was now trekking south and it would be miles and miles before it would be fully slowed to graze again.

"Pretty risky way to get rid of tracks," said Amiel, looking about him in wonderment. "But those animals are certainly a magnificent sight—my God, look at them!"

"Think it will work?" said Marcher unaccountably holding his rifle at the ready.

"Ought to be nigh as good as a blizzard," said White River rubbing the back of his neck like a man feeling fatigue. "Be daylight soon. Make sure those horses are fast and get some sleep . . . we got to move as soon as this herd runs out." White River followed Amiel's gaze to Ironfoot, who was down now uttering a medicine chant that could not be heard over the rumbling about them.

Marcher was rubbing his left shoulder, moving the arm up and down. It was almost normal again except for an ugly bruise that bred a fierce stabbing pain under the pressure of his fingers. He was swearing to himself.

White River, finally seeing Ironfoot rise, came toward him. "Reckon this is goin' to do it?"

Ironfoot nodded. "Buffalo plenty good medicine."

"Think this herd will get by before dawn?"

Ironfoot looked to the northwest where the herd was still moving toward them out of the darkness. "Plenty buffalo," he said noncommittally.

"Well, we can't stay here come daylight."

Ironfoot squatted down, White River beside him. After a moment or two the Crow said they would wait till the buffalo thinned out. Then they would spread out, leaving the least possible sign, and follow the trail of the buffalo into the northwest until they reached cover. White River asked again when the Crow figured they could leave. Ironfoot was silent. He thought this herd, large as it seemed, would pass before the sun would rise like a blazing shield and reclaim the world. But he could not be sure. In his boyhood he had seen herds so large they took days to pass, but that was long ago when the sky was a sacred blue and the sage-colored grass was tall upon the prairie . . . long, long ago, before the whites came and altered the Great Spirit's laws of life. In the end he said, "Ironfoot make good medicine—buffalo brother to the Absarokee, they hear."

White River stood up and turned away. He knew now his question was unanswerable, remembering wryly again that most questions that mattered in life were. Well, he needed a quick sleep. Fatigue was fraying his senses and making everything unnaturally heavy. He wedged himself between two rocks, noticing for the first time that the north wind was bringing a new chill into the air. He sniffed at it before he fell asleep. The weather was due for a change. God, how the seasons spiraled on, washing over the land, bestowing birth, decreeing death, in themselves the only consistent and visible will of the unknown, for to be sure they served no heart of man.

22

The little band that gathered in the hard dawn on the wooded hill with a rock facing seeping water were not saved by the buffalo. They were saved by the dream of Yellow Knife, the Minneconjou shaman. They would never know Yellow Knife, but he was Stone Maker's cousin and a man of many medicine dreams and magic spells, the people sitting in silence as he recounted his visions. Many wise ones said the Great Spirit spoke through the dreams and spells of Yellow Knife.

He had a dream the night before his powerful cousin, Stone Maker, left the Sioux camp. He told it in the morning to Wandisapa and Stone Maker, who came with their faces freshly painted, the impatient Minneconjous anxious to pursue the Arapahos crowding behind them. He made the many secret medicine signs as he talked, telling them they would meet a strange spirit on this journey, that they would not see this spirit but he would be there. He was neither good nor evil, but if he gave them a sign of anger, they were to come back.

Wandisapa and Stone Maker looked at him warily.

"Why do we not win the heart of this spirit before we go?" grunted Wandisapa, who knew of Yellow Knife's powers but suspected some of his spells had been inspired by whiskey. "Can we not make our sacrifices, our secret pledges to him?"

"He is a warrior spirit," said Yellow Knife cagily. "His heart cannot be won with presents."

Wandisapa wanted to say: *Bah! Is this a time for spirits that cannot be appeased with presents, pledges? We are at war!* But he gathered his robe about him in silence, knowing too well that such words would only put a shadow of bad medicine over his war party, the braves feeling that the spirit was angered and would turn against them.

"My cousin does well to bring us his strong medicine dream," said Stone Maker. "If we catch these Arapahos with the serpent's tongue, we will know your spirit is with us."

Yellow Knife did not share this spirit's taboo concerning presents. Stone Maker gave him a fine spotted pony before he left, Wandisapa grunting in faint derision as the pony was led off.

"He has great power," cautioned Stone Maker, his eyes fine slits that looked out on the retiring pony.

A vision of Red Moon with the many-shots gun in his hand crossed Wandisapa's mind. "It is not his kind of power we need, my brother."

The Minneconjou war party moved swiftly over the trail of the Arapahos, the braves eager for a fight but none completely forgetting the words of Yellow Knife. His strange spirit might be leading them, but Yellow Knife himself stayed in camp. An eagle coming from behind them and circling around to fly back in the same direction was sensed by some to be a sign to return, but Wandisapa said evenly that the spirit had sent the eagle to guide them to the enemy and having seen the enemy right before them as it circled knew it was not needed and returned home. Stone Maker said nothing.

The following morning a lone horseman was spotted to the east, but the scouts rushing up could find no trace of him. "It is the strange spirit watching us," said some, making a medicine sign. Others kept their thoughts to themselves as Wandisapa urged them forward muttering, "Come! We were looking into the sun. Was it not difficult to see? We could have been mistaken."

Stone Maker rode close beside him. "Do not talk so, my brother. There was a horseman. This much you and I know."

Wandisapa's eyes fought for sanity. "Is this then Yellow Knife's strange spirit? Does my brother say this?"

Stone Maker looked at him long and hard. "Stone Maker hopes this horseman was Yellow Knife's spirit—and not some Cheyenne sent to warn these Arapaho dogs."

The fury fled from Wandisapa's face and in a moment was replaced by a hard, sober cast. Wandisapa shook his head; he should have known. Stone Maker was right. Was not this land filled with traitors, were not these days burdened with betrayals that withered a man's will to fight and left the heart empty and weary of hope?

But Stone Maker was caught up with another concern. He was watching the braves move silently forward, secretly studying the terrain to the east and fingering their medicine bags. As a leader of men, he sensed trouble in the making. Wandisapa had been wrong. There was a horseman. It was foolish to deny what seasoned eyes knew to be so. How much better to have said the horseman was a Cheyenne scout sent with Black Water's warning to his friends, for surely this was the probable truth. Now it was too late. Once faith in their senses has been shaken in men going into battle, it cannot easily be restored. As he looked about him he could see in the eyes of some that this obscure fear had mounted the steed of imagination—it was only a matter of time before both would grow until a hoofbeat of dread deafened all other faculties of the mind.

Toward evening they came into a hilly place. The trail of the Arapahos had not grown fresher, so Stone Maker decided to travel that night in the hopes that if they continued south, they would overtake them by morning.

They sat quietly eating the *wasna* until the sun set. Then Wandisapa sang a strong-heart song while the braves chanted along in low guttural tones. But suddenly Stone Maker raised his arm. It was time to go. Scouts were sent ahead on foot. Travel at night required wolves to be far ahead of the main party to make up for the loss of vision. It was dangerous work. Night Dancer, whose medicine was said to be especially strong in the dark, was sent ahead with five seasoned warriors, Stone Maker again repeating the wolf calls they would use to signal danger.

When the main party finally started after them it had gone but a short distance when the first wolf call came alive in the dusk. It was followed quickly by three more that meant the enemy was coming toward them. "Hou!" said Wandisapa. "Will the antelope try his horns against the bear?"

Stone Maker ordered them from their ponies and started leading them stealthily forward on foot. This did not smell to him like Arapahos. As a seasoned warrior he knew the importance of seeing the face of the enemy before the battle was joined. In time he stopped. Why were there no more wolf calls? Why had Night Dancer not sent back a scout with word? The braves hung still in the darkness, the auguries of Yellow Knife's dream riding hard upon them. Then the Sioux war whoop lifted the night in the distance and a sudden movement in the brush before them became the figure of Broken Leg, one of their wolves.

"Speak!" said Stone Maker in a hushed command.

Broken Leg was nearly breathless. "Whites—three of them. Night Dancer has trapped them among some rocks."

"Who attacks?" demanded Wandisapa, the echo of the war whoop still in his ears.

"Our brothers—they will strike many great coups."

The braves began to mutter among themselves, growing restless at this mention of easy and profitable work for the war club. Wandisapa silenced them with a hiss. He was seething again. Would these braves never learn that wolves are not sent out to fight? "Are these whites armed?"

"There are many guns among them."

"Then why do we not hear them?"

Broken Leg looked behind him. He had no answer for this strange thing. Surely whites with courage enough to come so far into Sioux country would have gotten off a shot or two.

"*Ayeeeee!* We have won a great victory!" said one of the braves standing close.

"Our people are not so quiet in victory," said Wandisapa, knowing at once this too was a mistake.

Stone Maker looked long into the darkness. "We will go forward carefully. Let no one speak or shoot until Stone Maker gives the hunting yip of the wolf."

No sooner had he spoken than a weird, unnatural cry rose in the distance. The braves heard it, held still for a second, then shifted uneasily. What then was this?

Wandisapa looked forward into the darkness again, this time his anger was thick in his throat. "It is a trick!" he said hoarsely.

Stone Maker stood silently beside him. He thought with Wandisapa that this was surely a trick, but still there was something seriously wrong here. Where were their scouts? Why had they not signaled? He drew a breath of air and gave the two loud wolf howls that meant *Where are you*? No sound rose in answer in the silence that followed. A dangerous murmuring started among the braves.

"They are stalking the enemy and cannot betray themselves," snapped Wandisapa with a tinge of fury.

"Is this not then the cry of Yellow Knife's spirit?" hissed one of the braves.

"It is our warriors twisting the tongue from a captive white," ranted Wandisapa, making little of the fear in the other's words.

Stone Maker grunted in caution.

The weird cry rang out again.

Some of the braves began to move back to the horses.

"Who calls himself a warrior this night?" shouted Wandisapa cuttingly, his acid tone reaching out to sting the warriors through the darkness. But they were under a far more sinister lash now. The day of anxious wondering had hatched many fantasies, each seeming harmless as it rose to flutter a moment and then roost at the edge of the mind. But now flocks of them rising together were far too much for even the strongest medicine to call back a man's courage.

"It is enough," said Stone Maker under his breath. He had seen braves preyed on by such fearful premonitions desert war parties before. It was a bad thing to have happen. It weakened a chief's place among his warriors. It made the people restless with him when he rose in council.

"We will camp by our ponies," he said evenly. "At dawn we will raise our war clubs against these snakes who crawl unbidden across our lands. Tomorrow we will count many coups, all will be good."

Mumbles of assent along with grunts of relief rose from the warriors, who moved quickly back to the horses. By dawn Stone Maker sensed a few might be gone but he hoped not many. Daylight would surely stiffen the hearts of the fierce Minneconjous.

Wandisapa turned to him in the dark with near-agony in his voice. "Are we children that we let our many warriors sit under their blankets out of fear for a handful of whites?"

"It is not the whites."

Wandisapa looked around in the dark. He knew there was no helping matters; night was a forbidding time to die. To the warriors it meant a spirit forever wandering instead of one at peace in the great victory lodge that blazed beyond the stars. Though many a brave would risk it once success seemed assured, few could be brought to dare if the matter lay in doubt. He sighed in grim resignation. "The Arapahos have picked their enemies well."

"It is not a thing to be met with anger."

"Let us smoke, then. I would hear what is in my brother Stone Maker's heart, for the heart of Wandisapa is on the ground."

Stone Maker looked strangely into the darkness toward where the weird cries had risen. Then he looked up at the pitch-black night that engulfed them. "I would like to look upon his face," he said thoughtfully.

"His face? Whose? The face of Yellow Knife's supposed spirit?"

"No. Night Dancer's."

At first light, Wandisapa and Stone Maker led the watchful and wary braves into the rock pocket. An old wolf scampered away from the body of a dead Minneconjou as they appeared. In time the bodies of the three disemboweled warriors were discovered, the last being Night Dancer's, his head almost wrenched from his body, his features hideous in death. The moon was still prominent in the sky as light flooded the east. It was a strange moment. Wandisapa and Stone Maker stood together and chanted as the sun rose, some of the braves joining in.

"I will go alone," said Wandisapa as they finished. "The will for war has left the hearts of my people."

"Stay with us," said Stone Maker. "There will be another time for our tomahawks—a new day when the taste for battle rises strong again in our mouths."

Wandisapa looked about him. Yellow Knife's spirit was as alive in the eyes of these warriors as the brilliant sun now fast stripping the secretive darkness from the land. All about them was open sign that these whites were merely men, led by a daring Indian who in desperation had attempted the ghost medicine. But all that was of no avail. He had no words for his feelings, but recalled that many years ago a dark-robed white had tried to tell him that superstition sees only what supports it. Ah, were the whites not wise and lucky to have but one God and he always with them, from birth to death. Theirs was a constant ally, a mighty one, who did not permit minor spirits meddling in the way of things.

"I will go south," said Wandisapa. "There are whites along the river." He pulled his pony closer to him. "If the Arapahos delay, I will teach them to talk with straight tongues."

"My brave brother should return with us," said Stone Maker clearly. "Our people need you."

"A man is what is in his heart—my people do not need what is in my heart today."

Stone Maker dug his moccasin into the earth. "Does my brother send words to his lodge?"

The war chief looked to the north, to the land of hard yellow rock and coursing streams and the great stretches of earth that he had always felt would one day claim him again. They seemed far away now and like this dawning a little unreal. The hunts, the taking of Blue Wind as his bride, the calling to council, the *heyoka* dances, the village set stirring in the early morning by excited children when it was known that they would travel that day to a favorite place. Somehow he seemed apart from it as though only his spirit was looking back on a fruitless life bereft of meaning.

Stone Maker grunted anxiously.

"Tell the people not to wait for me," said Wandisapa firmly. "Tell them Wandisapa has followed his heart and has gone the warrior's way."

Murmurs of shock and protest rose swiftly from the braves on every side, but Wandisapa's hand was in the air. "Wait!" he cried, "three Minneconjous will not see their lodges again because my medicine was weak. I do not wish to hear their squaws keening in the darkness. There are other strong ones to lead you. Listen to their words."

Stone Maker was standing tall before him. "Brother, is there not a sickness of spirit that comes for a time upon great warriors when they look upon defeat? Wandisapa, let us smoke. Then we shall hunt for fresh meat. In time all will be good."

Wandisapa turned and mounted his pony. A murmur of sadness slipped through the warriors. Stone Maker stood like a man weary of life, his heart embittered and heavy in him, his mind seeing ahead to the scenes of his village that now must come. But there was no hope to stand against it. An Indian's right to choose his own time to die was sacred.

"Hou!" said Wandisapa to those about him. "Hear me now. You will not hear me speak again. I have been your war leader these many seasons. I have led you against the Crees, the Assiniboines, the Crows and have twice counted coup on the hated whites. I have been mighty in battle, but a thing is in my heart now and it speaks to me as the voice of the Great Spirit. Remember me as a warrior, remember me only as you see me go from you now." With that he raised his voice in a great war cry, one to make the air tremble and pick at the skin along the spine. Then with his mount rearing high in the air, he swung about and started from them singing loudly a brave-heart song that told once again of man's ancient faith that for the true warrior total victory and glory can only find their full measure in death.

23

In the first gray of morning, Ironfoot pointed to the dark hump of mountain the Sioux called Innyan Kara. They were approaching it from the east and its black eminence looked in the dim light like the back of a giant buffalo sleeping on the plain.

White River came up alongside Ironfoot and looked at the sky. Ironfoot grunted. There were only a few minutes left when they could risk moving about. Ironfoot had caught sight of a dark oval cap of foliage in the dip just ahead. It spoke of water. He was making for it silently. White River did not speak; there had been few words that night. Though they were all weary, they wore their weariness now as men do an injured limb that in the press of life must first be accepted and then finally ignored. It was the knowledge that Ironfoot had grown markedly morose that took their thoughts now.

He had returned with a deer he had brought down with his bow the evening before, dropping it silently, slumping down beside it to hold his head in his hands, refusing to talk, eat. White River waved the others off to a low fire where parts of the freshly killed deer were hurriedly scorched and eaten. White River did not have to be told that Ironfoot was suffering from bad medicine, but he also knew there was no helping it. Ironfoot had seen some sign during his hunt, a diving bird, a silent, watchful wolf, the strange behavior of a snake, and whatever its significance, whatever it put him in mind of, it had left the brave with his spirit shaken.

In the dip they spread out, making do with scant space. White River quietly noticed there was no ready place to post a lookout.

Marcher's motions told of a new excitement that had taken him. He settled between White River and the Crow.

"We're there—aren't we!"

"Likely," said White River, not looking up.

Marcher had the map in his hand. He spread it out on the ground and a new energy lightened his voice. "This looks like it might fit the landmarks scratched out here."

White River threw a glance at the oft-studied map. "If this be it—shouldn't be more 'n a half mile yonder."

"Good, let's get started," said Marcher, folding his map again.

Ironfoot grunted.

White River rose and looked about him. "We sure don't figure to find it come dark," he said quietly. Even Marcher knew his words were directed at Ironfoot.

"Come on—I'm ready." Marcher's voice sounded like steam hissing through the now growing dawn.

"No take pony," said Ironfoot.

"No—we'd best hoof it," agreed White River, moving to take his rifle from his saddle. "Comin'?" he said idly to Amiel.

"Not on your life."

"It's been a long trip—this may be the only high doin's."

"I hate to tell you, but I hope you don't find it." Amiel was studying the ground, looking for a suitable place to sleep. He moved slowly, his weariness showing in every move he made.

"We will," rasped Marcher defiantly. Then to White River, "Come on!"

It looked at first as though Ironfoot were not planning to accompany them, but as White River turned to go, he found himself behind Ironfoot at the west end of the dip, peering through the foliage, obviously preparing to move out on the slope of the plain that rolled in an unbroken sweep to the hills in the southwest.

Less than a half hour later, they were standing with the sun upon them at the second gully that meandered to the south, its way marked unevenly by little exposed places that were usually in the crook of a bend where spring waters had swirled about and reached down to the rock face below the soil.

White River surveyed the long quiet reaches about them. A few birds were working back and forth over the plain and a hawk drifted high over Innyan Kara, but beyond that nothing moved.

White River looked at the map Marcher had opened again and held in his hand. "We might's well spread out," he said, shifting his rifle and looking warily at the sun. "Marcher, you and Ironfoot can work down this gully. I'll work up—if you see anythin' try to keep it a secret, we ain't exactly set up for sudden company."

They moved apart almost soundlessly, Marcher watching the ground for a telltale pile of rocks, White River and Ironfoot sweeping the wash in short stretches, then warily patrolling the land on either side. It was many hours before they worked back together again, Marcher swearing quietly to himself.

"Take it you come up dry," said White River. Then, not waiting for an answer, he pointed to a break that cut across the land to the south. "Might be that's worth a look."

Ironfoot looked at the stretch of land to the east from which they had come. White River turned his gaze that way too but saw nothing. The noon sun had lost some of its strength with the shifting of seasons and the land was easier to look at. But it was empty and still and hinted at no threat he could see.

"Company?" he said idly, noticing Ironfoot was still looking.

"Eagle," said Ironfoot simply.

Thus guided, White River lifted his eyes above the land and finally saw a speck that grew larger as it moved slowly at an angle to them and passed to the southwest. There it circled slowly and went east again.

"Likely huntin'," said White River.

Ironfoot said nothing but instead looked hard to the south where White River had noticed the break. White River did not press him. This country had a language all its own. Sometimes it shouted, sometimes it whispered, and sometimes its only signal was silence. Its main means of expression, however, was its game. Animals, particularly large ones, rarely ran. When they did they had a reason. Unless they were young or rutting or on the attack, their movements were nearly always a slow perpetual quest for food. If one got a feel for their ways early in life it never quite left. But the birds took a subtler eye, perhaps because they often carried the subtlest messages of all. An eagle could see vast distances and as a sentinel had no peer in the land. A Mandan Christian had once told White River that the eyes of an eagle were second only to the eyes of God.

"Quick," muttered Ironfoot finally, nodding at the break. "We look quick, then all go."

They moved off over the plain to the south. Here they shortly found another dry stream bed and began to work along it. An hour slipped by and White River began to wonder at the folly of delaying longer. Ironfoot repeatedly scanned the sky overhead, obviously waiting for the eagle to reappear. At times he looked long and hard toward the east, where a haze was gathering and the unnerving silence still held its grip on the land.

Marcher went from rock to rock almost as though he fully expected to find messages written upon them or that they would by some magic whisper a secret they had long held for his coming. But as time went by his temper heated up, and he kicked savagely at the earth where a rock proved nothing more than a rock. Ironfoot seemed to show the least interest in the search, yet it was he who stopped at a long, sweeping turn in the dry bed after the others had wandered ahead and called them back with a meaningful grunt.

White River and Marcher swung about and then retraced their steps, both wondering what the Crow could have found in a stretch where so little could have been missed.

They found him with his toe pointing to a long brown object that White River saw at close inspection was a bone. "Man bone," said Ironfoot noncommittally. Marcher looked at it and then about him with incredulity. "This can't be it—it's supposed to be a grave—a mound of rocks!"

White River studied the ground above them, sobered by what he had missed in passing before. Ironfoot had clearly got his clue from the rocks that lay about them beyond the rim of the wash. Someone must have thrown them there. There was simply no other way they could have moved from the dry bed. White River smiled faintly at Ironfoot. "Look's likely enough, we'd best smell around here real careful—got a feelin' we're a mite late, though."

"Hell—this can't be it!" argued Marcher.

"Season or two can make a heap of changes in a makeshift grave—'special when there be varmints 'round to help." White River began moving slowly over the ground, Ironfoot doing the same. Only Marcher stood contemplating them as though they were losing their reason.

Ironfoot in time grunted and kneeled to pull up what turned out to be some finger bones lying almost concealed in the reddish earth. Neither he nor White River said any more. They saved that until they turned up half a skull, lying just beyond the lip of the wash, meshed firmly in a clump of dried grass with several blades growing through it. Ironfoot did not touch it, but White River worked it up and turned it over in his hand. The skull had been split by a sharp instrument and beneath it lay a small section of jawbone containing three teeth, one of them gold.

"Varmints 'pear to have gotten a heap of help, reckon," said White River resignedly.

"You two trying to say this is Paul's grave . . . that that's Paul . . . his skull?" sputtered Marcher.

"It's a white man's," said White River.

"How do you know?"

"Injuns don't come by gold teeth to my rememberin'."

"Even so, that doesn't make it Paul!"

"Likely him—or what's left of him."

"Could be anybody."

"Marcher, there ain't been five white men passed this spot since creation. Everything fits . . . signs are clear as hell. There was a pile of rocks over this till someone pitched 'em off and used a hatchet where it weren't needed no more."

"I don't believe it, not if he was dead. Why would anyone do that to a dead man?"

"Oh, Injuns will carve up a dead one quick as they will a live one—once't they got the notion."

Ironfoot was looking to the east again. "We go now," he said tautly.

"What about the crucifix?" shouted Marcher. "That's got to be around here somewhere—aren't we even going to look for it?"

"We go," said Ironfoot, his voice dropping low now in a way that was meant to remind Marcher that for them secrecy was one with survival. The effort was wasted, for Marcher shouted again.

"I'll be damned if I'm running off—go if you want to, but I'll be damned if I'm a bloody enough fool to risk my neck for months getting to this blasted spot and then go running off without even a decent look!"

"You seen all you're likely to," said White River. Somehow he knew this would be the way of it from the beginning. Anger was beginning to stir in him. If Marcher wished to stay he could, but Ironfoot was clearly reading trouble in the air and now he himself could feel something in the deep of him vaguely signaling, telling him that it had been too quiet too long.

"You've forgotten they wouldn't take his crucifix," challenged Marcher, the gauntness about his eyes seeming to grow deeper. "They consider it bad medicine."

"Best you forget talk such as that—Injuns just naturally figure a dead man's gear to be their own."

"I was told they're scared to death of one—think it brings the white man's curse. By God, I bet they probably threw it around here somewhere."

"We go," said Ironfoot and for the first time an inkling of impatience and impending fear rode in his voice.

"We're headin' back," said White River with finality. "You can stay if you're a mind to, but we figure to be leavin' at sundown. If you're not back by then—cut your own trail."

"Damn!" Marcher's eyes seemed to try to transfix them, but they were shifting about, uneasy at something unknown and unmindful of him.

"And keep an eye peeled, hear!" White River looked to the east, then glanced over the wash where Paul's bones were strewn. "Trouble 'pears to cotton to this place."

Ironfoot had already started to move away. White River fell in behind him.

Evening began with three crows, alerted by their sentry's call high in a cottonwood somewhere, rising noisily from the decayed remains of a jackrabbit they had been feeding upon on the open plain.

White River's eyes blinked open. He had been dozing, preparing for the night's travel, thinking vaguely of the consequences of Marcher's disappointment. He found Ironfoot standing above him looking in the direction of the raucous crow.

"Trouble?" he said in the controlled and hushed tone that had become almost constant between them. The long weeks of imminent danger had schooled all outward emotion into submission.

"Him not come back!" responded Ironfoot with an urgency that said that trouble was there. White River looked to the south. There was a slight rise in the land that would cover Marcher until he had gained the last quarter of a mile. "A fool with gold on his mind gits powerful careless," he said half to himself.

Amiel was asleep on the other side of the dip.

White River stood beside Ironfoot and gazed with him upon the far hills to the east. "What d' you figure—somebody workin' our trail?"

Ironfoot looked away impassively for a moment then back. "No, village come, big village."

"Village?"

Ironfoot pointed eastward to a far reach of plain and to what looked like a thin shadow that should have been only a harmless harbinger of night. It was some moments before White River realized that it was moving slowly, like a drugged serpent. A large village on the march. So it was this that had been moving toward them all day, this that Ironfoot had sensed as it approached, aware of its coming almost as soon as that vanished eagle.

"Well, I'll be," he half whistled. "Come to think of it though—it's a sight better-looking than a war party. If they anyways knew we was here they wouldn't be amblin' along out there like that."

Ironfoot did not answer. War parties came out of villages that size like bees out of a jarred hive. He knew White River knew this too but was working toward an argument to wait for Marcher. This was a serious risk in Ironfoot's troubled mind. With evening coming on that village would have to stop any moment. It was already late in the day for a village to be on the march. They must be driven by something important. But once settled, their camp would spread out in every direction; young boys and braves immediately herding the horses out to graze. Sentinels would have to be posted, for they were near enough to Crow country to expect night raiders or even outright attack. Marcher, where he was, was likely to be discovered. Afoot, his loss would be certain, but seasoned and trail-wise warriors would know he did not come afoot. In time they would discover the dip, the horse tracks, and then their weeks of stealth would be wasted.

"Me go," said Ironfoot, starting toward the south and Marcher.

"No, you best stay here," said White River, opening the breech of his rifle and blowing it clean. "If it comes to a rumpus, get movin'." He moved up the side of the dip. "Wake up Amiel and get him ready. Might be we have to get shut of this place real sudden."

He bent low as he looped over the ground heading south, grateful for the shadows thrown by the nearby mountain. When he reached high ground he could see the dark stream that had been the moving village working itself into a ball and growing larger. That could only mean they were making camp, that they would for various reasons drift far out onto the plain about them and that the menace had mounted. Why wasn't that damned Marcher coming?

He kept on, wondering when he came to the second break why he saw no sign of the other. Surely he had not wandered farther, surely he had not forgotten the direction they had come from. Marcher had learned a lot in these past weeks. White River doubted if he could be lost here in such simple terrain. Yet he was not in sight, and that seemed the only answer until White River came to the final wash and there he found Marcher at the spot where the bones had been discovered, lying flat on the ground, a knife in his hand with which he was gently spading dirt. There was something unnatural about him. White River approached slowly, but Marcher spoke only when White River's boots loomed within inches of his face.

"Came back, eh?"

"Get up."

"I'm digging."

"There's a Sioux village asquattin' down not more 'n a mile or two from here. They figure to be over here like itchy ants any moment makin' sure they got this patch to themselves."

Marcher looked at him vaguely for a moment and then went back to digging. "So we're running again, eh. Well, I've got a feeling that André Lewis Marcher is all through with running."

"Not if he figures to stay alive he ain't."

"Poor argument, friend." Marcher pulled something from his pocket and extended it to White River. "You were right, I guess, it was Paul. I dug this out of the earth."

White River took the object, glancing with open concern over his shoulder at the plain beyond. The settling darkness was killing visibility but he could still make out the disturbed and growing area of the camp. Somewhere a drum was already set up and a low beating began to resound.

The object was metal, round, and dull black. The thin rusted thread inside said it was the top of something. Some of its black coating had been scraped off with a knife and he could see writing lay underneath. White River could not make out the writing, but he allowed the disk was silver and badly tarnished.

"Well, what the hell does it say?" He handed it back, his interest elsewhere.

"Victoire."

"What?"

"*Victoire*. It's French. It means victory."

"Get up!"

"You don't understand. It's the lid of a snuffbox Paul used to carry. He put that *victoire* on himself. He used to put it on everything. It was a kind of hobby of his. My mother has a set of kitchen pots that . . ."

"Forget that damn nonsense 'n let's get to humpin'."

Marcher lolled back and looked up at him.

"What for? I failed. I've been nothing but a God damn fool. Ben was right—a God damn fool, taking on like a conquistador and ending up with nothing but the God damn lid of a snuffbox." He ended almost with a laugh. "A God damn fool chasing some other God damn fool's mine. Jesus, blow taps, sound the death march!"

White River looked at him steadily for a moment. The Sioux, real as they were, clearly held little peril for Marcher at that moment. He was like a boxer stunned beyond the fear of another blow.

White River, looking about uneasily, crouched down beside him. "Listen, Marcher, you got here, didn't you?"

"Sure—I got here and what the hell good did it do me?"

"A sight more than your settin' to allow."

"Oh, come now—for Christ's sake! Don't start with any of that sonofabitching nonsense about . . ."

"Some fellows would figure you finally got some rope on the truth."

"What truth?"

"Truth about that uncle of yours—dyin' 'n being buried here 'n all."

"Hell—I knew damn good and well that was true before I left home."

"How?"

"Don't ask me—I just knew it was."

"Well, there could be some of us who don't smell upwind that good—this more 'n likely makes the rest of it true."

"Huh . . . so it does, eh! . . . and after the abuse I've had to listen to . . . sure this proved Paul's partner was telling the truth . . . and if he told the truth about this much why in hell should he be lying about the rest?"

"Figure that way myself—so mebbe now there's a mine to be tracked down."

"Maybe there's a mine to be tracked down?"

"Yep."

"Without the map?"

"There is a map—it's in that crucifix!"

"But . . . oh come on! . . . that's crazy. The crucifix is gone. Where the hell would a man start . . ."

"Don't know. It's a big country for a fact but not as many hands to go around as you think."

The drum in the distance suddenly stopped. In the silence that followed Marcher's voice sounded louder and frighteningly out of place.

"You must take me for an idiot! You're jabbering about something that's—oh, Christ—one chance in a thousand."

White River had him by the arm and was bringing him to his feet, starting to guide them both up the side of the wash. "That's a pretty tolerable chance considerin' the odds if you're fixin' to stay here."

Marcher was quiet and suddenly deep in thought as they paused at a rise of land they had angled behind and from which White River peered toward the east. The plain was dark and seemed empty, except where the village's flickering eyes of fire seemed to brighten at the returning rhythmic throb of a drum.

Ironfoot watched Amiel wake up. The horses had finished feeding and were standing quietly together now. He was glad that the wind was from the west so they would not grow restive at the scent of horses in the village, particularly the stallions, who were bound, considering the season, to catch some mares in heat.

But that village was a mounting menace. He was hoping the excitement of settling camp and its very bigness—Indians grew careless with size—might delay the sending out of wolves. But by morning, at the latest, their presence or their passage through here would be known and this night was their one chance to run for freedom. With a good enough start they should escape easily. The season of war was over, the Lakota moon of Calves-Turning-Black was upon them. Energies of horse and man alike would be needed to prepare food for the coming winter. The Sioux were not likely to wander too far from their lodges now unless seriously provoked.

He took himself to the east end of the dip and settled with his back to the other to rebind his braids. Then he put on fresh paint, drawing white lines across his cheeks and a yellow wavy one across his brow. Under his lip he drew a yellow triangle and opening his deerskin shirt made a secret symbol on his chest. As he worked he sang a medicine song to himself, one he had made up during the previous days. One that told of a great burden he carried, a burden that could not be lightened by human hands.

O secret spirit, hear me now
I cry from the mountains
From the wide heart of the land
My heart is silent like a stone long forgotten.
I know you are angry, secret helper,
Your signs say you are very angry.
Ironfoot did not follow the wisdom of his medicine dream
His heart did not go like a true arrow to Black Shield's grave
His secret spirit will not help him now.
His heart is like stone under ice.

He stopped and waited patiently for his sign; none came. He chanted quietly again.

I will wait for a sign, secret helper.
For many snows Ironfoot has made many good pledges—
His heart is waiting.

And now the drum in the village below began to preoccupy him. It was not a dangerous sign. The drummer was obviously getting ready for a gala evening; likely a social dance was going to be held. He would know shortly. But surely they should be on their way.

The darkness was throwing a thin veil over the plain now and in a few minutes movement would be all but impossible to detect. Surely White River and Marcher were waiting for that. But minutes passed and they did not appear.

24

Ironfoot moved noiselessly over the withering growth of the plain. Even though his own sight was limited to a scant fifty feet, he still moved cautiously as though he were visible from half a mile. The presence of that village opened up a dozen dangers, none of which could be reasonably predicted. Had it been a small village, sentries would have been dispatched long ago. But there were other possibilities haunting him. Young and unauthorized war parties avoiding the Sioux warrior societies, the Akicita policing the village, and slipping off at night, coming west toward the land of the Crows and Shoshones. Or braves carrying their sweat lodges out to dream on Innyan Kara. Or young lovers seeking privacy away from the old squaws of the camp. An encounter with any of these would in time ignite the entire camp and its many swift claws would be reaching for them.

The drum in the camp changed its rhythm and now he knew it was a social dance. He could see, as he stood on his toes to peer in that direction, the long line of braves drawn up beside the fire, dancing to and from the line of young girls. The sight of it moved him strangely and he thought of home and Goes-Walking and how she would keep his lodge clean and warm, not even knowing if he would return from such a dangerous mission but perhaps praying to herself he would. Black Shield had been their pride. He was not like Snow Runner, his younger son, who was renowned for his great winter trip but who seldom returned with horses or with scalps to be sung about.

Surely White River and Marcher could not be far now. He moved toward the second break, aware in a dim, uncomfortable way that he was already too far from his horse and getting farther all the time. Ah, this was inviting death. He stopped, deciding in a flash to give his owl hoot twice, their old signal for trouble. It was as much as he could do, if there was no answer he would return and leave. He cupped his hands about his mouth tightly, but the sound of the hunting owl never emerged. Had he been looking anywhere but southward, the call would have gone forth, but his eyes were on the inky horizon and he saw as clearly as break of day a fire arrow leave the horizon, arch upward, and then turn down again. It was surely miles to the south, but it was a signal that was picked up by someone in the village for the drum stopped in the middle of a beat and the fires sputtered and threw sparks frantically, as though hastily beaten, and then went out.

Ironfoot stood motionless in the darkness. His instincts told him that this was too big a thing to be explained by their presence alone. That fire arrow was miles away and would not have been put up because of a handful of strangers found near such a large camp. Something more frightening was happening—his mind struggled for a feeling for the way of this thing, but it was as impenetrable as the night that surrounded him.

In the weird silence that now hung like a pall over the land, the owl hoots seemed all too risky. The village below had clearly read a message in that fire arrow. A bad one. It would send scouts in all directions now to steal surprise from any threat buried in this night. But who or what could threaten the mighty Lakota in their own land? The whites maybe? Striking back for the many killings of the bloody summer?

A movement on his right and slightly ahead made him freeze. Someone was coming. Keeping its outline covered with his body, he brought up his bow. After a moment or two he knew it was White River and Marcher. At last! They came almost directly toward him, but his cover was less complete than he thought. At fifteen feet White River threw himself downward and brought his rifle up.

"Not shoot!" hissed Ironfoot. The figure on the ground brought itself up slowly again, its dim outline becoming that of White River.

"Where's Amiel?" whispered White River, scanning the dark plain. "There's trouble a plenty round here."

Ironfoot motioned for silence and led the way back to the dip. As they approached it, unexpectedly they walked into Amiel crouched thirty feet from the south lip, his hands up in warning. "Listen—we've got company."

White River's face came within inches of his in the dark. "Company? What kind?"

Amiel motioned him to follow. They slipped down into the dip, and as their eyes adjusted to the heavier darkness White River began to make out the form of two squaws slowly walking along the bottom, bent over, apparently picking grass.

"Where'd they come from?" White River whispered.

"They came along the wash," said Amiel with real concern. "Before I knew it, they were just standing looking about. There wasn't much time to think. I hid up there. It was just before that drum stopped. I suppose that means they've been missed."

"No—it's too soon for that. But they will be."

Knowing what had to be done, White River and Ironfoot both crept up stealthily behind the squaws. In what seemed no more than a moment, the Sioux women were sitting back-to-back on the ground, their hands tied behind them.

Both captives looked glumly at the ground, saying nothing. White River lifted one's chin. Though her features were obscured by the dark, she was obviously a young girl and painted for a dance or for some ceremony. The other was an older woman, also painted, but it was too dark to make out the heavy patterns on her face.

"What were they doin'?" he asked abruptly.

"Collecting weeds or something," said Amiel. "Had this basket with them."

A hand-woven basket lay a few feet away, its contents spread awkwardly over the ground. Ironfoot picked up one or two sprigs and then threw them down again.

"Medicine grass," he said coldly. "This one medicine woman." With his bow he pointed to the older one.

At Ironfoot's voice both squaws looked up quickly and now they shifted about with the first hint of unease. White River understood why.

There was no code of chivalry among the Plains Indians. Killing a woman carried almost the same honor as killing a man—an enemy was an enemy. There were few practices the whites were more appalled at. Occasionally a young woman would be kept as a wife or as a slave, but that was more uncommon than thought—and always unpopular with one's own tribeswomen. Ironfoot methodically took out his knife and settled in front of the younger one.

White River was quickly beside him. "We'll take them with us and turn 'em loose come mornin'," he said, a tinge of command tightening his voice.

The tip of Ironfoot's knife picked up the edge of the young girl's ear lobe.

"Who is headman of your village?" he said in halting Sioux.

The girl's head was motionless in the dark, her eyes closed.

The knife point went up a notch.

The girl's eyes blinked open and the bright paint showed where a line had creased her forehead. "Gray Owl," she said sullenly.

"How many lodges in village?"

"Many."

"The Oglala will let this Crow watch his own scalp being danced about their fires," spat the older one.

"You will not be one to see this thing," grunted Ironfoot, removing his knife from the young one's ear and placing it against the older one's throat.

"Easy!" said White River. "A dead medicine woman can fetch more trouble than a barrel of free whiskey."

The blade of Ironfoot's knife was partly covered by loose rolls of fat on the squaw's neck. However, there was pressure behind it and she was clearly fighting an impulse to pull away. Her dark eyes still met Ironfoot's steadily. White River watched this happening, hoping it would soon end. He understood it though. The savage code was to take the power of pain from the enemy's hand and if need be to die in the way which would give him the least pleasure. Ironfoot moved the knife slowly to a more threatening angle. His motion was casual. Patience was required to pare away at the victim's will, but other pressures were mounting. Amiel was coming forward aghast. Even

Marcher was about to speak. White River only silenced them both by indicating Ironfoot's threat was mere bluff, an attempt to get information that might be worth having. Yet even as he did this, he himself was fighting a concern at the passage of time. Surely they had delayed here beyond all reason.

"The fire arrow flies in the south," muttered Ironfoot to the squaw. "What does this thing mean?"

The squaw looked at him. Even in the darkness her determination could be felt. Ironfoot turned the knife another fraction. A strange gurgling could be heard in her throat.

Suddenly the younger one forced her head toward Ironfoot. "It is High Elk and his Cheyennes. They warn our people the black men are coming."

The black men? Ironfoot pondered this, then released the knife. "The Utes?"

"Yes. Runners came to our village many suns ago saying a great war party was coming into our lands. The people of High Elk and Gray Owl have come to meet them."

"That shapes up to be some war party," breathed White River, who was just able to follow the hurried words in Sioux.

Ironfoot looked up at the sky, the tip of the knife now against his own finger. But he questioned the young squaw slyly. "Is there wisdom in war when the grass withers and the frost giant waits behind the wind?"

"They came into Cheyenne country for a great buffalo hunt during the Moon-of-Making-Fat. Some of our warriors helped High Elk's people surround them at a bad time and many scalps were taken. Wounded Bear's two squaws and three sons were killed. Their hearts are bad against us."

Ironfoot stood up, quietly weighing what he had learned. White River stood beside him, following the same line of thought. The Utes, close relatives of the Comanches, and supreme in their mountain fastness to the west, had attempted a hunt on the broad Cheyenne plain spreading out before the Medicine Bow range. It was some time in June. They had been surprised while their men had been spread out and their women and children were busy butchering the kill. Without warning it was suddenly their turn for slaughter and the entire family of their chief, Wounded Bear, had been put to the knife. That alone smacked of desperate losses. Ironfoot would not know until later, but he could imagine now how in the dark valleys and lonely parks, and beneath the tortured clouds that forever seemed impaled upon the snowy knuckles of the great granite peaks, Wounded Bear would sit in his sweat lodge or in some cave he preferred now to his empty tipi and wait as the red pipes of war went far to the west and to the south. In time his tribesmen would begin to appear—a hardy mountain breed with strong and spirited horses. They would come with their faces painted; they would sit about mutely, remaining silent about this massacre of their people but all knowing it must be avenged. Then when the last had gained the camp, a great war dance would be held. And now they were here in the land of the mighty Lakota and the fearless Cheyennes, and whatever the Cheyennes had seen in the south, a great village had suddenly drenched its fires and was hugging the night.

"Get mounted," said White River. "Put these squaws on that extra pony. We'll turn 'em loose at dawn." His knife was busy cutting the bonds at their wrists so the older one could hold to the horse's mane.

"Not leave basket," said Ironfoot scooping the scattered contents back and thrusting the basket up to the younger one perched behind.

"Is there trouble brewing down there?" said Amiel, mounting beside White River and nodding toward the valley.

"Nothing that concerns us."

"Keep together," cautioned White River again. "Sioux will mebbe have troubles of their own come dawn, but don't count on it—now let's get movin'!"

Ironfoot finally led off, holding the rope of the spare pony that carried the two squaws. He seemed more than a little concerned about them and looked back sharply from time to time. White River was well behind. The land about them was level to the sharp slope of the mountains to the west, and the Crow, heading almost directly north, was moving at a pace that indicated his only interest was distance. There was no hope of covering their tracks. They simply had to get beyond reach.

Marcher maneuvered his mount until he was alongside White River. He was full of interest now in what was happening on the plains behind them. White River, glad to see he had shaken off his mood of the wash, was still annoyed at his questioning, and only informed him in curt, staccato phrases of what they had learned from the squaws, then dismissed the subject with, "Reckon it fits likely enough."

"Sounds like they'll be too busy to mess with us for a spell," called Marcher. Then he leaned over his saddle, turning his dark face sideways, making a remark White River would never forget. "Bet that will be a hell of a fight back there—kind of thing a man could hate to miss."

25

The only incident that marred the night came when Ironfoot reined up quickly and swung about to the two squaws. Before the others could circle him, he had released his bow and was whipping both of them soundly.

"What in hell's got into you?" called White River, coming up.

Ironfoot tore the basket from the younger squaw and thrust it forward. It was almost empty. They had been dropping sprigs and roots to warn trackers, who could have followed them anyway with childish ease, telling them that they were still alive and captives.

"Might as well dump 'em and be done with it!" declared White River.

Ironfoot thought otherwise. Captives inevitably forced more caution on pursuers. He had another plan for releasing them, and besides, this night he felt his medicine would speak to him again. Kicking his heels into his horse, he started away now like one who sees easily and knows how to use the secrets of the land. The Arapaho pony with the two squaws came hard behind him and he did not stop again until the wet gray of dawn.

At dawn a bone-shaking chill was in the air. Amiel felt his teeth rattling and Marcher swore quietly as he tried to work his blanket around him.

There was a wet, crawling mist over the plain that made them feel as though they were moving through some netherworld, where only occasionally could they see a small clearing in the heavy vapor clouds that billowed with maddening slowness across the earth. There was no wind, but the ghostly mist had fingers that crept along the skin and made the body huddle to protect its pockets of warmth.

White River did not like it. Blinded by this fog, they could stumble into anything and anything could stumble into them. He drew his hands across his bearded face and tightened his coat about him. Damn, it was cold. He watched Ironfoot rising high in his saddle to peer forward.

"Higher ground, eh?"

Ironfoot did not answer at once. He had not foreseen a morning like this. In his own country he could have moved up upon the mountains, getting above this treacherous cloud layer. But here the hills were running out and the flat lands leading to the streams beyond would be more thickly set with mist than here.

"Not good here," he said at last. "Maybe sun bring wind . . . sweep prairie."

"God damn risky," muttered White River. "If we aren't goin' to hunt high ground we'd best squat and stay quiet—sound travels like all get-out in this kind of doin's."

Ironfoot nodded and led the way to a little knoll just visible ahead. Here they dismounted, with White River warning the others not to let bridle-chains rattle or metal strike metal. "Keep it quiet as a church-yard, and if you've a mind to cough, work your head into a blanket."

"Can we risk a fire?" inquired Amiel.

" 'Twouldn't nothin' burn," allowed White River, looking at some nearby wet pines that seemed loaded, vaguely oppressed, with large gray drops of moisture. "Get those squaws down and offer them some grub. Likely they'll take to some meat."

When motioned down, the squaws slid readily from the pony and settled on the ground, their robes seemingly keeping them indifferent to the cold wet yellow grass that carpeted the underwash of the knoll. Amiel took some of the deer meat he had left and offered it to them. The younger one tore off a strip and commenced to chew on it, but the older one sat rigidly, her face resembling stone; her only response to Amiel's repeated offer was silence.

They sat about glumly and in frank discomfort, the vein of frost in the air warning each one in a different way that shelter might soon be a condition of life. White River and Ironfoot knew the weather should hold for a few more weeks, but when it broke there would be no compromising with proper cover. A quick unexpected fall blizzard could and often did sweep these plains, covering in white and unbroken silence its toll of the unwary. This was blizzard country. Often frigid winds brought high strings of telltale clouds days before—but not always.

In time it was clear that the sun, which registered only as a lighter form of gray against the eastern half of the sky, would not dissipate the mist. The temperature went up a few degrees but the wind remained feeble and the smell of sodden earth lay around like lazy smoke. White River took his jacket off and shook it. It kept him itchy to think he could be within a hundred yards of skulking Sioux and neither one would be visible to the other. Complaining wasn't likely to help, but it was impossible not to talk about it.

"Figure a scout or pushin' on to the river would make some sense?"

Ironfoot looked back over their tracks to the south. He had been measuring a real danger there. The mist would present few if any problems for trackers. The leaking rain would have little time to revamp the soft earth. The freshness of the sign would warn them that they were getting close and the arrows should be brothering the bow. But now the sign directly behind them was several hours old, and a trailing party could come upon this knoll with only a moment or two's notice for either side. Ironfoot looked down bitterly. Ah, how was one to see or hear one's medicine in this earth-sealing mist? Occasionally rain peppered out of the sky and its fall against the drenched soil caused a fine din that in time weakened the ear which was their last desperate sentinel.

Ironfoot stood up. "Ironfoot watch black trail—see danger come quick."

White River screwed his face as he looked up into the rain that had swung about now on a slight freshet of a breeze and was coming in from the south. "How far back you figurin' to set up?"

Ironfoot pointed to a stand of trees just visible through the mist and indicated he would go as far beyond that as they were to this side.

Amiel and Marcher, seeing them conversing, came over.

"Hope we're planning to move along—much more of this and some of us are bound to get ill." Amiel's eyes were bloodshot and the hair on his face lay wet and flat. Slow-forming drops of water dripped from his hat as he looked at them.

"Why the hell don't we try and get a fire going?" rasped Marcher. One side of his face hung differently from the other as slivers of wet grass showed where he had tried to sleep.

"We'll wait a spell longer—then we'll mosey. This weather's fixin' to clear." White River had pulled his rifle from under the soggy blanket. "Meanwhile Ironfoot's goin' to set up backaways. I'm goin' with him just in case there's somethin' back there already we can't see. Don't you go too far off—looks like easy country for a man to lose himself in."

"We supposed to just sit here?" said Marcher, clearly overwrought from hunching against the ground soaked through and inactive for too long.

White River looked at him quietly. With things the way they were, a man's mind held better when he was given a chore or two.

"Nope—nobody's just a-settin'," said White River as though he had planned it an hour before. He looked about, biting his bottom lip for a moment. "Marcher, you get up ahead here and keep a sharp lookout. Don't move if you see somethin' unless it sees you first. If that happens fire one quick shot and get back here. Amiel, keep an eye on those squaws—if anything happens, tie 'em together in a hurry and don't turn your back on 'em for too long—they bein' quiet don't mean they got their minds on prayin'."

Minutes later he and Ironfoot arrived at a brief drop in the plain that began its falling off with a cluster of red-streaked boulders.

"This should be as good as any," said White River, knowing the words were unnecessary, that the other had the same thought.

Ironfoot looked patiently about him. The whisper of a breeze that had stirred a while ago was back now a little stronger. "Soon the robes of the cloud spirit will be taken from our eyes," he said as though this thought were mother to many others.

"Can't be too soon," said White River, low. "If'n it lets up a little, we'd best move anyways." Ironfoot said nothing but continued looking around. "Got a feelin' we're not alone," finished White River, his eyes working against the mist.

He left Ironfoot and made his way back to the others, noticing as he went that visibility had increased a trifle and that billows of mist were beginning to rise as though anticipating a marshaling call before the wind.

As he approached the wet campsite, his thoughts were shattered by a war cry that broke out behind him and clearly came from where he had left Ironfoot. White River swung about with his rifle, crying, "Marcher . . . Amiel . . . get in here!" He had gone to the ground immediately and drawn a sight on the mist behind him, knowing he could not shoot with Ironfoot in that direction until he was certain of his target. Amiel appeared running low, his rifle on the ready. White River motioned him to a position about ten feet away.

"Where's Marcher? . . . Ironfoot?" Amiel's voice had a slightly frantic pitch that almost failed to force its way through the heavy air.

"Not here, for a fact . . . keep down."

"Sioux?"

"More 'n likely." White River began to move forward in the grass. "Cover me best you can," he called. "Got a notion it's quieter out there than 't ought to be." White River started wiggling forward in the grass, but he stopped suddenly. Three figures were appearing through the mist. Three! No thought now of Ironfoot. His elbows dug for firmness in the sodden earth as he fired at the middle one. But instead of the sharp bark of his rifle, he heard only the sickeningly empty click of a firing pin striking futilely against its cartridge head.

Amiel, watching from the rear and realizing what had happened, hurriedly swung his own rifle up. Only later would he look back in awe, convinced that any man in creation caught in White River's place would have worked that hammer a second time. But White River behaved like a man whose mind is set against thinking. He was rolling in the grass almost as though the deadly click had been his signal to spin. He came up several feet away with his pistol blasting into the mist, but the figures were already ducking down, and his shots, like Amiel's, did no more good than the arrow that wopped into the ground marking the crushed grass where he had just lain. When Amiel looked again, the three figures had disappeared.

White River finally shouted to him, but his only words were "Damn if those squaws didn't light out. Amiel, hold those horses. Could be we'll have us a shootin' spree afore long."

"What about Andy?" called Amiel, unaware of the painful edge of concern that was in his voice.

"Can't do no more than we're doin'—savin' his horse. He's bound to have heard that shootin'. Likely he'll come in if he can."

A sound in the brush nearby startled them, but it turned out to be a buck, startled itself by something further back in the mist, and bounding in upon them it suddenly rose and seemed to change direction in midair as its white eyes met theirs. In a moment it was gone again into the curl of mist wafting across to the east of the knoll.

"Weather's fixin' to lift," said White River now softly, ignoring the deer. He had already reloaded his pistol and retrieving his rifle, fed it another cartridge, his eyes contemplating the long gun as a man does a situation that has to be accepted. "You can never tell."

Marcher heard the shots rising behind him and turned to make his way back to the knoll. A wind was moving in from the north now and he could see one stretch behind him where the earth was clear for almost a mile.

A movement on his left made him stop and squat down. Someone was running. The rifle stock was high against his cheek when two figures emerged from the mist and made their way across his sights. It was the two squaws. He was about to press the trigger to fire in front of the first one when a thought stayed him. If they were making off like that, the camp had not been overrun by Sioux. Recapturing them, on the other hand, would be dangerous and would surely reveal his position.

He started forward again, pleased with his reckoning of the situation. The mist ahead was still heavy, but the breeze was firmer now; it would soon clear off. It occurred to him that he had come farther from the knoll than he thought, and surely farther than White River had intended.

Rumph . . . swish. A buck bolted from the break on his right. It was a furry blur of action that almost immediately, and seemingly blind to him, leaped in front and disappeared in a few swift bounds into the mist. "Damn," he swore to himself, tensely aware that something besides himself had flushed that deer. He crouched down, trying to peer beyond the still shimmering brush where the buck had lain. He saw nothing. He looked about him. A stubble of trees that had not been visible moments before was coming into view. The mist was surely lifting. He decided to wait, settling on the ground, the feel of the rifle cold against his hands, the knowledge that he was soaking wet clawing for attention in some dim part of his mind. The rising mist finally gave him his reward. Another figure was crouched beyond the thicket on his right. He could see it beginning to move now, circling toward his position. He worked his rifle to his shoulder. He would double this one up proper. The figure was drawing nearer now, in a moment it would be impossible to miss. His eye carefully marshaled the sights, his finger drew up on the trigger. Then all of a sudden the figure was gone. Vanished as though the ground had sucked it up. "Jesus," he swore to himself a little too loudly. He succumbed foolishly to the reflex to raise himself a few inches higher, but still he could see nothing. The mist was clearing quickly now and he could see the ground where the figure had vanished. There was only one slight depression to the right of where the deer had bedded innocent of their presence that could possibly conceal anything. He leveled his rifle at it determined to shoot at the first inch of flesh to appear. But it was only a moment before he suddenly saw something above the depression waving back and forth. It was a dark bow. Someone was signaling him. He eased up on the rifle. He recognized that bow and the otter skin that hung from it. It was Ironfoot's. In a moment the Crow himself moved cautiously into view again and, bending low, started running toward Marcher.

"I thought you were way the hell over on the other side of camp!" hissed Marcher as Ironfoot came down beside him.

Ironfoot looked at him stoically and then motioned for him to follow. They moved cautiously forward now toward the knoll which was visible suddenly through the mist, its right flank bulging and uneven where the horses were bunched together, held by Amiel. As they moved and cleared their vision around it, they saw Amiel, who raised his arm in a quick warning signal, and finally White River on the opposite side of camp, kneeling for the partial cover of some brush.

The tone of their coming together was set by Ironfoot's quiet nonchalance, which everyone took to be a good sign, and in spite of the wetness and the reawakening of that familiar drag of fatigue, they congregated in a mood of men secretly relieved.

"Mighty quiet," called White River, coming up slowly and surveying the land that was clearing rapidly as the mist lifted on the wind.

"Suits me," allowed Amiel coming away from the mound. "Can't get quiet enough."

"Who freed those squaws?" challenged Marcher.

"No one. They just lit out," said White River, his eyes on Ironfoot. "What you make of it?"

"Small party," grunted Ironfoot, putting up three fingers. "Two young . . . one old brave."

"Funny," mused White River, looking around again.

"Warriors needed to fight Utes," reasoned Ironfoot. The only danger he sensed was losing the horses. He had circled around to cut them off if they tried slipping up on that quiet and likely side.

"Well, they got their women so they can go back now and jaw some 'bout being heroes." White River was looking at his rifle again. "Reckon we'd better mosey along all the same."

Ironfoot mounted first, looking up at the sky. The mist was moving fast now, swirling and bunching in the wake of the wind. He studied it for a moment; its mad pattern suggested moving forms to his fancy. One he watched on impulse till it swept around and became for a fleeting instant the thin head of a fox. A trace of smile eased his features, which had been hard and morose for days. There was no other sign and no other sign needed, for in the secrecy of such things lies their strength. He moved his mount off into a breeze that threw its deep-fingering chill against their wet clothes. The long land was clearing about them now and a man could finally see in relief a lonely arc of sky.

PART FIVE

CROWS

26

In the year of the big snow that came to lie upon the Beartooth Mountains until the late arriving chinooks melted it and swelled the streams racing northward to add to the turmoil of the already brimming Elk River, Ironfoot—he had not earned that name yet—stepped from his father's lodge and saw the hungry and sickly people of his village preparing for a hunt. It had been a winter of devastation and near disaster. The Piegans had come to steal most of their horses just before the first heavy snow, and the raiders' tracks and the horses with them had been lost in the storm. Game was scarce, and the coughing disease, which some said came from letting their women give themselves to the sickly whites at the fort, had carried off many of the old and almost as many of the very young.

Ironfoot had lately been possessed of an overpowering but joyous idea. He would go off into the Beartooth Mountains and dream. He would discover his secret helpers and come back with strong medicine to aid the people. "Strong medicine does not come because we wish it, my son," muttered his crippled father, "such medicine comes only at the will of Ah-badt-deadt-deah."

Ironfoot remained silent out of respect but later went to the lodge of his uncle White Tail. White Tail was a pipe carrier, a warrior with grown sons of his own. After they had smoked, he asked his uncle to help him prepare for his dreaming, leaving the present of a good knife before the old man. White Tail, knowing how it was with the young in this painful year, looked down in silence for a moment, then said, "Bring willow sticks for a sweat lodge in the morning, but do not leave your tipi today or talk to anyone of this thing."

The sweat lodge was put together in secrecy, his uncle rubbing him with sage and a strange-smelling grass, painting the secret symbols on his face and chest. Then he was taken high in the mountains where he lay in his robes listening to the wolves howl and facing the torment of days and nights without food or water. When the dreaming finally came upon him, it filled him with dread. Suddenly he was stunned by a great light in the form of a young man shining over many prancing horses while in front of him a fox and an otter barked fearfully and pointed to a dark figure beyond the light. The dark figure suddenly grew larger and came toward him, spreading its wings like a great bird of evil, quickly consuming the light and leaving him in cavernous darkness, choked with fear.

How long he lay there he did not know, but when he opened his eyes he found White Tail standing over him, whispering, "It is time." He returned to his sweat lodge, where weakness made him so faint he had to be carried to his father's tipi. Only after a long sleep of exhaustion did he awake to the smell of strange herbs his father had thrown over the fire.

"Let your spirit be strong," said his watching father knowingly, "there is often wisdom in dreams that leave a heaviness in the heart."

Blue Ice, a medicine man who could read the spirit talk woven into dreams, was sent for, and after they had smoked his father murmured, "My son has dreamed. He will speak of it and Blue Ice will help him find his message from the spirit world."

Ironfoot took a deep breath and began to relate the dream that now chilled him as he spoke. Somehow he knew it for a dark prophecy. He told it truly though, and they listened in silence, not one of them lifting his eyes from the fire until the heavily breathing youth had finished.

Blue Ice waited for long moments, as though gathering many difficult thoughts together in his mind, before he finally said, "This is a dream one should not speak of many times."

His father's eyes rose grave with agreement.

Ironfoot felt his heart going cold within him. His premonition had been right. Still he sat in miserable silence knowing there was nothing he could do. A dream dreamed was beyond changing.

"The fox is your secret helper," said Blue Ice, his eyes now looking up at the dark dome of the lodge, "and the otter will serve you faithfully in times of danger. Sew some otter skin upon your bow to keep it strong and straight-shooting in the face of enemies." A long silence ensued before Blue Ice went on. Ironfoot sensed it was growing hard for the old man to speak. It made him want to cry. Surely this thing must soon end.

Blue Ice sang quietly to himself for a moment, then said, "A young man, but one strong with horses, will come into your life. Yet he will die young and the bird of evil will visit his grave. It is an ill omen. The great darkness tells us the way ahead is not to be known."

Such was the message the young man spent three bitter days and nights in misery and fright to hear.

The years now lay heavily on Ironfoot, his father telling him each spring to dream again, but for this he had no heart. He made a secret medicine bundle from the dried vital parts of a fox and carried it under his shirt. He tied the skin from the hind leg of an otter upon his bow. He went finally on a large raid against the Shoshones, taking two scalps, one from a man he had struck and knocked to the earth with his left foot. His father danced the scalp for him and sang of his new warrior's name, Ironfoot. Ironfoot was very proud that day and took many horses to the lodge of Big Mountain where he tied them to a stake to show he wanted the slim and pretty Goes-Walking for his wife.

Big Mountain accepted the gift and his daughter's heart sang.

Now in his own lodge Ironfoot saw the Absarokees fall upon good years and he shared them. The buffalo were plentiful and war party after war party came back with horses and booty that swelled the wealth of the village and made the hearts of the squaws full. Ironfoot counted many coups and became a pipe carrier, some thinking the day would come when he would be a great war chief.

Goes-Walking gave Ironfoot two fine sons, one of whom grew into a great athlete and a wizard at handling horses. He was given the name of his father's brother, Black Shield, a renowned war chief who had been killed a year before defending their village against the dangerously mounting visits of the Sioux. So skillful was the young Black Shield at stealing and breeding horses that his herd often numbered over a hundred. Ironfoot and Goes-Walking were proud of him, more proud than they were of his younger brother, the one who would one day be called Snow Runner and stand tall and honored among his people. But Ironfoot had never told Goes-Walking about the dream of his youth, and now as he watched Black Shield prancing by on his splendid swift ponies it began to trouble his mind and bring upon him long spells of brooding. Often he warned Black Shield about going so many times against their enemies. But Black Shield loved the excitement of the warpath even more than he did the young girls who danced between the fires toward him.

Ironfoot was also worried that Black Shield had tried twice himself to dream and had failed. It was a bad sign. Too bad for restful sleep and the secret peace so sought in a father's heart.

The increasing attacks of the Sioux finally led to a desperate one led by White Man's Medicine, he who wore the white man's cross about his neck, in which Goes-Walking's brother and his sons, returning early from a hunt, were cut off, surrounded and killed. Black Shield had been close to these young men and he cried as he slashed his arms, painted his face black, and swore to avenge them. Another young brave, Yellow Runner, agreed to go with him, and the two left quietly at night on the trail of the retreating Sioux.

Left behind, Ironfoot, with his younger boy, watched over his son's great herd, trying not to think of the many bad signs that filled each day. He prayed to his fox medicine to protect his son and pledged many sacrifices for his safe return. But one morning he found a sick and dying fox behind his lodge and he knew his son, Black Shield, had fallen upon trouble.

It was a long wait for Yellow Runner's return and word that Black Shield was no more. After hearing this Ironfoot sat for many days before his fire without speaking. His younger son gave some of his brother's horses away for it was coming winter and there were too many for him to care for, let alone protect against the plundering Sioux. And that winter the Sioux came, when all conditions said they would not, when the snow was on the ground and the frost giant breathed upon the land each night. But it was said that the Sioux chiefs were angry at the death of White Man's Medicine and thought they would surprise this Crow village and wipe it out.

The Crow chiefs knew that warriors were always dying and that, in reality, behind this attack in the dead of winter lay the long Sioux greed for Crow hunting grounds. Defeat and even destruction of the Crow nation had been the Sioux goal for too long to be ignored. And the chiefs knew the situation was too serious for smoking or waiting for signs that would not come. They were surrounded and no horse however swift could get through the deep snow. The warrior societies, pledged to die in battle, took their positions around the village. There was much talk of victory and taking Sioux scalps, but most of the stoic, war-scarred warriors knew their one hope was the River Crows, who were in winter quarters many miles away. A fleet youth with the heart and stealth of a mountain lion was needed to slip by the Sioux scouts at night and run for help. It was a terrible decision, for even if safely past the Sioux a horseless man in this country, made naked by the all-revealing snow, would move at great risk and be helpless if discovered or tracked down by the crafty and determined Sioux.

Red Warbonnet, their greatest war chief, looked at the four tight-faced youths who had marched proudly behind old White Tail to his tent suddenly aware of their new importance. He regarded them mutely, then gave them the desperate facts in his quiet, war-hardened way. The chosen "warrior"—a subtle elevation caught by the ready ears of the young—must leave at the first dark. He must slip between the Sioux scouts, run all night so to be at the camp of the River Crows before the sun climbed too high in the sky on the morrow. He might evade the Sioux now but they would surely find his tracks at dawn and, guessing his mission, would send their speediest braves in pursuit.

The youths, among them the silently praying Snow Runner, drew lots. Snow Runner wanted that short stick. He had long secretly nursed a tormenting desire to prove himself the equal of Black Shield. This was surely his chance. Being an athlete like his brother, he knew he could make the other village before he was caught. He would make it and know the tribe's tribute or he would die and avoid the shame. It seemed a fair bargain.

A chief's son who walked proudest of all got the shortest stick. He stalked away with it, circling the camp so as many as possible would see him. But after waiting for darkness, and his father and uncle praying over him for hours and paying him many honors, he fell into a dead faint almost at the moment to leave.

Seeing this, Red Warbonnet grunted like a man who has long suspected he was watching beavers paw the air like bears, but Snow Runner electrified the sober, bitter face of the great war chief as he snatched up the short stick and raced behind the lodges, swinging under the ropes where the horse herd was held and then disappearing at its outer edge as Lazy Owl of the Big Bellies—a warrior society guarding that spot—crouched as sentry, half raised his spear before realizing the fleet ducking figure was leaving his own camp and not coming from the direction of the Sioux.

It was a thing too sudden to stop, but as the people put their hands over their mouths in astonishment, old White Tail and Red Warbonnet exchanged glances. It is the first mark of a warrior that he considers dangerous missions to be his business and that he avoids talking about matters when it comes time to act.

The chief's son was carried to his uncle's lodge, his father beginning to mourn for him as though he were dead. The boy would awake to find he would forever be called Sleeps-Like-Squaw and no warrior society would ever admit him.

Snow Runner did beat the Sioux to the camp of the River Crows and returned with over sixty warriors to join in the hard fighting that still remained before they could dislodge the determined foe. But during the long night Ironfoot kept a vigil for his second son, not knowing Snow Runner would live through this great thing to hear the whole village sing his praises and give him his name so that this deed that saved the people would not be forgotten.

Also during that long night Ironfoot chanted a medicine song and pledged he would give Snow Runner all of Black Shield's horses if he returned safely. In his growing grief that he would be sonless he pledged that he himself would visit Black Shield's grave before the next snow and see if the vision in the dream of his youth had been borne out. There would be much praying and fasting before this thing could be done, there would be many smokes and words about the site where Black Shield lay in his shallow grave. He had heard Yellow Runner's story about the death of his courageous son, how he had fulfilled his pledge, had slain the Sioux chief and taken his white man's medicine from him, had almost made good his escape when his horse went down in a rocky place, breaking its leg and bringing death to its magnificent rider. Yellow Runner had buried him as best he could, for the Sioux were up like hornets, but Yellow Runner returned in black despair and lived only till the next raiding party, from which he did not return. Ironfoot sat through the long lonely winter, knowing now what he must do.

• • •

When the spring grass made the ponies sleek and strong at the bit, word came from the Kiowas that they would like to trade for horses. Snow Runner decided to take part of his now vast herd of horses south, for the Kiowas had many things from the settlements of the southwest to trade with. After much thought, Ironfoot agreed to go with him either at the end of the spring buffalo hunt or in early summer. In the back of his mind he had decided to leave Snow Runner once they had disposed of the horses and go east, circling the no man's land between Sioux and Crow country and make his way up to the Belle Fourche and Black Shield's grave.

Goes-Walking cried as they left, knowing in the way of a woman that Ironfoot's days of praying and fasting could not be explained by a trading visit to a friendly tribe. She had heard him speak to the brooding Yellow Runner of Black Shield's death, heard him chanting quietly through the night. But she was only a woman, she must wait. She must wonder at every word and at the lack of any. She must lie lonely in the lodge. The people about her might in secret be sorry for her, but she must walk proud.

Even though Ironfoot's prayers and fasting had brought him no visions, that spring on his first night in the Kiowa camp he had a dream. An old man dressed in the skin of a white fox with its long head protruding over his had appeared before him and in a chanting voice had said he must go straight as the true-drawn arrow to Black Shield's grave or an evilness would overtake him there. Ironfoot awoke in a cold sweat to find Snow Runner bending over him.

"Is my father ill?" said the soft-speaking Snow Runner.

"It is nothing."

Snow Runner went back to his robe. "The Kiowas have given us much of the white man's food. It is difficult to sleep."

Ironfoot arose and kicked the dying fire back to life. Then, settling on his blanket, he took his pipe from its beaded cloth and smoked. Across the lodge Snow Runner pretended to sleep, but he was awake and waiting and worried, as Ironfoot well knew.

"I will go in the morning, my son."

"Does my father wish his son to go with him?"

"It is a thing a father should do alone."

"When does my father return?"

"When the Great Spirit above wishes it. Sleep now, my son."

Ironfoot began to smoke again and the night passed with the silent Snow Runner lying quietly in his robe, far too quiet for one asleep.

27

The evening Ironfoot approached the island in the Platte, his heart was beginning to feel the burden that a man knows when his every step takes him closer to his son's grave. The knowledge that the sight of Black Shield's bones would mean the handsome, dashing youth was forever gone grew unbearable for him. He had moved carefully, for to his surprise, he had found signs of Sioux war parties all along the Platte country, and they seemed to have swept the earth of the whites and their wagon trains with the slow-moving oxen making their way to the mountains in the west. He moved steadily east until one night the sight of fires burning warmly on the island told him that some whites, defying the Sioux, had gathered there.

He started fording the river carefully, getting only close enough to the island to be seen but then patiently standing in midstream while waiting for the camp to recognize him. If recognition was not immediate, it was unmistakable when it came. A rifle ball fired at him by a shouting sentry went wide of its mark, but the same sentry's shouting turned the camp into a frenzied anthill. Ironfoot, watching the armed figures appearing hurriedly on the bank, called out that he was a Crow and a friend, and at that a tall figure in front started motioning him in.

That was the beginning of his slow drift away from the good words of his medicine spirit. Surely he had done wrong to allow it to be so.

But, now as they moved along the stream, the yellow sky of an autumnal dawn hanging before them, a quiet lay upon the earth, a dreamlike stillness through which flowed the clear fresh waters of the Belle Fourche. Ironfoot was leading them along the north bank, his eyes hard on the growth that hemmed in the river and swept back and forth to engulf clumps of trees whose leaves matched the pale pigments of the sky. He knew the country well; it had once belonged to the Absarokees. At times he led them through the trees well away from the stream, stopping often to look intently at some small elusive game or a flight of birds. But his instincts told him the land was empty.

Finally they circled sharply back to the stream again, Ironfoot watching for and finally seeing the rocky stretch where Black Shield's powerful stallion must have gone down and sent its daring rider to his death. He stopped, looking far down the rocky wash where in the past years the river must have made its bed. In time his eyes picked out what his heart told him were the bleached bones of the dead stallion. Now he must be very, very close. He moved slowly, the others following him at a distance, suspecting by his manner that he wished to face this thing alone.

The huge leg bones of the horse lay yards apart and one single hoof lay upright, a fungus growing in its pit. Ironfoot looked about him knowing Black Shield's grave, if indeed a grave remained, was behind one of two immense boulders nearby. There is something unnatural about a father gazing on the grave of his son. It seems to rupture time, to disturb the fundamental order of things, to raise the dreadful specter of a seed line dead beyond recall, to settle winter in a man's secret mind, a winter dark and destitute of any hope of spring. Ironfoot chanted a little medicine song, spoke to his spirit helpers, the fox, the otter, pledged many sacrifices in return for their help and then ended by looking at the sun steadily for many minutes.

Then he rose and moved toward the boulders. As he circled the one on the left he found it bare, with only a few undisturbed flat rocks at its base. But he could already see the mound of hastily piled rocks behind the other. He walked toward it knowing his journey had ended. The rocks were large enough to keep wolves and coyotes from getting within, but they had been put together hastily in the dark and he knew small rodents and insects could come and go at will. Black Shield's bones would still be here but little else. He started to remove the rocks. White River came up and quietly knelt to assist him. They worked slowly, the white, cleaned bones beginning to appear beneath. Marcher and Amiel came up, Amiel quietly pulling his hat from his head. Soon the lower skeleton of the body was uncovered, a rusting knife lying beside the right hip. Up they moved exposing the ribs, the great empty cavity of the chest that showed the power of this horse-loving youth. Ironfoot was standing as White River took the last rocks away from the head and the gleaming white bones of Black Shield lay exposed, the rotted headband still holding tufts of darkly matted hair to the skull.

The silence that should have commanded this moment perished in the gasps that escaped from Amiel and Marcher, and the low groan that fought its way through Ironfoot's tightly closed mouth. There was no way of preparing for it, only Ironfoot knew of or believed in the bird of evil, but there it was. Ah, why had he not come alone! Around the neck and lying to one side, distorting the symmetry of the left shoulder blade, was a thin black chain leading to an even darker metal object that lay eerily in the new harsh light, its dark, tarnished form all too clear beside the white of Black Shield's bones. It was the last thing in the world that should have been there. It fitted neither time nor place. It was a crucifix with a large nugget at its back.

• • •

The Crow war party was around them at dawn. Ironfoot, long awake, built the fire up to signal them in. They came well mounted, their faces painted and some of their young braves giving the Crow war cry that served in their wild, exuberant way as a greeting. White River, alerted by the noise and the change in the fire, got up matter-of-factly. Marcher and Amiel sat up in half-halting motions and gazed about trying to measure the cordiality of these frightening new faces.

Ironfoot and the war leader greeted each other warmly, then settled by the fire to smoke. The war chief was Fire Wolf, a River Crow, and a relative by marriage to Goes-Walking. Some of the older braves also came forward to smoke and Ironfoot waved White River into the circle, an invitation that told the dark, watchful faces that this white was one that Ironfoot held above the others.

After the pipe had been passed, Fire Wolf said, "My brother, Ironfoot, has been long from his village."

"True. Many moons."

"It has been a summer of much fighting."

"Ahh. Truly the Sioux never sleep."

"No, not the Sioux. They have sent their great war parties against the whites. Their chiefs have been too busy with their victories in the south to come against us, but the Piegans made much medicine this season and they have come against us three times. We finally defeated them on the Big River near the mouth of the Musselshell, but we lost Red Warbonnet and many good men."

"Ahhh," sighed Ironfoot. Not only the Sioux but the powerful Blackfeet were after their lands. He looked at the parfleche containing Black Shield's bones. Would there be a piece of land that would belong forever to the Absarokee where these bones could lie in peace?

"Did my brother find that which he went to seek?" Fire Wolf's tone was low, his eyes down out of respect, the pipe motionless in his hand. The reason for Ironfoot's absence was long suspected.

"Ironfoot has found that which his heart sought."

"It is good."

Ironfoot stared at the fire for a moment. A chill wind was gathering force above them. It was two days' travel to Red Lodge Creek. They had best be on their way.

"Does Fire Wolf journey with us to our lodge?"

"No. It is time for a little fall hunting and perhaps some fresh skins to strengthen the tipi. We have been out many days now, but the land is empty. Our enemies are gone and the wise ones are saying the squaws have keened enough for this one season."

Everyone was on his feet as the war party left, Ironfoot swiftly indicating to the others that they should eat quickly and get on their own way. A peculiar tension that had gripped the group at Black Shield's grave had now mounted to where it was beginning to bring strange and unsuspected lights to their worn faces. At the discovery, Marcher had been first to the crucifix and with his knife had worked the chain loose and then the cross from its sheath. So rapidly did he move that he almost tore the dried deerskin wrapped tightly inside.

"God! By God!" he shouted. "Here it is!" Then, looking down at Black Shield's remains, he went on breathlessly, "And damn if this isn't the bastard who killed Paul!"

Ironfoot had whipped out his knife, but White River was standing between them and shouldered the Crow back. "Keep your damn foolish notions to yourself!" he spat at Marcher. "Your uncle has been dead for years—this boy got killed hardly a year ago. Got to be 'nother answer!"

White River pushed Marcher away from the grave with a sharp thrust that sent the other reeling several feet before he regained his balance. Marcher came up and his eyes grew steady with fury as he and White River confronted each other. It was a long, painful moment. Nothing was said, but it settled something deep between them and both were glad.

White River drew Amiel away as Ironfoot went to his knees, looking at the handle of the rusted knife and the few shreds of clothing that remained to identify in their own macabre way the bones of his beautiful, thrill-loving son, that boy who had seemed so long to laugh at death.

Amiel's voice came up in a shocked whisper. "God, this is unbelievable!"

"A man ain't got no choice but believin' what he's seein'," muttered White River.

"But how?"

"Could work thataway given a few twists and turns here and there."

"So there really is a gold mine after all."

"The story 'pears to shine for a fact."

Amiel let his breath out in dismay. "More trouble . . . I'll wager on it. Damn, if this doesn't beat all."

White River's hand tried an uncertain grip on his mouth. " 'Magine so."

Farther away, Marcher had the deerskin spread out and was bent over studying the crude map scratched upon it.

"Isn't very God damn clear," said Marcher, clucking to himself. In the left-hand corner there was an obvious starting point. Three scratched lines—he decided they were streams—joined to make one that seemed to go upward between two dark places. They could have been mountains. In the center of the skin a dotted line went around another dark blob and seemed to move up the back of it. There a large *X* appeared with the words "Victoire" and "Paul's star at sundown" scratched beside it. Behind the words was the outline of what could have been the top of a mountain, but there was no directional arrow to indicate from what side the mountain, if that was what it was, was being viewed.

Marcher got up slowly. "Well, by Jesus, this is still going to take some figuring."

Marcher lifted his eyes up slowly over his map and caught the stooped back of the quietly working Ironfoot. He knew that it had been a stupid mistake to anger the Crow. He had lost the value of this man's intimacy with the land. Something told him he would pay a serious price for it. He took the shaft of the crucifix and started to work loose the long, thin nugget that had been imprisoned by softening and bending the wide trim of the prongs bent around it. He had to use his knife and it soon scraped through to the quick gleam of silver. Ah, a silver crucifix holding a nugget of gold. He smiled to himself at the incongruity. Then, with a final wrench, he worked it free.

The nugget lay in his hand. It did not look remarkably different from other stones he had seen. He rubbed it hard on his sleeve and then held it up to the light as though expecting to see something in it shimmer with a warm golden glow. He decided at last it looked very much the same.

Marcher cradled it in his palm, judging its weight. It did not seem heavier than one expected it to be. He moved slowly with it over to Amiel. "Must be gold ore," he said, holding it out in his hand.

"What of it?" snapped Amiel, not looking at the proffered stone.

Marcher still held the crucifix in the other hand. He raised it and looked at it contemplatively. "Wonder how the hell this ever got here."

White River looked straight up. The pale, lemony sun was high now and hung in a hard blue sky. Autumn was in the land. Then he looked over to where Ironfoot was finally working the many bones of Black Shield into the tight leather cover of the parfleche. "Well, all we can say for sure," he replied slowly, "is two gents had a hand in it—and both of 'em's fair dead."

28

They came to the Crow camp on Red Lodge Creek on the afternoon of the second day. A boy tending the grazing herd saw them coming and raced to the village with word, so that on their arrival old White Tail and other headmen were already awaiting them, surrounded by squaws and young children raising a deafening din.

Ironfoot saw Goes-Walking standing before a lodge well away from the main circle and knew at once how it had been with her. But first he dismounted and spoke to his uncle White Tail who had become an old man chief.

"Our brother returns," said White Tail, his feeble eyes misty with hidden emotions.

"It is well," said Ironfoot. "Ironfoot has grown lonely for his lodge." He turned to other headmen of the warrior societies that policed the camp. "These men are guests of the Absarokee—let our people see that they are fed and sheltered."

The whites dismounted and were soon being led into the skin lodges by eager Crow women summoned forth by the genial shouting of the braves. Then Ironfoot smoked with White Tail, hearing patiently again the dire straits of the Crows. Only after did he go to his lodge to stand close to Goes-Walking. It was a good moment, even though the air about him as he walked to his tipi was full of the sense of many missing and an unspoken fear gripping his people that their enemies were too great for them.

Still there was feasting as evening approached to welcome the guests and a short dance put on by Snow Runner and a handful of braves who returned just before dark with some good paloose horses they had stolen from the Shoshones. These horses, bred carefully by Indians far to the west for power and speed, had come from beyond the great mountains and were much prized by the far-traveling Crows for their strength and endurance. They also brought back three Shoshone maidens, who sat dismal and doubtful of the future between the old squaws who settled down beyond the fires to watch them.

After he had choked down some food, Ben slipped into his tipi and rolled himself in a thick robe he found lying there. His chills had grown worse in the last day or two and in the past hour he was sure he had developed a fever. He knew his body was suffering from exhaustion and needed some decent food and rest, but this was neither the time nor the place to get sick, not in this primitive camp with danger on every side. After an hour he heard the drums beating outside and forced himself to get up. Behind his tipi he had noticed a cool, flowing stream and his parched throat urged him to quench his mounting thirst. Still, when he knelt down, the last light of day cast back a reflection from the water that appalled him. Fighting to keep from trembling in the evening breeze, he pulled at the heavy growth of hair that now almost concealed his face. The sight of it made him return to the tipi and make signs to the old squaw, Yellow Leaf, who had come to tend his needs, to heat some water. In his long neglected pack he found a razor and a sliver of soap. An hour later the beard was gone, but his face was cut in a thousand places and sore as a scraped shin. Still, sick as he was, for the moment it revived his spirits.

Exhausted from the task he wandered unsteadily out to the circle where the drums were beating and White River was seated with Ironfoot, White Tail, and some other braves. Snow Runner and his war party were still dancing and chanting their brave deeds. In the distance he saw the Shoshone captives and asked in a puzzled way as he settled by White River, "Where did those girls come from?"

"Somewheres back in the mountains, I reckon. They're Snakes."

Amiel rubbed his flushed face, aware that White River was suddenly looking at him uneasily. "And what will they do with them?" he said firmly.

White River's mind was not on his words as he continued to stare at Amiel. "Don't know—they parleyin' on it now."

Amiel looked at the silent White Tail. "What do they usually do?"

White River turned away slowly. "Oh, after the boys that brought 'em in get through with 'em, some braves might marry them or use them as slaves—or just do the things that naturally gets done to girls." He swung back, a trace of tension now in his voice. "Ben, are you all right?"

Ben ignored the question, but he avoided White River's eyes as he said, "But surely that's nothing but pure savagery!"

"Reckon that's right."

"Well, don't say it like that, can't it be stopped?"

"Nope—not by us."

"It seems to me we have to try."

White River turned away again, creases of concern etching his face. "Ben, these people have been livin' like this since Adam could crawl. They've got their own beliefs and ways of doin' things. It don't pay to be forever tellin' them they got to do different."

"Say what you will, but I just can't sit here and . . ."

"Hush up for a spell! I've got me a notion these three might just be goin' home."

Amiel looked at him uncertainly. "What makes you think that?"

White River nodded toward Ironfoot and gestured for Amiel to let the matter lie.

Ironfoot was sitting beside White Tail, listening to their aging but greatly respected war leader, Big Owl, speak of their tribal plight. Behind Big Owl sat two renowned warriors who were visiting from a neighboring River Crow village and had long been in council with him. White Tail was regarding the visitors mutely, the oft-smoked council pipe in his hands.

"Snow Runner must understand," argued Big Owl. "The Absarokees need allies, not more enemies to come against them." He turned his head like a man bothered that a truth so obvious had to be spoken.

"Then why the Shoshones?" muttered White Tail. "Are not the Flatheads or even the Nez Percé better warriors?"

"Very well, then, send the pipe to the Flatheads and Nez Percé too," ranted Big Owl. "Every tribe fighting the Piegans should smoke as brothers against them."

"And what of the Sioux?" questioned White Tail. "Will they, the Cheyennes, and those thieving Arapahos sit in their lodges like squaws when the grass comes to make the ponies strong?"

One of the visiting braves sitting behind Big Owl grunted, and Big Owl drew himself up as one reminded of strong words to be said. "In this brave's village runners have come from the forts to the south. The whites are asking our young men to ride as scouts for them against the Sioux. The Sioux have killed many of their people this summer, but the whites, who are against war only until it is made on them, have gathered great numbers of their horse soldiers, warriors who have no lodges of their own and who live only to fight. They have many horses and many guns. Even before the snow comes they are going against the Sioux and their allies. The Sioux will need peace when the grass comes to strengthen their ponies again and hunt for food."

"Ahh!" said White Tail. "Are you telling us the slow-moving and noisy whites will find the restless wolves of the Sioux asleep?"

"No. But even without our young men they already have many Pawnee scouts who will find the Sioux villages and these will have to be moved far away or they will be burned. Remember, the whites carry the good grain food for their horses in their great wagons. The Sioux ponies like ours will be weak from lack of grass. It will not be an easy winter for the Sioux. The new white soldier chief at the fort is very angry. He has already hung two friendly Arapahos accused of selling the many-shots guns to a Brule chief."

"What if the Shoshones refuse the pipe?" queried White Tail, lifting his proud face.

"If we send these three women back unharmed with presents and an offer of friendship, their chiefs will accept. The Blackfeet have long given them good reason to." Big Owl looked straight at the old chief as he spoke.

Ironfoot grunted. "Your words are good, Big Owl. I will speak to my son. It will be as you say."

White Tail studied his pipe. "Why do we not ask the whites to help us or at least give us guns, many-shots guns and many bullets?"

Big Owl looked again at the visiting braves behind him. These warriors had been silent up to now, but here one lifted his head in anger against the darkening sky. "The whites do not feel an Indian's pain until it becomes their own. I went with our old man chief to the fort to ask for guns. They sent us to a black robe, a good man who made many good words in spite of the whiskey on his breath. He said guns are things of war and should not be wanted by men of peace. We told him of our great fear and the many guns of the Piegans and Sioux, but he said only bad people depended on such things. There was much trouble hearing his every word as the sun was going to sleep and great wagon guns were roaring behind us and many soldiers with long knives on their guns were shouting together as they marched around the fort."

"But they wish our young men to act as scouts against the Sioux," said Ironfoot, noting that Snow Runner had stopped dancing and was now approaching.

"Only a few have gone," said the other, his face caught in a curious frown. "The white soldier chief said he wanted only braves who were strong in battle. When asked if they would help us against the Piegans if we helped them against the Sioux, they said they could not help us but would send word to the Piegans to stay at peace." He paused and grunted like a man vexed by his own words. "The Absarokees will need their young men to hold their hunting grounds."

Night had drawn upon the camp and the fires that were built up threw a lonely yellow light on the long brooding faces of the Crows.

The following day White River came into Amiel's tipi and looked down at him shivering beneath the many robes Yellow Leaf had piled upon him. Ben's eyes were dark hollows and his skin was the color of red chalk. White River shook his head.

Ben tried to smile up at him. "It probably looks worse than it is."

The old squaw, Yellow Leaf, mumbled something to White River and pointed to her tongue. White River quietly questioned her in her own language for a few moments then she scurried out as though struck by some urgent thought. "So you came up with a big fever last night, huh?" White River was running a quick restless hand over his worried face.

"It didn't last long. I'll be up and about in a day or two."

"Listen, friend, best you stay put," replied White River, his tone approaching a command. "There are fevers in these mountains that can kill you."

Amiel looked weak and seemed to be having trouble speaking, but he pulled at the pile of robes as though annoyed at White River's words. "How long do these fevers last?"

"As long as it takes the critter who has them to die." White River settled on a blanket a few feet away. There was no mistaking the alarmed edge in his words. "They're going to start feeding you what will look like cold soups, some of 'em are thick with the bitterest herbs ever to reach the pot. Drink them, and don't worry if you can't keep them down, they'll give you plenty more. Stay under those robes and get as much sleep as you can. A medicine man will be along to chant over you. He ain't gonna cure you but we'll give him some tobacco anyway. Crows like a little magic on their side. Now I'd best fetch your brother."

"Fetch Andy? What for?"

White River looked at him uncertainly. "Ain't much a man can be sure of round here, Ben, but for a fact you're sick enough to be talking things over with your kin."

A few minutes later Marcher, dressed and clearly ready to ride out of camp, arrived. He looked concerned at his brother's flushed and feverish face, but as Ben pressed himself up to reassure him he wasn't feeling all that poorly, Andy began to grow restless. "You probably just needed a good rest, Ben. We've put in some mighty rough weeks. I'd better get out of here so you can sleep. Don't worry, I'll drop by as soon as I get back."

"Get back? Going somewhere?"

"Sure am. You haven't forgotten I'm still hunting for that mine, have you?" But later that night when Marcher returned, White River, Ironfoot, Big Owl, and White Tail were huddled over a small fire in Amiel's tipi, and Ben was ranting and far too delirious to realize who was there.

• • •

White Tail and Big Owl had seen the rash on Amiel's face and the fear in their hearts for their people had left them near speechless. White River, who had witnessed one of the decimating plagues along the Missouri, knew that as bad as Ben looked, it was not smallpox. He suspected the joint-racking and often deadly mountain fever. Marcher, when he came in, was confused and almost incredulous at the turn of things. He quickly argued that Ben like himself had been inoculated and couldn't possibly have smallpox. But the Indians had never heard of such powerful medicine. Certainly it had never been offered to the Crows or other tribes in distress. They greeted his words with stone faces sullen with doubt. And so they sat through the night, waiting for what the dawn would bring, Big Owl and White Tail making it clear that if tiny raised pustules were found on Amiel's body at dawn, the whole village was fleeing and the whites must remain behind.

White River was not surprised. The Plains Indians feared smallpox more than any of the white man's diseases. Whole villages and even tribes had perished from it. He knew from the Indian point of view the tribe's survival was at stake. But the light of day showed Ben's skin to be clear, his fever down and the rash beginning to recede.

Still it was evident to all that Ben remained critically ill, with the fever continually coming back and his joints aching till he moaned in misery. It took several days of careful nursing before he had the strength to sit up and talk. A medicine man came regularly to chant over him, but White River would not allow the shaman's favorite treatment of a long spell in the sweat lodge and then a cold plunge in the icy stream. Buzz Matlock had always said that as many seriously sick and weakened Indians had likely died from that body shocking and deeply chilling experience as were killed by the diseases it was supposed to miraculously cure.

29

Many weeks were to pass before Ben Amiel was able to take short rides or even walks along the slopes without returning exhausted to his robes, yet his health gradually returned and the wait served other purposes. The whites after some time in the camp began to feel more flesh over their bony parts and the leaden clamp of fatigue lifting from their limbs. The skin lodges were comfortable enough, but the nights in these mountains were growing colder and one morning they awoke to find a thin, light snow had fallen upon their camp on Red Lodge Creek. A wind with the will of the mountains behind it hurried pewter-colored clouds across the sky until a wan afternoon sun finally broke through, bringing light but only a trace of heat.

White Tail stood before his lodge and looked at the rim of hills to the northeast. Runners had been coming to the camp in a steady stream, bringing word of many matters that made the headmen ponder long into the night and led to much smoking and councils that troubled the heart. The Shoshones had accepted the alliance and would send a delegation early in the spring to smoke with the Crows. But the Flatheads, the Nez Percé, the Kutenai, and the Pend d'Oreille had all held back. It was said the Blackfeet had many guns and even now were raiding into the mountains for more horses. It was said that Blood-on-His-Moccasin, the great Piegan war chief, would smoke with the Bloods and the Blackfeet proper, bringing together the three tribes of the powerful Blackfoot nation, whipping up their already strong craving for war. Some friendly Crees the Crow runners met along Big River had warned of great war parties coming south by spring.

All this was bad enough, but what troubled the Crow chiefs the most were the bad words coming from the south and east. One of their own warriors, wounded and sent back from the white expedition against the Sioux, told of white soldier chiefs who would not listen to their Indian scouts, who moved too slowly and were too easily decoyed away from the retreating villages. The Pawnees and Crows had trapped a few stragglers and there had been some hard fighting with Sioux warriors who were circling the white supply columns and getting away with good horses and many guns, and most serious of all, ammunition, the metal shells the Indian could not make for himself. Truly this was troublesome news, no one saying outwardly what in the end it could mean.

Old White Tail had closed his lids wearily when he heard these things, muttering to himself in the way of old men, "Ahh, the Sioux have seen our young men helping the whites—will they not remember?"

The old chief looked around him as though he were looking at a land he had already departed and which he was trying to recapture in a dream, for surely they could not hold these rich hunting grounds against so many powerful and determined enemies. Surely they would one day be like the thin white goats that lived in the mountain vastness and took only that part of earth too gaunt and austere for others.

Had it not been for these trying times, the whites in the camp might have caused less trouble. For though they came together, they were not of one heart and moved about like strangers wary of each other's intent. The one called Marcher had been taken up in secret council for he was looking for the yellow metal that affected the minds of the whites and wanted the Crows to help find it. Ahh! One does not leave honey on the ground of the lodge to bring a million ants to foul it. Though some felt they recognized the place where his picture paper said the yellow metal lay, all looked at it in wonder and made the sign for not knowing. Some braves, anxious for the presents Marcher offered for help, took him on long, fruitless trips, once to the Crazy Mountains up above Elk River and once as far south as the Popo Agie. But mostly they took him but a little ways from camp and then moved in wide, lazy circles. The other two, White River and the man called Amiel, seemed good men. They hunted for game and kept their own tipis as well as a few of the poor of the village supplied, and the one called White River was a good warrior who had helped drive off some swift-appearing horse thieves who had tried to surprise the village herd.

From the ridge above White Tail could see the two of them now returning from the high meat racks along the river where they had hung the fresh carcasses of two deer. Some squaws were gazing up at the meat, their cutting knives looking small and black in their hands. High above an eagle was passing on its daily hunt along the river. So high did it soar over the village it hardly seemed to move against the sky.

Amiel squatted down in the spacious lodge that he and White River decided to share to keep him company during his long illness. He was slowly working his hands over a dim red eye in the white fire bed, coaxing it back to life with dry twigs. "Perhaps we ought to be making plans to go, getting south of here before we're snowed in and haven't any choice."

"Where did you have in mind to go?" White River was settling on a big robe, getting himself into a comfortable position to clean his gun.

"To the fort, I guess. They say it's only three days' travel."

White River shook his head and screwed up his mouth. "Ever winter up in a fort?"

"Of course not."

"Explains your thinkin'."

Amiel looked at him questioningly. "You know whether it's safe or not to stay here?"

"Safe as anywheres—Crows are good people, better than most."

Amiel glanced seriously into the fire that was beginning to crackle with the sticks he was slowly feeding it.

As the days passed, no figure in camp caused more comment than Marcher. His quandary was like a slowly exposed nerve that in sudden and unexpected movements spread rivulets of pain and bred its own hell. He could see winter closing the land, he could see the reluctant Crows heavy in their robes murmuring among themselves, as one or another finally accepted a bribe to lead him on futile quests into promising hill country or along some distant stream.

Sometimes he would return in a mood of near violence, convinced that he was a fool but knowing he was helpless to change things. On one occasion Marcher, furious at the latest bland deception of the Crows, accused Amiel and White River of not helping him when it was clear they could. Amiel smiled cynically and simply agreed with him. White River, after a long silence, put the matter where it had to be put. "If these Crows ain't helpin' you likely there's a reason, and likely it's a better one than we could come by for buckin' them."

Marcher's tipi was kept clean and warm by a slender young girl whose name was White Bead, a niece of White Tail. She was not often to be seen, keeping mostly to White Tail's lodge, but when she was she caught the eye of every man who viewed her, for her face was finer and narrower than those of her sister squaws and her eyes had a surprising glint of green. She for one admired Marcher and had come willingly. She would sit silently at night watching him devour the meat she had prepared, a thin spot of vermilion on each cheek and in the part of her hair. Marcher paid little or no attention to her, though he gave her some trinkets and a piece of bright cloth. On a few occasions he ranted at her about the slyness and subterfuge of her people, as though she were the Crow nation rolled into one. She watched his wrath with her greenish eyes, slowly warming to his gestures like a woman wanting, but for all that she didn't understand a word.

But however little notice Marcher paid White Bead she caused comment enough between Amiel and White River. They found speculating on her impossible to avoid. "She sure looks different, not like the others," ventured Amiel. He could have been musing over some odd and interesting literary point. "Only native I've noticed with that color eyes."

"Figures to be a breed," muttered White River, "pretty one to boot."

"A what?"

"Half-breed." White River settled back on his elbows, unlimbering his long body. "More 'n likely French. They was trapping up hereabouts afore most. Heard tell them Frenchies shined somethin' fierce at lovin' up squaws."

Amiel cupped his hands gently over his mouth, absorbing White River's blunt but convincing words. "That could explain it, I suspect," he sighed in almost rueful acceptance. "Could it mean trouble for Andy?"

White River smiled to himself. "Not likely. She's White Tail's niece. She's there by her own choosing. Don't fret it, Ben, she could mebbe be the proper medicine for him."

"I see," mumbled Amiel, still fingering his mouth. "Poor child."

Ben had no way of knowing, for White River could find no way to express it, that the Indian girl White Bead, with her lithe body and cool, lustrous eyes, reminded him strangely of his Lydia. It was not so much her appearance as the way she moved about. There was something deeply feminine and graceful in the sway of her body that rippled under the thin deerskin dresses. She could not have been more than sixteen but he was sure she was the prettiest Indian girl he had ever seen, although some of the Arikara girls he had grown up with, even shared a blanket with, were not easily forgotten. Again he had no words for it, and he suspected White Bead herself was unaware of it, but it was the motion of her body as much as her looks that aroused every male who eyed her walking through camp. Yet she had chosen Marcher, despite his indifference to her, and dutifully tended his lodge while keeping her eyes down when passing the many high-standing and important braves who could have brought her great honor and who clearly desired her.

30

In time the long trips on the cold slopes changed Marcher's mood. He grew secretive and kept to himself. His many excursions, if nothing else, were giving him a familiarity with the land, a knowledge of the Absarokee tongue and a growing understanding of how things were and how one stayed alive in this strange, beautiful but treacherous country.

Once they ran across some wagon tracks and followed them to a cache of whiskey jugs, discovered under some hastily gathered brush. The scouts squatted over a pair of heavy boot prints and another of light, worn moccasins. Marcher was able to piece together that a whiskey trader whom the Crows, unlike their neighbors, did not allow in their land, had brought an Indian scout along to warn him of trouble. The scout had seen Marcher's party coming and had advised flight. They only had time to conceal the cargo under the clumsy cover, probably intending to recover it later and cart it into the mountains. There was some good trading for whiskey in that mountainous country to the west. The Crows laughed as they began to break the jugs with their tomahawks. Marcher dismounted and saved two for himself without knowing why, for the smell of the fluid going into the hard earth reminded him of harsh-cut tobacco and turpentine.

His bribing of scouts had left him almost poor. His blankets were gone, along with his knives and metal cup and what cloth was left in his pack. Even his razor he relinquished, deciding he had no interest in shaving or cutting his hair. His clothes were almost in rags now and White Bead, seeing his need of a squaw, made a deerskin shirt for him and cut some leggings from a strip of well-chewed leather. Seeing him go by, White River rubbed the back of his neck gently and muttered to Amiel, "There's a gent what's fixin' to squat here a spell."

But Marcher did not give up his guns. He guarded his two repeating rifles jealously and carried his long pistol with him at all times. Big Owl had offered him four valuable horses for one of his rifles, but he shrugged the offer off and turned away.

Although he could not see it clearly, the semblance of a plan was forming in the back of his mind. His instincts warned him he would need those guns.

It was on his last trip that a thing happened that suddenly changed Marcher's standing in the village, and earned him an undeniable degree of respect among the Crows. He and two scouts were moving up to a small valley at the edge of a sweep of trees when his leading scout signaled them into cover. There were traces of snow on the ground and it was iron-cold as they sat motionless inside the tree line.

It was many minutes before Marcher saw the reason for cover. Four young braves were herding a half-dozen horses at a gallop down the narrow valley. The two Crows had dismounted and were now taking up positions at the rim of the trees, one with an old breechloader and the other with only his bow. It was clear that they were going to ambush these riders who Marcher gathered from their low grunts were young Sioux braves returning from a small secret raid on some Crow village for horses. He dismounted too, moving behind them with his repeating rifle at the ready. In the back of his mind he was reasoning that this ambush had to work or this desperate young war party that had them outnumbered might somehow get in a lick. The Crows watched him out of the corners of their eyes as he took up his position. The raiders were coming slowly toward them, their own attention on the captured horses and on the vamp of valley stretching behind them, from which they rightfully suspected pursuit might come. Marcher waited until he heard the far Crow's rifle crack in the frosty air before he opened fire. Almost immediately two braves were down, another clearly wounded with an arrow in his stomach and hanging on to his pommel. The fourth lost his mount as it wheeled at the volley. The two Crows leaped from cover and ran out to pull the wounded Sioux from his horse. He came down with his knife out, but his eyes were heavy and out of focus and did not change much when a tomahawk made a sharp gravelly sound against his skull.

The last remaining Sioux was on his feet and running clear of the horses that had started to stampede. He tried to swing about and mount one as it raced by, but Marcher's rifle snapped again and he rolled down limp and unbalanced, his arms uncurling with the impact of his fall. Immediately Marcher fired again and the brave's chin rose slowly in that high, still angle of death.

The Crows took the scalps, rounded up the many horses and hurriedly rode back to the village. They held the scalps high and whooped as they entered, Marcher riding steadily behind them. Somehow the whole experience elated him. Word of a victory was soon everywhere and people gathered about the singing and dancing scouts, who openly told of Marcher's two kills. White Tail and other chiefs came to smoke with Marcher, a thing the people watched, knowing it was a great honor, hoping Marcher would show respect for their headmen.

Marcher ate quietly by himself that evening, the warm food feeling good after a long stint in the cool air. When he had finished, he smoked for a while, looking into the fire and thinking of all he'd been through since he'd left on this long trek, thinking of how long it had been since he had had a woman, thinking of these Crow girls and the way they looked long and quiet at a man.

In time he decided to try some of the raw whiskey he'd saved from the whiskey trader they'd frightened away, and by mixing it with water and sipping it he found it went down with a minimum of torment. Just when he was not sure, but suddenly he knew he was feeling its effects. It made him lax and drowsy and before long he was rolling into his robe to sleep. How long he slept he did not know, but when he awoke during the night he found White Bead standing over him looking down silently, the tiny light from the fire marking the soft coloring of her eyes. He reached up and took her hand. She responded by coming down to her knees. They looked at each other closer now, their breathing a trifle more audible. Then he opened the robe and bending ever closer, she allowed herself to be drawn in.

31

That winter little raiding parties from the Crows' many enemies continued. No serious fighting took place, but once some young Arapahos, after horses and loot, were trapped in a gully and Marcher came up with his rifle to help drive them out. Big Owl cautioned him on getting too close, but Marcher ignored him, as was his way, and pressed up almost to the rim. The Crows were murmuring in warning as he thrust his rifle barrel forward, but it was too late, for immediately the barrel was grabbed by one of the enemy and wrenched from his hands. Marcher was digging desperately for his pistol and the Arapaho was rising up, the rifle level with Marcher's head, when Big Owl's war hatchet spun by and caught the Arapaho in the forehead directly above his left eye. He went down without a grunt.

The other Arapahos escaped in the melee, but Marcher was badly shaken and only with effort did he hold the rifle still when it was returned to him. It was some moments before he realized he had seen something impossible for him to describe, at least in that moment, for that hatchet had been thrown from nearly twenty feet and its timing . . . He looked strangely at Big Owl, knowing he owed him his life, but Big Owl made little of it, though much of the fact, in a way of dark warning, that Marcher's rifle in the Arapaho's hand would have meant Crow lives. Here was a lesson Marcher would not forget.

The following day he went to Big Owl's lodge and asked to buy the hatchet. Big Owl invited him to smoke and then explained he could not sell it, as it contained secret medicine things he could not part with. However, he offered to make Marcher one in return for the use of one of his repeating rifles in the spring hunt. Marcher agreed and offered to make it two hunts if Big Owl would teach him to use the hatchet. Big Owl grunted in agreement and Marcher's lessons began that very day.

It was a regular hatchet with a slight curve in the handle and the heel thinned down to make it lighter. It was kept in balance by a slim oval stone bound by thongs on the off-blade side. In spite of the bright decorations along its handle, broken by three black bands of leather at the grip, it was a lethal-looking weapon. Amiel and White River regarded it apprehensively as they saw Marcher swinging it about.

"Never seems to put it down, does he?" Amiel lifted his eyes to study the sky, which seemed gray and foreboding.

"Reckon he's got a reason." White River had discovered he did not like to talk about Marcher, so little more was said.

White River realized the season was closing in and another year was passing. By his reckoning Lydia should be fourteen by now, a young woman with a budding woman's needs. Girls matured and married early in the west. Why this would bother him he did not fully understand, for surely Lydia would find men to love her, men to cherish and care for her. She would never lose that indefinable warmth that drew people to her. Yet in his often-recurring fantasy that little girl with her strange, mothering eyes and the growing grace with which she moved her slender body, of which White Bead's lithe figure kept him mindful, belonged to him and he to her. Looking down at his long, gaunt figure clothed in tattered pieces of cloth and hides, he could only smile at the thought of a girl ever wanting to belong to him, or finding out that he belonged to her.

But the coming days were to prove him wrong. A tall, shapely widow called Blue Lodge had caught his eye across the village fire. He knew the meaning of that look, and while, with her broader face and darker skin, she was not nearly as pretty as White Bead, neither was she a wanton. She held herself proudly and left the decision in his hands. Maybe, he began to think, that was an answer to his growing restlessness. Maybe he needed a woman to touch. Maybe he had lived too long in a world that had vanished with Buzz. Maybe Lydia had already found another world. The young were quick to take a new hold on life. Maybe he was asking too much of her, of her memory, of life itself. Maybe . . . it would be a long winter.

Suddenly he realized explaining such a move to Ben could be difficult. He had never noticed Ben responding to the many squaws that flirted with him, although he seemed more amazed than shocked when White Bead went to live in Marcher's lodge.

But quiet, courteous Ben was more observant than he thought, and awaiting his chance, broached the matter himself. "Don't see how anyone can stand my company as long as you have."

White River smiled at Ben's way of showing understanding. "Been planning to give you some time for your lonesome."

Ben grinned.

White River looked at him, hoping to encourage his own interest. He knew Ben was lonely. "It's a heap warmer when it's two, Ben, and it shortens the time the snow sits."

"Must be getting old," said Ben good-naturedly, but in the back of his mind he knew another woman would only remind him of Melody, the only woman he ever made love to. His heart told him no amount of lust would ever cure his loneliness. He patted White River on the back and two days later offered a willing hand to help White River and Blue Lodge set up their tipi next to his.

The following day snow began to fall, lightly at first but then like a curtain drawn against the day. It finally stopped in the afternoon and the herders bringing together the stock discovered many horses had been stolen, among them Big Owl's favorite war pony. A tracking party was assembled immediately, and Marcher, weary of the idleness of camp, decided to go along with it. His popularity was growing with the braves and the presence of his many-shots rifle always made them feel strong.

However, the snow made for poor tracking, and Big Owl, leading the way, seemed to be going by some secret sense that saw in the snow swept from a single branch of pine the way to be pursued for a mile. In less than an hour they came to where the raiders had been when the storm lifted and now it was child's play to follow the many fresh hoofprints in the snow. They were heading almost due east and Marcher gathered from the braves' grumbling that these thieves were surely Sioux.

As the trail got fresher, the Crows began to press forward, for it was beginning to get dark and there was great fear they would not overtake this small enemy force before it escaped completely under the cover of night. They agreed that there were four in the raiding party but there were nine of them, including Marcher, and the Crows were confident. Their quirts resounded again and again against their ponies' flanks.

But they did not overtake the Sioux until dark, and then they found them in a strong place from which a single bullet suddenly raised snow around the hooves of the winded Crow ponies.

The Crows dismounted quickly, circling their enemies, but Big

Owl, shaking his head in quiet anger soon saw the Sioux were well hidden in a high wooded place with the stolen ponies probably corralled somewhere beyond.

"It will not be an easy fight, my brothers, for we cannot cross the open snow even in the dark."

The braves grumbled, feeling a file of cold sharpening the air about them. "Let us wait for them, then, Big Owl," said the youngest brave among them. "They must come from this hiding place in time even as does the winter-slumbering bear."

A tall Crow, looking through the dusk to the east, remarked knowingly, "We cannot sleep, for they will surely leave with the wind."

Big Owl studied the situation for a moment, then gave commands for the braves to spread out around the wooded area, posting two braves on each side except on the east, where he placed three. He told them to build fires but to stay out of range and keep their horses and weapons close. It was clear he and Marcher were to watch from the south side, where they presently stood.

Marcher was glad of the fire. In spite of his blanket-coat, the cold had numbed his limbs, and the prospect of waiting out the night began to pall upon him more and more. Yet there was nothing he could do. He wanted the Crows to think of him as one of them and leaving now would injure a plan that was slowly forming in the back of his mind.

How that night passed he did not know except that on rare occasions he and Big Owl talked. Mostly he stood clapping his hands or holding them over the fire to keep some feeling in them.

Just before dawn the frigid wind seemed to let up a little and Marcher was beginning to doze lightly. His first knowledge that the fight was on came with the crack of guns to the east and the Sioux war whoop suddenly hard against his ear as the surrounded ones tried to break through. Big Owl was already mounted and gone as Marcher, quickly rallying himself, swung onto his horse and began to follow. As he lashed the pony toward the sound of the fracas he was suddenly aware of another rider coming the other way. The other rider was looking behind him and their mounts collided with a sickening thump. Marcher pitched forward in a rough roll that separated him immediately from his rifle and scraped his face savagely against the hard surface crust of snow. He came to his feet stunned but with an almost animal instinct that the other was on his feet and rushing at him. Something made him reach inside his blanket-coat for his hatchet just as the other stormed into him and brought him down. In desperation, and unable to find the breath to shout, he grabbed the wrist of the hand that had plunged a knife into his left shoulder and rolled with the furiously struggling figure until he himself was on top. Aware another figure was approaching, he pulled away from the knife wielder to brace himself on one knee and free up the hatchet. But Marcher hesitated a moment too long and the downed figure lunged forward to get inside the swing of his weapon. Again he was pinned to the ground. This time he turned the hatchet to its flat side and bashed it with all his remaining strength against his attacker's head. At that, the figure slumped and rolled still.

Marcher came up quickly, expecting another assault, but he discovered it was Big Owl coming up to him, holding his lost rifle and looking at the hatchet even now rising slowly in his hand.

The fight was over. The other three Sioux were dead but not before they had managed to kill the youngest Crow warrior. The rest of the braves were rounding up the horses and by the time they came forward, dawn was already opening a thin cherry fan in the east. The stunned Sioux still lying at Marcher's feet began to groan.

Marcher saw Big Owl bending over the prone body and found himself quickly turning away, certain the Crow was going to slit the enemy's throat with his own knife. But when he looked back he found that Big Owl had merely tied the Sioux's hands behind him and was even then pulling him to his feet.

The other Crows grunted as they came up and dismounted. Without any words they pushed the Sioux up on one of the stolen ponies and tied his feet under its belly. Marcher could see the body of the dead Crow tied across another mount. He discovered the cut on his shoulder was not serious, his heavy coat having absorbed most of the blade, and his face was only bruised and tender around the eyes and chin. He knocked the snow from the barrel of his rifle.

Finally, with the dawn flushing scarlet behind them, they started back. With the coming of light the Sioux proved to be nothing more than a boy, but upon regaining his senses he began to hurl insults at the Crows, shouting at them, giving out as though in contempt the Sioux war cry.

They ignored him as though he were already dead. Marcher sensed from their dark manner that the young Sioux would have much to shout about later.

In time he and Big Owl were riding in the van of the party, the others surrounding the captive and the recovered horses to the rear. But it was some time before Big Owl muttered, "When one fights with the war hatchet, my brother, he does not think like a wolf looking on two trails."

Marcher knew now that Big Owl had seen him hesitate in the fight.

Big Owl looked long and hard at the far horizon where an icy blue sky met the frozen white rim of the land. There lay a coldness in his eyes that matched the arctic scene they looked upon. "Teach your fingers to grow about the grip, so at a touch you will know which way the blade faces—make it a part of your arm, an arm that moves without thought, as a man's hands go before him when he falls."

Marcher now knew the secret of Big Owl's incredible way with the weapon. Quietly, as he reached inside his greatcoat to finger the grip, he decided that before long he must master it too.

32

In the Crow village winter was setting in, and the snow, coming more and more often, had begun to pile in high drifts along the valley floor. Travel became difficult, then impossible, and the fires frequently leaped high in the morning cold of the lodges.

The endless thud of Marcher's hatchet striking wood kept many ears and eyes aware of his growing skill, particularly when he roughened its handle by tying the old yellow bandana, now stained and crusted with dirt and age, above the bottom rawhide strap. It steadied his grip and made the weapon whirl through the air like a giant angry bee. It was not long before young braves, admiring this sudden new power, were calling him, out of respect, Yellow Hatchet.

Yet the matter that really held the people's minds as the snow rose about them was the young Sioux captive whom Big Owl wanted to put to death. But others had come forward to stay his hands and ask more and more often for the pipe. Particularly firm in resisting this action was White Tail, but Ironfoot and others were soon with him.

The captive's extreme youth would not have normally helped him, but now it was used as an argument for adopting him into the tribe. Big Owl scoffed at the thought. The young brave would escape on the first horse he mounted. Actually the others knew this was true, nor would it have been surprising if he took a Crow scalp or two with him, but in the back of White Tail's mind, and he sensed Ironfoot now shared this desperate hope, was the thought of returning this youth in the spring to his people as an emissary of peace. As their war leaders knew, they were already overmatched by the Blackfeet; to have the Sioux moving against them at the same time raised serious questions of survival. Yet this was Big Owl's captive and so they had to talk on.

Ironfoot had another reason for avoiding, or at least delaying, this young Sioux's torture and death. He had visited the captive a number of times and had seen that he was well treated. At first the young Sioux was haughty and defiant, but patience and good treatment and a hope that one could almost see starting to jump in his young breast that he perhaps was going to live after all soon changed his demeanor. He began to talk to Ironfoot and soon Ironfoot realized he had made the right decision. This young Sioux had known about the chief, White Man's Medicine.

The story came out slowly, but it had the ring of truth about it. This chief had once killed a white near Innyan Kara and had taken from him a cross which everyone knew as the white man's medicine. He did not plan to keep it, as it was thought to be bad luck, but in traveling south he had run into a party of well-armed whites who were going to kill him till they saw the cross. For some reason that made them let him go, and he decided that for him at least this was good medicine.

He started to wear the cross and people now called him White Man's Medicine. Surely he was a great and successful and popular war leader. But one night after returning from a raid, he went out to the hills to pray, taking with him his two squaws. Then long after dark one squaw returned wounded and on foot to say that the war chief and her sister, his other wife, were dead, having been ambushed by a Crow.

It was discovered that there were two Crows about the camp, perhaps stealing horses. What happened after that no one was sure, but the Sioux camp had become a seething caldron—White Man's Medicine had to be avenged.

The Crows could not be caught, but one was followed to his village and the chiefs smoked solemnly, saying to themselves that that winter the village would be destroyed. Ironfoot needed and wanted to hear no more. He rose, saying to the young brave, whose name they discovered was Little Hawk, that he should always be brave and never desert his friends in battle. Little Hawk nodded and rubbed his sturdy shoulders as though this were not a thing a Sioux needed to be told.

In the end Ironfoot and White Tail prevailed upon Big Owl to spare the Sioux brave and the pipe was finally put to rest. Little Hawk was told he was going back to his own people in the spring, that he would have some freedom about the camp but he was not to leave it without permission.

He listened to this stoically, but Ironfoot and White Tail smiled at each other when they left as they heard him dancing and singing in youthful exuberance behind the skins of his lodge.

Big Owl, however, drew his robes about him gravely and walked through the camp pondering a matter that drew closer as the moons turned in the sky. The people would often watch him as he stood staring off to the north, knowing what was in his heart. As a rule the skies to the north wore a curtain of moldy gray, but on clear days they wore a blue so deep it looked like evening approaching at high noon. Big Owl dwelt on those skies, for he knew they could see what he could not. He knew they arched on and on over prairie and river to the Eagle Hills. He knew one day they would turn a light azure and become sun-filled, and at that time beneath them would be stirring the dreaded Blackfeet.

PART SIX

BLACKFEET

33

The great northern plateau washes westward, breaking around the many rump ranges that warn of the wall of the Rockies beyond, for it is at these mountains that the mighty plain gives out and the eye so used to the hypnotic sweep of space must turn northward to hold the spell. To the north, along the eastern wall of the granite giants, lie the rich headwater countries of the Missouri, the North and South Saskatchewans, names around which the bloody history of the Northwest hangs as the chant and mystery of sea and old sail cloaked the rock-worn coasts of New England.

Here are grasslands and swift-flowing streams and strange red and yellow abutments of rock. There is an easy roll to the land that says it is very old, that eons of waiting have worn it down beyond recall, that hills once sharp against the sky have become valleys and are at peace. In summer roving game abounds, and the puma and the wolf are but a twinkling of death in a restless sea of life. The terrain is alive with berries and rich grasses that range everywhere, halted in their march only by the dark stands of conifers along the gentle slopes. But the summers here are not long and those who laid claim to this land knew it. They broke their year into four uneven parts, the largest of which was winter. They were a hardy, aggressive and savage people and their power in the Northwest such that they saw no need of peace. But even they, the mighty Blackfeet, "the Devil's Own," could not fight the hour when the sun drifted south and the deathly cold that slept in the great white peaks to the west rose to ride the wind and lay its reign upon the land.

Sometimes in winter the sky would break scarlet and blue at dawn with the air as clear as gin, but the wind rose sharp and steady, and the temperature would plummet down, ever downward, mocking a sun that could only light up the snow mantle to a brightness that stunned the eyes but brought no more heat than the blue-tinged moon that mounted in its turn in the sky. Sometimes the wind would briefly lower and a quietude that said the land was dead as far as every horizon troubled the mind, and it was hard to believe that life still hung on under the snow, waiting.

High on the frozen Marias River, the Piegan camp was huddled in the lee of sharp-rising bluffs that followed a bowlike bend of the river to the west. Smoke drifted up from the great circles of conical tipis, and a rangy dog lunged through the snow, angrily followed by three others, howling for part of the dead pup it carried in its mouth. Upstream from the village stood the horse herd nibbling on tiny strips of inner cottonwood bark cut for them by young boys. It was the only forage left in a frozen land. A lone sentinel, huddled in his robe, watched them from a ledge on the frigid bluff above.

Within a few miles there were other Piegan camps strung along the creeks and streams that stretched their frozen fingers into the Marias. Within twelve miles the entire Piegan tribe, the largest group of the Blackfoot nation, had made their winter quarters. The fall buffalo hunt had been good and most of the camps still had meat enough, but the winter had been a hard one and fresh game to flavor the pot or sweeten the stomach was nowhere to be found.

Some forty miles to the northeast of the Piegan camps were the Kainah, the Bloods, a smaller tribe, wintering around the headwaters of the Milk River and talking endlessly of their victory that year over their Cree and Assiniboine enemies. Every tipi, its red markings bright against the snow, had its feathered scalp pole and warriors reciting their many coups, their *namachkani,* over and over again. The tribe's war leaders had said in many smokes an even greater victory over the

Crows might come that spring. The young men were jubilant and sang as they worked on their weapons. But some of the old men sat silently behind the wide eagle fans, wondering what talk rose above the keening in the camps of the Assiniboine and the Cree, two tribes who had the whites at Fort Union to arm them and, perhaps, even as in the past, to lead them.

Finally further to the north where the ice of the Bow River bent into the frozen bank of the South Saskatchewan, lay the camp of the Siksika, the Blackfeet proper, the smallest of the three tribes that made up the Blackfoot nation. They huddled in their winter quarters eager for the spring and the raiding parties that had made the tribe rich in horses and slaves. Several decades ago the white man's spotted disease had so reduced them that the remaining men determined to bring back every female captive they could and lie with her to swell their numbers. By now they had some of their old strength back and their medicine was strong again. They were anxious for the war drums, the shouts and war whoops of the attack, or the stealthy horse raids that made a man rich and gave him importance in the tribe.

Deep in the main Piegan camp that ran along the Marias, Blood-on-His-Moccasin sat quietly in his lodge, a great buffalo robe about his shoulders, his small deep-set eyes trailing across the many robed figures about him. They were headmen of the hunting camps nearby, except for Jumping Calf, whom the others regarded as chief of all the Piegans. It had been a winter of long waiting, and Blood-on-His-Moccasin sensed that both spring and its vital grass would be late this year. Secretly this had made him morose and ill-tempered, for he was weary of the smoky lodge and the long days of idleness. A warrior with the ache for combat in his bones, he did not like empty talk or storytelling, even of brave deeds, as other men did. Yet his restlessness showed only in his little, quick-moving eyes, and of the robed figures about him only Jumping Calf saw it there.

"It is said that Shoshones will come to smoke with the Crows," said one of the headmen, putting aside the pipe he had been drawing on.

"Shoshones are squaws," rumbled Blood-on-His-Moccasin, disdain bending his features.

"When the buffalo returns and the thunder speaks for the pipe ceremony, we will find fresh meat for our old and young ones. After that we will show these Crows some real warriors." It was the tall, thin Jumping Calf speaking. He threw a bone he was chewing on into the fire.

Blood-on-His-Moccasin grunted. Jumping Calf put too many things before war, but he was a brave man nonetheless, and Blood-on-His-Moccasin respected bravery above all things. Now he turned slowly to the others, among them the hideously scarred War Belt. "Will our brothers, the Kainah and the Siksika think we are strong in war if we wait until our bellies are full before we lead them to our enemies?"

Jumping Calf kept his eyes on the fire. "Our weak ones must eat."

Blood-on-His-Moccasin smothered his long seething dislike for Jumping Calf. A scene in the Pend d'Oreille camp a few years before still hung like an open sore between them. "Can we not leave hunters and young boys to make a surround? I say the Crows will not be ready if we come before the buffalo returns."

Jumping Calf looked heavily at Blood-on-His-Moccasin. "Has Blood-on-His-Moccasin forgotten that the grass that brings the buffalo is needed to make our war ponies strong again?"

War Belt grunted in agreement. "My best war horse is thin and could hardly carry me here this day."

"Who speaks of horses?" defied Blood-on-His-Moccasin.

The others looked at him in quiet surprise. Finally Jumping Calf said cautiously, "We have not smoked here to speak of warriors going on foot to steal horses. My brother has been making many brave words of war."

Not only War Belt but others grunted in agreement. Jumping Calf, thus encouraged, went on. "Would Blood-on-His-Moccasin take us into the land of our enemies afoot? Surely he must know the Crows have horses and good ones. Surely he must remember the rivers rise like serpents when the snow leaves the mountains? Surely he has not forgotten our horses saved us in our last battle when the Crow medicine was strong."

"Saved us because the Crow horses were strong and could carry their warriors. Now their horses are as weak as ours. Besides I have smoked with the chiefs of the Kainah and we have a plan for stealing their horse herd first."

"Ahhh," said Jumping Calf almost to himself. So a plan had already been smoked on with the war chiefs of the Kainah. A faint distrust of Blood-on-His-Moccasin and his intent began to edge along Jumping Calf's mind. It was not the first time.

"So they have come to us with more plans," grumbled War Belt dryly. "Our squaws are still keening about their last brave words for war."

"They are great warriors," defended Blood-on-His-Moccasin stoutly. "Did they not gather many coups on the Cree and their allies during the hunting season and scatter them as the bear does rabbits from a hutch?" Blood-on-His-Moccasin's anger was alive in his small eyes. "When I killed Red Warbonnet, the great Crow chief, and brought his scalp home for our victory dance, you did not speak with these squawlike words."

The others sat quietly, carefully weighing these things said in anger. Some remembered the old Crow chief riding before his warriors and going down when his horse was hit. Though the Blackfeet swarmed over him the old chief fought like a grizzly and did not die alone. The enraged Crows, charging in and struggling bitterly for his body, had struck down many good men, among them the son of Jumping Calf. In truth, it was a close and costly thing. Jumping Calf bit silently into the stem of the pipe, his eyes closing as the strange loneliness that was his son's death rose within. What then was this loud talk of a victory dance?

War Belt leaned forward and gripped his knees. "Let us fight the Shoshones first," he said. "It is said they have many horses fed in the white man's way. Horses who are strong even after the long snows."

The eyes of the others all gathered to his cruelly scarred face, and for a moment only the wind through the smoke hole above could be heard. Here was a wisdom worth smoking over.

The pipe was refilled, lit, offered to the earth and sky and the four corners, and then passed slowly around, each chewing over in his own mind, as it went, War Belt's words. Finally Blood-on-His-Moccasin said, "My brother War Belt speaks well. The Shoshones get the dead grass of the whites from the Black Robes that live among them. To take these horses would be the work of children. The Shoshone ponies will give us victory over the Crows."

"Where are the Shoshones?" asked Jumping Calf evenly.

"Our scouts will find them as the weasel finds sleeping mice," muttered Blood-on-His-Moccasin.

"How many horses will they have? And how many will have eaten the dead, strange grass of the whites?" persisted Jumping Calf.

"We will know when they are ours."

Jumping Calf and some of the headmen exchanged glances, then Jumping Calf pulled his robe about him preparing to rise. "Does our brother Blood-on-His-Moccasin wish to hold his victory dance now?"

Many of the listening headmen tried hard not to smile, but Blood-on-His-Moccasin's face froze and he gripped the handle of his knife under his robe. He would remember that Jumping Calf had mocked him.

"We will sleep on this thing," said Jumping Calf. The others looked at him as he stood before them, an impressively tall man and a keeper of the most sacred beaver medicine bundle. Few were his equal in wisdom. "When the snows begin to go, the Kainah and Siksika will come to council with us for we have sent them gifts of tobacco and asked them to. When they come, we will tell them our thoughts and hear their words, for they will be our brothers in war."

He left the tipi, the other headmen, lumbering to their feet like old bulls, following him out. It was a chilly trip to their own camps and many wished to be beside their own fires before dark.

War Belt, leaving last, stopped at the flap of the tipi and turned to Blood-on-His-Moccasin. "You know we two are brothers, but once you did a bad thing to Jumping Calf. Give him many horses and make his heart good again. If you do not do this thing, your medicine might be weak and there might be great trouble when we go against the Crows."

Blood-on-His-Moccasin sat brooding over his fire. Was he not their greatest war chief? Why then did they not follow him as warriors should? Why did they stand about haggling like squaws or carrying anger from the long past? That half-breed Pend d'Oreille girl Jumping Calf had taken prisoner, and that he, Blood-on-His-Moccasin, had forced into his robe while Jumping Calf hotly pursued their warriors further into the mountains—was she so big a matter? He had only used her for a while, but Jumping Calf refused to take her when he returned her—an open insult—giving her instead to the warriors. But was this a thing to come between chiefs?

He sat watching the coals, thinking of the strange manner and words of Jumping Calf and the headmen who grunted in support. Ah, was there not some secret menace there? Well, he, Blood-on-His-Moccasin, was still strong among the warriors. They would follow him whether Jumping Calf would or not, for they wanted and needed horses, booty, women. Only Blood-on-His-Moccasin could promise them all these things.

Anger, spawned by a gnawing resentment, brought him to his feet. He took his medicine bundle from its perch beside his great Kiowa war horn and holding it before him sang his medicine song. He sang it many many times while overhead the wind droned and the strange spirit lights that none could account for began to dance in the northern sky.

34

As winter deepened so did the confusion and frustration of the two whites held fast by the steep drifts of snow surrounding and, with sudden high winds, threatening to bury the Crow camp. Marcher, shunning everyone but White Bead, had settled on the side of the camp opposite Amiel and White River. The men saw little of each other, an arrangement all three were content with.

Still, Marcher and Amiel shared something unknown to each other. In their own ways both were withdrawing within themselves and away from this strange and for them alien world. Marcher had become morose, given to ugly fits of anger and frustration; Amiel became more and more apathetic. They both seemed lost in some dark preoccupation brought on by endless fields of snow that stretched in unbroken sweeps toward every horizon.

One day Marcher stared into the small, stained trade mirror he had taken from White Bead and propped on a sagging lodge pole. He appraised his beard and weather-worn face indifferently before grabbing a handful of ragged hair, slashing at it repeatedly with his hunting knife. It was a slow, occasionally painful process, but in time he rounded off the unkempt growth sufficiently for his taste. Time was something he had plenty of in the way a forgotten prisoner has time.

He knew he would survive the winter, but there were things that took getting used to, such as finding the mornings dark and snow heaped as high as one's shoulder against the lodge flap. There were shrieking winds so cold a man had to move his bowels in quick, short releases or his genitals would go numb. Within the lodge though, once he had adjusted to the grease-scented smoke, there was warmth enough and even some rudiments of comfort. White Bead was a good squaw, or as good as he figured squaws got, tending to his needs and speaking little. His growing command of Crow made talk between them simpler. The only English word he taught her and then forced her to use was "Yes." So whenever he muttered to himself about the weather, cursed himself for his bad luck, or just ranted against the eternal idleness that ate like acid into his nerves, she simply mumbled "Yes," not knowing if it was a fitting response or not.

Yet even here in his agitated misery a slowly growing confidence began stirring in the depths of his thinking, telling him that in spite of disappointments and seeming defeat his instincts had not deserted him. Something had been going on in the back of his mind. To get what he wanted from this land he had to become part of it. More than that, he had to use others who were already part of it. This mounting intuition in time bred a long evaluation of the forces about him that slowly and in some mysterious way unveiled for him the subtle fabric of a plan. Caught up and frustrated by his own weaknesses, he had forgotten the weaknesses of others, and in a curious moment in the half light of the lodge he suddenly perceived, like the sky opening after a frightening storm, the key to his predicament. He lay on the lodge skins looking upward for several heartbeats before he rose, his eyes closing in a grim inner-seeing, his hands gripping his head in a mock gesture of despair. Kicking the dirt floor, he stood with his hands on his hips, studying the lodge flap for long moments, then he began to mutter to himself as he pulled on a heavy robe and reached for one of his repeating rifles, carefully kept in its covering of dried skin beside his robe. As he made his way toward the flap his voice rose in smothered rage. "You're an ass, Andy Marcher, a stupid blind blue ribbon ass!" He squirmed his way through the lodge flap, his voice growing dimmer as he moved away, "Yep, just a twenty-four-karat ass!"

"Yes," murmured the silently watching White Bead, her face almost lost in the dark reaches of the lodge.

As Marcher made his way through the heavy snow to the camp center, he knew something was bothering the Crows. As the winter drew to a close, it was quietly pervading the entire camp, making the men unaccountably quiet and the women, settling deeper into their robes, more watchful of the men. Sometimes he would see White Tail and Big Owl standing behind the circle of lodges, looking at the sky, saying nothing. Marcher concluded in the end they were beset by some problem discussion could not diminish. Had he been more interested, as were Amiel and White River, he might have discovered it for himself, but Marcher had one interest and only one.

What had just fallen together in his mind, however, was the way Big Owl looked at his repeating rifle whenever he passed by. At first he thought it was simply the admiration fighting men or devoted hunters hold for any superior weapon, but now he knew it was more than that. Now he was recalling the compelling sequence he should have noticed from the beginning. It was Big Owl who had offered him four sleek and valuable horses for his gun, Big Owl, because he was watching intently, who had first seen the Arapaho in the ravine seize the gun barrel and had sent his hatchet in almost the same instant to dispatch him, Big Owl who stopped first to retrieve Marcher's rifle while Marcher was still in his death struggle with the Sioux. What if that Sioux had gotten his knife up in time? Who then would have owned the gun? And now he saw Big Owl again returning the gun he had borrowed to rid the camp of some wolves that were preying on the camp's dogs. The Indian's expression was that of a father offering up a son.

He winced as he pulled upon the flap of Big Owl's lodge, for almost as heavy as the robes that sheathed its conical shape was the rancid air inside. He knew at once that others were gathered there, their indistinct figures rimming the long, low fire, but it was not until he settled on the ground that he recognized White Tail across the tiny fingers of flame and Big Owl seated on his right. The others soon proved to be well-known warriors, men of many coups and proven leaders in war.

Marcher, blatantly unaware of the discourtesy involved in his crude entry into what was obviously a serious council, made the sign for wanting to talk. Big Owl, noticing at once the repeating rifle lying across his lap, lifted an uncertain hand in response. Keeping his eyes from the others seated about him he said, "His words will be as welcome as is Yellow Hatchet in the lodge of Big Owl." Several of the others grunted—but they fell far short of grunts of approval. Marcher, his senses alerted, picked up this warning tone and realized impatience had made him blunder again. He would have to recoup.

He motioned for the pipe, which they patiently relit and passed around the circle. When that was done, Marcher turned slowly to Big Owl, his gaze also taking in White Tail whose quietude did not erase the fact that he was headman of the tribe.

"We would hear the words of Yellow Hatchet," Big Owl murmured, watching Marcher lift the rifle to a more prominent position on his lap, as the silver nameplate on the stock picked up the glow of the fire.

"Yellow Hatchet feels the heart of his Absarokee brothers," began Marcher in their tongue. "Their hearts are heavy. Can their brother, Yellow Hatchet, make them light again?"

There was a long silence, and in the end it was the grim White Tail who answered, "Do brothers need to be told what lies in each other's hearts?"

Marcher measured these words carefully, ruefully realizing he was being told his ignorance of what lay beneath their long-standing worries belied his words. Fool! he thought. Wisdom, had he had any, would have warned him to come sooner and be aware of their troubles. Now he would have to gamble, a dangerous thing, he had discovered, when dealing with Indians. "The medicine of my brothers tells them a strange spirit is moving among their people."

White Tail smiled coldly into the smoke drifting above, clearly conveying he could see through these falsely offered words.

Big Owl, his face etched with concern, reached again for the pipe. He turned to his fellow tribesmen. "Yellow Hatchet has not lived long among the Absarokee. He knows little of what we hear in the song of the wind and the changing shadows the sun leaves upon our mountains. The Absarokee have long walked hand and hand with the whites. Let us remember that."

White Tail nodded, allowing these conciliatory words to stand, but his mind was clouded by the fact that two other whites in the camp knew of their fear of impending attack, had even smoked over it. Why had they not told this strange one?

Marcher rose, holding his rifle before him, his eyes on White Tail but his attention riveted on Big Owl whom he remarked with relief was staring steadfastly at the rifle. Drawing his robe about him he said in openly strained tones, "Yellow Hatchet will leave the fire of his brothers now. He will think upon their troubled spirits until wisdom comes. Then he will speak with them again and our hearts will be as one."

As he disappeared through the flap the lodge behind him was left in a long, uneasy silence, but in the council of the Crows such silences held the meaning of many, many words.

Outside the wind picked up a fleece of snow and swept it across Marcher's face, causing him to stop before Big Owl's lodge and stare at the far end of the circle where the dark streaked lodges of Amiel and White River stood. Those two would know what he now had to discover, but having avoided them for so long, he was ashamed to seek them out now. Damn! Every circumstance appeared to work against him. As he turned fretfully toward his own lodge a new and animated thought sparked to life in him. White Bead! She would know, probably had for some time and kept it from him. Why hadn't he remembered what sly bitches these squaws could be? His irritation, fueled by his many frustrations, grew as he made his way through the uneven mounds of snow toward his lodge.

Much had changed between Marcher and White Bead in the last few months. In spite of her bending to his every need, his growing chagrin with himself had found an all too ready and helpless object in White Bead. Clearly the closeness of the lodge did not help, but the lodge robes at least kept the camp from seeing the growing sordidness of the scenes within. It was while his whiskey still lasted that he took to handling her roughly, sometimes seizing her in cold lust, taking her before she was ready, forcing her to say "Yes, yes," as he pumped his body against hers. Even when his whiskey ran out he would take fits and strike her when she was bending over the fire or kneeling to mend their skin robes. Not once did she wince or whine at his abuse but turned slowly back to him, rubbing the hurt part, stoically watching him.

He came into the lodge, his eyes narrowing in the lesser light, peering about for her, while, as was his habit, he returned his rifle safely to its skin coverings. He sensed her coming toward him to help him off with the now loose-hanging robe, but how it started he could never later remember. The heavy robe came off awkwardly and momentarily they stumbled against each other. He turned and seized her with one hand to right himself, while with the other he struck her across the face with such force that he spun her completely around, her body crumpling till she was on her knees, her head going down to be cradled in her hands. Then as though his spleen was still not spent, he stepped forward to kick her pathetic figure that now seemed one with the ground. But then suddenly she was not on the ground but rising to meet him, her face stopping only inches from his, her cool, emerald-tinted eyes seeming to hang by themselves in the darkened lodge. It was a moment that paralyzed him with its unexpectedness, a moment when he felt the tip of a long skinning knife breaking the skin above his navel, her eyes and the knife holding him as one. He seemed to experience an eternity of faint terror before her breath wheezed at him with a throatiness he never thought could be hers. "Y-e-s-s . . ." she breathed. He drew back, unable to take his eyes off hers but she came forward with him, the knife still holding a fraction beneath the skin. Dazed, he raised his hands in the peace sign, but it was the words that rose in his mouth that seemed to release her. "No," he cried in English, repeating it many times before he was able to break into Crow. "No . . . White Bead and Yellow Hatchet not fight!" He shook his head in short, quick jerks from side to side. "No, no, no," he shouted, returning again almost helplessly to English. Finally, still watching him, she drew the knife back within her robe, but her eyes were still intense as she said, peering at him through the half-light of the lodge, "Yes . . . no . . . no . . . no!"

An understanding for which the human race has never found adequate words had passed between them.

35

The wind was still alive and moved with a wild, anguished scream through the mountains. The snow lay in long, uneven fields beneath the sharp heights that shielded them from the sun. Evening had put a thin bitter edge on the high rare air and some of the Blackfeet held pieces of blanket across the bottom halves of their faces as they lumbered behind Blood-on-His-Moccasin who was leading them in an exhausting climb toward the southwest.

It was just in the last light of day that they caught a glimpse of three figures before them, zigzagging back and forth on a little field of snow. The braves knew at once it was War Belt and two of their wolves, and the zigzagging meant a Shoshone village had been sighted. There was much grunting of approval, for they had been traveling eight days now, most of the time against the endless pitch of the mountains and the eternally rising valley slopes where the air came ever more slowly into a man's nostrils and had to labor its way through his body.

There was no thought of fires as they camped on the frigid slope. There was only the dry beef and the water that came from melting snow in the mouth. The braves huddled together silently drawing in their robes or white Hudson Bay coats, knowing that there would be no sleep that night, knowing they would have to move stealthily to where they could strike this enemy village by dawn.

No one spoke until War Belt came up to say, "We have found our enemies. Their village is at the bottom of the next valley and they have many horses."

"How many lodges?" demanded Blood-on-His-Moccasin, his face turned sharply toward the next valley mouth.

"As many as twice the fingers on a man's hands."

Jumping Calf grunted in vague surprise.

"And they have so many horses?" asked Blood-on-His-Moccasin, hearing now it was only a small village.

"The horse herd is in a closed place beyond, but Long Otter circled their village and got very near to it."

"Are these then the good horses we seek?" questioned Jumping Calf. There was more than a hint of impatience edging his words.

War Belt turned and signaled one of the scouts who had settled behind him to come forward. "Let Long Otter speak of what he has seen."

Long Otter was a tall, spindly man with a heavy crop of hair greased and braided to his shoulders. Now, from much running and crawling, many errant strands of hair were drooping forward and partially concealing the left side of his face. Though not a leader, he was known for his ability to move about noiselessly and to hold his mud-encased body in one position as though turned to rock for hours on end. It was his job to teach the young boys of the village the deadly and demanding disciplines of a scout. His medicine, a puma's claw wrapped in weasel skin, was known to be very strong.

"I crawled to the other side of the Shoshone village," said Long Otter, the exposed half of his face expressionless. "There are many, many horses. This I have seen."

"Do they look strong and well-fleshed from the winter feed of the whites?" queried Jumping Calf.

"There are many that do, yet a few seem poor and thin as antelopes."

Jumping Calf and some of the Siksika chiefs grunted uneasily. It was clear they thought this a strange matter.

"The Shoshone may only feed their good war ponies," said Blood-on-His-Moccasin. "It is their war ponies that count. They are the ones we have come for."

"My brother speaks well," declared a headman of the Kainah.

Jumping Calf and the Siksika chiefs stood together, their heaving breath audible in the darkness. A peculiar air of uncertainty seemed to hang over them. Finally Jumping Calf said, "Did you see any Black Robes of the whites in this village of the Shoshones?"

"I saw only one. But there was much smoke coming from the lodges, as though their people sat in council. Who can say whether there were others?"

Jumping Calf grunted again and looked up at a sky now freckled with stars.

Blood-on-His-Moccasin stamped his feet in irritation. "Our scalping knives will help us count them with the next sun. Now we must eat. When the stars have journeyed partway across the sky we will go forward again and take this village."

The weary village of the Shoshones was finally silent, and even the persistent and restless mountain winds seemed to be asleep, awaiting the first hint of dawn before they bestirred themselves again. Its few headmen sat dozing over their spent fire, for they had fought their fatigue the evening before and gathered to council on the great happenings of that day.

A very strong party from their main village to the south had arrived in the morning. They had come on lively, prancing horses clearly fed on the good winter grain of the whites. They were well armed and even accompanied by an unhappy Black Robe, Father Villiers. Splendid as they looked though, they had carried bad words in their mouths. The Blackfeet were on the warpath and the Crows wanted the Shoshones to smoke with them and become their allies. The Shoshone chiefs had consented and had sent this great party led by Rising Hawk, a remarkably able war chief, to their outlying villages as soon as the snow cleared the passes, to tell them they should move south as quickly as possible to join in the ceremonies that made the Shoshone medicine strong for war. That so many braves had come at first surprised the little village, for there were over sixty in all, but then at once they were told that the Blackfeet were already believed to be in the mountains and if the traveling Shoshones encountered them Rising Hawk wanted to be sure the Shoshones drew the first blood. This made the people's hearts glad, for hatred of the Blackfeet was a tribal obsession whose roots were lost in a dark time even the oldest grandfather among them could not recall.

The Black Robe, Father Villiers, did not want them to go to war. He spoke in council first, having lived with them for many years and having fully mastered their tongue. But the visiting warriors, and even the hosts to whom he had brought coffee and several cooking pots, greeted his pious words of peace with a patient but impassive silence. He was a good man and had done much to help their tribe, but his medicine was hopeless against the Blackfeet and they knew it. Over the years the Blackfeet had unhesitatingly killed two gift-bearing Black Robes who had sought them out to speak to them of peace. The Crows, the people whispered to each other, knew the folly of following the whites. In the end it was their own fighting men who held their hunting grounds. Their way, the way of the red pipe, seemed the better one to meet these murderous marauders and change these agonizing times for the long-suffering and embittered Shoshones.

After a respectful silence, the council talk turned to war and Father Villiers rose and left, unwilling to listen to words his faith told him were evil. He wandered about the village for hours, quietly praying to himself and asking forgiveness for his failure to Christianize these strange people. He thought of his many years of work and willing sacrifice, of the grain, of the trade he had brought to them, and then he stopped to stare at the mountain vastness about him, wondering, as he would many times before he died, at the inscrutable ways of God. It was he that Long Otter had seen.

Shortly after dark the visitors had left, their strong rested ponies and many spares bearing them quickly to the west, where they were told lay still another small village only an hour's ride. A young brave of the village, an excellent tracker, went with them as a courtesy, for they knew this land too well to lose their way. But idle as it was, it was this gesture that saved this brave's life.

He had been an idle dreamer in his youth, a good rider and tracker but shy of all girls except his younger sister. Her name was Little Rabbit. She teased him shamelessly, but he still left unexpected gifts under her blanket and laughed to see her find them there. He rode away now beside the mighty Rising Hawk, knowing his father's proud eyes were upon him. Still, shyly, he did not look up until they were clear of the camp. His name was Far-Away-Storm.

36

Ben Amiel peered through the flap of his lodge at the long lonely wastes of snow leading to the mountains. This was truly a land that threw a hypnotic spell over a man's mind. No wonder these savages put such faith in dreams, and the medicines they felt their sacred delusions left them with. The heart required a secret feeling it was not alone against the fierceness and isolation of this terrain.

He wondered what this land, this life, was doing to Andy, for something unnatural and menacing had entered his ways, something no desperate craving for Paul's gold could ever account for. He sensed their long eroded feelings of kinship had all but vanished, and he was helpless to conceal his revulsion at Andy's weird urge to become one with these friendly but primitive warlike nomads.

Were it not for White River's companionship, he sensed, his own loneliness and increasingly frequent depressions might have cost him his sanity. But White River, feeling his need, came by faithfully every day. Sometimes they rode or just walked together, and inevitably they hit upon and enjoyed little jokes: White River, peering at twelve-foot drifts slotted between their lodges and drawling prophetically, " 'Pears we're fixing to get a little snow," or Amiel, catching a glimpse of the scowling Marcher across the village and musing, with a lightness he rarely felt, "Getting harder to tell you two gents apart all the time."

He even discovered how White River had got his name. It seemed when he was still a stripling he had been out with an Arikara hunting party. It was late spring and the rivers were in flood. They were crossing the rapids of a large creek when they were attacked by a war party of Rock Indians, the ones the whites called Assiniboines. White River got behind a large rock in the middle of the swift, roiling water and with a lance taken from a wounded warrior kept the enemy from making the one long leap necessary to cross the raging stream. This momentary stalemate allowed the Arikaras to rally, and the Assiniboines, facing a growing cloud of arrows, decided to withdraw.

The Arikara, celebrating his brave feat, gave him the name of Fights-Where-the-River-Runs-White, but traders and boatmen along the Missouri with only a limited command of the tongue soon shortened it to White River. It stuck. Actually, as White River admitted, there was little choosing, as the missionaries had given him their own name, Kleinhorst, which no Indian could pronounce and no one else seemed to remember. Whatever name his poor dead parents had bestowed on him had disappeared, as did they, with all they owned, in the ashes of their wagon.

But there were other, more serious exchanges too. White River told Amiel repeatedly about the Crows' fear of the Blackfeet, about the menace this marauding tribe held for their winter camp, about the Crows' growing presentiment that an attack was imminent.

Ben found himself almost as incredulous as alarmed at these words. His response to these threats betrayed the white man's persistent doubts about Indian clairvoyance. "How could they know or suspect such a thing, friend? We haven't seen a blessed soul in months."

White River shook his head, aware of the futility of further talk, but his voice was firm enough when he said, "No accountin' for it, fer a fact, Ben, but listen to me and you'll likely live longer—Injuns just know!"

Ben regarded him quizzically for a long, awkward moment, finally forcing a smile to show the warmth he felt for this seemingly roughhewn, formidable, but deeply decent and, as he had discovered, deceptively sensitive man. "I guess I just can't see how even your Blackfeet can venture very far in this snow."

White River gazed back to him, his face lifting slightly as though he had long wondered why the whites refused to accept the Indian's ability to feel the presence of things invisible to them. And yet, he knew it was this very quality that kept the whites watchful and wary of these people. In the end he gripped his chin like a man who realizes his mind has drifted from the main point and is busy focusing on it again. "Chinooks are a-comin,' " he said meaningfully, "warm blows that can clear a mountainside in a week."

White River rose, reminding himself audibly of a talk he had planned with Big Owl. Ben let him go, amazed that he was secretly proud of the way the Crow chiefs admired this man, as did he, and valued his counsel.

Soon he was crawling into his robes and listening to the wind whine through the lodge poles above, thinking of the Virginia woodland he would return to one day. Still, that night, before he fell into a strangely troubled sleep, he had a vision of endless drifts of snow wrapped around him like a protective wall against whatever dark and faceless forms lay threatening beyond the horizon. Yet two mornings later he awoke to find a blackish moist margin of earth spreading itself inward from the rim of his lodge. He did not need to touch it to know what it was. White River's chinooks had come. The snow was melting.

Dawn came with a blast from Blood-on-His-Moccasin's Kiowa horn as the Blackfeet pounced on the Shoshone village with their characteristic savagery. Before the sun reached the horizon the few surprised Shoshone warriors and headmen were all dead. The remaining squaws and children were quickly herded into the center of the village where they broke into screams as they watched the Blackfeet mutilate the corpses of their men, ripping off scalps, stripping the bodies, and cutting away any valuables the attackers' eyes fell upon. Then the lodges were looted and some of the young girls and squaws put down on the growing heap of robes and booty and raped. But the worst was yet to come. Blood-on-His-Moccasin, who had led the attack, had sent War Belt to bring in the horse herd. War Belt dallied only long enough to take a few scalps and to mark two cringing young squaws as his own, then he and several of the Siksika braves started for the corral, which lay gray and indistinct in the wool of night still unraveling to the west.

By the time they returned, the loot was piled high beside the captives, and Jumping Calf and Blood-on-His-Moccasin were watching the bloodstained Kainah chiefs tormenting a young Shoshone girl in an attempt to discover if there were other villages nearby. Her eyes were wide but lusterless like a dying deer, yet her lips remained a thin line across her face as their knife points worked about her breasts.

"Ho!" shouted the excited War Belt, appearing among them. "There are but a few horses and their ribs are out and as sharp as horns!"

"What are these words you speak?" said Blood-on-His-Moccasin turning on him.

"It is true," cried War Belt. "It is only a small herd with ponies as thin as lodge-poles!"

"Then they have tricked us!" roared Blood-on-His-Moccasin and grabbing his hatchet pulled an old squaw by her braids until her neck lay open before him. "Where are the good horses we saw but yesterday?"

The old squaw looked at the dark head of the hatchet. She spoke no Blackfoot but she saw War Belt come from the corral and she knew what he meant. She raised her hand and pointed to the west.

Another squaw who had been captured by the Blackfeet and who had learned some of their language before she escaped came forward. She told them of the strong party that had visited the day before, but they had left after dark and gone west. She did not mention the other village.

The Blackfoot chiefs looked at each other, rage tormenting their faces.

"Our medicine is bad," said Jumping Calf, looking at Blood-on-His-Moccasin. About them the Blackfoot warriors grew quiet and grim-faced. "There is much booty here, but we cannot take it with us. We cannot even take these captives."

The Shoshone squaw who understood Blackfoot stiffened at this last remark and then whispered anxiously to those about her. A general moaning began immediately among the women and spread to the children for they knew all too well what it meant.

"We will still have our victory against the Crows," cried Blood-on-His-Moccasin, stamping his foot.

"The Shoshones will warn their new war brothers, the Crows, we are coming," said Jumping Calf. "We cannot walk faster than word of this day. Such matters travel on the wind."

"So it is," added a Siksika chief, his face set against Blood-on-His-Moccasin.

"Come, brothers, let us smoke on it," said War Belt.

"Yes," spat a headman of the Kainah, kicking a nude Shoshone girl from under him, "let us smoke. For though we have won a great victory we have no horses to take back and can take little else back without them."

Now many of the warriors looked at Blood-on-His-Moccasin and muttered as though they had long suspected the matter, "Our medicine is bad."

The sun was well up in the sky when the Blackfoot war chiefs sat down to smoke. Some of the things that had to be done were done. Sentinels were posted on high points on all sides. Some of the straggly horses in the corral were butchered to provide meat for a badly needed feast. The rest were killed and some of the meat packed. The children were summarily slain, the war clubs quickly silencing their pathetic, almost animal-like cries as some reached for their mothers, others for freedom. It would always defy the understanding of whites that had these same children been taken back to the Blackfoot village, they would have been adopted and looked upon as their own. The cringing and screaming squaws fared little better. They were made to help prepare the meal, after which the warriors used them any way they wanted before slaughtering them too. By noon the carnage was complete, but the Blackfoot chiefs sat stoically in the middle of it and passed their pipe. On a rise to the south, crows and magpies had begun to gather, jabbering back and forth and cocking their heads at the many bodies strewn below. To the east solitary wolves and coyotes, many far, far downwind from the village, curiously sniffed the air and then swiftly turned into the wind.

By early afternoon they were ready to leave. It was decided not to fire the village and the small hill of booty sitting at its center, for burning robes, many laden with grease, made thick black smoke and this might catch the eyes of scouts and hurry the alarm that would only open the eyes and ready the bows and guns of their enemies. If they had been lucky enough to kill everyone in this village it might well not be known for days.

But the war council had been an unsettling one, with the decision to go against the Crows finally prevailing. Jumping Calf and not a few others had argued persistently for a return to the Marias, but Blood-on-His-Moccasin, aided by the chiefs of the Kainah and finally War Belt, won out. There were many long tortuous miles separating this dead Shoshone village from the Crow camp to the southeast, but even War Belt and all too many others rose from the council knowing these camps were far closer together than the hearts of Blood-on-His-Moccasin and Jumping Calf.

A half hour after the Blackfoot war party departed, the little village had turned into a hellish uproar of wolves and coyotes snapping at each other as they gorged themselves on the slaughtered. Two eagles had swept down with the inevitable crows and other birds to flop about and pick at the dead. A puma slunk in, and after much hissing and clawing at the coyotes, carried off the body of a child. Nor did the melee in time die down. Instead, with the arrival of new scavengers, starved after a long bare winter, it grew until a constant frantic roar seemed to shake the air about the abandoned tipis.

The sun was starting its descent of the sky when the returning Shoshonean brave Far-Away-Storm mounted a high ridge to the west. He had been enjoying his trip back from the neighboring village. The pinto the visitors had given him was a good horse and he had not had such a ride for months. It was a great honor to have been picked to escort the party bearing the Shoshone war pipe, and youthlike and drawn to dreaming in his solitude, he was ascribing to it an importance beyond all reason. He was sure it meant he was going to be a great warrior. He sang a little war song he had been laboriously making up.

As he approached from the west it was the sight of the corral that first stopped the breath in his nostrils. It looked empty and yet it was not. There were dark shapes strewn about its confines and a curious, maggotlike movement that from this distance could only be smaller animals moving quickly about. It was when his eyes rose to the village that a faint terror slowly began to seize the fringes of his mind. He could see no details, but icy fingers touched his heart at the fanlike movements between the lodges where flocks of birds wheeled about and settled again as they do when they feed.

At first he kicked at the pinto and urged it forward, but as he closed the distance the appalling truth stunned him into stopping. There was no way he could fit what lay before him into his mind. The enormity of it started him saying to himself over and over again, "It cannot be! It cannot be! I am dreaming. I must wake up!"

Now he could see the wolves and coyotes and almost hear the furious fighting over the corpses. He knew from the way the animals ran in and out of the lodges that they were empty, and that there was no one left alive in the camp. That meant his father was surely dead. But his mother, two younger brothers, and Little Rabbit . . . perhaps they had been carried off as captives. It was a thing often done. He began to circle the village, aware now that this attack had come that dawn and that the enemy might not be far away. His growing fear put a taste like wet earth in his mouth. No longer did he feel he was a great warrior, but only a frightened youth afraid to enter his own village, afraid of the enemy, afraid of the nightmarish sight that tugged his eyes back to it time and time again.

He moved around to the north and then to the east, and saw how the enemy had crept up on his village. His heart sank at their numbers. Everywhere there were deep moccasin prints. Could the whole Shoshone nation send that many warriors against their enemies? At last he came to the tracks of the departing Blackfeet and studied them in growing desperation, knowing in the end no women and children had been led away. The village that was his life was gone. Not a human or animal was left alive except himself.

Perhaps it was the thought of his playful little sister running toward his lodge flashing through his mind that set it off. But suddenly a half insane craving for vengeance shattered his brain. He ripped out his knife and screamed the Shoshone war whoop. Over and over again it trilled from his mouth echoing up and down the valley and ending in an immense stillness that told him how very alone he was; that told him the Blackfeet could not hear, that they would not come back.

The sun was close to the mountains now and shadows from the peaks to the west were coming across the ruins of the village. Far-Away-Storm looked down at it from a little height, knowing when he left he would never travel to this place again. He looked up at the sky. A long string of clouds to the northeast was turning a dull then a fiery red. They lay toward the land of the Blackfeet and seemed an omen to Far-Away-Storm, for now he was no longer a youth dreaming of glory and shy at the mention of it but a warrior who had picked his way to die.

37

Big Owl came back into the Crow village with an uneasy heart. He had been to the Big River, the Missouri of the whites, on a scout and had seen the snows going from the slopes about him and the seeds of life quickening in the land. Ordinarily it would have been a time for rejoicing and preparing for the new coming of the buffalo. Ordinarily it meant the long bitter winter was spent and the easy nomadic life of spring and summer was upon them. But now a heavy brooding had come upon him and the news that his young son, Beaver Tail, had gone but two days before into the mountains to dream brought a strange, distantly troubled look to his eyes.

He sat for many hours in his lodge before White Tail, Ironfoot, and White River came to join him. The four sat for some time passing the pipe before White Tail said, "Did my brother learn much in his journeying to the Big River?"

"There is much silence in that country," responded Big Owl, his eyes nearly closed now and bent on his fire.

"It is early," considered Ironfoot. "Even a Piegan must eat before he can fight. They will hunt first."

White Tail leaned forward and said softly, "My brother, Big Owl, seems very weary."

Big Owl hesitated before answering. "I have traveled many days but met no one. Last night I dreamed that many enemies were in our lands but we could not see them." The four sat in silence for a moment. Then Big Owl continued, "Have the War Clubs sent out scouts?"

"They will go tomorrow," answered Ironfoot.

White Tail seemed to be meditating to himself. "Did my brother see these enemies in his dreams?"

"Not until they were upon me."

"You saw their faces?"

"I saw only a tomahawk bringing me my death."

Again there was silence in the lodge as the three men pondered this ominous dream. It fitted all too well their long preoccupation and anxiety. Even White River sat in tight silence, aware it would be wrong for a white to speak.

Ironfoot was the first to broach action. "In the morning we must bring our young men in from their dreaming. Scouts will be sent in all directions and our village fortified."

White Tail, his eyes suddenly narrower, his head lifting a fraction, nodded slowly in assent.

And now the four sat together in an even greater silence, the mood of Big Owl having claimed the others. Outside the deepening darkness came in from the hills like a living thing which had eyes and a mysterious will all its own. It was to be a fateful night for the Crows, a night that had already started several miles back in the low-lying hills where Big Owl's son, Beaver Tail, had gone for his dreaming. The boy had awakened frozen from the long lying on the frost-hardened ground. He knew he was ill and he needed warmth. He had built himself a little fire and was nodding over it, trying to recall the wild fragments of dreams that had flashed by in his near delirium. Finally he slept again slumped beside his fire and now a different but clear and dreadful dream began. There were enemies moving about him though he could not see them, and they were stealing up on him. A terrible fear that turned this dream into a nightmare triggered something deep within him and he began to rouse himself from his sleep. But even as he did, aghast at the rising terror that marked his awakening, a Blackfoot hatchet opened his skull, and even as White Tail, Ironfoot, and White River left his father's lodge the body of the young and devoted Beaver Tail was lying beyond dreaming, mutilated beyond all recognition and badly scorched in his own fire.

• • •

Later that evening Ironfoot, followed by Snow Runner, came to White River's lodge and found Amiel and White River starting a meal. Sharing food was an ancient courtesy equally binding upon host and guest, and the four ate quietly of the deer meat prepared by Blue Lodge. They were licking their fingers when White River, using their own tongue, finally said, "Ironfoot's heart has been made heavy with his thoughts. Will he share them at the fire of his friends?"

Ironfoot took the pipe Snow Runner had prepared and waited until the smoking had begun before, aware of Amiel, he answered in English, "We feel our people are in great danger. Perhaps Ironfoot's friends should ride now to the south."

"Danger?" said Amiel, his tone almost casual. White River winced to himself. He knew he had not mentioned the scene in Big Owl's lodge, but clearly, in spite of numerous warnings, Amiel was missing the stark mood of the moment.

"Why does my brother wish us to go?" said White River, a forced look of kindled interest lining his face.

Ironfoot's eyes flickered to Amiel. "It would be wisdom. As my brother knows we have decided to fortify this village in the morning."

"It's still blowing mighty cold," said White River, his words sounding cant, lacking conviction. "Doesn't hardly seem the season for trouble yet."

"In the old days," said Ironfoot grimly, "war was a game played by men who used the summer as the time to show their courage and remind their neighbors that their hunting grounds were sacred. Now it is no longer that way. The whites have taught us to come while our neighbors sleep or when hunger is upon them, and sweep all life from their village."

White River's eyes were turned speculatively to the fire. This was the ancient breach between white man and Indian, even here between Ironfoot and him. It was the white man's guns and horses that had put saber teeth into the Plains Indians' warfare. "Still so far there ain't no sure sign?"

Ironfoot shook his head.

"Well, we'll have a look come mornin'. Could be there's trouble afoot, but I always figure . . ."

Snow Runner's hands suddenly shot into the air in an unexpected gesture for silence. In what seemed the same motion Ironfoot glanced quickly up at the smoke hole of the lodge.

Amiel, turning to White River, waited a moment before he whispered, "What is it?"

Ironfoot, followed by Snow Runner, was getting to his feet. White River rose with them, looking at them curiously across the fire. They were obviously listening, and Amiel strained his ears for a long moment before he heard the distant if now distinct sound of an owl hooting. For one not alerted it could easily have passed unnoticed. Amiel suddenly felt unnatural being on the ground and started rising too, but before he was on his feet, Ironfoot and Snow Runner had ducked out of the lodge and White River, reaching for a bowl of water, was killing their fire. In the last light of the coals Amiel saw White River reach for his rifle and cartridges, then, turning to grasp his own, he followed the tall figure out into the dark.

Far-Away-Storm had tracked the great Blackfoot war party until he was sure they were going southeast into Crow country. Then he had exhausted his pinto getting to the large Shoshone camp on the Snake River, where he knew Rising Hawk's party carrying the pipe would be returning that day. Here the Shoshone chiefs heard with amazement, followed by a sickening fury, of the extermination of their little village. Those who had relatives in that camp began to wail, and young men began singing stronghearted songs and crowding around the council circle calling for war.

The party carrying the pipe was already in camp. A celebration had half begun. The scene was suddenly one of incredible confusion with both Father Villiers and Father DuBois trying to get a hearing before the council circle, which was almost invisible with the surge of people on all sides.

Then Rising Hawk stood before them, his dark, brooding, and badly pocked face looking fierce beneath the famous headdress made of twisted Blackfoot scalps. He fired his gun in the air and demanded silence. He was a strong man, strong enough to know fear in its most deceiving form. As a fighting man he sensed an element of panic in all these cries of vengeance. Fear of the Blackfeet was deep in his people, deep as a sickness that lives in a man's loins and is born in his children. For over a century they had suffered incessant and devastating attacks that would have meant extermination had they not retreated deeper and deeper into these great mountains. And now the Blackfeet had that critical advantage of numbers, brought on in part by the Blackfoot warrior's well-known lust, which had led the young ripening Shoshone girls into captivity for generations.

Rising Hawk knew the importance of this new alliance with the Crows. He had been the first to speak for accepting the pipe. The Crows were growing desperate themselves. Their offer of the pipe said as much. But desperate men fought well, and besides, they had withstood the Blackfeet better than any tribe confronting them. Something now must be done to make this alliance firm, for surely the Shoshones could not stand alone.

The camp began to settle about him, growing quieter as it did. Finally all eyes were on him. They were the eyes of men desperate for revenge—but clouded with an obscure doubt. Rising Hawk did not disappoint them. He called for war, but he called for an immediate force to overtake the Blackfeet, following them into Crow country if need be. The warriors eyed each other restlessly. But then Rising Hawk spoke cuttingly of how some tongues wasted words, of how sometimes he thought he heard young men pretending to be warriors howling a defiance that might as well have been the squeak of mice.

Immediately stung and furious, the young warriors rose with angry shouts that he was the one who was talking and not riding to battle. But it was as Rising Hawk wanted—he would torment them into a fury that would be vented on the Blackfeet. When the council finally broke up and the people started shouting to the war drums, almost a hundred warriors sat astride their best ponies circling the camp behind the towering figure of Rising Hawk. One of them was the desperate, thought-haunted figure of Far-Away-Storm.

38

It was Long Otter, the sharp-eyed Blackfoot wolf, scouting before the main party who found the Crow village just before dark. Long Otter signaled War Belt, as in victory, from his low ridge to the east. When War Belt finally came up to peer at the tipi tops through the trees his corded body seemed weary from the long day's searching. After a pause he motioned Long Otter back to alert the war party and bring the headmen up. But Long Otter stayed motionless, his eyes holding the other in a strange, probing look. War Belt, sensing the scout's unease, rubbed his hideous face and said he would circle the village to the north and locate the horse herd and that the warriors should be told to signal with three quick owl hoots when they came up and he would answer and guide them in.

Long Otter still did not move: only his eyes searched soberly for War Belt's in the growing darkness. A tension began between them, ending only when War Belt snapped in irritation, "Go, before I open your ears with my knife!"

It was a mistake.

Long Otter should have been left to scout the village. He was a natural wolf with the single-mindedness of the true scout. He would have gotten closer quicker and would have felt the way of things, the drift of enemy intent, the likely setting of battle, the realities of surprise. He knew War Belt was weary, drawn out by their long ordeal, pricked by doubts that gnawed at his reason. Scouts could not afford weariness, let alone doubts.

But, in truth, War Belt was more than just weary and on edge. He was brooding about the bad things he had seen happening among his own people, at the loud anger of Blood-on-His-Moccasin, at the quiet fury of Jumping Calf and others. Such things made the spirits frown and brought bad medicine, and when Long Otter left he sat down to chant a secret strength-giving song and paint a special medicine symbol, whose source he was not allowed to reveal, on his arms and legs.

By the time he rose to spy out the village, it was too dark to find readily the things that an attacking force calls upon for its advantages; the direction of the horse herd, its size, the number and position of the enemy's lodges, the approaches that would favor assault, the avenues of escape. He had only made his way to the stream's edge when he heard, poking lightly into the night behind him, the three thin hoots of the hunting owl. He let his breath out. That would be the others, obviously goaded here quickly by the impatient Blood-on-His-Moccasin. War Belt stood for a moment in the darkness and then cupping his hands to his mouth in what he hoped were distant muted tones, answered them.

It was a night of strange happenings for the Blackfeet. Blood-on-His-Moccasin listened restlessly to War Belt's false words about the returning Crow hunters that had kept him under cover and unable to scout the village. Almost without waiting for War Belt to finish, he sent Long Otter and another scout to crawl as close to the village as possible and report its strength.

As they were talking, warriors of the main party kept coming up and the hooting of owls finally grew so frequent that Blood-on-His-Moccasin sent War Belt back beyond the ridge, where he was told to hold the warriors in total silence.

The second scout was back first to say the village seemed to be asleep with but a few fires burning and one squaw keening in a distant part of the camp which was made up of perhaps forty to fifty lodges, all to the west of the stream. Blood-on-His-Moccasin grunted with satisfaction. The Crows would soon learn what the Shoshones already knew—enemies of the Blackfeet could not afford to sleep. He commanded the scout to return and wait for Long Otter, then sent word to the warriors waiting beyond the ridge to come up.

So many minutes had passed by the time the anxious second scout finally saw Long Otter rising beside him that he had already decided to leave and report the suspiciously long absence to the council he knew was being held beyond the ridge.

Long Otter did not speak until the scout whispered, "Did my brother go to sleep in the camp of the Crows?"

Long Otter looked wearily behind him. "Long Otter says that village is too quiet for sleep."

"Does my brother say they are dead?"

Long Otter did not answer.

Beyond the ridge Blood-on-His-Moccasin and Jumping Calf were sitting with the other chiefs and the now silent, morose War Belt.

"We will surround their village as a snake does the gopher," Blood-on-His-Moccasin was saying in a low, hissing voice. "These Crows have seen their final sun."

"How many lodges are in this camp?" questioned Jumping Calf, the long days of travel telling in his voice. When he heard there were forty or fifty, he glanced at War Belt. "Then their horses must be taken first."

War Belt was about to answer when Long Otter and the second scout appeared beside them, so it was Blood-on-His-Moccasin's voice that reached into the darkness. "Oh, our brother Long Otter returns. He will speak of what his eyes have seen."

Long Otter settled down beside them, his long thin face seeming like half a face in the dark. After a moment he said, "I have watched their camp as a puma watches the spring cave of the bear. The young bears are as quiet as rabbits, but today I think I would hunt deer."

Blood-on-His-Moccasin grunted. "What thoughts are these my brother brings?"

"I cannot say," said Long Otter, his head now bending forward, "but the village sleeps like an owl awaiting the rustle of mice in the forest."

There was a moment of silence, then Jumping Calf said, "And their horses—were there many?"

"I found no horses except those tied to lodges and they were but few."

"Perhaps they have sent out a large war party," said a Kainah chief.

"Perhaps," said Long Otter, his head still down.

"This is squaw talk," exploded Blood-on-His-Moccasin. "We will crush them tomorrow as the bear's paw does the chipmunk!"

Jumping Calf drew his robe about him. It was cowardice to desert a war party, particularly for a chief. And yet the thought had preyed upon him for days. He and the Siksika chiefs had discussed it guardedly. Still the only honorable release from such a commitment was to have a dream that warned of disaster. But this might one day be mentioned in council and such a disgrace would be impossible to live down. In addition, there was still the dangerous possibility that their own young men would choose to stay with Blood-on-His-Moccasin, and if he scored a great victory, bringing them much loot and honor, his rank in the tribe could no longer be challenged. The braves had been out many, many days now and though they had won a great victory over the Shoshones all they could take back to their nation would bring nothing but ridicule. Most of these young men were still poor and had come on this mission for horses and booty. It was the nomadic Indian's only way to affluence. So anxious were they for the power to buy brides and to ride proudly through their villages that nothing but certain defeat could turn them back.

Blood-on-His-Moccasin's anger was now turning on the quiet deliverer of doubt. His voice rose to reach the ears of the warriors waiting about them. "My spirit tells me Long Otter's heart is no longer the heart of a warrior."

Long Otter's shoulders stiffened at this cutting remark. In his long, perilous life as a wolf he had never shirked duty. Though he was not a chief, there were many chiefs here whose places at the council circle would have been empty had it not been for him. Slowly, as his hand tightened on his knife handle under his robe, he was filling with the rage of the faithful servant for the ungrateful master. He had a right to challenge this thing, but at the end he looked up at Blood-on-His-Moccasin and said nothing.

The brittle moment was broken when War Belt said, as though he were asking for an end to foolish talk, "Let us not talk of bravery. Even the grizzly walks around the fire."

"We will attack with the morning star," rasped Blood-on-His-Moccasin, rising swiftly as though the council were over.

Now Jumping Calf rose slowly to face him, and suddenly the towering form of Jumping Calf seemed immense and hard and defiant in the dark, as though he knew the other chieftains were with him. And they were, many of them secretly recalling their debt to the lionhearted scout whom Blood-on-His-Moccasin had just insulted. "We will attack when the eagle eyes of Long Otter tell us to. We are not crazed buffalo charging upon hidden stakes that will impale us."

There was a long silence in which Blood-on-His-Moccasin stared at the challenging form of Jumping Calf before the deep-brooding War Belt said, "Your words are good, Jumping Calf."

Blood-on-His-Moccasin felt the winds of approval blowing strongly upon the tall dark form of Jumping Calf from all sides. A miscalculation on his part could turn this rising wind into a storm. He looked casually at the night about him as though the moment meant nothing to him. "My brother speaks too quickly," he grunted. "It is this very thing, a signal to attack from Long Otter, that I have planned."

The Crow camp was stirring within moments and with a discipline bred by the eternal imminence of such situations, every fire but a few in the outlying areas went out and the braves began appearing in the center of the village, arranging their war things silently in their hands. White River, seeing even Marcher approaching, was reminded of the effect the fire arrow had on the Sioux village near Innyan Kara.

White Tail and Big Owl came to stand with Ironfoot in the center of the growing group, but there were few words to be said. The horses were to be brought to a place handy and easy to guard. Sentinels must crawl to the outskirts of the village and if possible beyond. The enemy's position must be made known. The squaws, children, and old ones must start thinking of a safe place to run. The warriors must agree upon a line of battle so they would not shoot each other in the dark.

Half an hour later everything but marking the position of the enemy had been achieved and several of the warriors crouched around their headmen and the three whites, White River, Amiel, and Marcher, to hear which way their counsel would now point. It was agreed that those stalking the camp were west of the stream, so the women and children were given some horses and told to move down the east bank. It was also felt the attack would come at dawn, yet there was no certainty of it. From time to time owls hooted again in the distance, and a feeling that these intruders were Blackfeet began to grow. A decision was finally made to leave, and even keep burning, a few small fires at outer points of the village to make the enemy think their presence was still unsuspected—a risky thing but worth the chance. The futility of sending for help was clear to all. No help could possibly arrive before sundown the following day. By then, one way or the other they would need no help.

Marcher, quickly asserting himself in an open gesture for acceptance, was all for moving up and taking them by surprise. The Crows heard these bold and foolish words in silence. White River finally warned him in a hoarse whisper it was nothing but addleheaded tongue-wagging to talk of surprising a war party of unknown size coming at you in the darkness with weapons at the ready.

Diving Hawk, the captured Sioux, who had become a familiar sight about the village and was beginning to talk to a doe-eyed young Crow girl, appeared suddenly before Big Owl. "Give me my weapons as you have given me my life—Diving Hawk will fight with the Crows against their enemies."

White Tail came forward, looking doubtful. "And what if they are your people—or even Cheyennes?"

"Then I will take them your words of peace." The young Sioux stood tall, sounding fearless in the darkness.

Big Owl looked quietly at White Tail. "I say give Diving Hawk his weapons. His heart is good. He has kept his word so far and has not tried to run away."

39

When dawn could be felt but not seen, the Blackfeet had moved to where they formed an arc that bent around the village starting at the north end beside the stream and ending at the south end again beside the stream. Yet they were well back. Only Long Otter, approaching across the middle, was nearing the camp itself. He held himself very close to the ground, moving only as a slight wind rippled through the nearby trees and seeming almost part of the night itself. He had been restless in his robe and gnawed at by Blood-on-His-Moccasin's remark. Once he had dozed and awakened quickly, realizing he had been dreaming of standing over Blood-on-His-Moccasin's dead form with a tomahawk in his hand. It was bad medicine to dream of killing a chief. Long Otter considered himself a brave warrior. It was not stealth but cunning that made him the unusual scout he was. He knew how to hold his body so that its outline would resemble anything but the human form. But Blood-on-His-Moccasin had said he did not have the heart of a warrior.

He was to enter the Crow village and if it was truly asleep he was to give the Piegan war cry as a signal for the others to attack. This made him grimly happy. It would put him in the forefront of the assault. He would slay three braves before the others could draw blood. His squaw would dance in the victory circle with the first three scalps taken hanging from a vermilion stick. The people would sing of him as a great warrior . . . greater than many who hugged the pipe . . . greater perhaps than even . . .

His anger and smoldering resentment were to be his undoing, for they cost him the single-mindedness of the scout in the house of his enemy. He no longer allowed the murmur of things to guide him. He began to read into them what his heart desired. He wished to open this attack and so he missed the fact that the objects seemingly strewn about the outer rim of the village lacked a reassuring random look. He was before a large leaning iron pot. He eyed it carefully, the faintest light in the east showing him its dim outline. His eyes roved over it, his lifetime of experience and a talent for ferreting out irregularities telling him the outline was faulty, telling him that something in the symmetry of the pot was off. He knew he could not be seen, with the night behind him and his face blackened with mud. He was almost on the ground and he knew he was indistinguishable from it.

His every instinct told him to be wary of that pot, but his pride had already started a process within him that blinded him to caution.

The camp was asleep and unaware, for there were no braves rushing to bring up their horses for battle.

Their presence was unsuspected, for there was not even the slightest stir or the growl of a dog in the nearest lodges, where death should clearly come first.

The attack would succeed, for there was nothing but stray gear to keep the Blackfoot warriors from charging the heart of the camp.

Such was the porous reasoning that displaced discretion.

He was about to rise and give the war cry. Then the iron pot caught his eye again and something deep within him forced him to narrow his gaze for a final time on the drift of its rim. Surely someone had thrown a robe over it to dry, surely it was nothing more, and it was time to open the attack, to open it before some young impatient warrior made it a thing already spoken for. Long Otter must open this attack. He must take the first scalps, he must show those who dared mock him how a real warrior leads in battle. That was the way a warrior with pride in his own manhood must go!

He rose and began the great Blackfoot war cry. He felt the air in his lungs rising and becoming a wild screech in his throat. His hand had found his hatchet and it was partly drawn from his belt. But then suddenly his senses began to record a flash—they never succeeded for it was only the faintest fraction of a second before everything was nothing and nothing mattered anymore.

For the Crows dawn came with the curious chirping of an invisible bird lost somewhere in a clump of bushes at the stream's edge north of the camp. There was little light, but every Crow warrior's eyes bored into the lifting darkness, looking for the faint but quick shadowy movements that would be their only warning of an attack. White River leaned over the sights of his gun, his body stiff from its long holding to the cover of a large tilted iron pot that had not been used since the last buffalo hunt. A second bird was now whistling somewhere to his left. The normal stillness of dawn was quickening with a secret life of its own. Somehow he knew they were moving toward him but as yet there was not the vaguest hint of where they were. Finally and almost unaccountably a figure rose up from the ground a few yards in front of him. He could see its head turning as though quickly studying the village. In a moment it was clear the Crow ruse of a camp asleep had worked. For the figure thrust his head back and gave a great war cry, the high-sounding *hi-yip, yip, yip,* of a screaming Blackfoot that was cut off at its apex as White River blew the emerging warrior's head off. Yet the thunderous howls of the Blackfeet rising everywhere to rush forward made this quick shot no more than the snap of a branch at the crest of a flood.

The Blackfeet were suddenly like a wall rolling forward, their broad painted faces taking hideous form in the near darkness. The Crows, sensing the numbers before them, began singing their death songs as they opened fire, the twang of the bowstrings being lost in the deafening staccato of rifle and musket shots. But in that first charge it was impossible to miss, and the Blackfeet, caught in the open and growing more bunched as they closed in on the rim of the horseshoe, were crumpling to the ground as though met by an invisible scythe. Yet had they kept coming the issue could have had only one end. At close quarters the badly outnumbered Crows would have been doomed. But the Indian concept of war denies the white man's brutal logic of strategic losses. A man may die if he chooses but for a war chief there are no expendable warriors. It makes a mockery of his medicine, a dangerous and irremediable disclosure, and marks him as one who has only human means at his command. Only moments before the

Crow line must be breached the Kiowa horn was droning from Blood-on-His-Moccasin's lips and the Blackfeet suddenly fell back.

Enough light was filtering from the east now to see the Blackfoot dead and wounded lying in twisted heaps, some of those still alive signaling their agony with a slowly moving arm or knee in the air. The macabre sight drove the Crow warriors wild. They started to shriek as they leaped from cover, intent upon the many easy coups that lay before them. White River, Big Owl, and even White Tail shouted to them to come back, but they broke into raucous war whoops as they ripped scalps from wounded and dead alike and began to despoil the bodies.

It was the sight of Marcher in the graying light wielding a hatchet over a wounded Blackfoot that brought Amiel in a stunned state, crying to White River, his face distorted by astonishment. "This is maniacal! My God, look at those animals! In the name of Christ, stop them! Stop him!"

White River looked at Amiel with a face that revealed only helplessness, and then turned away from this scene that was like a dawning in hell.

It was the Blackfeet who stopped the ravaging of their dead. They came on again, not en masse this time but slowly, their arrows and bullets driving the Crows with their many bloody war trophies back to cover. Marcher came into the long pit with an arrow still hanging from the fleshy part of his arm. A warrior who was busy cleaning his scalping knife reached over and pulled it out. Another appeared and hastily tied a band around his arm. It was clear the warriors were beginning to consider Marcher one of their own.

White River counted twenty-two bodies that had fallen in the onslaught. He had never seen such a massive attack carried out by Indians before and this was surely no mere raiding party. Had they kept coming it would have been over now, with the only luck a man could ask for being to die quickly. But the danger was still with them. He could feel it in the silent chill that ran before the true dawn.

The fighting then became desultory, but it had its deadly side nonetheless. The Blackfeet crept up on all sides, keeping to cover themselves but riddling the Crow village with shot and high, looping arrows. The whites and some of the Crows returned as much fire as their dwindling supply of shells would allow. But it was not enough. The Crow wounded mounted, and when the sun blazed fresh in the eastern sky it was clear the Blackfeet were getting the upper hand.

And now individual Indians began rushing forward to grapple alone with the foe—proving the mysterious truth that Indian warriors were not truly soldiers but gladiators at heart. One Blackfoot after another rushed a Crow position and killed an Absarokee or was killed himself in the attempt. This brand of fighting was clearly on the side of those with numbers, for even when a Crow warrior, waiting desperately until he could not miss, managed to double over an onrushing Blackfoot, he all too often had to expose himself to insure success and immediately caught the deadly fire of the many Blackfeet covering the attacker.

One tremendous Blackfoot warrior, whose headdress was a mass of twisted snake heads and whose body was streaked in curving red stripes, broke through the Crow's withering outer defense line. He caught a Crow brave trying to reload and killed him. He turned to another, but a young warrior streaked out of the pit and took him from behind. They went down together, rolling over one another, making it impossible for either side to shoot. But the warrior from the pit had his knife in the Blackfoot and in time the red-streaked body lay still. Then the other, obviously wounded, tried to stumble his way back to the pit, but at its very edge a Blackfoot slug caught him in the back of the head and he fell forward, dead.

Big Owl came up and grunted in dismay as the Crows turned the limp body over. It was the young Sioux, Diving Hawk.

By noon White River was in the pit with Big Owl, Ironfoot, and White Tail, trying to get them to agree to abandon the village and make a run for it across the stream to the east, hoping the Blackfeet would be too busy looting the undefended village to follow. But Ironfoot and White Tail both pointed to the many wounded that would have to be left behind and said with that incomprehensible pride unique to the Indian warrior that this was the day they had chosen to die. Big Owl, studying the rim of the western ridge and then glancing into his powder horn, said nothing.

An hour later with the faint drone of a distant horn the shooting stopped completely and all knew the Blackfeet were preparing to storm the village again. The Crows, sensing what was about to befall them immediately began singing their death songs, some waving poles with the freshly taken Blackfoot scalps upon them over their heads for the Blackfeet to see. White River shook his head slowly at Amiel. "Braver 'n hell, these Crows, but it ain't goin' to be 'nough, I'm thinking."

Marcher was suddenly with them. "These bastards will make it in here this time," he shouted excitedly, "but they've got a hell of a lot of fighting to do before they down us." White River and Amiel, listening for the thinnest fiber of fear in his voice, heard none. Amiel's face was still distorted by the horror that invaded it while watching Marcher's bloody hatchet hack at the dying Blackfeet.

"Reckon they're planning to scuffle, sure enough," said White River with irony. "How many shells you got left?"

"Twelve."

"Leave off wrestlin' with 'em till there's twelve less to wrestle with—hear?"

Marcher smiled. "I'll be wearing eagle feathers in my hair when this is over."

White River looked up slowly. Overhead vultures were drifting in lazy circles like so many kites held by an invisible string to the dead flesh that lay strewn about the village. "Could be them's the eagles you're figurin' on up there," he muttered in wasted sarcasm. Marcher was already moving forward like a man possessed.

A thunderous volley that broke from the ridge beyond, which was the western horizon for the village, took everyone by surprise. White River knew at once, when the sing of lead failed to torment the air about him, that the village had not been fired on, but a great din shook the near woods as the Blackfeet could be heard screaming and beginning to fire in return. White Tail looked about him, not knowing what the moment demanded. Ironfoot, moving sideways to keep his eyes on the ridge, joined him.

White River, coming closer to the other two, was the first to speak. "They've been hit from t'other side. We'd better get out there and give whoever it is a hand."

"Could it not be a Piegan trick?" cautioned White Tail, mindful of the deadly risk that lay in leaving cover.

"They have no need to trick us," said Big Owl, making his voice heard over the roar that continued to grow on the ridge. "No more than a bear needs to trick a sick calf."

The Crow warriors showed little inclination to leave their cover, and perhaps would not have had not a thing happened that made Big Owl allow a grateful smile to soften the deep lines so firm in his granite face. A wild, penetrating yell was rising above the uproar, and everywhere weapons were being raised. No seasoned warrior needed to be told he was hearing the shrill war cry of the Shoshones.

White Tail, the full measure of a chief, now stood tall in his own village, lifting his voice to reach the rising Crows who suddenly saw him standing unafraid in their center. "Come, my stronghearted brothers," he roared, "the brave Shoshones have come to help us—let us go like the warriors we are and show them we know no fear of death but only of not standing with our friends against our enemies as men!"

40

The Shoshones had been moving toward the sound of sporadic firing for over an hour. Their horse-holders were keeping the mounts well back, while the rest of the party crept up on foot like so many stalking lynxes bent on a dangerous prey. Rising Hawk wanted and needed the surprise and shock that lies in the strike of plunging eagles. He knew the Blackfeet had him outnumbered and that they held his people's fighting prowess in contempt. He knew that the first sign of weak medicine would send his warriors running for their ponies with all hope of victory gone. He knew the Shoshones must lose their fear of the Blackfeet if they were to survive, and that surely required a great victory, a very great victory with many Blackfoot scalps and few men lost. He mumbled some medicine words to himself and watched his young men moving grimly forward. They were very close now and down the line to his right he could see a Shoshone brave pausing and pointing forward with his gun, signaling he had sighted the enemy.

The Blackfeet were aligned along a ridge directly before them. There appeared to be a hurried council of war going on with the braves working with and readying their guns and bows as though they knew they would soon be fighting again. Studying the many moving blotches of red and white that made the Blackfoot camp seem like a weird serpent perched along the ridge, Rising Hawk knew that every moment he delayed the risk of detection grew. He picked out a second, lower ridge spotted with small spruce that lay between the two forces. It was an inferior position to the one held by the Blackfeet, but it was within good gunshot range of the enemy, and the dread of waiting, which was rising cruelly within him, warned his warrior's heart that there was no time to find another. He gave the signal to advance to the lesser ridge and the Shoshone braves went forward again, but now they embraced the earth and pressed themselves forward like marmots blinking at the shadow of hawks. Surely they would never attain the spruce-lined ridge without being discovered. And yet miraculously they moved on, miraculously there was no outcry or shot from the Blackfeet ranks as the Shoshones began to squat behind the chest-high trees atop the minor ridge. One warrior after the other began to feel that this day their medicine was surely strong.

Rising Hawk's eyes told little of his thundering heart, which held the knowledge that he was now committed to battle. The last of the Shoshone braves were still struggling into position when the sight of two Blackfoot wolves coming on the run toward their position told Rising Hawk he could not wait. A glint of color or the sheen of a rifle must have been picked up on the opposite ridge and the war-wise Blackfeet were quick to read its possible menace.

Leveling his own rifle against the lower trunk of a stout little tree, he waved his hand behind him and turned quickly, opening fire. It was their signal for all-out attack.

The volley struck the Blackfoot camp with a queer jolt, and its strange colors quickly shifted, many disappearing, only a few becoming still. The two scouts shot up in the air from the impact of lead penetrating their bodies. Arrows, arriving after the shot, disappeared into the young foliage beyond, their shafts seeming tiny and ineffectual at the distance, though their arc gave them a deadliness denied even the leaden balls. Then there was a split second of silence before the Shoshone war cries filled the air.

Had the Shoshone volley killed a few braves and wounded a few others the Blackfeet might have found their combined enemies too formidable to promise victory at a price Indian reckoning was willing to pay. But most of the Shoshone braves were aiming at the council circle where they knew the headmen would be sitting, and Jumping Calf and War Belt and many of the headmen of the Siksika and Kainah were slumped in death before the roar of the volley settled.

This only infuriated the Blackfeet, and they began to fire back, aiming at the little trees that logic said were the only concealment their enemies had. Blood-on-His-Moccasin, miraculously unscathed by the hail of lead and assured by the rising war cries that these newcomers were Shoshones, immediately ordered his braves to move down the ridge on both sides and outflank these contemptible and craven people who had so long fled before the mighty Blackfeet.

Rising Hawk could see immediately that their attack had not routed the enemy. The returning fire was beginning to grow and to come in from his flanks. The little spruces were no more protection than cobwebs against the Blackfoot fire, and the Shoshone braves were beginning to hug the ground and sing their death songs. Rising Hawk tried to rally them but the growing cries of the Blackfeet and the steady increase of their fire were already making a brave here and there break for his pony. A few clearly wounded, crouched painfully on the ground, were calling to their friends for help. Rising Hawk did the one thing he could, the one thing left open to him, the thing that had not been done in his memory—he shouted to his warriors to stand and charge their enemy—a Shoshone war party charging a Blackfoot force of superior numbers.

A handful of warriors rose with Rising Hawk and began to run with him toward the Blackfeet. A few more jumped up and came after him almost in a single file. Finally the remainder came to their feet and lumbered awkwardly forward. It was a formation that invited disaster, and the Blackfeet were quick to sense it. Discarding their guns, they came from cover with their lances and war clubs high in the air. Blood-on-His-Moccasin, seeing a victory in his grasp, was greeting them with a great blast on his Kiowa horn.

Rising Hawk tried to bring his war party together, but they were stopping, taking time to pour powder into their guns and fit arrows into their bows. The Blackfeet coming in from their flanks were already reaching those at the first rise on the greater slope. The young Shoshones being overrun fought desperately, but as they were so strung out the Blackfeet slowly began a methodical slaughter that was outdoing in its fury the massacre of the village.

Rising Hawk knew now there was only death for him, but he knew in the same moment he did not wish to live. He had failed his people. From this defeat they could never recover. So weakened, they would be hunted down like rabbits, the Blackfeet killing the men and the old ones and taking the children and the young squaws back to their lodges. The spirits had failed them and it was too late for prayers and fasting and the secret oaths that made a heart strong.

A Blackfoot appeared before him and swung a war club that was covered with blood. Rising Hawk stepped inside the blow and opened the Blackfoot's body with his knife just below the rib cage and from one side to the other. The Blackfoot's eyes closed in pain as Rising Hawk thrust him from him and now Rising Hawk made the last decision of his life. It was made as the piercing drone of a horn sounded just before him. He knew in a flash this was Blood-on-His-Moccasin, the dreaded war chief of the Piegans. This man would join him in death. This man whose very name was a nightmare to the Shoshones had danced his last victory dance under Shoshone scalps.

Rising Hawk went toward him, killing another Blackfoot with his hatchet as he did, but the Blackfeet, knowing now he was the headman of the Shoshones, were crowding about, anxious for his scalp and weapon. Blood-on-His-Moccasin was also coming toward him, knowing him now for a chief who had taken more than a few Blackfoot scalps, which he wore as a headdress. They were almost upon each other when a Blackfoot brave coming from behind caught Rising Hawk about the neck and raised his knife to plunge it into his chest. But Rising Hawk, with the dreadful calm of a man who has accepted death, parried the knife with his hatchet and flung the Blackfoot over his head. He knew before his life left his body he should not have taken the moment it took to bend over and kill that brave for that was the moment in which Blood-on-His-Moccasin buried his hatchet in Rising Hawk's spine, and the great warrior fell back helpless to the ground. He lived for a few moments while the Blackfeet with their deafening shrieks began to carve up and despoil his huge body. But he did not live to see the Shoshone brave who, in the excitement of his chief's death, had gotten behind Blood-on-His-Moccasin and, grabbing him by his braids, had pulled his head back and opened his throat with a quick blow of his hatchet. Another swift blow or two and the head was severed from the body and the Shoshone brave was holding it high above him, giving the Shoshone war cry.

The Blackfeet were thrown into silence for a moment. The head of their war chief was now holding their eyes like a suddenly fallen oak. Then, as the nearest brought their clubs up to give this daring Shoshone his death blow, a second volley roared out from behind them and Blackfoot warriors leaning over freshly slain Shoshones started to topple over their victims.

The Blackfeet and a tall Siksika who was their only remaining chief had had enough. The Crows rushing up from their village were now in possession of the ridge the Blackfeet had just descended from. The Siksika chief gave the signal to fall back and this time toward the north, for the cries of the Crows told him that the ridge they had but minutes ago commanded now held only death. Immediately the remaining Shoshones took heart, and Rising Hawk's dream that the Shoshones would one day drive the Blackfeet before them was finally realized.

Far-Away-Storm was wounded, but he still held Blood-on-His-Moccasin's head in his hands. He stooped for the dead Blackfoot's Kiowa horn and rifle, managing to kill another of the retreating enemy as he emptied the latter. Then he turned and walked slowly up the lower ridge. Here he offered the severed head to the sky, muttering something that was not clear above the still resounding shots of battle from those straggling about him. But there was one heart at least that knew why the mighty and dreaded war chief of the Piegans, Blood-on-His-Moccasin, was really killed. He was killed and beheaded because of a playful little girl child, who would play now only in the memory of her brave brother and whose name had been Little Rabbit.

PART SEVEN

PAUL'S STAR

41

The buffalo milled around slowly as though aware something threatened them. Several bulls stood at the edge of the small herd looking heavily at the long grass and scrub pines that ridged around them. The young sun of spring hung in a sky of bottomless blue and there was no wind save that which touched the cheek to tell a man he was out of doors.

The Crow hunters crept to their position, many wearing animal skins but others merely stripped down to loincloths, their bodies rubbed with pungent weeds to keep the man-smell away.

The horsemen kept back until the hunters were all in position. Then, at a signal from White Tail, they came forward on all sides screaming and waving blankets, their nimble ponies helping them to turn the herd in a clockwise swirl. The buffalo at once began to brawl and bolt in blind panic, first this way and then the other, but slowly they fell to swinging about in a rough circle, and as they did the hunters' guns and arrows began to bring them down.

Marcher, having stayed back with the others, began moving forward now and was soon in the outer circle leveling his rifle at one beast after the other. The small buffalo herd was soon down to half its size, with many of the calves already exhausted in their run and stopping to bawl and nose the udders of dead cows.

When only a handful were left, a young bull unaccountably broke out of the suicidal circle and charged through the line of hunters. It was immediately followed by others, some with arrows in their flanks, a few with puffs of blood spraying from their mouths. Largely because the hunters were out of arrows or shot these few made it to the open prairie, but for some it would be only a brief respite. Sooner or later the wolves smelling the weakening wounded would bring them to earth and leave their bones to whiten in the sun. But the Crows had lost interest in them now, for the squaws were coming up and running to the dead and dying animals to make meat, the children streaming behind them for the bits of raw liver dipped in gall that their winter-lean and half-starved bodies craved.

Above birds began to sweep in quick circling flights and the quick yip of gathering coyotes soon came lightly against the ear. Marcher was up and sauntering about, watching the meat making, smiling to himself as did the braves who were collecting their arrows and finishing off animals who still struggled to get up or worked a helpless hoof against the air.

"There'll be feasting aplenty for a week, reckon," said White River almost idly to Amiel. They were sitting on their mounts a few hundred feet from the noisy slaughter.

Amiel's eyes were on Marcher, his lips pressed firmly together with a thought he did not share. "Surely quite a sight," he said in a tone unrelated to his words.

White River looked at him and then followed his gaze to Marcher. There was little to be said except what saying couldn't fix. Marcher was looking around him and across the expanse of prairie like a man who had finally all the things he wanted for the taking. The Crows called to him as he moved about, and many jokes laced with a flattering lewdness were thrown at him by the squaws. Marcher joked back at them, his growing mastery of the Absarokee tongue impressing even White River.

White Tail and Ironfoot watched this thing too, but no one knew their thoughts.

The tribal feasting began several hours later with pots cooking everywhere and the sweet scent of cooked meat making the dogs whine until the squaws, tired of throwing them scraps, drove them off. Horses were still coming in, piled high with robes and meat. From the south a breeze was beginning to comb smoke from the village as overhead three perfect wedges of geese passed high in the sky.

Marcher sat in his lodge with White Bead. She was busy preparing his food and he was examining his second repeating rifle like a woman handling a baby. He had watched Big Owl returning the gun after the hunt, watched his eyes that held to it as though it were part of a man that had made him momentarily greater and now its leaving must make him less. Big Owl had killed seven fine buffalo with it that day, more than twice the number brought down by most of his neighbors. Marcher smiled to himself. Tomorrow he would talk to Big Owl and the long, patient game conceived so many long months before would soon be over and won.

The feast lasted until the drums began to shake the first crisp comings of evening air and the young men stepped forward together in a growing circle, sporting buffalo horns and shouting what great hunters they were. Many good kills had been made that day.

Large fires began to appear and the young girls drew closer to them, giggling as they lined up for the social dance that the village crier said would shortly come. A sudden merriment had struck the camp, and the hard days of the past year seemed washed from memory and forgotten. The whites looking on were struck by the Indians' capacity to live for such moments, living as though knowing they could do nothing about things ahead or those behind or their final moment or its way of coming.

Marcher sat watching them, drinking the last of his cooling broth. He was warm with his own inner turnings and one side of his mouth drew his face into a half smile as he rocked slowly with the drums. In time Amiel and White River saw him laughing and clapping his hands among the old ones sitting at the side of the circle, and as they watched White Bead came slowly toward him and, taking him by his hands and moving back and forth with him, led him proudly out into the dance.

Big Owl worked his way down from the escarpment, making the hopeless sign at Marcher's deerskin map. "There is no other mountain to fit the medicine skin, my brother."

Marcher looked back at the far plain where they had turned away from the stream formed from three small creeks. The map had been perfect to here. This rump range two days' travel from camp seemed to fit the map perfectly. But now they were on the mountain, near its peak, just where the line seemed to end in *X* followed by the cryptic words "Paul's star." Yet here there was nothing except high rocky shoulders and little gullies where wind-driven rains and melting snows deepened their seams with each season.

Marcher began to move about cautiously, studying the slope as a man does when he is sure he is missing something too obvious to be easily seen. They were near exhaustion, for it had been a long trip made rapidly through a dangerous country and their ponies had to be left below to rest. "Must be something we're missing," he grunted mostly to himself.

Big Owl suddenly saw and stared at a low cloud closing quickly from the west. The sun was beginning to set and would soon be behind it. The cloud had long streamers hanging below it and Big Owl knew at once it meant rain, heavy rain.

"Heap storm," he said casually, knowing Marcher would not be easily talked off the slope.

"Rain be damned," said Marcher, kicking at a flat rock and starting it down the slope. "It's around here somewhere. I know it is. It has to be!"

For several minutes they moved along the slope in silence looking for upturned earth or displaced rocks or a star chipped into one of the many rock facings, or any minute sign of the lode that would be Paul's only legacy. Big Owl's eyes, however, watched more than the earth. This was both country and season when two men alone on an exposed mountain slope were already in the shadow of the surround and courting death. He wondered how their horses were faring below. They would be getting some rest but not enough if it came to vigorous pursuit. He looked at the repeating rifle in his hands. This was very strong medicine. His heart could not turn from it when Marcher offered it for leading him to this place, but his mind kept traveling to situations where he knew it would not be strong enough. Indian-like, he mumbled a little *"Ai-yee"* to himself.

A fork of lightning finally came out of the fast-closing cloud and the sky turned dark as a wind laden with hail and water began to mow along the foot of the slope. It distracted Marcher for a second and Big Owl spoke up quickly.

"Lightning bad. Maybe make horses run. Better we go back."

Marcher fixed him with a look that drifted slowly, too slowly for Big Owl's ease, from contempt to abject concession. "Guess maybe we better had. Be dark by the time that squall quits." He looked around him like a man who does not accept what he sees, then started down the mountain in desultory fashion, Big Owl following him, two figures dropping down into the storm, disappearing as the hail rising to meet them finally roared around them like pebbles in a mighty gourd.

The following night they made camp by a little stream that was nothing but a trickle through a green basin, and there they roasted strips of venison from a young deer they had killed at dusk. Marcher had been moody all day, riding slowly and forever looking back to view the stretches they were leaving. Big Owl had become stoic, refusing to show his impatience at their slow pace, which he knew Marcher would challenge as weakness, but Big Owl kept a sharp lookout. Every brave knew that when making tracks in dangerous country you made them as quickly as possible, for hostile pursuit is a constant peril which grows as the line of slow travel lengthens.

Their little fire was well covered and made of dry wood which threw off little smoke and then only when melting fat from the venison hit it. As they finished, Marcher took his saddle and placed a folded blanket against it. Above them a shower of stars was filling the sky, making the heavens seem cheerier than earth and putting a man's mind to wondering if perhaps they weren't.

Big Owl was down on his knees drinking quietly from the stream. Below, the hobbled horses could be heard munching grass and shaking themselves against the eternal gnats that bedeviled them.

"Come morning—I'm heading back to the mountain," said Marcher as though they had been discussing the issue all day. Big Owl's face came up with but little surprise, for in a sense the Indian knew they had.

He took his own position opposite Marcher and waited long moments before he replied. "Plenty danger back there—Big Owl fears his white brother will not see his lodge again."

Marcher grunted, "Coming?"

It was a while before Big Owl answered, but Marcher had long ago learned that part of parleying with Indians was sheer waiting. Indians could rarely be quick-talked into or out of anything, particularly if it went against their medicine, and they often had an oriental set against changing their minds in a hurry, feeling it somehow involved a loss of face.

"White brother," said Big Owl at last, "the yellow metal is like a bad spirit in the white man's mind. It makes him gore the earth like a wounded buffalo thinking it will make him strong again. Do not think of returning to that place in this moon. The Sioux have finished their hunt—as we have—and many war parties, with scouts whose eyes are as sharp as eagles and whose noses would match those of hungry wolves, will be traveling that way. Come back to our village where we can smoke and watch our young ones play before the lodge. The many good things of earth that were given us by the Great Spirit are there." The Crow seemed to ponder his own thoughts for a moment, then finished with, "Big Owl has spoken these words with his heart."

Marcher lay in silence for a time. He knew he had just lost Big Owl, a turn that tripled his risks. Yet one man alone was less conspicuous than two and he began to think he had learned more than most about the stealth needed to traverse this country unseen. After a bit he was weighing his chances in a way men do when desire has already decided matters and reasoning is required for pride alone. He could make it back to the rump mountain, hide his horse, and scale the slope on foot. He would wait for sundown, for that surely had something to do with finding Paul's star, which was the key to the mine. Paul was no fool. He would make discovery of that mine something the intellect alone could master. Somehow the answer lay in being on that high spot at sundown, nothing else made sense. The map's mark of *X* over "Paul's star at sundown" had to reveal the mine.

Well, he would sleep now. Big Owl already seemed asleep. From all those who had started on this quest, only he, Marcher, now remained. That would make it his by every right known to man. He had remade himself in every way necessary to get here. He could cope with this inscrutable land now and with the savages that claimed it, and that made him superior, for he still retained the white man's higher powers of logic and firmness of purpose.

The following morning, when at the edge of dawn Big Owl awoke, Marcher had already disappeared.

42

He just made it before sundown, his lean body bracing itself against the still ovenlike rocks, the bareness of the land around him telling him he was finally and utterly alone. In his anxiety to be there before sundown he had not eaten all day. The climb up the ridge had narrowly challenged his final strength. He rested a moment or two against the boulders, trying to will away his weariness, and then began to circle to the right, peering into gullies and at rocks that seemed in positions that defied the pull of the terrain. One looked like a sentinel and he labored toward it, but a glance at its base told him it had not been moved for epochs. He examined it for faint scratchings but found none. He studied the downslope, looking for a dry bed that might hint at its source and betray the lode. But those he could see came up to dissipate in crevices that spread like the veins on a hand and then dried up. And then it was sundown and he settled in near exhaustion to watch the sun slide below a far ridge that was the western horizon. The gall of defeat was gathering in his throat. He felt his body demanding rest, his exhausted limbs occasionally quivering in warning of uncertain responses. A low surging in his brain signaled the imminence of a coming collapse, one that he knew would tug at basic care and even dissolve the desire to live. But this his thoughts desperately struggled against, for he did not dare consciously concede he had no way of dealing with defeat. Uncontrollable tears rose and moved in slow, uneven trickles down into the matted hair that covered his face, but he was not even aware of them. He felt only a numbness as though his body was partly frozen and would soon be inert and incapable of any motion at all. For the first time he glimpsed the fact that no amount of fighting could force this thing his way. For the first time he realized that no passion of his, however powerful, could possibly prevail. It had taken the barren faces of these rocks to stay him, to overcome him, to make him nothing more than a momentary intruder whose presence was meaningless and who even with his death could make no meaningful mark on time.

He turned about and threw himself face down upon the slope. Somehow he wanted to shut out the sight of that thin rim of the sun disappearing beyond, bringing on a night that could now be for him the front paw of death. Somehow he felt if he did not see it disappear, it would remain, at least in his distraught mind, in the sky. But as he turned his eye caught something that held him and then slowly brought him up again. It was a light somewhere on the long ridge to the northeast, a light almost like a star, but a light that grew slowly thin and then completely faded out. It was not a fire. There was still too much daylight to see a flame at this distance. What was it, then?

He had raised himself half up, trying to fix the spot where he had seen the light, but his mind began to doubt its own recollections and after a minute he could not tell whether it had been a mile or five miles away. And what in Christ's name was it doing there? He began to rub his body, trying to restore life to it. Strange emotions began to sweep through him. One was pitched up from the kiln of fear and carried the sudden weight of Big Owl's warnings. Could it be a Sioux wolf signaling his presence, making his death on this mountain rim already a certainty? In the end even this terrible thought could not compete with others that crowded into his mind. Dimly he sensed he had reached Paul's secret and he lay on his side for hours, trying to measure his strength and knowing finally it would not carry him to that taunting ridge beyond.

Somehow he had to plan, to plan to get down from this mountain. He had to have food, rest. He would have to force himself into command of his reasoning or he would surely perish here. But he sensed he had seen Paul's star and a dim, obscure hope began to fuel his resolve. He would sleep for a while, then work his way back to the grassy ravine where he had left his horse. In the morning he would shoot some game, small game if necessary, and eat. Then he would rest during the day, leaving long enough before sundown to climb here again. This time he would post himself and watch in the direction of the light. As he fell asleep, a thing too deep for his overwrought mind to ponder told him that the light would be there.

A chill wind woke him before dawn and he started to slowly feel his way down the slope, often on all fours, his shins and elbows receiving bruises that seemed dim to his drugged senses. His mind was slowly pulling together the happenings of the evening before. He knew they centered about a light and from that he reconstructed his plan to use this day.

It was dawn before he saw his mount looking at him apprehensively in the coming light, and then, satisfying itself, dropping its head down again into the lush grass. He went a little ways beyond where his saddle and gear were and settled himself, his rifle in his lap. Here he dozed again, but was awakened by birds that had gathered to pick at bugs attracted by the dung of the horse. His eyes blinked open to see an enormous jackrabbit that had come to a curious halt fifty feet before him. The big wide eye of the hare was clearly visible as it fixed him in doubt and Marcher brought his rifle around as slowly as his poorly coordinated limbs could manage. He did not wait beyond the touch of the stock to his shoulder, for once the great hind legs snapped against the earth the chance would be gone. The crack of his rifle left the jackrabbit in a kicking sprawl, part of its snout blown off. Before Marcher could reach it, it was dead. He picked it up and carried it back to a stony wedge in the ravine where he laboriously built a fire, and as the small flames began to climb and build on the dry brush he took his knife and started to clean the rabbit.

An hour later, after eating, he cleaned the bones and distantly decided to make a broth of them for dinner. But that would come later. Now he pulled himself into the shade of the southern ledge of the ravine and, turning his saddle for a pillow, fell asleep.

Coyote-Singing came out of his crouching position and stood up slowly to his full height. His face turned to the northeast like one suddenly alerted and puzzled at the same time. He had been bent over, sharpening his knife on a smooth stone, awaiting the return of Big Blood and the two other braves who were out seeking meat before their party moved any deeper into Crow country. Suddenly a faint snap like a distant whip told him he had heard a rifle shot and his senses warned him that it had come from the wide valley that opened its mouth to the northeast.

He stood for many minutes weighing this thing in his mind. His own hunters he knew had taken only bows and arrows. So this was a thing to be wondered at. He held his breath expecting to hear other shots, but none came. And still he could not turn away. Finally he pulled the strong-seeing glasses from his war gear and trained them up the great valley, but even after much looking he saw nothing.

Big Blood, his enormous shoulders broadening as they let the carcass down and finished their task, watched Coyote-Singing descend from the spike of rock and come toward him. It was still very early. They had not planned to move until nightfall, when darkness would help blind the enemy. But now Coyote-Singing was pointing to the northeast. "Did my brothers hear a shot?"

Big Blood looked at the others questioningly and seeing their silence said, "We heard no guns. What shot is this my brother speaks of?"

Coyote-Singing quietly told them of hearing a distant shot that he sensed had come from the valley to the northeast, but as he finished they still looked at him questioningly, Big Blood finally turning to look that way too.

"Was it not a rock from the cliffs sent by the spirits to sleep on the valley floor?"

"It was a shot," said Coyote-Singing as though he had little intention of saying it again.

They all stood there looking to the northeast in silence. This was not without good reason. Their war party was not a normal one and its origin had made them more wary. They had left against the will of Red Moon, who had said that the Brule warriors should stay with the camp till after the spring hunt and then the Sioux nation would go as one against the Crows. This was to be a major war and every man would be needed.

But the terrible winter that had just passed had driven the Sioux braves to distraction. Being forced by white troops through the endless snows would have been great enough travail, but there were well-mounted Crow and Pawnee warriors helping the whites, bringing their Indian cunning into the balance so that both old and young had been lost and many brave men had had to stay behind and taste death to save villages. Never had vengeance so infected the Sioux. The Hunkpapas had chosen to go against the Pawnees, but the Oglalas and the Minneconjous and Brules were determined to leave the land of Absaroka a land of blood.

The Akicita had done its best to keep the warriors in camp, but even some of its own members had slipped away to return with scalps, as well as arms and legs and not a few heads. But the dancing and the frenzied singing seemed to do little to reduce the hate.

Coyote-Singing settled on the ground, the others around him. About his chest he tightened the snakeskin that had been given to him in a dream that spring. He hoped that it would be strong medicine. The pipe was unsheathed and lighted. It was passed around many times. Finally Big Blood broached the issue.

"My brother would go into the valley beyond?"

"It is a thing that grows in a warrior's heart."

"We have made medicine to go against the Crows."

"I will do this thing myself and this day return."

"We had better go with you. One shot does not mean one gun."

"No, Coyote-Singing will do this thing alone. My brothers will rest here. At nightfall I shall return and we will go against the Crows."

"And if you do not return?"

"A warrior lives with death, my brothers. We Lakota are surrounded by it. We cannot hide from our enemies like the grouse with the broken wing. We must strike against those who come into our lands as a spring grizzly does those who approach its den. If I do not return, Big Blood, slay many Crows and make the hearts of our people glad."

• • •

Marcher awoke again in the late afternoon. He felt a little more strength in his limbs now, but he was still hungry. He took the small round iron bowl from his pack and filled it with water from the seepage that mothered the trickle running through the ravine. The first bowl he drank, the second he put over a small fire he had started on a flat rock and, breaking the rabbit bones, put them in. His horse was standing on the shady side of the ravine looking at him, the smell of the fire making it back away a few steps.

After an hour he drank the broth, but it was thinner than he had hoped. He belched as the last of it went down, and swearing that his stomach needed filling all the time, slung his rifle over his shoulder and started back up the slope.

It was a long, weary haul and he was panting badly when he reached the summit, his rifle off his back and hanging from one limp arm. It would still be almost an hour until sundown so he settled himself upon the warm rocks to study the rough line of ridges running to the northeast. As he lay there he tried to fix exactly where he had seen the light the evening before, but in the end he could not for the life of him tell. Yet it would reappear, of that he was certain.

As the minutes slipped away his gaze grew more and more intent. The sun was bending to the horizon and the shadows on the slope below were reaching toward him. He stood up straight and posted himself on the large rock, his eyes riveted to the line of ridges beyond. The rim of the sun was almost on the horizon and still there was no . . . but then, suddenly, he saw it—the light. It was shining at him and immediately he started toward it. Heedless of his footing he broke into a staggering run and he knew what it was now, he should have known all along. It was a piece of mirror fixed to reflect the sun's rays at sundown and carrying a message all its own. It would give him the secret to the mine. He had won at last, he had won, he had won, it would soon be his.

After a half-mad run he knew finally he was getting very close to it. He could see the light beginning to dim out, but now he had marked it in his mind and there would be no losing it again. He was only a couple of hundred yards away and unaware that he was shouting to himself. The ground seemed to have flattened out here, enabling him to move a little faster. He was on the verge of victory and in that moment it had all been worth it. In that moment all pain was erased and he felt a rising passion putting new power into every joint and spending itself in a long meaningless yell.

Why he fell he did not know, but his first sensation was of pain as though an enormous insect had bitten him on the ear and knocked him off balance. It was only as he lay in a sudden haze that he realized a rifle had been fired and he had just missed death by less than a centimeter. His rifle had spun from him as he went down and now instinctively he clawed for it, finally reaching it and shaking his head desperately over it to clear his vision. As his eyes steadied he saw a figure far off, almost as far as he had run, looking toward him and then, as though not seeing what it wanted, disappearing suddenly behind a spike of rock.

43

Coyote-Singing took his mount swiftly to the valley mouth, then began to work his way from one high point to another, scouting the land carefully before he covered it. There were no tracks in the occasional ravines, but he studied each one carefully as he moved along. Shortly after noon he came upon the tracks of two horses, but they were old, too old for any thought of pursuit. He followed them cautiously for a way and was rewarded by coming across the tracks of a single mount. These were fresher and told him he was not dealing with a large party, since this horse's tracks matched one of the other two. Two men had come this way and left, and only one had returned.

He lost some time circling one ravine so that he could get to high ground on the other side and inspect it, but the ravine was empty. He kept glancing at the sun. The day was passing and he had to return to Big Blood and the others. He would like to have tracked that horse openly, but the valley floor had spread out and ran along the slope of a high ridge which rose till it turned and folded in against the summit of a mountain. To have stayed with those tracks would have made him visible for miles. Instead he kept himself under the slope using his strong-seeing glasses to follow the tracks farther out on the valley floor. It was slow work and he had nearly tired of it when a wisp of wind teasing the edge of the slope told him that a cooking fire had been lit somewhere ahead. He saw the next ravine cutting into the slope and reaching further in than the others. He saw also the horse's tracks ended there. Here he would have to be as cunning as a mountain cat. The ravine would be hard to surprise, for it had a wide, treeless front and the advantage would lie completely with any occupant behind the growth within. Nor could he get above it, for the valley wall rose steeply here and a man caught on the open face of that rock would be helpless.

Time began to concern him. The sun was lowering into the west and it was a far ride back to the others. Yet he was sure he had found his quarry. All his instincts told him it was in that ravine and no real warrior could turn back now.

He tied his horse behind a great boulder that threw a shadow large enough to cover them both. Then he took his rifle and strong-seeing glasses and moved to the first cut in the mountain slope that bent around to start forming the ravine. Here, holding himself close against the coppery green rock facing, he brought his glasses to bear on the foliage within. At first he saw nothing, but then he saw flecks of motion which he knew were the slow movements of a hobbled horse, but more than that he could not see. He would have to expose himself for that. Ideally he should have waited for nightfall, but staying here till night fell meant the war party would go on without him.

In mute anger he began to examine the slope above. But the prospect of approaching from that direction undetected mocked sanity. Still he had to find a way to get into that ravine without losing the all-important element of surprise. As his glasses played on the stretch above he suddenly grunted, for here he saw it—the figure of a man moving slowly up toward the summit. He was already too far for a safe shot, but it gave Coyote-Singing the heart to chance a more daring penetration of the ravine. He reasoned that if he found only one horse it was likely the man was alone and his scalp as good as taken.

Slowly he came further and further around the steep ravine wall, and with each step he slipped forward with more confidence. Finally he reached the thin line of foliage, and seeing through it knew at last he had been right. The horse lifted its head and looked at him in a long gaze and ended by whinnying and standing as though it was ready to shy. But Coyote-Singing was not interested in the mount now. He eyed the saddle and gear and decided he would take these valuable things along with the horse on his way back. Now his eyes were turned up the slope where the slow-climbing man was becoming a tiny figure almost at the summit.

Coyote-Singing made two decisions simultaneously. One, it was approaching sundown and he would have to stalk his victim before dark or he might lose him. A man alone on an open mountainside with a rifle was a different proposition from one sitting half asleep over a camp fire in a ravine. Two, he would have to accept the fact that Big Blood and the others would go on without him. Well, perhaps at dawn he could trail them. With two strong horses he stood a good chance of overtaking them or of avoiding pursuit if he ran into a superior number of enemies. Through his glasses he determined the man had stopped near the summit and was on the ground looking in the opposite direction from his camp. Coyote-Singing wondered what he was doing there, for surely he was not hunting. He started to crawl his way up the steep slope slanting behind whatever outcroppings of rock he could use for cover. It would not be very difficult if the man stayed where he was and this he was clearly doing, for he had not moved in long minutes.

Some half hour later with the high air cool and still and the land below them darkening in the pall of night, Coyote-Singing had drawn within rifle range of his prey. The man was up now and watching something beyond to the northeast; with his glasses Coyote-Singing saw a repeating rifle hanging from his hand, one such as he had taken from the Pawnee. But, incredibly, not once had this foolish one looked behind him. Surely it was a strange way for a lone man in this war-worried country to behave. Standing on an exposed summit without glancing in the many directions from which trouble might beset him. And what was he watching?

Coyote-Singing brought up his rifle and braced it against the rock, thinking of the fight in which he had claimed this weapon he now held. It had been a formidable war party with the renowned and powerful Red Moon carrying the pipe and his own father, Strikes-His-Enemy, a man many said could dance with death so strong seemed his medicine. He could still see his father, as they attacked the soldiers' supply wagons on the Sweetwater, jumping his horse over the enemy barricade and using his quirt on the face of the soldier chief. Surely it was the end, thought watching braves, to this unusual and spiritually unyielding man. What warrior, they asked themselves, with a cruelly twisted leg and empty eye socket would still have such courage for battle? But miraculously, Strikes-His-Enemy had thrown his head back in a great war shout and turned to make his way out again, singing an ancient strong heart song as soldiers' bullets chopped feathers from his headdress and so creased his pony's flanks and legs it had to be abandoned. Coyote-Singing grunted in satisfaction. Was this not a father for a warrior? Behind the stoic face he showed his fellow braves, like Big Blood and Hawkfoot, lay a deep pride that he, Coyote-Singing, had sprung from the loins of such a man.

But it was not a journey to put on the great robe. Clearly from their slow shooting the soldiers had only the single-shot weapons. With only one many-shots gun, taken from the brave Pawnee, they returned to the Medicine Water where those with wounds or injured parts entered the sweat lodges or sought poultices of herbs from the wise ones. It was there he remembered Black Water, the courageous Cheyenne, sitting alone thinking of the young White Fringe, whose body had fallen so close to the wagons it had to be left for carrion.

But now the man was suddenly moving, crouching over, his body like a limp, disjointed finger against the sky. He seemed to be bending forward as though peering into the distance. Coyote-Singing, steadying his gun and taking a deep breath, began squeezing the trigger, but at once the figure dropped down and disappeared. He released the trigger and came up to a kneeling position. He knew he could not have been seen. Something beyond had drawn the man over the crest of the summit. Coyote-Singing started up after him, coming into the almost horizontal sun rays that still brushed the tops of the range. He was breathless when he reached the spot where the man had been standing, but immediately he saw the man moving far along the spine of the ridge and running toward a light that looked like a brilliant star.

Coyote-Singing started after him, still struggling for breath from his climb. He could tell from the other's gait that the man was running heedlessly and wasting valuable breath at this altitude by shouts that bordered on screams. Surely this man was running toward some strong medicine, medicine that was hiding in that strange light which even now was beginning to recede. Coyote-Singing stopped and kneeled. The man was nearing the spot where the light had come forth. Coyote-Singing decided he must not reach it. It would be a long shot, a risky one, but he squeezed the trigger and saw the figure pitch forward, the rifle spinning from the man's hand.

Coyote-Singing came to his feet slowly. It was hard to see in the gathering dusk whether the figure was still moving, but he peered patiently for a moment. A warrior learns that a wounded foe can often be more dangerous than one free to run.

Then he saw the man was moving and had recovered his gun. There was not an instant to waste. He threw himself behind the nearest rock.

44

Big Blood and the two braves grew disgruntled as the day wore on, and the swift pinto of Coyote-Singing did not appear from the valley mouth to the northeast. It would be a bad omen, a very bad omen, if he were lost. This was a matter that festered and grew bigger in Big Blood's mind. Strikes-His-Enemy would have to be told he no longer had his favorite son, and Red Moon would surely close his eyes when told he had lost a favorite warrior—and all this on a raid forbidden by the tribal council. Big Blood had long been a strong leader among the warriors, and his following had often set bold or idle tongues to gossiping that one day he would be chief. But among the warrior societies there were those who felt he was more interested in killing and coups than he was in the people. His reputation would suffer from the loss of the young popular Coyote-Singing in this rash murder raid against the Crows.

An hour or two before sundown he motioned the other braves to their ponies, and with only a questioning look at the sky swung his quirt vigorously into his sorrel's flank and led the way at a gallop toward the valley mouth.

It was dark on the valley floor by the time they had followed Coyote-Singing's devious tracks to where they discovered his mount. It was darker still when they entered the ravine and saw the good chestnut and the gear, and the fire remains which said a white man was making camp here. The sun was just ready to leave the high peaks above them when, as they looked up at the summit which towered above the slope and to which all tracks seemed to lead, they heard the thin, high, clear snap of a single shot.

Marcher brought a bloody hand back from his ear and wiped it on his buckskin shirt. His head was aching but clear now and he was trying frantically to piece together his plight. How insane could one man be? He had been so mesmerized by that mirror, he had ignored every rudimentary rule of survival in this land. Running along an open slope, shouting like a banshee, never checking his backtrack. Fate had not forgiven him. Some cold, penetrating feeling that moved from his body to his mind told him death was astride every possible move. He was cut off from his camp and horse, he had no food. He had only his weapons—his gun and perhaps fifteen rounds, his hatchet, and his knife. The strap on his field glasses had broken as he fell and he had to twist his head to see the uptilt of one lens socket lying behind him. He would have to back up over some loose boulders to get at them, but they must be recovered.

He lay there undecided, not really daring to move. In gratitude he watched the darkness claiming the ridges and sprays of stars beginning to appear as pinpricks in the sky. He thought of moving toward the stone he had seen the figure disappear behind, but that was a two-sided coin which could fall either way. If he let his attacker come to him, a gamble, he would have the advantage of hearing the other's movements, allowing himself a target. If he moved, he risked being heard himself. But if he could move silently he might gain an edge on someone thinking he was still lying where he had fallen. After pondering both sides he decided to move. First he crawled backward until he recovered his field glasses. He had to tie the leather straps together before he could set them on his neck. When he did they sat up tight, barely allowing room to clear his face. Then he started forward again, drifting slightly to the left.

After he had crawled for twenty minutes along the off-side of the ridge, which swept downward to the southeast, he stopped to rest. He knew he should be thinking of escape. He should be making use of this darkness, which was his only and transitory ally. There could well be others stalking him, and in the morning they would raise him in this open country as easily as wolves flush a lame deer. As he lay there the night chill that played along the spine of the ridge began to stiffen him. He swore at his miserable luck and then at himself for being a fool, a fool among fools. All reason demanded his horse and gear were gone and he was now afoot in this tormenting land. He had little more than a narrowing choice of deaths. And now he thought again of the mine, of the mirror on the cliff wall behind him, of the future that was almost his. A rage thickened in him and he swore again. Damn if he wasn't cursed.

The mine put him to thinking of other causes for this predicament. Perhaps these were not Indians, but white men pretending to be savages and really after his mine. If they were, he had led them to it, and he was twice the madman for it. The strange cry of some night bird and the distant yip of a coyote left him peering into the darkness. No, by God, they were Indians sure as sin.

He decided he would stay on high ground. There was little cover here, but if he found the right position he could at least ward off surprise, and there was always the chance it was a few passing bucks, having found his horse and hoping to take his gun and scalp to boot. By morning the intruders might be gone and he would at least have another go at that mirror and the key to the mine.

He rose quickly now and made his way carefully back to a point almost a quarter of a mile beyond the spot where he had first perceived the light. It took him some time to find cover that would enable him to still see the ledge which held the mirror as well as the sweep of ridge. But in time he judged a space between two angularly pitched boulders would suit. The night seemed to grow darker, and it wasn't until after midnight that a soft moon rose to bathe the ridge and the peaks beyond it in a thin blue light and assure him he was right.

Coyote-Singing came into the dark ravine knowing Big Blood and the others were there. The coyote signals had surprised him, but it was good to hear his friends had not left him to carry out their raid alone.

But when Big Blood came up in the darkness, his greeting was terse. "Does my brother bring us the scalp of this stupid white?"

"It will be mine with the next sun."

"Coyote-Singing forgets the scalps of his Sioux brothers hang in Crow lodges. Let us take this one's horse and leave him afoot. There is but one coup here. We have made medicine and have come for many."

Coyote-Singing looked up at the ridge, his eyes moving to dark slits as he studied the back of the summit against the dark blue of the sky. "No. This one has the many-shots rifle. Coyote-Singing wishes to have it. He will bring it to Red Moon's lodge. Red Moon's heart will still be good toward us."

Big Blood grunted at the truth of this.

"What is this white one doing here?" questioned one of the braves following Coyote-Singing's gaze to the heights.

It was a long time before Coyote-Singing answered, then he answered slowly, "Coyote-Singing does not know this thing, but there is an evil spirit up there. Coyote-Singing has seen it."

Big Blood grunted again. "What have the eyes of Coyote-Singing seen?"

"A strange light toward which the white one runs. Coyote-Singing will make strong medicine tonight, for it is the eye of an evil spirit and Coyote-Singing will destroy it."

45

Dawn began with a faint haze to the east. Marcher watched it as it lifted the cowl of night from the slopes and made the mountains glisten in spots where a heavy mist had dampened the dark obsidian rock facing on a clifflike drop to the north.

With his glasses he studied the ridge before him, traveling over it slowly, finding nothing that called for caution. It was only when the sun finally broke through a sharp wedge in the range to the east and dappled the ridge in the young fresh light of a new day, that his glasses picked up a figure lying fully prone between two boulders near the spine of the mountain, its only movement being the top of its head, which was swinging toward him. It was an Indian with a small pair of field glasses sweeping the terrain. Instinct made him recoil behind his rock cover as the distant lens turned in his direction.

He waited a few minutes and then brought his glasses around to the off-side of the rock. The Indian was looking the other way now and seemed to be signaling someone behind him further down the slope in the direction of his old camp. More minutes passed before two crouching figures crept up beside the one between the boulders. They too looked around, but they used only eyes seasoned to the broken blade of grass and the mark of a boot-nail on a weathered stone. For many minutes they looked about as though confident that what they sought was there, then they came slowly forward, standing upright on the ridge. The sun, getting clear of the range to the east, lit their dark skins, their brightly painted bodies and feathered headwear, making them seem like toys in the distance. They stood together making signs in the direction of both slopes. Marcher decided they were going to work the softer ground farther down each slope in order to pick up his trail. They did not seem rushed. They knew he was afoot and they were well mounted. It was a matter time would easily master.

As they moved across the ridge he decided they were just within safe range but he could never get the three of them at once, and without a horse he decided his best bet lay in avoiding detection. And now they were moving down the ridge and away from him. The one with the field glasses and a snakeskin about his chest was leading the way. Marcher, suddenly getting a peculiar feeling, raised his glass beyond them and finally found the ledge where he knew the mirror lay fixed by the hand of Paul. They were still a way from it but they were moving steadily and with purpose. He watched them for a few more seconds and then, as though he had divined their terrible intent, he rose from his cover and started after them. Insanely he began to stride along the ridge, one hand before him as though he were cautioning them against danger. On they went, and he began to move more rapidly behind them. By the time they approached the ledge which held the mirror, he was abreast of the ravine that held his camp. Miraculously they had not looked back once as they reached and stood before the ledge, looking up at it, pointing to something. He stopped and helplessly brought his field glasses up. Surely they were arguing about what to do with the mirror. He had a maniacal desire to shout at them to leave it alone, they did not know its worth, that it was his, that a thousand curses hung over the hand that touched it. But even as he suppressed this desire, he saw the one who had led the way take his rifle stock and smash it against the ledge. Thin slivers of light needled the air for a fraction of a second, and then the brave was pounding something to dust beneath his feet.

"No!" roared Marcher, a frenzy gripping his voice. "No, you God damn fools! No! God damn you!"

The Indians turned toward him, their rigid postures showing their surprise. A second later a rifle shot sliced the morning air and a whining slug plowed angrily into the rocky bed behind Marcher. Shaking, he brought his own rifle around and fired two rapid shots. They drove the Indians from sight, which said he had missed. His mind was fighting itself for control. "Damn fools!" he shouted again, but he had just opened the door of death. Another bullet, droning closer than the first, warned it was creeping in. His only chance was to move before they surrounded him. That would buy him at least a few minutes, or at best hours, but the only real hope was his horse, and now he realized he was right above the ravine where he had made his camp. Before the idea was completely formed in his mind he was reeling down the slope, one hand holding his rifle high in the air for balance. In the back of his mind he knew he could beat them to the ravine and that everything depended on whether more braves were waiting below. Like a man who can take any risk when the alternative is certain death, he ignored another bullet coming from the ridge far to the right. The downward angle and the jerking motions of his movement were making him difficult to hit. He bent all his attention to the ravine below. No matter the odds he was going to have to fight, he knew enough about Indians now not to be taken alive. As he neared the ravine he could see the Indian ponies tethered on either side. There were four in sight so he had at least one Sioux to get by. But where was his own mount? As he tried to keep his feet, for he was half falling down the slope, his eyes ravaged the ravine, but the chestnut was nowhere in sight. He was already in the ravine and running for one of the Indian ponies when his chestnut came through the foliage at a dead run. On its back was a Sioux brave. In the absence of the others he had taken the hobbles from the horse and was testing the mount's speed, but at the shouts he had raced back. Now he was coming directly at Marcher. Marcher tried to get his rifle around, but it was too late. The Sioux swung his war club and Marcher, fending it off with his rifle stock, had the gun knocked from his hand. Without thinking he grabbed the brave by the wrist, which the downswing of the club had straightened before him, and with a backward surge tore the Indian from his horse. Again it came as a thing beyond planning, but Big Owl's training had taken hold well enough now for him to get along without thinking. The hatchet was in his hand and the brave looked up just in time to take the blow across the bridge of his nose. When Marcher pulled the hatchet out, one of the Sioux's eyes was pumping blood and the Indian's head went down to take the next blow at the nape of the neck.

Far above him the Sioux war cry was rending the air and Marcher, his breath fighting both in and out of his lungs, fell upon his rifle. Somehow he saw it all clearly now. He had fought his way back from the final drumbeat of death and it was this killing that had kept him alive. Coming to one knee he shot the two Indian ponies nearest him and then forced himself up and fell upon the shying chestnut. He had no time for his saddle and gear, but he swung to the other side of the ravine and grabbed the single rein of the two remaining ponies. Then, pounding the chestnut wildly with his heels, he went at full gallop through the line of foliage and out of the ravine. The mountain was still throwing a great shadow across the valley and there were fingers of mist which looked like some eerie forms of growth that could be seen clear across to the sun line on the slope beyond. Above him more shots were ringing out, but the hoofbeats of the three horses swamped his hearing and if they came close he would never know. At the cut of the ravine he knew he was out of range, he knew he had beaten them, he knew he was riding off with his life, but he knew also they had defeated him. The dream that had sustained him for so long was dead. The wind that washed against his face and the sharp morning colors of rocky peaks lofting their reddish and whitish buttresses into a coral and blue sky did nothing to remove the sight of a Sioux warrior with a snakeskin about his chest driving his rifle stock against a distant ledge and bringing forth a flickering shower of speckled light. What he did not know, what he would never know, was that the stock of that rifle carried a silver nameplate upon which was engraved the name Benjamin Amiel.

46

The excitement and confusion which spread over the Crow camp served to conceal Marcher's return. The village was preparing to move to the east, where large herds of buffalo had been sighted, and everywhere squaws were bringing down lodge poles, screaming at dogs and children, and packing household articles on their horses and travois.

White Bead had been slow to her task until she saw Marcher approaching, leading the two strange war ponies. At this sight her eyes came to life as one who feels suddenly whole again and she began to shout back at and harry as well as outpace those around her.

It was not until the village was under way that White River and Amiel remarked that Marcher had returned. Ben refused to approach him. Since seeing Marcher running amuck with his hatchet among the Blackfoot wounded, Ben had found himself sickened by even his presence. But White River, remarking that the horses were Sioux war ponies and smelling possible trouble, came riding over. He was aware at once that Marcher had little yearning for talk.

"Been on a horse raid?" he said, casually eyeing the two Sioux ponies.

"You know damn well I haven't," said Marcher irritably.

"You look clean beat," drawled White River, noticing the gaunt quality had returned to Marcher's face.

"You got something you rode over here to say?" Marcher was searching the sky like a man preoccupied with the weather.

"Just bein' neighborly," muttered White River.

"Well, you've paid your respects. Now I've got some thinking to do."

A few minutes later, White River and Amiel had pushed their mounts to the vanguard of the moving village. There was less dust there and less noise from the raucous procession that now stretched out for a quarter of a mile, moving like a serpent on the great rising slope that swept to the east.

Amiel was looking back at the slumped, slow-riding figure of Marcher. "My God! What's got into him? I'll wager he didn't find his mine."

"I'll bet a bull boat full of Tennessee brewed he found some red skin though. Those ponies look real slick. That type don't come for askin'."

"Maybe they're just strays."

White River's eyes narrowed as he bent to his habit of hunting the horizon. "Strays don't come with rawhide bits and war paint on 'em."

Amiel considered this for a moment, then, accepting it, said, "Believe now I'd rather not know how he came by them."

"Might have just run off with 'em." White River was watching a Crow wolf riding up to White Tail and making the no-enemy sign.

Amiel muttered, his interest fading, "Just like that, huh?"

White River glanced back at Marcher. "No, I'm thinkin' he got 'em in a fracas."

Amiel turned away, his eyes becoming far-gazing. "How do you figure something like that?"

"Well, talkin' ain't turned him back yet, and his ear's nicked like a coon dog's as got careless and he ain't got around to cleanin' that hatchet."

The long march ended where a large creek ran into Elk River, the Yellowstone of the whites. The creek was broad and full-flowing at its mouth and to the south and east scouts reported large herds of buffalo moving toward them from the Horn valley.

The fourth day after they arrived in camp the racks were again piled high with buffalo meat, and to the west of the camp dozens of buffalo hides were being stretched and scraped. The hasty arrival in camp of three scouts that had been sent across Elk River caused great alarm until it was known that they were only reporting the Black Lodges, the River Crows, coming to join them for a long-awaited summer reunion. It was decided a feast should be held to welcome them, and the old village crier went about shouting, "The hunts have been good. Fill your cooking pots. Many friends are coming. Life will be good. The Great Spirit smiles on the Absarokees."

White River looked over the campsite, protected as it was on two sides by the creek and river, and decided White Tail had made a wise decision. This was a veritable fortress, a handy arrangement so close to Sioux country. White River was lying in the sun in front of the lodge he and Amiel had helped Amiel's housekeeping squaw, old Yellow Leaf, put up. The patient, ancient Yellow Leaf, seeing his desire, had spread a robe, and he had driven two sticks into the ground to make a backrest from some strips of deerskin cut from leg wrappings. It was the only luxury a man could manage, and White River lay enjoying it, contentedly puffing the stone pipe Blue Lodge had brought him.

Most of their clothes were worn out now and they were wearing comfortable and snug-fitting skins cut for them by Blue Lodge. A man easily enough got used to them though and skin didn't seem to take to dirt like cloth.

Amiel, seemingly struck more and more frequently by sudden and disturbing moods, had taken to wandering off by himself, watching the game graze in the distance, often just looking for long periods at some sun-bathed cloud crossing the sky. At times he bent to study a rash of blue or yellow flowers, pulling a fresh blade of grass to chew or holding a skin-tight knuckle to his mouth. White River watched him, a secret uneasiness growing, but said nothing.

Yet stretched out there and drawing leisurely on his pipe he noticed how the season was getting on. With the weather turning fair they had quietly allowed time to start slipping by them, and not even Amiel appeared ready to pack out. Perhaps they needed this rest after the grueling winter and the physical and nervous exhaustion brought on by their close call with the Blackfeet.

Ah, but it was pleasant. He shook the ash from his pipe and loaded it again. He thought of Blue Lodge and how she looked at him across the campsite or when he rode by, and how she had come when he wanted her back on Red Lodge Creek. By rights he should have approached her family with some presents and many good words. It was a thing the Crows expected, but he was doing something maybe more important, keeping them supplied with food.

The Absarokees were in a good mood, there was much laughter and merriment beyond where the lodges opened into a half circle facing the river. He took another look at their present encampment. It was truly a strong position, but comfortable as he was, something in his mind was not at ease. They were perilously close to Sioux country and this hunting camp was far too large not to have been detected. Lately he'd been thinking more and more about Buzz and how he had once saved an Omaha village. The Omahas were corn Indians, for a good part of the year abandoning war and patiently raising their crops. But the Sioux raided them incessantly, stealing their horses and sometimes their women. The Sioux were far better horsemen and surely better warriors, but the Omaha were closer to the whites and had more rifles. Buzz had noticed the Omaha squaws scooping out shallow pits in the earth for their men to lie in and shoot from. This helped their defense, but the Sioux warriors soon learned to ride over these pits from different directions and use their lances on the helpless occupants below. Buzz showed the Omahas how to scoop out a second pit behind the first, warning the rifleman in the second pit to concentrate on shooting only at warriors trying to ride over the first. As long as the first pit held their village was safe. The raids soon stopped.

He looked around the campsite again, and taking his pipe slowly from his mouth, he pursed his lips for long moments in thought.

The appearance of Marcher surprised him. Andy was suddenly stepping from behind his backrest, looking different in a new buckskin shirt and pants White Bead had made, chewing the edges soft for him. On his feet were moccasins with flaps that rose above his ankles and were tied there firmly by white strips of rawhide. In his belt were his hatchet and knife, but he carried no gun.

"Got time for some talking?" said Marcher abruptly.

"Can make some, reckon," said White River without moving.

Marcher settled down before him and pulled his knife out to scratch the earth as he talked. White River saw he had started to shave again but had let his hair grow, keeping it tied behind him Indian style. "Been thinking of making a deal."

"Mmmmm?"

"Oh, not with you or Ben," answered Marcher coldly.

White River looked about him as though faintly amused. "Crows is easiest to deal with when their paunch is empty."

"Naw, they won't fit—scared to go south."

"South?"

"Yep, I'm heading for Denver."

"Denver?"

"Right. There's miners there. Probably an assayer. Men who know what they're doing. I'm going to make a deal with the right ones to hunt out Paul's mine."

White River stared at Marcher as though he were missing something in the other's words. "It's a fair piece through mighty rough country—Cheyenne country, I'm thinkin'."

"Don't worry, I'll make it."

White River mulled over this prospect for a moment. "Ever been in a raw minin' town before?"

"No. Why? Something wrong with mining towns?"

"Heard tell."

"What?"

"Mostly that they're full of gents like you, bustin' their guts for claims and puttin' gold before God or gettin' breakfast."

"I can take care of myself."

"Reckon. Reckon mebbe you can. Those Injun ponies you rode in with weren't no gift, I'm thinkin'."

Marcher looked away sullenly for a moment, then said quickly, "Those Sioux bastards broke Paul's star."

White River looked at him queerly for a moment. "You found that star?"

"Yes. Sure as hell did," said Marcher haltingly. He told White River what had happened on the mountain and ended by working his knife into the ground and cursing that he had not managed to kill them all.

White River was silent for a long stretch as though he were weighing these doings in his mind. Then he said abruptly, "This ain't hardly what you came over here to palaver about, is it?"

"No, it isn't."

"Figure you best get on with what you minded."

"I want you to keep an eye on White Bead."

"You're joshin'!"

"No, God damn it, I'm not! Some of these bucks around here have been studding up to her. Enough to sicken a man!"

"Then you figure on comin' back."

"I'm planning to."

"Ha!"

Marcher was on his feet. "Just keep an eye on her. I'm having her move her tipi next to yours and Ben's. They won't bother her if they see you're of a mind to stop them."

"Well, I'll be go to hell!"

Later, when Ben returned, White River motioned him down and told him about Marcher's visit. Amiel pulled his deerskin cap from his head and looked at it long and hard, the early afternoon sun causing a mist of sweat to glisten on his exposed forehead. "You mean he really cares what happens to her?"

"Way of puttin' it, I reckon."

Amiel sat looking in dim wonder across the camp where Marcher and White Bead had pitched their lodge. After a while he got up and went into the tipi. White River could hear him asking Yellow Leaf for water spiced with whiskey.

It was a thing impossible to explain, for it happened more and more often.

The old squaw Yellow Leaf, whose son was lost against the Blackfeet and who more and more often slept in Amiel's lodge, rose up on her elbow to listen to Ben cry out in his sleep. Above her the wind whispered through the lodge poles; in the distance a dog barked against the night. She shook her graying head in dismay, her mucused eyes, left almost lusterless by her many years, blinking slowly in the darkness. Oh, what a good and gentle being was this white man she tended, one who should have taken an Absarokee maiden into his robes to beget sons and proud walking daughters to make his coming years a time when the heart rose full and the spirit knew peace. But there was a bad happening in this one's life; it had left him with a loneliness long frozen within and which now none of the common joys of living seemed able to thaw. Again he cried out in muffled terror, his head swaying strangely, his breathing heavy and uneven. Resignedly she turned back into her robe, knowing there were things only the medicine spirits could account for. Humbled by this knowing, she lay in the darkness, sighing quietly till the sudden soft drone of light rain against the lodge skins lulled her back again to sleep.

Ben himself was grimly conscious of a dark despondency slowly claiming him. Almost daily he thought of Andy and the hideous sight of his hatchet plunging down again and again, despoiling the bodies of dazed and dying Blackfeet. No amount of telling himself they were enemies bent on his own destruction could lessen the horror of that sight. He wondered at night if it was possible this taint of savagery could be festering in his own mind; after all, they were half brothers. But that thought was unbearable. Surely his father, a good, honest, and religious man, a lay preacher who lost his life refusing to use firearms in a slave rebellion, could not have sired so degenerate a son. Surely Melody, that fragile, sensitive girl, could not have given herself and her love to a man who would revel in the gory slaughter of wounded men. But these were only words. That bloody hatchet continued to rise and whirl through his mind. He had already seen what this wilderness and the druglike blood lust of these fierce peoples could do to a man.

Secretly he was growing disturbed by other things, events he had once let pass without notice. He had shot a deer and watched it die, its great startled eyes upon him as the light of life faded from the wide frantic orbs. In his mind he kept seeing that frightened deer dying all day. Inevitably he began thinking of all the wild things he had killed, cutting off their lives as would a wicked god. He knew he was becoming unnaturally morose and depressed, but he couldn't help it. The sight of human scalps outside many lodges, and the way these natives, even children, ran to gorge themselves on the blood and the still warm flesh of dying animals, was filling him with the eerie sense that he had entered a world without mercy and compassion, where mankind had not advanced beyond the mentality of wolves.

White River watched him from a distance. He had seen cultured, pious, and sensitive Easterners shocked into near demented states by the raw savagery of Plains Indians before. There was no cure for it. Amiel simply had to leave. Even then, it might be years before he would feel normal again. Something happened to a man's deepest convictions when he realized the line between man and animal was in fact a lofty illusion that could only be sustained by a carefully nurtured faith. Marcher was a different story. He fitted this life better than some, like White River, who had been raised to it. He was a born predator who found his natural habitat here, where unfettered expressions of hostile human emotions knew few restraints. White River turned his thoughts to getting Ben to Laramie, where passage to the east could be arranged; Marcher he mused on grimly for only a moment, then forgot.

But the long, bothersome quandary about himself remained. Shouldn't he be leaving too? Shouldn't he be going east to find work, maybe even setting up a spread somewhere? He had heard that government land was going cheap, sometimes for little more than filing a claim. Most vexing of all, had time eroded his dream of having Lydia again—eroded it beyond repair? Should he even go on hoping?

White River spent a day or two pondering these mixed urgings of his heart, aware that the patient, devoted Blue Lodge, sensing his mood, was watching him quietly, her fears apparent. At the same time, Amiel sat behind his lodge skins, sinking into an emotional morass no amount of common sense, repeated over and over again, could stave off. He had taken to dreaming stark, frightening dreams, dreams of his father praying over Melody's grave, praying for his son's, Ben's, salvation. Vainly he tried to call to his father, telling him he would be saved, he would not descend to this heathen life. But the dream would vanish as he awakened to a hoarse crying out that he realized was his own voice. One night the dream suddenly turned into a nightmare, with Melody rising from her grave to pray beside his father, then both of them turning to him, their faces grotesque under vermilion war paint. He screamed into the gloom of the lodge, awakening himself and surely old Yellow Leaf. He lay looking up into the darkness, his skin wet under the coarse robe, his heart pounding, his mind helpless to fend off the fear that seemed to fill the lodge. In vain he tried to will himself back into sleep but only succeeded in drifting off for short, restless moments till dawn.

That morning, noticing Yellow Leaf had disappeared, he stayed in his lodge thinking of how he would ask White River to guide him back to civilization, what he would say in farewell to the Crow headmen, how he would avoid facing Andy. But now that his decision was made he felt better. What he would do when he arrived at the lonely farm, what he would say to his mother about his half-mad brother, these thoughts he put off for another day. It was enough that he was escaping from this barbarous country, that he was still sane, alive, that he would one day be back in a Christian world and know peace again. So enthralled and relieved was he at this prospect that he hardly heard the excitement that was coming from all sides of the camp, or noticed the smiling Yellow Leaf who was pulling back the heavy flap of the lodge and greeting him with a shout that the River Crows had come.

PART EIGHT

CHEYENNES

47

The arrival of the River Crows brought much excitement and opened a scene that would hang in the minds of many as what life should have been like, as Ah-badt-deadt-deah had meant it for the Absarokees, with feasting, dancing, courting, relating of tales, renewing of old friendships. Food was plentiful and the ponies were sleek from good grass. Small groups that had wintered in the south by themselves kept coming in. Contests were held for the bow and the fleet of foot, and many spiritual offerings were made to keep the good times and the good feelings with the people.

Marcher delayed his trip to help White Bead move her lodge and to trade with the River Crows for the many things they had brought, which they had gotten in a raid against those strange, distrusted gypsies of the high plains, the Red River breeds, who belonged nowhere and were hated for their guile and white man's ways. Among the things brought along were bright cloth, salt, surprising quantities of shells, and gallons of the cloudy gut-grabbing Red River whiskey. The Crows did not plan to drink the whiskey themselves, but they had learned its value in trade with other tribes.

The morning Marcher was planning to leave, trouble suddenly arrived. Scouts rode in hurriedly from the east, partly swimming their horses in haste across the creek and rushing with a growing train behind them to White Tail's lodge. A knowing stoicism swept the faces of the chiefs as the scouts entered. Perhaps it was because there was a thing that slept in the heart of every warrior, a thing he knew could be awakened at any moment. The headmen listened to the words of the scouts in grim silence.

The Sioux had appeared in a great encampment only one day's ride to the east. They were not alone. They were already sending out many wolves, some of whom must surely be watching the Crow village at this very moment. After weighing these anxious words, one of the chiefs asked solemnly for the number of enemy lodges, and after many exchanges between the scouts it was clear the Absarokees were outnumbered by at least two and maybe three to one.

Spotted Horse, chief of the River Crows, was the first to offer counsel. "Should we not go back to our winter camps where we can better protect our weak and old ones?" His words seemed to make the air heavier and more hopeless, for there was no place that they could go where the Sioux could not follow.

"We have too many enemies," said White Tail. "We should smoke over these troublesome words and perhaps send a peace pipe to the Sioux. Perhaps they are as weary of war as we."

"Ha!" said Big Owl, his eyes rising to the little patch of blue above where the lodge poles met. "They are thinking of our young men helping the whites against them when the land was bare and their ponies were weak. They will offer us peace beside our fathers."

"Will not the whites help us?" asked the River Crows.

White Tail brought his eyes back to the circle. "The strong arm of the whites is many suns and many long smokes away," he said betraying the emptiness of the hope. "Indians killing Indians does not break the medicine law of the whites."

"The Absarokees have made a mistake to befriend these whites," snapped Spotted Horse. "They will always be further from our hearts than ever could be the hearts of other red men, even our enemies."

The wisdom of this statement silenced the circle for a few moments, then Ironfoot finally spoke. "The whites are not all the same. Those who live in the forts and fight for pay money do not care whom they go against—they have no lodges, this is not their land, they come only to do what their own Great Spirit tells them is wrong, though I have heard them pray to Him to help them do it. Yet there are other whites who come as brothers to know our hearts, to help us in time of need, who stand beside us in war. Let us ask them for their counsel—they will speak with straight tongues."

Everyone knew he was speaking of White River and perhaps Marcher, and after a long silence it was clear that no voice of objection would arise from the circle.

When Ben and White River arrived at the open council lodge, it was already encircled by a growing number of tense and sober faces and the air was heavy with sun-touched clouds of drifting pipe smoke. White River was not surprised to find Marcher already seated in the inner circle and even speaking. Amiel was stunned, particularly when he saw White Tail listening to his brother, the lines of the chief's mouth heavy with disapproval, that the Crows would allow this troublesome white such recognition. But White River knew, among Indians, even chiefs had to acknowledge the words of successful warriors. The two war ponies Marcher had led into camp had not been wasted on the Absarokee braves, who had turned to smile and grunt in admiration. Ponies of that caliber came only from important Sioux fighting men and could have only been taken with enormous risks. Whites revered their own soldiers for saving them from defeat or subjugation, but Indians often looked to their warriors to save them from extinction.

Marcher was now sitting with all eyes on him, his faintly haughty manner hinting he was, at least in his own sight, approaching the status of a war chief. White River settled beside Ironfoot, and motioning Amiel down beside him, wondered what really lay behind Marcher's strained and excited words.

"You say the Sioux are planning to attack this camp," Marcher shouted. "I, Yellow Hatchet, say the last thing they expect is to be attacked themselves. Give Yellow Hatchet fifty warriors and he will strike their camp tonight. We will spill enough of their blood to spoil their taste for war. Meanwhile the Absarokees can make haste and return to their mountains. I say after our attack the Sioux will have no heart to follow."

A smattering of young braves sitting far back in the outer circle gave brief, if uncertain grunts of approval, but the faces of the headmen were grim with concern. Big Owl, who wondered what really lay in the mind of this strange white who had tantalized him with that rifle until he led him to the stark mountain where the yellow metal hid, knew Marcher was not concerned with the safety of his people. His brave talk about attacking the enormous Sioux camp with only fifty warriors was the prattle of a child going to pee on a prairie fire that in a flash could sweep up and consume him. But one thing was clear. Marcher did not want to stand and fight, he wanted to flee. Fear was hardly the answer for that one. There was something else in that strange mind.

Most of the warriors still regarded Marcher with interest and respect as White Tail raised the pipe and tonelessly thanked him for his strong words. They understood and accepted the arrogance of brave men. One day many of them hoped to emulate it. But experienced heads in the council lodge knew their chiefs were really waiting for the quiet taciturn White River to speak. The braves would remember Marcher raging against the Blackfeet, but the chiefs saw the deadly efficient killing skills of this unassuming man who organized the horseshoe defense and left before his slot in the pit a small windrow of charging Blackfeet shot through the head.

White Tail glanced up at the lodge covering. "Do others wish to speak to the heart of their Absarokee friends?"

White River looked about thoughtfully, saw their waiting faces, and knew it was time to speak. He leaned forward and placed his two hands upon his kneecaps. He spoke now in their own tongue. "White River's heart is good toward the Absarokees. He counts many friends among their chiefs and warriors. He knows you to be strong in battle and has seen your braves drive back your enemies. If the Sioux have danced their sun dance and are sworn to war, putting things off won't help. Better to stand and fight, and fight here in a strong camp where the creek and the river can help hold them off. If you run now the Sioux will only follow you. If you split up into small parties they will track down as many as they can and butcher you. And if they don't fight you this summer, they will come with their war clubs raised in winter.

"White River says this is a strong camp. If the Absarokees make it stronger as he will help them to, the land of Absaroka will be as a robe painted with their enemies' blood. We have food, guns, ammunition, there is water in the creek and river, our hearts are good.

"The Sioux are many but this will make them careless. I say when they are fewer they will leave the Absarokees in peace. These are your hunting grounds, do not run from them as though they belong to others—for by the next sun they will."

White River sat back. In the silence that followed, White Tail looked at Amiel, who had been listening to White River's words and was somewhat taken aback by them. The thought of more fighting turned his stomach and dried his mouth. He knew he should say something, even if he had no counsel worth the hearing. It would have eased his mind somewhat had he known White Tail turned to him only out of courtesy. The Crows knew this one's nature was too soft for war.

He came forward very slowly, clearing his voice self-consciously, for he had never been asked to speak in such a council before, and he began in a voice that unlike White River's or Marcher's carried nothing of the steel ring of a warrior.

"I am not a man of war," he said a little hesitantly, realizing as soon as he said it that for the hard faces about him it was a poor beginning, "but the Absarokees have been good and generous friends and have shared their home with me. If there is trouble I will help if I can." He settled back again, aware that he had said nothing of interest or value to the council.

White Tail held the pipe before him thoughtfully, then spoke as though his mind were elsewhere. "It is good to know the hearts of our white brothers."

"Their words are good," said Spotted Horse, looking at White River. "Our brother, White River, has reminded us the swiftest warrior can not outrun the truth. These are our hunting grounds. If we run from our enemies now they will stay here and say this land is theirs. Let us fight while we are all together and strong. The Great Spirit will help us for we are fighting for the land he gave us."

Big Owl lifted his eyes from the fire. Few noticed he looked straight at Marcher. He began to suspect why that one wanted to leave. "I say we *must* stand and fight here! If we travel from this spot we cannot protect our weak ones as we move our village west. The Sioux will send their warriors on swift ponies, while we must stay with the old ones and our slow-moving travois. It would be as one riding a turtle going against one riding an eagle."

White Tail, looking at Big Owl and remembering Beaver Tail, said low in his throat, "Are our young men alone in the hills?"

Ironfoot, his mind turning to Snow Runner, looked at Big Owl whose eyes by now were down. "The young men must be brought in from the hunting—they must be called quickly to the village and warned of danger."

The others gave low grunts of agreement, but White Tail's eyes were lost in some inner scene burdening his heart. There were few who needed to know the cause of it; once again the thinning ranks of the Absarokees were having to bite back their fear and strive to match the strength of a stronger enemy.

• • •

Amiel knew when they left the council lodge any plans for leaving were forgotten. The Crow chiefs had committed their tribe's fate to White River's counsel. There was no way he could leave now. The thought of more shrieking violence and death appalled him. He wondered if his sanity would survive another lunatic scene of dismembered bodies. More and more Crow warriors were hurrying by, their faces painted black, the color of death, and everywhere medicine drums were pounding that incessant beat that began to feel like a felt hammer against his head.

"Don't think about it too much," muttered White River, eyeing him quietly. "Thinking about Indians just makes 'em seem bigger and meaner-lookin' all the time."

White River turned to view the pits being dug along the creek's edge. A barricade, built mostly of rocks from the creek bed, was quickly forming behind them. Neither spoke as they spotted Big Owl leaving the work and coming toward them, his eyes to the west.

"Maybe much trouble may come from where the sun sets," he said, his mouth tightening up in the way of a man becoming aware of a new and ugly reality. Amiel noticed Big Owl was wasting no time calling on medicine spirits or squatting in his lodge, painting his face.

"Best plan on it," said White River, turning and gazing with him. "Sioux are bound to try everythin' afore they quit."

"Your words are good. It will be as at the creek, pits like two diamond-backed snakes," said Big Owl, starting in that direction.

"Yep," said White River, "and bring 'em clear around to the river." After a moment he shouted to the retiring war chief, "Put your strong medicine boys in the front pits and the best shots you got behind 'em."

Big Owl looked back, smiling wryly but making no answering signs. Here was one Indian, thought White River, that would probably trade a wickiup full of medicine bundles for one wagon gun.

At the sign of a rider on the east slope the two started to their lodges. Tension was visibly mounting in the village. Scouts coming into camp were being watched more and more closely, for their faces more and more often carried messages as forceful and as frightening as their words.

48

The Sioux encampment stretched along the great curve of the stream almost as far as the eye could see, and beyond that the bright white tipis of the Cheyennes held the eye for a moment against the pull of the horizon. Across the stream, where the south slope of the hills rolled under a deep robe of grass, the Northern Arapahos were hurriedly pitching their tipis and sending runners to the Sioux council lodge to accept an invitation to feasting and dancing.

It was late afternoon and the air in the bottom was filled with a dark fleece of smoke that came against the nostrils, rich with the tang of burning meat. Some young boys, just freed from their herding duties, raced their ponies about the outskirts of the camp and shouted to each other in mock war.

The three tribes agreed to come together after each had finished its spring hunt and held its sun dance. And the fact that they were already in the country of the Crows left even the children in little doubt as to the words arising after the many smokes in the council lodge.

The Brules, Red Moon and Strikes-His-Enemy, were there, along with Gray Owl of the Oglalas, Stone Maker of the Minneconjous, Black Water of the Cheyennes, and many others. When the Northern Arapaho chiefs came to take their place in the circle, the course of things had already been set. The whereabouts of the Crows was well known and though their hunting camp to the west was larger than expected, it was still dwarfed by the great village now made up of the Sioux and their allies. Yet this bigness was a problem too, a problem that only rare leaders like Red Moon and Strikes-His-Enemy understood. Strength of numbers tended to make warriors reckless and careless of their chiefs' counsel. In spite of sightings of Crow scouts, small war parties would be forever slipping off, as they had all spring, looking for personal honors and revenge. Even the medicine of the brave Coyote-Singing, the son of Strikes-His-Enemy, had been bad, for he returned afoot without his favorite war-horse, fasted for five days, and spoke to no one of where he had been. A brave that had gone with his party had not returned, and Big Blood stayed moodily in his lodge with many thinking he had lost respect in the eyes of the Lakota.

Though only a few whites had been seen among the Crows, their hunting camp had remained where it was. The last scouts reported the hunting had stopped, yet there was still no sign of leaving—a thing to be wondered at, for it went against Indian reasoning. Red Moon frowned over it as did Strikes-His-Enemy, but they shared no words. Experienced fighting men do not need to remind each other there is a reason in war for everything.

The assembled chiefs now took turns at speaking, many making loud and bold claims of visions of victory, but this was only ancient custom and ceremony, for the plan of attack was already set by the Sioux and clear to all. One party would cross the Elk River and circle to the north, recrossing the river beyond the Crow camp and taking the enemy from the rear. This would also cut off their retreat. The remainder would attack across the narrower creek, although the scouts said it was still high, which made a few wonder at the wisdom of this thing. Yet there was little doubt of victory and much boastful talk of revenge. Only Strikes-His-Enemy, who spoke last, put a whisper of warning against this storm of loud talk.

"The Crows have taken the whites by the hand—already they have found that hand empty, but their wolves have seen our great village and they have not run away. Tell your warriors not to fight foolishly, thinking only of coups and honors. We have other enemies and every brave is needed."

Yellow Tongue, a chief of the Northern Arapahos, spoke up at these seemingly soft and almost squawlike words. "If the Crows wish to stand and die, that is well. Our braves carry arrows and tomahawks enough to kill them all."

Strikes-His-Enemy looked in curious surmise at the quick-talking Yellow Tongue, his one eye calmly fixing the other's two. At another time he would have dealt more cuttingly with these foolish words, but the council was over and he was already rising as he said, "Men who have decided to stand and die do not often die alone."

Marcher kicked the ground impatiently, angered at the silent forms of Amiel and White River standing relaxed, coolly watching him. White River was leaning forward with his hands on his hips, Amiel behind him with his hands folded, his face void of expression.

The three were well behind White Bead's new lodge, where they had met, Marcher having just returned from watering his already loaded packhorses at the creek.

"God damn those Sioux bastards," Marcher said as much to himself as to the others. "I wish to Christ they were all roasting in hell."

"Shootin' gets them there faster than talkin', for a fact." White River's tone implied he was waiting for an answer.

Marcher turned to tighten the pack slung across the horse. "Well, the hell with it—it's not my fight. I gave them a chance to get away and they didn't take it. Besides, I've got other business I've got to get on with."

An awkward silence hung between them for a few moments, telling them how far apart they were, how the days had hardened their feelings, how no threat, however big, could bring them together now.

Then Amiel said, "And what about White Bead?"

Marcher looked at him, a cold, challenging jest making his dark eyes seem darker. "What about her?"

"Can't be playin' nursemaid to her if the Sioux get down to serious business," answered White River.

Marcher turned back to working with his horse. "She'll be all right." He faced away from them as he spoke.

"You're bound to go, eh?" mused White River.

"Yep."

"Ain't many thinks a sight of a man who lights out leavin' a woman with this kind of trouble makin' up."

Marcher spun around and confronted them in sudden rage. "Jesus! All right then! I don't need you buggers to preach to me. I'll take her with me! Now go to blazes and get to hell out of here."

White River snorted in open derision. "You ride into Denver with a squaw and you won't hardly get a white man to jawin' with you let alone joinin' up. Denver's damnation on Injuns."

Marcher strode away, pulling the packhorse after him. His fury had him on the verge of a run. They watched him stake the horse to the right of the new lodge site, and even at this distance they could hear him swearing to himself as he kicked the ground again and disappeared behind the flap of his lodge.

"He'll stay," muttered Amiel, as though the thought did not particularly please him one way or the other.

The other nodded. "Reckon—but 'taint because we're askin'."

Amiel sighed, raising his hands to rub his temples. Around them the camp was noisy and roiling with activity. He took a half turn and studied the ground uncertainly, as though the sound and motion of so many disturbed him.

The Sioux chiefs sat their ponies on the rise east of the creek, where the Crow camp first came into view. The wind freshening from the west made the feathers of their headdresses and lance points flutter with a low, burring sound that could be heard against the enormous silence that in a moment came upon this mighty force.

The sun was now already a few hours in the sky and its strength was fast growing like fire spreading through dry pine. A cloud or two passed far to the north, but beyond that the sky was blue and deep as a gypsy's dream.

The chiefs with their white feathers sat mounted in an irregular line that became the crest of a sea of brown braves behind them. Red Moon and Strikes-His-Enemy sat near the middle, their gazes fixed on the flow of the creek and the long rows of pits that marked the bank beyond. Black Water and his Cheyennes, along with most of the Arapahos and a few Sioux, were to have crossed the river during the night to circle and attack the Crow camp from the rear. All knew their signal from the far rim of hills beyond the Crow camp should be coming soon. As they waited, several chiefs looked about them in silence. There was little that could be done for the moment and they were empty of words that had seemed to come so easily in council. Only Red Moon and Strikes-His-Enemy spoke and they only to each other.

Strikes-His-Enemy was murmuring like a man puzzling through a treacherous thought. "Does the angry wolf take the frightened porcupine in his mouth?" he said, his gaze on the fortified camp.

Red Moon, looking thoughtfully through the narrow slits of his eyes, was long in answering, but as all knew, that was his way. "We have painted our faces to teach the Crows a lesson—does my brother's great medicine tell him we have come to learn one?"

Strikes-His-Enemy gave a long, curious sigh, as though he had a vague pain in his chest. "When I was young," he said, raising his one eye to the bright sky, "the Lakota drove enemies from our lands as the grizzly scatters coyotes from the kill, then our wise ones taught us that in war surprise is a shield that makes a single warrior seem like ten. We are fighting these Crows as the stupid whites fight, bringing as much death upon ourselves as upon our enemies. It is not the Lakota way."

Red Moon weighed these words with his head up and turned at an angle, like a man hearing a faint but unfamiliar noise. But then a noise did intrude upon his thoughts. It was a deep murmur from those about him, and thus alerted, he looked ahead and saw a faint puff of smoke rising from the distant hills to the west. Black Water had succeeded in circling the Crows. The jaws of the trap were open. Now the stout heart of warriors must snap it shut.

"The long thoughts of council are over," he said in a hushed, throaty voice to Strikes-His-Enemy. "Let the Lakota and their brothers lift their war clubs as one."

Strikes-His-Enemy did not answer. Again he was looking at the sky, something tugging at his heart in the old way, the way Wakan Tonka had led the people when the wind was young and before the long shadow that was the hand of the whites had crossed the land. Behind him he heard a brave calling for courage from his companions. "It is a good day to die."

White River and Amiel followed Ironfoot's pointing to the light puff of smoke that hung like a tiny stain on the blue sky just to the west, the many Crow warriors about them murmuring to each other like men whose long uneasy suspicions had finally fallen together in fact.

"No more than we figured," said White River casually.

"How many do you think will come that way?" shouted Marcher, bringing his rifle up as though already there were lines of Sioux to be shot at instead of a simple wisp of smoke being steadily dispelled by the wind.

"Hard to say," said White River, looking back to the east. On the slope the bright colors of the immense war party looked for all the world like gay trimming on a great basket that a man could only feel was pretty and harmless. "That's likely to be the main shebang up yonder."

"God—but they seem endless." Amiel's eyes were following the ridge to the river as though he were watching a shooting star falling to the horizon.

"They're not," said White River matter-of-factly. "And we won't have to kill them all to discourage what's left."

Black Water, his buffalo headdress on and his face lined with white stripes, was experiencing that ancient blight of war, divided command. Though by virtue of his Cheyennes' numbers and his own high standing as a warrior he was the ranking war chief of the party sent to trap the Crows, Yellow Tongue of the Northern Arapahos was still stubbornly pointing to the south and demanding that they send part of their force in a sweep in that direction to cut the Crows off from their last corridor of escape along the west bank of the creek.

Black Water, seeing the other stop, dismounted and settled bitterly to the ground in a sudden council, his anger growing as the pipe was lighted and passed around. This was wasting time, time the Crows could put to good use, time that would cost Cheyenne lives. Yellow Tongue was a new chief, still heady with fresh power.

Black Water wondered at the wisdom of any words at all, but he said solemnly, "Yellow Tongue knows our Sioux brothers are waiting for us to strike the enemy. Yellow Tongue knows the sun moves even when our warriors do not."

"We will win a great victory with many coups and many scalps," said Yellow Tongue, "but only if these Crows do not escape."

Victory, victory, thought Black Water. How easily victory mounted in the minds of the young. Black Water bent forward, steeling himself against his own fury. "The Crows do not try to escape. They are waiting for us in their camp. Let us go and fight them before darkness throws its robe across the land."

Yellow Tongue had held on to the red pipe, a thing Black Water did not miss.

"We must put one of our strong arms to the south," insisted Yellow Tongue.

Black Water hit the ground impulsively with his rifle butt. "There are no Crows to the south," he snapped, finally losing patience.

Yellow Tongue rose to his feet, turning to speak to the warriors who had dismounted and were standing in a straggle of clusters watching this uneasy thing among their chiefs. He gave a long and loud talk that made Black Water seethe with rage, for in it lay what had driven this foolish man to upset their well-laid plan of attack. The Sioux, shouted Yellow Tongue, were great warriors and good friends, but they were not the only ones who understood war. Should the Sioux chiefs decide how to fight when others were sent to do the fighting? He, he told them, had had a dream in which his medicine had warned him that the Crows would escape by way of the creek. He and his Arapahos were riding to the south to keep this bad thing from happening. How many warriors here would join him?

The few Sioux that had come along began to move forward as he spoke. One, a giant of over six feet, stopped when he had made his way to the front of the group.

"Does the Arapaho think we will listen to his bad words about our chiefs?"

Black Water came to his feet. He glanced about him, seeing in the faces of the warriors what he most feared. "Let us not make foolish words like old squaws," he cried. "Here this day we must stand together like brothers and warriors."

The Sioux braves came closer and settled on the ground. "We will smoke with Black Water and hear his counsel," said the tall one.

A second, with a wide vermilion stripe down the center of his face, grunted in tightened anger. "We have heard the Arapaho speak of medicine dreams that would send his braves where there are no enemies. Now we will hear the words of our war chief."

Black Water knew that this thing must be handled with all the skill that a warrior leader could muster. The braves were beginning to think their party carried weak medicine. The seated Sioux and many of the standing Cheyennes were looking at Yellow Tongue in quiet contempt. Even some of the Arapahos gazed painfully at the silly and dangerous price being paid for this young chief's pride.

Primitive emotions were now astir. Black Water rose to his task, knowing it would take much talking to return this force to the weapon of war it was meant and had to be. He looked at the sky. The golden sheen of the afternoon sun was slanting westward in an endless canopy of blue. The day was waning. Could he mount once again that faith in victory that must throb like a drum in the words of a leader in war? He would try.

The great wall of Sioux began to move down the slope in full view of the Crow camp. Like the wing of a giant eagle it stretched forward, covering more and more of the land that rolled toward the river until the land itself seemed alive and moving too. The bright colors grew brighter as they drew nearer, feathers from headdresses, lances, and shields covered the slope like a battle flag unfurling in the wind.

They stopped just short of gunshot range, and now their chiefs seemed to be looking up at the sun and then over the Crow camp to the far west, telling the Absarokees that they were waiting for their other party to attack before forcing the creek. The young Crows began racing up and down the bank, making signs of defiance at the Sioux. The Sioux braves were soon answering back and a display of riding took place that made Amiel grunt in admiration in spite of the growing tension.

"Regular doin's with Injuns," said White River, looking on with him. "Mostly it's showin' off, but it gets their horses second wind too."

Marcher was on the opposite flank of the camp, surrounded by a group of braves who were watching him study the land to the west through his glasses. White River could tell by the way he swept slowly back and forth he had found nothing.

Beyond, the Sioux were beginning to dismount, their chiefs gathering together as though in council. A strange thing, thought White

River, for their plan of attack was clear now and there was little to hinder their getting on with it.

Ironfoot, coming up and taking a long gaze to the west, said simply, but in the knowing way of an aging Indian, "War ponies can bring enemy quick—no enemy—maybe bad medicine there."

Long before the first touch of evening the Sioux on the slope to the east broke into groups and built enormous fires.

"They figure to wait till dawn," said White River, as racks of meat were brought into the Sioux camp from the rear. After the meat, small groups of squaws began to arrive and some young boys appeared, racing about gathering up the ponies and leading them off to feed. Finally the old men came, leading mounts that were laden with robes and drums. It was clear the Sioux did not intend to spend the night in silence. It was almost dark, however, before the party to the west could be seen approaching the Crow camp. They came on slowly as though they knew they had missed their moment, stopping as did the others out of gunshot range and settling down to build fires and take food from their war packs.

"Heap Cheyennes," said Ironfoot, watching the large center of the party.

"More 'n Cheyennes, I'm thinkin'," said White River. But it was now too dark to make the others out.

The Crows, not to be outdone, lit their own fires and as evening turned into night the three camps filled the darkness with great pyres of light. A stranger coming upon the scene might have thought a colossal celebration among three friendly villages was going on, the kind of celebration people might give if they thought they were spending their last night on earth.

But the fires on the slope to the east were not built for light alone. In the great Sioux camp drums began to sound and they grew until there were over a hundred. Above them the many rattles sounded, some made of skulls and carried high above the shaker's head. The sudden screams of warriors working their way into the dance began to split the night, and finally the whole camp seemed to be writhing in a great, frenzied circle that for all its savagery tingled the skin of the watching whites with an edge of ecstasy.

It was the war dance of the great Teton Sioux, a tribe with a reputation for boldness and barbarity that had reached the cozy parlors of Boston and New York and to some lands beyond the sea. They were a people who had conquered and held territory greater than that of many nations of Europe.

But the Crows, boldly answering this menacing scene across the creek with shrieks and savage cries, started their own drums, and their warriors began to twist and turn, dancing, brandishing their weapons and whooping as though going into battle. In time they worked their way into a wide circle that ran around their three largest fires.

"God! What a frightening spectacle!" said Amiel, half shouting so that White River could hear him over the din.

White River looked knowingly at him. When he spoke, his voice seemed to carry better than Amiel's. "That's what they're tryin' to do sure enough. Frighten the lights out of each other." He looked for a moment over to the camp to the west where Ironfoot had seen Cheyennes. "Yonder is mighty quiet."

Amiel was too enthralled to pay much heed to White River's last words. He had seen Indians dance before, but this was more than dancing. These were men singing of their own savagery, Sioux and Crow alike—men ignorant of any saviors and unsuspecting of the world of saints, men being moved to a murderous pitch by fear of one another and delirious at the thought of delivering each other's death.

Beyond the nearest fire Marcher, stripped to the waist, could be seen making obscene gestures at the Sioux and filling his lungs to shout. His words were lost in the deafening roar, but his feet began to pound the earth as he moved about, his sweating and glistening body picking up the beat of the drums.

Some of the Sioux chiefs caught up in the hypnotic rhythm of the drums and rattles were up and dancing with the warriors. Others watched, dancing within and remembering other moments when the body shook and the chest throbbed and the secret heart was made strong for the perils of war.

The warriors danced up before the few seated chiefs, some boasting and making the many movements of war. "I will kill a Crow chief!" shouted Big Blood, driving his long feathered lance into the ground. "I will count coup on him!" roared Coyote-Singing, coming up from behind and leveling his own war club at a spot beside the lance. The two danced about the imaginary body of the slain chief, mutilating it, decapitating it, shouting out the many parts they were hacking off. Another brave joined them, stamping the ground with his feet to show nothing of the body remained. Then all three went forward together, giving the high, piercing Sioux war cries to show they were scattering what remained of their enemies.

Strikes-His-Enemy watched the dance from his seat behind Red Moon. He was thinking of his son, Coyote-Singing, and how something had changed in him since the last bad raid when Coyote-Singing had come home in disgrace without his horse. Ahh, such a foolish thing to do and against the words of the council. But the young would not listen to the old, a bad happening, making the secret spirits angry and then, perhaps, who could tell? Strikes-His-Enemy had hoped that one day the people would make Coyote-Singing a chief, but that seemed a distant and only wishful thing now.

There were other matters that held Strikes-His-Enemy's heart down. The attack had had to be delayed, never a good thing when done for reasons beyond a chief's knowing. He sensed more Lakotas should have gone with the other party. The Lakota were the main lodge pole of their allied camp. It was not well to put the way of war into the hands of others, even tested warriors like Black Water—and finally there was that nagging memory of the new and unseasoned Arapaho chief, the fast-talking Yellow Tongue, one whose skin was smooth with youth but who made words like the wind when scarred warriors were sitting in silence, waiting for their spirits to point to wisdom in war.

Red Moon, too, looked ahead in silence. Some noticed this, for it was his habit to stand and shuffle about, singing an old medicine song on such occasions, but now he only sat. It was not that his heart did not occasionally throb with the great pulse of drums and pounding feet that surrounded him. The dance was in fact his idea. The years had taught him it is wrong to keep young warriors idling too long before battle, and when he saw the attack would have to be delayed, he spoke with the other chiefs and it was decided the dance would be good to keep the braves worked up, proud, alert.

But a part of his mind was to the west where Black Water and his warriors were sitting quietly about their fires. This together with the Cheyennes' late coming made Red Moon uneasy and a little tight inside, like a lone buck catching some new sudden scent on an unexpected turn of wind.

The words would have had to come sooner or later, working up at last from his long, long thinking; and they were simple enough. "Our brothers, the Cheyennes, do not dance tonight," Red Moon said to Strikes-His-Enemy.

Strikes-His-Enemy raised his head slightly and gazed to the west. The Crow camp was alive with its wild dance of defiance and its many fires throwing back the night, but the camp beyond was silent with its fires already weakening and beginning to fall away.

Strikes-His-Enemy gazed for long moments before he said almost sadly, "Warriors seeing bad signs do not dance."

Red Moon grunted half to himself. "Can Strikes-His-Enemy tell his brother, Red Moon, how his heart can know that these words are true?"

Strikes-His-Enemy cast his one eye down to the ground. His words were the last between them until dawn. "Does my brother, Red Moon, dance?"

Amiel lay awake in the tense darkness of his lodge. From without one could still hear the muted screams of gyrating warriors finishing their dance or the throb of a lingering drum or the faint, gravelly voices of skulls still rattling somewhere in the night. All about him he could feel the clutching ooze of death curling forward, embracing the campsite and the flow of waters beyond. Impaled in his mind was the growing and unbearable knowledge that the first pink of dawn would bring the great wanton dying, the inchoate roar of human savagery, the blood of young men soaking into the coarse, unfeeling earth, the frenzied din of women and children foreseeing their own slaughter. Oh, in God's holy name! What was he, Ben Amiel, doing in this satanic setting? How had he stumbled upon this terrain ruled by some insane god?

Strangely enough, he had no sense of being a coward. The fear of death was of little consequence in his tormented mind. It was just the things he was willing to die for he could not die for here. This was blind, unrepentant savagery. Clearly he was expected to fight. The Crows would not forgive him if he did not bring out his repeating rifle to hammer back the Sioux as he had the first wave of Blackfeet. Their respect for these lethal weapons was beyond belief. Marcher and Big Owl, he knew, would take a deadly toll of the attackers. He was sure White River's plan depended upon it, but he winced as he realized White River would of necessity be depending on him too. The thought irritated and distressed him. That damn gun was forcing him into the caldron of senseless killing because it made him a more effective killer. White River had warned that only heavy early losses would discourage the Sioux. The fight must be too costly to sustain. This prospect soured in him, for his heart told him these Sioux were only primitive and superstitious men, like these Crows, savages perhaps but humans too and capable of friendship, valor, loyalty. They had wives like White Bead and Blue Lodge and doubtless were proud and caring of their children.

As he sat looking into the darkness, he began to think in some eerie way of the mighty struggle Christianity had for the mind of Man, a struggle his glimpse that evening of Marcher brandishing his hatchet over the fire said was far from over. Trying to resist the rise of a morbid mood he sensed another's presence in the lodge but realized at once it was simply his father's words echoing in his mind. His father, a poor, struggling, but passionate and pious man, must have known his own agony, his own doubts, but he faced death in that Negro uprising rather than kill another. "Subjugation of the flesh is His price for peace of soul." These words kept marching across his mind till he felt the morbid mood of the moment dissipating, and a strange feeling of somehow being free filled him.

He sat there for hours knowing a transformation was taking place in the depth of him. Finally, only dimly aware he was drenched in sweat and emotionally drained, he rose and left the lodge, the repeating rifle held away from his body as though the touch of it were strangely forbidden. He found White River standing sentinel near the western pits. Without a word he thrust the rifle at him and turned to go.

"Ben." White River was reaching for him, turning him, seeking his eyes in the darkness, but only the whispered words managed to penetrate the gloom. "Ben, come daylight every hand is gonna be needed."

"I'm through killing, friend."

"Sioux ain't."

"Doesn't matter."

White River stood silent for a moment weighing the finality in Ben's tone, weighing all that he had seen and understood these past months, weighing the way life forsakes a man whose only offerings are simple love and devotion, the only things little Lydia had to offer but maybe the only things that counted. Then he reached resignedly for his revolver, but, suddenly hesitating and seemingly thinking better of it, he turned and extended his old breechloader. "Best take this."

"Just told you. I'm through. . . ."

" 'Taint for you to use agin them, Ben."

"You mean . . ."

"I mean if our luck shouldn't hold—don't be round to see how it ends up."

49

Black Water knew that dawn was almost upon him. He looked about him in the darkness like one who needs no light to see what a strange heaviness in the heart says is there.

The long council of the day before with Yellow Tongue and the many warriors who felt that the bad talking between their chiefs was perhaps a spirit sign to be smoked over had drained him badly, and then it too, after all, had barely touched the threshold of success.

They had finally agreed to go on, sending a runner to circle to the south, telling the other party that they would attack at dawn. But the braves were overly silent as they slipped up on their ponies and Yellow Tongue still hung back as one in whose breast still licks a small flame of anger.

As they made camp to the west of the Crow village, many watched the loud excitement of the warriors beyond, friend and foe alike, some munching a little dried meat or resting by the fires. But no drums sounded among them to draw the thoughtful braves to the dance. Black Water watched quietly, hearing them singing low to themselves or making the private medicine signs, or whispering the sacred words that would give them protection in the fight ahead. But as the evening wore on most sat sucking pensively on their pipes, watching the fires beyond, their eyes weighing matters well beyond words.

Who could say how an invisible blade of doubt works its way through the shield of a warrior's spirit? But Black Water knew and felt the signs. Somehow he sensed as can those who live close to their inner selves, accepting the heart's mystifying power to weigh the way of events, that his long, painful hoping was over, that the weight of things would be swept forever from his aging body, that he was about to stand and breathe in the air of his last dawning. He was not fallen in spirit. Rather he felt a sense of clear and almost sensuous relief. There was truly no end to war, no victory that could bring peace, no treaty that could bind the hearts of their endless enemies—particularly the whites. He saw his Cheyennes ready in the dark, ready to hear his commands to attack the Crow camp, ready to add to the legendary bravery of their people, ready to die.

The silence and solitude at the south end of their camp said that Yellow Tongue and many of his Arapahos were gone. Ah, it did not matter. Yellow Tongue had had his dream, he was young, knowing the days when dreaming still drew back to a man's heart the hope that kept drifting from it, when spirit medicines still seemed stronger than what every chief's eyes and the death of a people said was so.

There would be a day when Yellow Tongue's dreaming would run out, a day when his medicine would have to match the metal bullets that each year grew larger in the hands of the whites.

Black Water drew himself up and raised his painted arm toward the east. By now a chill wind was sweeping along the river murmuring a low, faint song older than Man and even the mountains he looked in awe upon. It was the last thing many heard that morning before the Cheyennes rent the air with their war cries and threw themselves against the rifle pits of the Crows.

Beyond on the great slope, the hanging gray darkness making their numbers difficult to discern, the Sioux sat mounted in endless rows, the new breeze coming off the river making a rustling among the many feathers that decorated the things of war. But it was the only sound that arose from that great multitude. The white face paint of a brave here and there betrayed his looking off into the sudden raw wind, but not a word was said. All knew that they were almost out of the womb of night, that daylight meant that they must ford the creek and sweep these strangely defiant Crows from the earth.

Red Moon and Strikes-His-Enemy sat forward with the chiefs. They were as silent as their braves, knowing too well that now there was little worth in words and less in any sign that might betray concern. Some of them sensed that events had claimed them, that the plans which seemed so malleable days before in council were now beyond the power of any one of them to change. In truth there were curious omens which troubled the hearts of many, but here again there was no value in voicing them. The arrow of decision had already left the bow and could not be retrieved. It remained only to see if its arc would vindicate their aim.

Red Moon looked behind him to the east. A faint tinge of higher gray was etching the far horizon. He looked back again to the west.

"We must be ready now, my brother," was his whisper to Strikes-His-Enemy.

Strikes-His-Enemy rubbed the stock of his rifle thoughtfully and then brought that strange and sagacious face slowly forward on his mount. "We are all ready, old friend. We have sung our death songs and we have reached the years when there is only yearning and a wisdom that knows no trail of hope."

• • •

The Cheyennes made the rifle pits on their first charge. The dark western sky behind them kept the nervous Crow fire ineffectual and the Cheyennes kept coming with their characteristic courage. But the wisdom of the second pits became apparent at once. Cheyennes raising their war clubs and pointing rifles over the first pits were caught in a withering fire from the supporting pits but a few feet beyond. Within less than a minute it was clear they could not hold. The shrieking Crows, feeling the Cheyennes give way, began shouts of victory and, in spite of White River's and Big Owl's frantic warnings, some hungry for coups left their pits only to be caught in their own fire.

Black Water had been wounded twice and his buffalo headpiece had been struck again, but he brought his determined braves back, knowing full well that bravery could only bring death beside that maze of pits. It was lighter now, and the chance to break into the Crow camp was swiftly passing. Besides, he could hear the melee along the invisible creek to the east and he knew the Sioux were coming against the other side of the camp.

The Cheyennes were huddled in a long, sweeping depression that ran in an arc till it disappeared in a common vamp with the river. Some of the braves, like Black Water, were wounded. Others were hurriedly loading guns or struggling to repair weapons. Still others looked starkly toward the pits, thinking of companions whose bodies could not be retrieved, which the Crows would mutilate and despoil.

Black Water decided they would try the river end of the Crow defense. They would have to concentrate on one place and get behind those pits or the Cheyennes would suffer a shameful defeat. There was no time for council. They must move at once. "Follow me," he said, his voice loud but low in his throat, and he began to make his way along the depression to the river. The braves followed him without question. Those too wounded to walk pulled themselves up to the edge of the depression and began firing toward the rifle pits in the experienced way of warriors who sense the need for distracting fire. As the depression rounded to the river, Black Water saw the rifle pits again, this time more clearly in the growing light. Blood was running down one arm and from the calf of his leg. There was nothing to be gained from hesitating. He looked back and saw the faces of his braves watching him intently. Among them he noted the big Sioux with the red band running down half his face. Once again he said, "Follow me." A Cheyenne brave standing directly behind him muttered, "It is a good day to die, Black Water."

Then they ran forward. Their first steps they took in silence, but as the Crows spotted them darting forward and screamed in alarm the Cheyennes broke into their war cries and bore down on the rifle pits at the river end of the line. Bullets chopped at them and arrows came whirling through the air, some ending their flight with the quick ringless thud of punctured flesh.

The Cheyennes began to fall, some already with their death wounds, others stunned and spiraling to the ground like winged birds that flop forward again. Still they came on. The big Sioux had overtaken Black Water as he reached the first rifle pit. Black Water fell in upon the single Crow within, knife in hand. The Sioux dived over him to the second. Fire from further down the line began to hail in upon them, but Black Water had killed the man in the pit, and when he rose he saw the Sioux bringing his war club down on a figure in the second one. Black Water was about to rush forward again, taking the rising Sioux with him, but at that instant a bullet struck the tall Lakota, making a smashing sound, opening white bone where the red streak had crossed his forehead, and that strange warrior's life was over before his great body could reach the ground.

Black Water drove ahead and was calling for his Cheyennes to follow him. If they could get among the lodges, the Crows would have to leave the pits to fight them or see their families annihilated. He could hear a few feet running behind him, but they did not seem many and now something seared across his ribs like a claw of fire and he knew he had been hit again. Yet he kept going. The lodges were before him now. He could hear the screaming of the squaws as they scattered. But then suddenly a figure was running beside him and he knew it was not a Cheyenne. The figure was clearly trying to hit him with something. Black Water went down on one knee as the Crow gun barrel passed over his head, the power put behind the blow spinning the warrior to the ground. Black Water was on him with his knife, plunging it in again and again between his ribs. Figures were converging on him from all sides now. Some must surely be his Cheyennes. He screamed at them to get in between the lodges and to make the Crows come to them, but no Cheyenne war cries rose to confirm his calling. Instead he heard what he knew was a white shouting to the Crows not to shoot in the direction of the lodges and with that he turned to find himself surrounded by almost a dozen Crows and at once he knew his death was upon him. His long hatred for the whites helped him decide his final moments for among the Crows closing in on him was a tall, heavily bearded white. Black Water went toward him, his knife in one hand, his war club in the other. He had almost reached him when the white's hand came up, the dark barrel of a revolver in it. The barrel spouted a long, ugly serpent of flame. Black Water felt the shaft of pain through his chest and his legs gave way for a moment. But then they steadied and he went forward again. Again the ugly orange tongue licked toward him and again his body seemed a thing apart, and he could not command it to go further. He tried to raise his war club to throw it, but the effort was beyond him and incredibly it fell from his hand. He thought the ugly flame was reaching for him again, but he was not really sure, he did not know. Suddenly he knew only that he was going down, down, down, softly as though he were watching himself fall from a far distance. And somehow he knew down there where he was falling, he would find a land beyond the whites, perhaps even find again the long-sleeping youth, White Fringe.

Where the great slopes swept up to the creek, the Sioux were urging their ponies into the water and their silence had given way to a frenzy of shouting that drowned out even the gunshots that sprang from the waiting Crows. "*Hoka-Hey,* charge!" The creek proved deeper and a little swifter than the first warriors liked, but they drove their ponies across it and were soon mounting the opposite bank. Here the Crows swept them with a torrent of lead and arrows that did not kill many braves but worked like a scythe among ponies struggling out of the water. Everywhere the Sioux were afoot and trying to crawl against the rifle pits. Behind them came more Sioux. While those afoot could not immediately reach the first rifle pits because of withering fire from the second, they kept the Crows down so that more ponies began to climb the bank. From the height of their mounts the Sioux began now to fire into the first pits, and the second pits had to open on them. More ponies went down, some of them kicking and lunging disastrously backward, throwing their riders against those behind. The smoke and confusion on the west bank of the creek was like a chaotic caldron aboil with jerking forms giving hideous cries of battle, many cut short by the sing of a slug or the feathery flash of an arrow.

But the Sioux, rallied forward by Stone Maker, came on, and soon the first rifle pit fell. Marcher and Ironfoot, posted behind the barricade, concentrated their fire on this weakened point and the breach grew no larger. But now that pitiless and macabre plague of attacking armies, their own dead, particularly the many ponies, was making the west bank harder and harder to climb. Where there were openings, the concentrated fire of the Crows was immediately drawn, and soon the gap was clogged and others had to be found.

Red Moon and Gray Owl, watching from the east bank, knew they would soon have to reinforce those fighting across the creek or pull them back. They glanced at each other in a dark knowing that everything seemed to be going against them. The warriors on the east bank could not shoot for fear of hitting those on the west. The warriors in midstream held their fire for the same reason as they tried to pick their way up the bank. But they could not come across fast enough, and the wounded now trying to make their way back put an increasing burden on the attackers. Badly wounded braves trying desperately to recross the creek began to slip beneath the surface of the water, and they could be seen turning helplessly with the current and moving toward the river.

Then it happened. Stone Maker took his mount up and tried to jump across a pit in the second row, his rifle ready to fire down into it as he did, but his mount shied at the last second and the pony sprawled backward, wildly rolling the chief off and into one of the adjoining pits. The Crows were on him in an instant and moments later were holding his head aloft, impaled on his own rifle.

It was enough to fracture the faith of the attackers, enough to make the Crows master of the moment.

The Sioux on the west bank broke and the bloody retreat across the stream began. The Crows, raising screams of victory, turned the creek into a bed of swirling carnage that only the Sioux on the east bank, when their field of fire cleared, were able to stop. Out in the stream, where streaks of blood looked like vermilion snakes that widened out and joined each other in pink clouds, the bodies of the dead and badly wounded were moving in a ghastly procession down into the river. The Sioux on the east bank watched this in anger and anguish, but every brave attempt to reach them only added to the grim flotsam.

The Sioux had lost over forty braves and many wounded were being helped beyond the eastern ridge. But they were still a mighty army, and most of the warriors had done no fighting at all.

The chiefs came together in council. The young sun was up now, though clouds were forming over it and a salmon-pink rash flushed the eastern dome of the sky. The only plan of attack possible was clear to all those who had witnessed the devastation of the first assault. The braves on the east bank had to cover the Crows with fire while others crossed the creek on foot and crawled upon the rifle pits. Horses were a menace, as they could not move quickly enough through the water and up the bank; they kept a brave high enough to become an easy target while at the same time blocking his supporting fire. It was decided to attack at once.

Gray Owl lined his Oglalas along the creek bank and Red Moon was to send his Brules and some Minneconjous across the stream and take the first pits by stealth and the second by storm.

The ponies were hurriedly taken back and the many braves were rushed into position. Strikes-His-Enemy saw Coyote-Singing taking his position at the head of one of the many parties, readying himself to cross the creek. Big Blood was moving to lead another, Hawkfoot a third. This would surely be a day for the Brules to remember. He glanced at the rifle pits across the stream and the barricade behind them. This was not the Absarokee way. He shook his head in a new foreboding. No, this was the work of the whites. Ah, the whites, the whites. Was there no other way but theirs?

Red Moon brought his spear down in the signal to advance, and the braves began slipping into the stream. Immediately the Crows opened fire, but the Oglalas kept them low in their rifle pits and the braves in the creek began to cross midstream. The Crows, sensing this new mounting danger, screamed to their second pits to pin down the Oglalas, but they were no match for the fusillade bearing down upon them, and the Sioux now began to mount the west bank. Now the Oglalas had to raise their fire and again the Crows rose against the warriors crawling toward them. And here and now the most savage part of the fighting began, with the Sioux coming to the lip of the pits, their tomahawks striking down on the Crows within or the Crows thrusting the muzzles of their muskets in the faces of the attackers, often leaving them headless. But slowly the pits began to fail and the second line was beginning to be breached. It was only because of the barricade that the Sioux did not open a broad swath between the crucial center pits. Here the desperate fire kept up by Marcher, White Tail, Ironfoot, and a few Crows became the frightening margin of survival for the camp. Yet it was not enough. Led by Coyote-Singing, Big Blood, and Hawkfoot, the Lakota came on with a cold fury that told White Tail and Ironfoot at least that their enemy was now confident of victory and the annihilation of their village was at hand. Some Crows were singing their death songs and throwing themselves upon the attackers, but it made little difference. The wedge of Sioux grew greater and greater. In a moment they would be rushing the barricade and then the great dying must begin.

Marcher's barrel was so hot a shell jammed it and it would not fire.

He swore at it and, casting it aside, drew his pistol and continued to shoot. Big Owl, coming up and firing more slowly, kept his rifle going, but he could see the menace growing and he shouted to Ironfoot as he looked around for White River, saying finally to no one but himself, for no one could hear him in that melee, "Great Spirit, save us—save our weak ones!"

Ironfoot needed no warning. He was singing as he threw aside his muzzle-loader and reached for his bow. Beside him was his stone tomahawk—he had found his place to die.

Then suddenly, just as the Sioux rose up and raced toward the barricade, White River and over twenty Crows, having thrown back the Cheyennes attacking from the west, came running through the lodges and hurled themselves behind the barricade wall. The Sioux could not have seen them, for they continued to move forward boldly as though they faced but few.

Hawkfoot, leading the way, paid for this ignorance with his life. White River's bullet hit him in the mouth and he spun like a man in a weird dance before his arms went limp and he went down. Then a volley from the barricade jolted and cut down the front runners and drove those behind them to the ground. And now the balance had shifted again. The Sioux were caught with both flanks and the front exposed. Immediately brave after brave, seeing their peril, leapt up in an attempt to race to the barricade or fling himself into the pits that remained on their flanks. But they died in their helpless frenzy and the slaughter went on. Big Blood shouted to his braves, "Come! Let us kill these Crows who fight like squaws. They are not warriors!" And with that he started for the barricade with "*Hoppo!* Let's go!" Every frenzied Lakota who could stand and run followed him. The snap of rifles and the whirl of arrows began to whittle at their flanks, but still they came on. Big Blood, running in front with his lance held high, took two slugs but still came on. The Crows and whites behind the barricade fired as fast as human hands could work, but still they came on.

White River knew they were going to breach the barricade and shouted for everyone to fall back, but the din of gunfire and shouting Sioux drowned his words and only a few went with him as he turned to retreat to a new line.

Men who have forsaken life are hard to fight. Big Blood, leading them, an arrow pinioned in his thigh, was first over. Others followed. A Crow trying to use his rifle as a club died under a Sioux stone tomahawk. Another was disemboweled by Big Blood's lance. Marcher dropped two with his revolver and wrestled another to the ground and killed him with his hatchet. Then, recalling the effect Stone Maker's death had had upon the Sioux and seeing Big Blood leading the attack, he tried to get a bead on him, but the fury of the fight made it impossible. He tried to work his way toward him, suddenly alive to the need to kill. He must kill that leading brave or they were done.

Suddenly, in the inscrutable way of battle, a new figure was molded into the scene. It was Amiel. In horror he had been listening to the rising and now almost unbearable clamor approaching his lodge. He knew—for his senses were screaming it—the Sioux were winning, the camp was falling. The great slaughter was about to begin. His eyes fell on the breechloader. He should never have taken it. Dying by one's own hand was as great a sin as killing another. If the camp and all in it were going to die, he would die with them. He would not be taken by the Sioux nor would he leave this gun for them to kill others. Somewhere in the camp the Crows would be defending their women and children to the end. He would give it to them.

He stepped from the lodge, shocked by the frantic closeness of the fighting. He must hurry. But where? The scenes about him were like tableaux from hell. The camp was in its last extremity, squaws rushing toward the fighting, skinning knives in hand, hysterical children screaming at the top of their lungs. He saw a large Sioux with an arrow in his thigh stabbing wildly with his war lance and struggling toward him. He was in the very vortex of battle. Something struck him in the shoulder and stunned him so he had to steady his body and change his grasp on the old rifle, catching his fingers in the trigger guard. He was only dimly aware now that an arrow was protruding from his upper arm, and his eyes, focusing again, were becoming fixed on the bloody lance which the great warrior before him was raising to impale him. With a choking sound breaking in his throat he instinctively thrust the gun barrel forward to avert the blow, but at that moment the old rifle, with his fingers trapped in the trigger guard, went off, and a heavy slug was driven into the throat of the striking Sioux. Big Blood staggered backward, as though drunk, but then caught himself as his face stiffened in death behind its hideous paint. In the last effort of his life he swung the lance around and thrust it at Amiel, his great falling body driving it into Ben's chest.

White River, pouring his fire into the braves still scaling the barricade, saw this out of the corner of his eye and knew Ben Amiel had taken his death blow. Big Owl and Ironfoot, finally seeing White River's new position, pulled the braves with them to the left flank to catch the Sioux in a cross fire. Ironfoot, though wounded himself, dragged old White Tail's now dead body with him, but he stopped to grab a loaded musket from a dead Crow and shoot a Lakota who had come up to strike again at White Tail's body. The attacking Sioux fell as though struck with an ax, but the action pulled Marcher's eyes forward to the sight of Ben Amiel's body on the ground with that curious arch of the neck which means coming death. For a moment he could do nothing. The scene had to fight its way into his mind. And then something exploded in his brain and he crossed a threshold he would never recross again. He grabbed his war hatchet and went running toward the Sioux. "Murdering bastards!" he shouted, facing a Sioux who rushed against him. With a swift drive of his foot, he knocked the man off balance and smashed his skull with a single blow. Two more Sioux appeared before him and he lunged for one, but he would have forfeited his life had not Ironfoot, taking another wound in the action, come up and engaged the other. White River, finding more braves coming up from the other side of the camp got them into line, and once again the bloody tide began to turn. The cross fire was beginning to shatter the reckless onslaught of the Sioux. Coyote-Singing, seeing that they were wavering, tried to drive them forward with a war cry, but it was useless. The will of warriors, once allowed to slip in battle, is not easily reset.

And now Marcher was pressing forward with a growing frenzy, for he had seen something. He saw a warrior with a snakeskin about his chest trying to rally the enemy and he knew this was the one who had smashed his mirror, deprived him of his treasure, made all his work and suffering meaningless. That Sioux was going to die and Marcher was going to kill him.

He still had his pistol in one hand and his war hatchet in the other, and he was shouting insanely to the Crows about him to help him fight his way through to this Sioux brave who was wildly attempting to make a stand. Ironfoot tried to follow him but was suddenly on his knees. But then Coyote-Singing began making the odd, disjointed movements of a man taking hits and he too was falling back in a half daze into the stream. Marcher pursued him like a man possessed of a demon. Into the stream he followed him, swinging at the retreating Sioux about him with his war hatchet. Bent on retreat, few of them struck back, and now Marcher began to close on the wounded Coyote-Singing.

On the east bank Strikes-His-Enemy watched his wounded son trying to recross the stream, but he saw also the maniacal surging of a white struggling to overtake him. Within moments he was in the water pressing through the retreating braves to reach Coyote-Singing. All three came together in midstream, where Marcher swung at Coyote-Singing with his war hatchet. The current was coursing against him and the blow missed, but it caused Coyote-Singing to turn and face his assailant. At that moment two fateful things happened. Marcher fired his pistol at Coyote-Singing's head and Strikes-His-Enemy put his arms around his son. Marcher was still off balance and the shot only grazed Coyote-Singing's scalp, but the powder flash blinded him. Weakened by loss of blood and the shock of the blast, his mind slipped away, and only the will to survive remained. His hand went for the knife at his belt and, feeling arms about him he grasped back at the other's body and began plunging the knife into it. Strikes-His-Enemy screamed, "Son! Son!" as he tried to hold the other's flashing blade. But it was too late. Coyote-Singing had brought his father what a thousand enemies could not, his death. Only dimly did he know he was clinging to him as his own loss of blood sapped his consciousness. But they held on together as their bodies began to swing with the current, and, still embracing, they slipped slowly into the river and quietly disappeared, seeming to those watching aghast from the shore to find peace beneath its rolling surface in a tragedy without name.

Marcher had recovered his balance and dispatched another wounded Sioux, but now suddenly he found himself alone. He called for the Crows to come on, but the Crows had had enough. There were many dead, including old White Tail, and wounded enough to make the squaws hurry forward in half screams as they came to their men. Children were sent scurrying for herbs or medicine men of which there would never be enough to go around. White River and Big Owl, knowing in the way of born warriors that the fighting was over, were carrying Amiel into a tipi, both knowing that death was closing in on their burden.

Beyond, the Sioux had had enough too. They had lost Stone Maker, Strikes-His-Enemy, many lesser war leaders such as Coyote-Singing, Big Blood, and Hawkfoot, and in every heart it was known that the full count of warriors lost was still the secret of the stream.

Red Moon and Gray Owl signaled the entire encampment to move to the east. Bad weather was making up and the wounded had to be gotten under cover. Later they would learn, as some already suspected, that they had also lost on this black day their firm ally the courageous Cheyenne Black Water and many of his irreplaceable braves.

• • •

They carried Amiel into the tipi and settled him on a robe, the wound in his chest pumping slowly against the bloody roll of cloth White River held. Many stood or knelt about him, White River trying to bring him to consciousness with soft words that did not seem to belong to a big man.

"Ben, Ben," he muttered softly.

Ben's eyes finally opened, but he did not speak. For a while he stared above him, his eyes opaque slits, as though fixed on something deep inside him. A squaw laid a wet rag over his forehead, but his eyes showed no sign he knew it was there. Marcher hurried in but was immediately silenced and in a moment was bending down on one knee, looking intently at Ben. After a long moment he said, "Looks awake—must be thinking something."

White River glanced at Marcher but said nothing.

Ben Amiel was thinking of something.

He was thinking of things which transcended this wild, unanointed life which was all that those gathered about him would ever really know of him. Somehow he had meant to but he was not thinking of God. Instead, he was vaguely musing, almost without concern, on how much of a man's life on earth is really painful. How most lives—when the truth is thrust up naked to be known—were really trivial, like his, and therefore tragic. How most virtue is born of man's fear of perdition. How his father's and Melody's love for him and his for them had been drained of comfort by time. How most people die lonely and alone, yet know it doesn't matter. Had he ever really lived his life or had it merely happened to him? Did he really care now about death? The years stretched out before him, lonely and lacking promise. Did he want this vagrant heathen life, without compassion, without beauty, without grace? He decided he did not. He was thinking that when he died.

Goes-Walking could not bring Ironfoot to his lodge. Some braves stopped to help her, their faces down and held tight against the sight of his many wounds.

They gently propped him against some skins in his lodge and sent for a nearby medicine man. But Ironfoot knew he was dying. He opened his eyes and looked long at Goes-Walking. "It has been good between us, woman," he said, his voice barely audible.

She was bent over him, trying to stem the bleeding from his side.

He put his hand on her. "Where is our son, Snow Runner? I would see him," he whispered. She looked at the deep wound intently and then turned away, avoiding his gaze.

Outside she called to some young boys rushing about with water and herbs. "Find Snow Runner and bring him to his father's lodge," she pleaded dismally.

Snow Runner, though an excellent shot, was one who had asked to be put in the forward pits and near the center where true warriors belonged. They found his body under two dead Sioux, a Lakota tomahawk in one hand, his own battle knife in the other.

With effort they freed his body and carried it to Ironfoot's lodge. Some people saw this thing and followed them in. The medicine man who was chanting above him was weakly motioned away by Ironfoot as they entered, and when Ironfoot saw how it was he slowly beckoned the dead body of his son to him.

In silence he held Snow Runner to him, and then tears rose in his eyes and a low moaning began as he started to cry. The others backed away. Even the medicine man knew what must be, and retreated through the lodge flap as Goes-Walking picked up her knife and went to the rear of the lodge. When one who is dying cries at another's death the gods alone should listen, for they alone understand.

PART NINE

MARCHER

50

A high wind heralding fall caused White River to narrow his eyes as he turned to gaze at the Crow encampment stolidly readying itself for winter in a small valley cut abruptly into the first rampart of a steeply rising mountain.

Most of that summer he had been churning over in his mind how the deaths of individuals could bring almost unendurable physical suffering, choking and hysterical sobbing, wrenched by an indescribable and unbearable sense of loss, while the death of multitudes brought only shock and disbelief, the mind refusing to register such a grotesque reality. The Crow nation had withdrawn from the battleground like a gladiator stumbling back from a near-fatal blow. Their losses by Indian standards were appalling, yet there was no consolation or even compassion. The need was too great for any human heart.

The trip back, not a few dying along the way, took many long weeks that were soon to be missed. For beneath the morbid countenances all thoughts were on the winter ahead, on the many widows and orphans that must be fed, on the dread knowledge that cartridges and even powder were low, very low. And there were other frightening signs. Near the mountains the birds were already wheeling silently like transparent fans, preparing to leave early, and above them a few geese could be heard honking, their swift wedges moving to the south. At night wolves and coyotes howled incessantly and the heads of stallions rose in the horse herd to hold rigid, listening for long moments. It was to be a winter when the ice would be reaching for the heart.

Marcher had told a grateful Big Owl he would fetch powder and shells from Denver, but there were those who knew he had other reasons for going. White River, heading out to hunt while the weather held, hesitated at the camp's edge to watch in curious surmise as Marcher left. In spite of his new quietude since Ben's death and his help in defending the Crow camp while it moved, something told White River there was still trouble and tragedy afoot in that man. He shook his head at the way of things. Could be he should be moving along himself. He had secretly hoped this would be the year he would start his search for Lydia. After much pondering in the keening-filled nights he had found himself tempted to leave more than once, but Blue Lodge's pathetic drawn face, and the quietly pleading eyes of the Crows, who saw in the guns of these whites their only chance of salvation, left him sighing and turning once more to organize a hunt. In reality, nothing disturbed him so much as the sight of pretty White Bead, whose lissome body had rounded somewhat in the past year, but who still moved with that strange grace that reminded him of Lydia. Lydia would be approaching womanhood by now, her body filling out. Were men somewhere watching her figure flow beneath her clothes and wondering what magic lay in the sylphlike form? Sometimes he felt the girl in his memory and the girl in his fantasy were no longer the same. Time had separated them, made them strangers. Then he would pause at some high mountain pass and gaze at the azure canopy of the world, knowing she was out there somewhere, waiting.

For all White River's forebodings about him, Marcher looked lean and hard riding out in his well-worn buckskins, the war hatchet still by his side, even some strange medicine symbols gotten from somewhere by White Bead stitched across his bags. Sun and wind had long since made Marcher's skin brown and leathery, and he had learned to put grease on it to keep it from cracking. His hair was still tied behind him Indian style. Like most men too long in the wilderness he had forgotten how much it and its ways had changed him. As he left he was leading a pack pony loaded with skins, his gaze fixed before him like a man who sees a point in time many long days ahead.

White Bead's trim figure stood motionless before her lodge as she watched him go, her eyes narrowing in her soft olive face till his figure disappeared among the first brush of rolling hills. It was only when she turned resignedly to enter her lodge that White River glanced across the camp circle, noticing a young brave, partially concealed by drying skins, whose quick downward motion betrayed he too had been watching the soft and now lonely figure of White Bead.

It was not easy country to travel through, but Marcher was secretly proud of the way he had made his way to Denver. He went south along the Wind River range, across the Sweetwater and then southeast until he crossed the North Platte. He watched the great Medicine Bow range rising on his right as he moved southward till he crossed the South Platte and there he picked up the Denver road.

He was proud of his feel for the country and lived off it with ease. He saw no signs of Indians or even whites until he was but a day's ride out. Then he passed a few parties that he hailed, and while all hailed back, the few he stopped to swap words with regarded him apprehensively, the women and children disappearing in the wagons and the men quietly sizing up his hatchet and repeating rifle. Some even ran their fingers over the beadwork on his pack bags as though they were mildly puzzled. White Bead had sent many fine skins, some decorated, for him to trade for rifle shells and some bright cloth and trinkets for her. Many of her friends had added to the load and his pack horse was growing thin under its burden. But Marcher pushed on from these edgy meetings, occasionally looking back to see the men still watching him riding off, a few with their heads cocked, their arms akimbo, their minds clearly wondering.

As he drew near Denver he began to see Indians, but these were surely a poor lot, mostly beggars, the riffraff and shuckings of a number of tribes, Utes, Omahas, Arapahos, even some Southern Cheyennes. The men, those who were not lying in the sun drunk, made pitiful signs to him to give them tobacco or money or whiskey or anything. They ran a few steps beside his horse, pulling at his leggings, their hands extended. The women, even young girls hardly approaching puberty, offered themselves openly. Disgusted but beginning to know his Indians, he watched to see if there were any Sioux among them. He found none.

In time he discovered he was passing through a long line of adobe shacks, where Spanish laborers and herders watched him in silence from beneath their immense and shabby sombreros. It was clear they regarded him with suspicion. Only one stout, overdressed man, sitting on a bench before a long, rambling house and twirling an unlit cigar, deigned to even smile at him. "*Buenos dias, amigo*. You have come veree far, no?"

"Plenty. How much further is it?"

"It is but a leetle ways. But I think that you must rest here."

"Why?"

The figure gestured knowingly to the house. "Ah, *amigo,* we have here tequila, *señoritas* . . . everything to make the eye bright again and the heart happee."

"Well, for Christ sakes!" Marcher half laughed, looking at the house. "Got no time."

"You be much sorry."

"Why?"

The man got up and came over. Marcher could see his face was like a prune that had been dried out and then soaked again, the light traces of wrinkles remaining.

The round, swarthy countenance contracted and smiled in a snickering way, then the stubby hand pointed with its cigar to the road ahead. "You will find many things different over there, *amigo*."

Marcher looked at him demandingly. "Just what the hell are you talking about?"

The man spread his hands in mock courtesy. "*Perdoneme*. Miguel wish only to help."

Marcher pushed on until he came to the main street of the town and found almost immediately a trading store. He hitched up in front of it and, ducking under the hitch rail, walked into a large, barnlike room that was rank with the smell of hides and oil lanterns.

Two men standing in the rear looked at him curiously. One wearing a dark vest over his white shirt took a step forward. "Something you wanted?"

"Yes, yes," said Marcher hurriedly. "I've got some skins I'd like to sell or trade for. You interested?"

The two men looked at each other, obviously more shocked at his accent and diction than what he said.

"Well, sure," said the one in the vest. "Bring 'em in."

Marcher labored back and forth getting the enormous pile of skins and robes in while the two men handled them and whispered together.

"Come down from Injun country, I reckon," said the one with the vest, who Marcher could now see at close quarters was sickly pale, partly bald, and had hanging lips that failed to conceal his three gold front teeth.

"What's your offer?" queried Marcher, ignoring the other's implied question.

The two muttered a few times to each other as though they were dubious of the furs and doubtful of the deal. Marcher watched them with a growing contempt. Civilization hadn't changed much, had it?

"Ain't much of a market these days as you likely know—best we can do for the lot is a hundred and fifty dollars."

Marcher knew nothing of the fur market, but his instincts compelled him to put his arms around the top furs. "Any other traders in town?" he said caustically.

"None you can trust."

"Figure I'll still be better off with them."

"Now hold on a minute," said the bald man, pressing the skins down and leaning on them. "We aim to deal fair. What did you have in mind?"

Marcher tried to judge the range of their connivance. Finally he said, "Three hundred dollars, plus some rolls of bright cloth, plus some trinkets, plus two hundred rounds of cartridges, powder, and oil for my gun."

The pale man weighed his words for a moment, then said in slight discomfort, "Be pleased if you'd give me and muh partner a minute to sort of discuss things and . . . er . . . chat."

Marcher nodded.

The two drifted to the back of the store and whispered for a few moments; then the man with the vest came forward again.

"It's a deal except for those cartridges and powder. We've got a few laws around here—been plenty of trouble as you likely know."

Marcher regarded him with irate skepticism edging on disgust. "What kind of laws?"

"Laws about who we sell ammunition to."

"You're selling it to me!"

The man seemed helpless to keep his eyes from shifting between Marcher's hatchet and his long bound hair. " 'Taint who's buying it," he said uneasily, "it's who's using it that's got 'em stewin'. Injuns aren't allowed in this town"—he fingered his mouth nervously as he took in Marcher's pistol—"nor is wearing guns. These furs came from up north . . . Injun country . . . there's Injun sign all over them. You didn't get 'em for nothin' and money don't hardly count much up there." His tone suddenly became placating. "Now look, mister, if you'd like some real fancy bolts of cloth we'll . . ."

"Well, damn you for an idiot!" shouted Marcher as he turned toward his skins again. "I'll bet you every dishonest dollar you've ever come by there's traders hereabouts not so finicky when it comes to selling a man what he wants and needs for himself."

Marcher was tugging the top skins from the pile, swearing at the job of packing them again, when the two traders came around the counter, their hands making little consoling motions in the air.

"Now hold on a minute," said the bald one, who seemed to be doing all the talking. "We're businessmen if we ain't nothin' else. Now you just give us your word those cartridges ain't goin' to no hostiles and we got us a deal."

"I won't give you a God damn thing—if you don't believe me, I'm not swearing to anything."

"We believe you," said the other one, speaking for the first time.

"Well, damn it, give me what I want so I can get the hell out of here!"

By the time ammunition, bolts of cloth, trinkets, and cans of oil were strapped in the pack bags and the money counted and in his pocket, Marcher discovered it was almost dark. He found the whole dealing had soured his gut, and his mind settled on a drink. Remembering the warning against side arms, he took off his pistol and put it in the pack, but he left his hatchet in his belt, running his fingers over its handle as he looked around. At the end of the next street he could see the yellow lamps of a saloon. Some men were loitering outside as he approached, and coarse laughter and an occasional mock squeal of a female began to reach his ears.

At first he was surprised to find it so dark inside, and he made his way to the bar with only a dim sense that others, whose eyes were already adjusted to this darkness, were looking at him. Somehow he realized it was suddenly much quieter, and a bartender with a broad handlebar mustache was leaning toward him.

"Whiskey," said Marcher.

"Sorry, we don't serve no breeds here—try Shawnee Joe's two blocks down. Whiskey is the same there as here."

Marcher's hand shot out, and grabbing the bartender by his shirt, pulled him even closer. "Who in hell are you calling a breed?"

It was his eastern accent and clean-cut features, devoid of any trace of Indian blood, that saved him. He had much to learn about Denver.

The bartender slowly drew himself back. "Sorry," he said again as though he were long used to using that word when he didn't mean it. Mechanically he put a glass and a bottle on the bar.

Marcher poured himself a shot and threw it down. It was then he became aware there was now an almost absolute silence in the place. Beside him was a man in rough homespun clothing who was clearly drunk. Now the man turned around and took to studying Marcher.

"Well, what d'ya know," he said in the halting voice of a drunk long insensitive to the serious side of things, "he ain't no breed. Well, 'pears to me if he ain't—his paw fetched him up a sure enough squaw to suckle on."

There was a ripple of hard laughter.

"Mind your own God damn business!" snapped Marcher.

A big man with the shoulders and girth of a prize bull got out of his chair and came toward the bar. His face was dark and unshaven, but his eyes flickered like candles caught in an uncertain draft.

He stood behind Marcher, slowly rubbing his immense thighs. "Could be you spoilin' for a fight, squaw man?"

Marcher turned slowly, his hand slipping casually to his hatchet. He confronted the other quietly for a tense moment before he said, "Can't say that I am, but if you try that 'squaw man' on me again, friend, I'll finish whatever it is you're fixing to start." His eyes were steady and his voice rolled in that even way that bespeaks its own menace.

The big man's eyes caught the hatchet for the first time and he seemed to hesitate. "You figure to fight fair?"

"I figure to win."

The bartender suddenly appeared. "We don't want no trouble here—you two want to fracas, git outside."

Nothing was said for a few moments. Then the big man spoke again. "I'd be gettin' out of Denver was I you." This time he didn't use "squaw man."

"I come and go when I'm ready."

Another man from a nearby table joined them, a short man with a broad forehead and a hard, square chin. "Leave him alone, Jeff," he said with a half-jesting authority. "If he starts anything you'll have the law on your side."

The big man called Jeff looked Marcher up and down and then turned and moved slowly back to his table.

"First time in Denver," said the other to Marcher. He used a new tone now. This one was not unfriendly.

"First," answered Marcher, still watching the muscled hulk that had sullenly withdrawn to his table.

"Well, there's been lots of trouble lately. Whole family goin' east was massacred last week—folks is a little edgy, I guess." This man wore a well-fitted shirt and coat and light leather boots, but he had a commonsense way about him.

"Have a drink?" said Marcher, turning to the bar again. He didn't really want company, but he needed information and this stranger might be a start.

"Wouldn't be polite-like now, would it, for me to turn you down," smiled the other.

The bartender, openly relieved to hear amiable talk, set up another glass. And now the noise rose again as the customers, tired of silence and deprived of excitement, turned to their liquor, which was as coarse as the laughter that soon followed.

"Dickens is my name," said the other man after he had downed his drink. "What brings you to Denver?"

"Looking for an assayer," said Marcher cautiously.

"An assayer?" repeated the other, his eyes opening a trifle in interest.

"Yeah—and maybe a couple of miners with the savvy to smell out a mine."

Dickens looked searchingly at him for a moment. "You talkin' about gold, fellow?"

"Your hearing is tolerably good tonight, Dickens."

Dickens shook his head, smiling as though he were enjoying some internal joke. "What d'yuh say your name was?"

"I didn't."

Dickens smiled again and rubbed his broad forehead. "Mister, you've got sittin' in this saloon no less than ten of the best gold gophers that ever swung a pick. You don't need an assayer if you've got any samplin' stuff with you. They can tell you what it's worth down to a dime."

"I like the assayer better."

"Have it your way, stranger, but better miners than these don't breathe. If you wanted to reach hell in a hurry they'll tell you exactly where to dig."

"You a miner?"

"No siree, not me. Got too much sense. Besides, don't want to be that rich . . . run a little store down the street."

"Sounds reasonable enough," allowed Marcher agreeably. "Guess I'll find what I'm looking for though."

Dickens swung around impulsively and said, "Well, I'll get 'em up here and you can take your pick." Before Marcher could stop him,

Dickens was shouting, " 'Tention, 'tention, everybody. We've got us here a gent who thinks he has a find. He's huntin' a pair of shovels that know where to dig—I told him we got the best diggers this side of hell—now, if you're not already too rich and got a hankerin' to hear more, step up."

The room changed its character almost at once, as nearly every man stood and came forward, some elbowing others aside to be closer to Marcher.

Marcher had turned around, his elbows back on the bar, to confront them. He was annoyed to find the man named Jeff standing almost at his right.

"Speak your piece, partner," said someone in the crowd.

Marcher felt a little respect in the tone. His backing Jeff down hadn't been wasted on this crowd. "Wasn't planning on talking business tonight," said Marcher easily, "but before you get all fired up, maybe you'd better chew over the fact that it's in hostile country and if it's your habit to get by on luck and not guts, you'd better get back to your drinking."

"Hell with that," shouted one squat miner. "I'd fight old Harry himself for a sure enough find. Where's it at?"

"Wasn't planning on telling anyone," said Marcher easily again. "Just planned on taking him there."

"How come we got to take your word there's a sure enough find, friend?" It was Jeff speaking, and there was no warmth in the final word.

Marcher turned slightly to free his right hand. "Nobody's asking you to."

"He's got some samplin' with him," said Dickens encouragingly. "Goin' to see an assayer in the mornin'."

Marcher wished to Christ Dickens would keep his mouth shut, but he knew the man was trying to help. He was the fool for having talked too much.

A lean man standing to his left with eyes like an uncertain watchdog piped up. "Meanin' no disrespect, you don't look like no prospector—how come you kick up a find?"

"It's a long story."

"We got time," muttered Jeff.

Marcher turned around and pushed the bottle to the back of the bar. "I haven't." The bartender had been hanging close, listening to the exchanges. "What do I owe you, mister?" asked Marcher.

"No charges, partner. Anyone brings in a find—drinks are usually on the house."

"I'd rather pay."

The man with the watchdog eyes interrupted. "Can we get a look-see at that ore, friend?"

"I think not." Marcher was putting two silver dollars on the bar.

"Go on!" said Dickens good-naturedly. "Let 'em have a look. One piece of ore ain't tellin' where that mine is."

"Let's see her," said the squat man anxiously. "By Jesus, I believe I can smell gold a mile upwind in a blizzard. Might save you a trip to the assayer's office. They don't consider assayin' funnin', you know. It will cost you money."

Marcher could feel the weight of Paul's stone in his pocket. His curiosity was stirring. After all, nothing this crowd could say would be final and Dickens might be right, maybe they could tell something from just looking.

Marcher turned about and faced them. "All right. I'm putting a piece on the bar—but don't nobody touch it, understand, *nobody*."

A number of heads in the crowd bobbed in agreement. The rest stretched a little to get a better view. Marcher took the stone from his pocket and laid it before him on the bar. He could feel the men crowding about him. "Bring a light," one shouted. The bartender hurried over with a bright kerosene lamp. "Damn!" whispered some-one. "If that don't look like it!"

But then it happened. A hand the size of a bear paw came onto the bar and started for the stone. "Lemme see that!" It was Jeff. A number of breaths audibly held up as incredibly a hatchet was out and its blade slicing into the oak bar, separating Jeff's hand from the stone by less than an inch.

Marcher's eyes were centimeters from the other's. "Your hearing is no better than your manners, mister—I said don't touch!"

Jeff's dark face took a strange turn and then the light in his eyes flickered out. But the great hand rose and closed over the hatchet as he muttered from somewhere deep in his guts, "Been waitin' to get that Injun tool off'n you—squaw man!"

Marcher tried to pull the hatchet out of the bar, but the other hand held it like a frozen vise. It was the miners trying to pull them apart and get between them that brought the hatchet free. Free of the bar but not Jeff. But now Big Owl's training on how to fight in close with a hatchet and Marcher's strange passion for it began to show. He knew he could not break the other's grip on the weapon, so he didn't try. Instead he drove his knee into Jeff's groin turning the heel of his hatchet up as he did. Jeff jerked forward and his forehead came against the heel of the hatchet. In that split second Jeff was stunned, Marcher wrenched the weapon free. Without hesitation it was whirling over his head and the heel was coming down to catch Jeff behind the ear with a long, bone-cracking whack. Jeff dropped like a heifer felled with an ax. And now Marcher, mistaking the hands that wanted only to restrain him for an attempt to disarm him, brought the hatchet in a wide swing to a position behind him on the bar. But here he succeeded only in smashing the kerosene lamp, which flew in a thousand pieces but left behind it a suddenly larger flame that started on the bar and then fingered down both sides of its wooden panels.

"Fire!" screamed a woman, and a general rush for the doors began. The bartender came running with a small bucket of water, but kerosene was still dripping from the lamp and he did little more than help spread the fire. "Christ, somebody help me," he shouted. "Somebody help me!" Marcher was backing away from the tremendous heat the growing fire was beginning to throw. Suddenly a bottle of whiskey sitting on the bar cracked at the edge of the flames and added its own raw complement of alcohol to a conflagration that seemed to rise up like a demon. In only moments other bottles began to go. The spot where his stone was lying was ablaze and rivulets of fire were now running over the sawdust-covered floor, reaching for the legs of the first pine table. He thought of grabbing a tablecloth and rushing in for his nugget, but already the fire had begun to roar and its many tongues were streaking outward like a thing alive.

Within minutes the saloon was an inferno and Marcher was driven through a window for the air that meant life. He came around to the hitch rack where a crowd was gathering and men were running with buckets of water from the public trough. Here, his hands trembling with shock and anger, he released his horse and, pulling it back, made the packhorse follow quickly as he moved off down the street. Behind him the people were still running up, still gathering, shouting. Marcher could only distinguish one voice. It was Dickens. It was his screaming, his frantic words, that finally ate into Marcher's fury-stricken mind. "Jeff is in there! Jeff is still in there! Christ and damnation, we forgot about Jeff!"

"*Carajo!* Is veree bad, *amigo.*" It was Miguel coming into the room where Marcher sat with a half glass of tequila in his hand. Not wanting to leave Denver and too exhausted to travel any farther he had decided to gamble and seek out the Mexican whose morals he suspected would not stand up to money.

"How bad?" said Marcher, putting down the glass and coming to his feet.

"Four people is dead. The one named Jeff and two men who take a woman upstairs . . . for making love, eh? . . . maybe they fall asleep, eh? But they are trapped in fire and die!" Miguel shook his head solemnly. "Many angry *hombres* look for you, *amigo*."

Marcher snorted. "Was the law there?"

"Si, and deese sheriff is very dangerous man, Miguel knows."

Marcher gave Miguel the twenty-five dollars he had promised him for his services and hitched his pistol belt up another notch. It reminded him he had not eaten since breakfast, but there was no time for food now.

"Is veree bad thing when peoples die," said Miguel looking at him thoughtfully. "A leetle fire—*caramba!* It is nothing! But four peoples . . ." He shook his head slowly as though he were stunned at the magnitude of the disaster.

"Shit, serves the bastards right!" Marcher was preparing to go.

"One moment, *amigo*. What you gonna do?"

"Leave—you idiot! What did you expect me to do, put on a pot of coffee for that posse coming in the morning?"

"Is veree dangerous to travel now."

"Why?"

"Miguel knows—but he cannot say. Is better you wait here one . . . two days, then when is quiet you ride out *pronto!*"

Marcher looked at the other in the dim light, but even in that half darkness the craft in the smooth-prune face caused him to pause and measure matters. His horses were tied, they needed feed. If he left now, Miguel would hurry back to town and curry favor with the sheriff and townspeople by putting them on his trail. If he stayed a day or two, a reward might be posted and Miguel would see that it was collected. Apart from what Miguel could charge him for his "protection," the Mexican would doubtless end up with his horses and gear. It was a sorry hand he held and he would have liked to turn it over carefully in his mind. But an answer too long in coming would be suspect.

"You got a stable out back?"

Miguel nodded. *"Si."*

"Let's get the horses in there where they won't be seen. I'll hang on for a day or two."

"Veree wise, *amigo*."

Together they took the horses back to the stable, Marcher taking off the saddle and pack bags and placing them in a corner as though they were to be there for some time. He left his rifle too, watching Miguel's eyes following it as he set it down. Then he saw to it that the mounts had plenty of hay before he returned with Miguel to the house.

"You would like some food, *amigo?*"

Marcher shook his head. "Too worried to eat," he muttered.

"Some more tequila, eh?"

"Not for the moment. I think I need sleep."

"Miguel will send a *muchacha* to sleep with you."

"Better not. I'm not in a studding mood."

Marcher was hoping his words carried conviction, for this Miguel was probably a demon at the art of deceit. But his instincts warned him that to take anything that might contain a drug would leave him without any cards at all. A *señorita* in his bed was as good as a sentinel at his door and he had noticed that he and Miguel always entered and left by the front door. There must have been others in the house, but Miguel was careful not to use them.

In his room again he decided to remove his clothes. It would look more convincing. Still he was careful to put his hatchet and pistol next to the wall on the ledge of a false window that ran below the edge of the bed. Then he crawled onto the cheap ticking under an old blanket and lay there listening. He could hear men coming and going, speaking in Spanish, and the giggling of girls interspersed with the clink of glasses.

Every once in a while he heard footsteps lightly approaching his room, pausing, and then receding again. Christ! What a fix he was in! He had lost Paul's stone, had got himself crossed with the law, and was huddling in this whorehouse like a rabbit in a briarpatch not knowing where and when to run.

In the great dimly lit room beyond other things were happening. Miguel was biting heavily on an unlit cigar and puzzling over matters in his mind. This strange gringo had said he was very tired, that he must sleep. But he did not snore. Miguel had been up to his door a dozen times, but he heard nothing. In Miguel's reasoning a very tired man snores when he sleeps.

Finally he beckoned to one of the slim, dark girls lounging about the room. "Teresa," he said to her in Spanish, "you speak a little English. Take a bottle of tequila and go to the bed of the gringo. If he sleeps you sleep next to him. Call to me if he gets up. If he is awake, try to get him to drink. Have a little party, eh?"

"But Miguel, Pancho will be here soon—he will ask for me."

"Tonight Pancho will take Tina."

"Ah, Miguel, you don't know how . . ."

"Go! *Pronto!*" He cuffed her and she backed away holding her cheek. Miguel ignored her and turned, smiling readily to greet a new customer just entering. "Ah, Señor Vasquel, where have you been? You have not honored us. . . ."

The girl placed a bottle and two glasses quietly on a table next to the bed. Marcher heard her clothes rustling off and felt her slip in, her warm, naked body touching his. But he knew why she was there. He lay still for a moment and then with the slow awkward movements of one being disturbed from sleep, he began to move about, finally ending up by turning a little suddenly toward her.

"*Buenas noches,*" she said softly.

"Oh! Well, hello—how long you been here?"

"A little while only. You want tequila, yes?"

He looked at her in the dark. She seemed pretty. The maleness in him stirred for a moment, but he forced it away, knowing he was being taken for a fool. Yet here was another tooth in this trap that held him. In the back of his mind he was struggling desperately for a way out.

"Will the lady drink with me?"

"*Si.* Teresa always drink wid de handsome ones."

She poured from the bottle into the two glasses and gave him one. "*Saludos, señor.*"

He took a mouthful, made a moan of satisfaction, then appearing to take a second swig returned the first to the glass. He kept the glass hidden in his hand. She seemed to be enjoying her drink and, relieved, he settled back like a man contemplating his pleasure.

Something told him she was attuned to voices from the other room.

"How do they treat you here?" he parried lightly.

"Veree bad. Miguel has no heart."

Marcher forced himself to sound comic and unconcerned. "Ah, but Miguel has tequila."

"Oh, *si, señor. Mucho tequila, mucho dinero*—but no heart!"

He looked at her, feeling the shadow of something in her mind. She was drinking again. "Teresa is unhappy," he said as though it mattered little.

She turned and looked at him. He couldn't see her eyes, but he knew from the pitch of her head there was anger in them. He had forgotten how much he knew about women.

He put his arm over her head as though to look at her and his drink slowly poured onto the ticking. He demanded she fill the glasses again.

It was much later when he managed to get to the outside of the bed, saying almost argumentatively he needed more tequila. Teresa was now talking about her Pancho. "Oh, *mi novio,* boyfriend, you understand, and this pig Miguel send heem to Tina."

Marcher, pretending the heaviness and carelessness of a drunk, muttered, "Shouldn't anyone . . . anyone ever . . . ever get in the way of love."

"Si. You *comprende, señor."*

He filled her glass again while she, as though in habit, wiggled against him in the ancient way of whores with men. "You do not like Teresa, eh?"

He ran his hand over her body. Pancho had good taste. "I like you real fine," he said as though he meant to take her in time. But the night was passing. The household had been quiet for over an hour, chances were it was well past midnight. He wondered if this girl could drink tequila all night and stay awake. But finally he could tell from her movements and her many repetitions that the potent fluid was making headway. He no longer had to feign drinking. She was hanging now in a little haze of her own where Tina, Pancho, and Miguel kept coming and going in her thoughts until she started expressing for one emotions she had felt all night about the other. "Teresa love Tina." He listened in desperation as she spoke more and more haltingly and more and more in Spanish. Finally she turned toward the wall and, dropping her glass as though her hand was powerless to hold it, fell asleep. Marcher waited for five minutes listening to her breathing. By then he was sure she was asleep. The bottle felt amazingly light in his hand; he knew if he had drunk as much as she had, a team of mules couldn't have dragged him from the bed. A man couldn't help wondering whether she had such staying powers in other ways.

Slowly and gently he rose from beside her, watching her head for the slightest movement. There was none. Minutes later he was in his clothes. He circled to the false window and retrieved his pistol and hatchet and in a moment he was ready.

He stood looking at the girl, fighting a thought. She might still come awake and give a cry that would be his undoing. He could see her neck arched as her head lay over the pillow. For more than a moment he fingered the hatchet—a way to make things certain. But he finally backed away and, working the door slowly open, slipped out of the room. The house was in total darkness, not a thing moved.

A full moon was throwing some light through the low windows in the main room beyond. He started toward this room where the front door stood, keeping his left arm wide and limber to guide him along the wall. Finally he knew he was almost at the door. He paused again. The moonlight threw eerie patches of light on the matted floor, but nothing moved. The place lay in dead silence. He stepped to the door and at once his foot came down on something soft which moved quickly beneath it.

"You make a beeg mistake, *señor.*" It was Miguel. He had Marcher's rifle. Marcher could see its barrel swinging up in the frail half-light of the moon. In the tiniest fraction of time it was over. Miguel was about to speak again, for he did not see the hatchet whirling above him near the dark ceiling and he never knew how it brought him oblivion as it cracked his skull open like an egg.

The hatchet came out with a thick sucking sound.

Marcher waited a moment or two to see if anything else moved, but the silence took over again and the house appeared to slumber on. He reached over and picked up his rifle, stepped over Miguel's body, and left the house. Outside the night seemed still and untroubled as he made his way to the stable.

By the next morning he was many miles to the north and near exhaustion, but he kept going. Just before noon he met a whiskey drummer hauling a wagon load to Denver. The wagon was long and low, with four horses pulling it and four others tethered to the rear.

"Want to sell some of that cargo?" demanded Marcher.

"Ain't haulin' it any further than I have to." The teamster, his cheek loaded with tobacco, sent an amber stream down the other side of the wagon. " 'Course you got to figure on payin' Denver prices."

"Figured on paying them." Marcher still had almost three hundred dollars on him, and where was he going to spend it? In the end they made a deal which included one of the extra horses the teamster had. His own packhorse could not have carried it all.

When they finished, the teamster pulled a bottle from under his seat. "Like a drink, partner? Be muh first today."

Marcher was so tired he felt drugged, but he needed a drink and knew it. "I'll join you."

The teamster watched him drinking, looking him over as he did, noting there was blood on the blade of the hatchet. "Don't mean no nosin' in, partner, but if you figure on sellin' that stuff to Injuns—be mighty handy if you didn't say you fetched it from me."

Marcher looked at him steadily for a moment, took another drink from the bottle, and handed it back. "You've got nothing to worry about, mister. I'd appreciate it if we agreed I never saw you and you never saw me."

"Done!" said the teamster climbing back onto his wagon. He looked down at Marcher and then at the bloodstained weapon in his belt, his face taking on a strange and sharp quality as he said, "Well, you know what them Injuns is all the time a-sayin'—bury that hatchet."

51

Big Owl had come to smoke with White River, his aging face heavy with the burden of his message. They had both seen Marcher coming into camp before the first snow flew. Ominously, he had ridden in drunk and darkly drawn about the eyes. He was leading a second packhorse laden with whiskey and thereafter for days he was either insane with liquor or morosely sober.

"Would my brother, White River, speak to the brave Yellow Hatchet?" murmured Big Owl after the pipe had been passed. "Tell him the madness the firewater brings is not the Absarokee way. Tell him our hearts are heavy for our long friend. Tell him our medicine ones will help drive out this new evil spirit that has entered him."

White River shook his head slowly, acknowledging the futility of any words. "Things get into a white critter's head, Big Owl, and mostly there's no getting 'em out."

Big Owl turned his eyes to the fire. "It will bring trouble. Our young braves look upon Yellow Hatchet as a great warrior. They will see this thing and then, who can say?"

White River looked away. "Reckon that be the way of things, sure enough," he muttered, his sense of helplessness draining life from his words. He knew Big Owl and his people found their margin for survival in the powder and cartridges Marcher had fetched from Denver, for the game was now too scarce and wild for the bow, but this new turning had put the aging chief into a painful quandary, one the passing of pipes could not resolve. Yet White River's eyes were soon peering beyond the troubled Indian as his mind started settling uneasily on the soft, proud, yet vulnerable figure of White Bead. It was a thing he had sensed growing in him ever since he beheld her watching Marcher depart for Denver, her smooth firm body as it turned into the lodge hanging in some distant part of his mind. It was not that he desired her as much as he felt akin to her, her fierce independence and struggle for dignity as she accepted the natural desires of her womanhood. Funny how a man could feel deeply about a woman even when she belonged to another man. Was it not White Bead's counsel Big Owl should be seeking? And just what counsel would her heart offer now for this morbid drunkard who took her supple and willing body under his robe?

The two sat in a long silence, each with his mute worry and wondering about the days ahead, while the fire between them slowly died and went out.

White Bead was the first to know of the evil spirit that was now alive in André Marcher. At first, making her heart heavy within her, he ignored her, brooding over his fire, swearing to himself, slugging at his whiskey, sagging finally into noisy sleep. He had brought her some cloth and trinkets but she had to unpack them herself and now they sat at the back of the lodge. She felt no woman's yearning to turn them into adornments that would brighten the eyes of her man.

White Bead had been approached by more than one brave in Marcher's absence, but she had resolutely driven them off. Once she had a near brush with rape. She had been bathing in a nearby stream when Black Feather, one of the River Crows who had stayed with the camp, had come upon her standing nude in the water and entering the stream grabbed at her wet, glistening body. She fought him off, even though he had pinned her against the bank, his erection rising. In desperation she bit deeply into his shoulder, screaming, "Yellow Hatchet will kill Black Feather for what he is trying to do to White Bead!"

With these words he released her, snarling defiantly, "Yellow Hatchet will not come back! He will find many white women with open legs in their big village! He will get drunk and not think of his Absarokee squaw! He will not come back!"

"That is Black Feather's only hope!"

The brave stood above her, the wild lust draining from his eyes. Warnings of Marcher's wrath were no idle threat. The name of Yellow Hatchet carried menace. "He will not kill me! He will not kill Black Feather—for then he would be driven from the tribe forever." This was a hard, inflexible truth. He who killed an Absarokee in their own village must leave the tribe for all time. Furious, but sensing his possible peril, he spat at her body, making a rude gesture as he turned away. White Bead watched him go, holding the breast he had wrenched so savagely when he first seized her. Oh, how their many calamities had changed the Absarokees. The high-born code of dignity among young men was gone. She remembered a time when Absarokee warriors would have turned their faces away in shame from a brave who would do such a craven thing.

But now with Marcher back she still did not have a man. She waited for him under the robes at night, but his foul words and drunken harangues were her only reward. Once she held his male thing trying to arouse him, but it lay limp and pliant in her hand till she realized he was too drunk to know her need. Tiny tears glistening in the firelight appeared in the corners of her eyes as she turned from him.

Worse scenes were coming.

One day White River came by. He had just returned from a hunt, bringing in several deer. He lowered a hind quarter beside White Bead, setting it down without a word. Even in the darkness of the lodge he could see the bluish bruise on her face and the scratch she had tried to cover with vermilion. It was a poor disguise.

Almost unaware of his gesture, he placed his hand on her shoulder in a soft, comforting motion, but innocent as it was it brought the half-drunk Marcher up from his sprawled posture across the lodge. "Getting mighty sociable, aren't you!"

White River's eyes, piercing into the half darkness, saw the heavy, dirty growth on Marcher's face. Contempt slowly contracted the corners of his mouth as he said, "She can't live on that panther piss you call whiskey, even if you can!"

"I can take care of my own!"

"Better start!" White River's mind flashed back to the brave, whom he discovered later was Black Feather, watching White Bead as Marcher left on his journey south. There were other things. "There's deer yardin' up in a valley back of yon mountain. Was I you I'd get there before a big blow moves 'em on."

Marcher sat up and clawed at his eyes as White River left. White Bead watched him stoically. The night before he had finally taken her into his robes, but after their lovemaking he had turned morose and hit her in a quick rage when she tried to come back to him. Womanlike and keeping her head down, she backed away, her hand reaching quietly for the skinning knife. But there was a thing that kept White Bead from using her knife, a knowing that made her pensive and played upon her secret self, in the end making her sit across the lodge watching the restless form of Marcher finally falling into a noisy sleep and raise a snore that seemed to gush from a thick guttural source in his throat.

Just before he had left for Denver she felt a change in her body, a slight shifting of moods and appetites, and long before her menstrual period failed to appear she knew she was pregnant. It didn't seem a thing to share with him then, with his leaving and all, but now she knew in only a month or two her slim form would give her secret away. She had hoped he would be proud and stand tall beside her, but her instincts told her that whatever evil spirit had entered his body in Denver it had made this the wrong time to reveal to him a child of his seed was coming to life in her.

He awoke one morning from a deep drunkenness, a drunkenness so numbing it had wiped from his mind all memory of what had happened the night before. But as the slit of his eyes opened he became aware of a thin line just inches from his face. At first he thought his sight had been momentarily affected by this unending consumption of alcohol, that it would disappear as his head cleared, but it did not. The line stayed there. Finally he moved one hand up to touch it and felt a sharp sting of pain as he became aware, in quiet shock, he had pressed his fingers against the stone-sharpened cutting edge of a long skinning knife. The knife had been stuck in the ground inches from his face, its menacing edge toward him.

It spoke in terribly unanswerable terms for itself.

He closed his eyes again, his inner turmoil stirring and slowly becoming unbearable. What had he done? It was some time before he could open his eyes fully to find White Bead sitting across the fire from him, nude. He stared at her and as his eyes gradually came into focus he saw the red welts around her throat and above and below her breasts. She let him stare at her for long moments, staring back at him in grim silence, her still beautiful olive face as immobile as marble. Then without a word she rose, put on her robe and left the lodge.

Hours passed before he could pull himself up, suddenly feeling nauseated and filthy, aware only of a burning need to cleanse himself. Moving clumsily, a pall of guilt pressing upon him, he heated some water over the lingering fire and awkwardly shaved. Then, almost stumbling, he fetched a second bowl of water from the stream behind the lodge, removed his clothes, and bathed himself. His mind was moving at random now. Somehow he knew he had to be alone, to get away from this depressing camp, to get by himself where he could think and breathe. He knew the weather was closing in but he didn't care. Slowly he packed his gun and gear, not realizing until he was almost ready to leave that grub was going to be his real problem. Grub for himself, which his stomach signaled hardly mattered for the moment, and for White Bead while he was gone.

After some thought, he went into a few neighboring lodges and offered to trade pieces of White Bead's trinkets, which still lay at the back of the lodge, for meat. It was a venture that made him grimmer still. The stony silences that greeted him in the dark lodges bordered on insults. Gratitude for his trip to Denver had all but vanished. It was not only their knowledge, impossible to contain, of White Bead's torment that turned their faces away from this whiskey-sodden intruder. The long, merciless winter stretched ahead, the game was drifting south, trinkets did not keep body and soul together.

How Black Feather found out he was struggling to trade for food Marcher never knew, but suddenly the sulky warrior came into his lodge with a shoulder of elk and some jerked beef.

Marcher had seen Black Feather about the camp, but other than that he was a River Crow who stayed on with the camp, he knew nothing more about him. White Bead had kept silent about his mischief at the stream. But the sight of meat relieved Marcher. His problem seemed solved. He picked up two strings of red beads and a pendant with a blue stone in it, but almost before he could offer them Black Feather was waving them away.

For a moment Marcher looked at him, suddenly feeling a strange distaste for this sullen Indian. There was craft in his manner, an uneasiness in the cast of his eyes. He first suspected Black Feather was going to ask for the colored cloth and the blue lariat lying across the bright red blankets, but Black Feather's gaze went elsewhere. He was looking at the remaining jugs of whiskey Marcher had sitting near the head of his robe.

Marcher followed his gaze to them before he grunted in genuine surprise, "Thought Absarokees didn't take to firewater."

Black Feather pointed to the meat and then to the jugs. "Two," he muttered as he held up two badly scarred fingers.

Marcher realized that Big Owl and many others in the tribe would violently resent this exchange, would accuse him of bringing evil upon their already overburdened shoulders, but he was feeling too empty, too involved with himself, too sick at denying his depressed feelings about White Bead, too anxiously wanting to get away and just be by himself to worry about any harm done to others.

"Shit!" he said, clapping his sides and rubbing his neck in frustration. He kicked at the edge of the great robe that covered the center area of the lodge, misery finally sweeping aside all discretion. "Take them, God damn it, and get the hell out of here!"

Half an hour later he had packed the jerk beef and a thin slice of the shoulder in his saddlebag. The rest he left for White Bead. In time she would return, knowing at least he had thought of her. Besides, though it was late in the season, he might still run across some game himself.

He was almost clear of camp when White River appeared before him, motioning him to halt. There was a new, uncharacteristic authority in White River's manner.

"Where you headin'?"

Marcher regarded him vacantly for a moment. "If I thought a man had any business knowing, I might just tell him."

"Was I you I'd do some tellin'."

Marcher tightened his lips in growing agitation but managed to mutter, "What the hell is this all about?"

"Swapped that polecat, Black Feather, rotgut for meat, didn't you? Don't you think we've got miseries enough round here a'ready?"

"Trading's fair."

White River looked like he was about to pull Marcher from his saddle. "If you were half a man you'd fetch White Bead and ask her how fair a whiskeyed-up man can be."

The mention of White Bead shook Marcher into silence for a moment. He glanced at the skies overhead. They were leaden. A few snowflakes were quietly drifting down.

White River's sharply lined face came closer to his. "Ain't you just afrettin' to know where she is? What's happened to her?"

"Bet you could tell me," Marcher spat back, losing his halfhearted attempt at a sneer.

"Bet I could! She's over at my diggins. Been there for hours. Blue Lodge has been patchin' her up with herbs and the devil knows what. What kind of nigger are you anyways?"

To this Marcher found no energy for an answer. All he knew was he had to get off by himself, had to think his whole sickening existence through. He backed his horse away from White River. "Tell her I'll be back," he said in a hoarse whisper and started away.

White River, watching him go, called after him, "Comin' back might not be as all-fired simple as leavin'. There's been welcomin' parties round here as has been a man's last!"

Two days of drifting in the growing cold and passing snow showers had left Marcher with a clearing head and a near starting point for facing the turmoil that boiled at some deep level in his mind. Above him unnoticed the wind slowly sharpened from the west. In truth, he was not exactly drifting, vaguely he knew where he was going, though he was not heading directly there or with any sense of haste. Nor did food or even fatigue prove a problem for him. He was in one of those emotional upheavals in life when a man is borne along by some psychic force that silences all demands of the flesh.

In time he was climbing to the ridge, the ridge that had held Paul's star, the growing power of the wind alive at his back. At the top the wind was whining in agony as it swept around endless boulders and turned into the downdrafts of the valleys beyond. It had swept the ridge clear of earlier snow and the country about lay in a lurking darkness, even though somewhere in his mind he sensed it was close to high noon. Slowly he made his way forward, approaching the ledge where the mirror had been lodged, knowing he had reached it when he spotted shards of glass still visible among the bits of shale and worn rocks scattered at the foot of the ledge. He picked up a few slivers, but they told him nothing except that the mirror had been black on the off side. The bulk of it was smashed to pieces as fine as sand, resembling mica.

He glanced up at the sky. The clouds were now like great purple ramparts massing to the west. The rest of the horizon was a steel gray. Bracing himself against the wind, he climbed to the top of the ledge; beyond it he could see three little valleys that came together with the faint trace of streams threading through them. They were clearly joining somewhere below his limited sight, but the plains beyond the valleys were empty, ominous. The wind suddenly seemed to pick up, gathering intensity. His every instinct warned him its new screaming was a tocsin those who chose to live dared not ignore. Yet here he was at the scene of his defeat. Would it not be better simply to stay here? Was there anything to go back for? "Damn you, Paul!" he cried. "Damn you! Damn your gold!" In his mind he heard strident laughter, but it was only the furies of wind rushing up the slope. Ben was the lucky one. He lay in his grave where scalding shame, humiliation, and defeat could never reach him. Strangely, he found it hard to remember Ben without remembering his oft-mentioned love for his father and Melody or their love for him. Was that what had made up Ben's life? Was his need of love what had made him unfit for this land of bloody struggles for survival? Were the things he had seemed bound to, like compassion and decency, really what drove him to a pointless and near sacrificial death? But Ben was a man unwavering in his convictions and accepting of his fate while he, Andy, had no creed but his own desire and raised a hatchet to all that opposed his will. Was that the difference White River felt between them from the beginning, and what lay behind his curious but steadfast respect for Ben and his obvious rejection of himself?

Bewildered to find himself annoyed, even dismayed, by this coarse plainsman's opinion of him, he was grudgingly beginning to admit in the keep of his heart that White River had a subdued nobility about him, a quiet knowing he was the match of any man, a dignity even imminent death could not lessen. Helplessly he realized White River's rejection had opened the agonizing question to which Ben's memory had long been leading. Had he, André Marcher, ever loved anyone? Had anyone ever loved him? The question seemed to echo through a frightening and expanding emptiness within him, a void that till now had been filled with rage and determination. The face of his whoring mother flashed before him for the first time in what seemed years. Of the myriad of faceless men who had ravished her body, surely some, unlike him or even his father, had known her love. But as he stared at this vision of his mother, her face became the face of the sensuous Margo, smirking at him from the dark swirling mists beyond, his stomach tightening at the thought of other men's nakedness joining with hers and thinking, as did he, her ecstatic intimacy was love.

Suddenly he had a sense of unspeakable loneliness, an infinite loneliness, his loneliness. It was White Bead who finally trapped his thoughts. Somehow he could not dismiss her. The flint-sharp skinning knife plunged into the earth beside his drunken body swept grimly through his mind. She could have built a scorching fire and left him, she could have killed him, she could have disfigured his face and body, even unmanned him. Again he saw her rising, nude, drawing her robe about her, and leaving the lodge, her face a mask concealing a terrible, even more terrible because it was unreadable, sentence.

The wind broke into a shriek, almost toppling him from the ridge. Slowly with his hands before him he started to make his way down, back to his mount. He found his horse whinnying and pulling against its tether. The imminent storm had panicked the animal and its flanks quivered as he came alongside. They moved out against the now demonic wind to start back, the animal instinctively drifting to the western side of the valley where the wind would have less force and the drifts would begin last.

In less than half an hour the snow swept across the land like a white canopy and Marcher's vision had fallen to a handful of yards.

52

In Denver, a U.S. marshal pulled at his heavy, graying mustache and shifted a wad of tobacco he had parked moments before inside his left cheek. "Anything more?" he asked gruffly as though talking for him was a chore.

"About all I can recollect," said Dickens placatingly, his eyes appraising the marshal, whose grim patience reminded him of the glacial pace justice often took in this land. "His nugget was found, as you a'ready know, raked out of the ashes by yours truly. 'Twas gold, sure enough."

"Huh," grunted the marshal.

"Folks figure he took off north . . . say he did that greaser Miguel in with his hatchet before he left. Mortally mean critter, I'd say."

The marshal glanced through the window. Snowflakes were still drifting down but becoming heavier and occasionally sweeping sideways as the rising wind heralded the onset of a blizzard. There was little he could do until spring. He had noted without comment that four people had perished in the saloon fire but the issue hardly concerned him. None of the victims, from the slim description he had been offered, appeared to be citizens most communities couldn't prosper without. Miguel's death he dismissed as a suitable end to a dangerous and degenerate pig, whose serious offenses he was reasonably sure went well beyond mere pimping or forcing poor Mexican girls into prostitution. But what did concern him was that large amounts of ammunition and powder could well by now be in the hands of hostiles, revenge-seeking killers, who in the spring would descend by night on white settlements, lonely ranches, or set up ambushes for small parties coming west. He had warned the traders who had done business with Marcher that if this proved true he was closing them down and putting them under arrest. A close examination of the skins Marcher had traded told his experienced eyes they had come from Crow country, which was surprising, as the Crows were known for their long hankering to keep peace with the whites. It was a thing that needed studying. He glanced at the snow again. There would be time to think on it.

Curiously, he had no name to go on, though the description should have been stamp enough. A tall gent with an eastern accent who looked like a half-breed and handled a hatchet as though he were born with it in his hand. Fitted a renegade right enough.

Moving along the street, his shoulder against the wind, he soon found the town sheriff, a cuss as short and fat as he was unsociable, in a nearby bar. The sheriff quickly finished his drink and swore as he saw the tall man approaching him, slapping his hat slowly, knocking snow from its brim.

"Bastard has been gone for a spell now, Peters," he had shouted, barely concealing his false geniality. "Better forget him."

The marshal, looking around him, quietly ignored this unsolicited advice. He stood a head and a half above the sheriff, grinning speculatively to himself before finally saying, " 'Pears he headed north."

"Most folks calculate sech to be the case."

The bartender was beside them filling the sheriff's glass. The marshal signaled his refusal of a drink as he shifted the tobacco wad again. "Anybody come down thataway about that time?"

"Don't rightly recollect," muttered the sheriff, his interest openly waning. He was really looking for a poker game to open up. The sharks usually let him win a few dollars to keep him safely neutral when quarrelsome greenhorns lost their stake.

The bartender, still within hearing distance, muttered meaningfully, "I sure enough recollect one!"

The sheriff gave him an indifferent look. "How so?"

"That whiskey drummer, Zeke, rolled in here a few days after that gent disappeared. Seemed fine till I told him a tall breedlike hombre with a hatchet had left four souls safer from sin than Gabriel ever was."

"That all?" piped the sheriff, struggling to show a trace of interest.

"You can say 'That all?' if you like," continued the bartender, spreading his hands on the bar and leaning toward them, "but damn if he didn't turn whiter than my old lady's Sunday drawers right as I was a-tellin' him, and downed a half bottle of that parrot piss he peddles before he could steady himself out the door. Damnest thing you ever saw."

"Zeke? Zeke, you say?" asked the marshal. "He still in town?"

The marshal came upon Zeke sitting in a combination brothel and bar, his hand under the dress of a young whore wearing enough makeup to shame a circus queen. The marshal placed his hat on the table and sat down.

"What-ya-want?" snarled Zeke, withdrawing his hand from under the skirt but forming it into a fist at the same time. He stank of liquor.

"Oh, might be just a few questions."

Zeke came forward in his chair, his unshaven face coming closer to Peters. The girl put her hand up to her hair nervously, instinctively alarmed by this dour stranger. "Who the hell do you think you are, bustin' into a man's party?" Zeke muttered thickly.

"U.S. marshal."

The girl was suddenly gone. Zeke settled back slowly, his eyes trying to clear. "Didn't do nothin'! Nothin'! God damn it, nothin'!"

"Somebody say you did?"

"Well, what the hell . . . ?"

"Heard tell you came down the north road with a parcel of whiskey a while back."

"Sure as hell did, 'pears to me a man's got rights . . ."

"Did you run across a hatchet-toting gent headin' t'other way?"

Zeke stared at him blankly for a moment, then something wary came alive in his eyes. "Don't likely recollect."

The marshal's great hand closed on his arm like a steel manacle. "Time to go, Zeke."

"Go? Where?"

"Courthouse."

"Courthouse! What in hell's name for?" Zeke was suddenly desperately struggling back to sobriety.

"Put you under oath."

"Courthouse! Oaths!" Zeke vainly tried to free his arm. "You crazy or somethin', what in shit's name for?"

"Oaths seem to help a man's memory, 'specially when he finds out lying to a federal marshal is a criminal offense."

The drunken flush left Zeke's face. "Hell's fire, Marshal, you don't need no courts, oaths and sech for me. I'm a man what's got respect for law . . . ask anyone . . . turn my own mother in be she only a flea's turd out of line."

The marshal looked at him quietly for a moment. He knew Zeke would have to be sobered up before any oath would be legal. Besides, it was clear Zeke was ready to talk. "I ain't asking this again, savvy?"

Zeke nodded with a willingness that amounted to pleading.

"Did you see the gent I mentioned?"

"Right as rain, I did."

"Talk to him?"

"Not a heap. Mean-lookin' critter. Short on jawin' but bought himself a surefired parcel of whiskey."

"Whiskey?" repeated the marshal.

"Sure enough. Needed a second mount to haul it. Paid Denver prices to boot."

The marshal knew now the man he was looking for had headed

north. Had he been going east he could have bought the whiskey cheaper as he drew near the settlements.

Whiskey was a powerful negotiating agent for most hostile tribes. Many braves became addicted to it almost from the first sip. But again, the Crows kept liquor out of their camps better than most. Well, he had time to ponder this growing puzzle. The blizzard was taking hold outside, rising like an angry giant, swinging signs and rattling windows and doors till its reign was complete.

Marshal Peters rose slowly, reaching for his hat.

Zeke seemed relieved but said as though he was desperate for assurance, "Everythin' set a'right now, eh, Marshal?"

The marshal drew the collar of his coat up as he prepared to leave. So deep in thought was he that he never heard Zeke's last urgent squeal. "If'n you catch up with that critter, Marshal, would be a mortal favor to me if'n you didn't mention my name."

As night fell, Marcher knew he was traveling almost blindly and that he and his mount were exhausted, needing food and rest. The wind, laced with a cold that came like a knife against his skin, seemed the greater enemy, sapping his and his mount's strength as they struggled against it. By some fateful luck the pony had once run wild as a colt in this country and instinctively kept to the western slopes, where the wind and the swirl of growing drifts were lowest. But it was not enough. Marcher felt a branch whisk by his face and knew he was next to a stand of trees. He dismounted and backed the pony into them, snow falling on them in soft thuds almost totally muffled by the high screeching of the wind. In time he backed against a huge hummock and crouched down, wondering what Indians would do in such a fix. Then it came to him. With his hatchet he dug into the base of the hummock till he had opened a notch big enough for him and his horse's head to escape the wind. He had food for himself, having eaten very little on his trip out, but he knew now it was food for the pony that would spell his only hope for salvation. No horse could fight this weather long without food. He kept digging until he reached the foot of the mound, where he began to uncover clumps of old dead grass. He loosened some and held them up to the pony's mouth. The horse nibbled for a moment and then with a whinny took it all. Encouraged, Marcher dug for more. His own exhaustion in time caught up with him and he stopped. From his saddlebag he took some beef jerky so brittle from the cold that he had to warm and soften it in his mouth before chewing. By now the pony was kicking the snow away with its hoofs and munching the dead grass down to its roots. Marcher, his limbs like lead, would have liked to sleep but he knew sleep was the first comforting claw of death to a weary man caught in a snowstorm.

He patted the pony's quivering flank, then, feeling a deadness creeping into his fingers and feet, stood up and stomped the ground, clapping his hands, his eyes peering into a white swirling darkness commanded by a sirenlike wind above that cried its warning to the helpless land below that death was afoot.

In the Crow camp Black Feather huddled over his remaining jug of whiskey and listened to the snow-laden wind batter the skins of his lodge. He knew Yellow Hatchet was out there somewhere, probably lost and awaiting death. If Yellow Hatchet did not return soon there was little to stop Black Feather from taking what he had for so long wanted. The slim, sensuous figure of White Bead swam before his eyes and he slugged again at the jug.

The other Crows in camp, aware of his whiskey ways and with that curious tribal prescience sensing some deeper evil, had been treating him with contempt, even turning their faces the other way when he passed, but that did not bother him. He did not intend to stay once he had his way with White Bead. But there was one presence that did occupy him from time to time with anxious thoughts. White River had been watching him lately. It was not a constant thing, but it was there for the flesh to feel. This one he knew to be a dangerous man, and one whose lodge White Bead visited often.

But Black Feather was watching too. He had noticed that White Bead went to her own lodge at night and that White River stayed with his squaw, Blue Lodge, rarely emerging until dawn. It was now an hour after dawn and he could see no tracks around White River's lodge. It was well. If the storm continued and Yellow Hatchet had not returned by night, Black Feather was ready.

When dawn came, the storm seemed to let up, but Marcher knew it was far from over. Blizzards did that from time to time. With the coming of light his mount and he were moving again, but the snow was deep and most of the time he walked holding onto the saddlehorn as the pony dragged him along. He had his collar up and tied about his face, but the icy wind still entered his nostrils and lungs like a sharp icicle.

The storm actually lifted enough for him to catch a vague look at the grayish eastern slopes, and now his familiarity with the country played a vital card. He pulled his horse's head further to the west, which meant turning more directly into the wind, but when after an hour or two he felt the ground rising to his right he knew his chances of reaching camp had brightened.

Yet it was a long way and the cold was bitter beyond belief. The little Indian pony put its head down and did its best and Marcher held on, trying not to notice the thickening whiteness growing rapidly again to the west.

Blue Lodge watched White River across the fire, her eyes down but her mind on him. "You think of her?" she said shyly.

"Hard not to." He looked up from the fire abruptly. With his mind deep in reverie, incredibly he thought she was speaking of Lydia but then grasped it was White Bead she meant. She had noticed his protective looks at Marcher's woman.

"Will her man come back?"

"No way to rightly tell." Then, getting the full impact of her concern, he added, "Blue Lodge is plenty enough squaw for White River."

Still watching the fire she smiled briefly. "Black Feather will soon leave, the Absarokee have turned their faces away from him—do not bring trouble."

He looked at her, realizing she had missed nothing. Strange how squaws said so little but kept a close watch on their men, sometimes even seeming to read their thoughts. "Trouble ain't hardly a fittin' word for things that need doin'," he muttered.

With that they sat silently, listening to the relentless howl of the wind overhead. Finally they took to their robes, the fire slowly dying, leaving only a red eye in the night.

Marcher knew his pony was dying; the daylong struggle had been too great. He had held on to the lee side of the saddle for hours, while the pony pushed ahead. Twice he had tried to dig through the snow for dead grass, but both times he had reached only rock or barren earth. It was growing dark again and he had hoped to reach camp by then, but it was clear now that the wind had been driving them south and they were lost. He had finished the beef jerky and then found the elk frozen solid. He chopped bits of it with his hatchet and held them in his mouth till they thawed, but his body was iron cold and he was moving more clumsily with every effort.

They stopped at the foot of a great outcropping of rock and, finding there some protection from the driving wind, tried to rest. But it was not possible. Rest would only lead to a slow paralysis of the body and finally death. Even as he thought this he found himself almost helplessly going to sleep and had to shake himself vigorously, realizing how close he had come to the thin line between living and dead in this frigid whiteness. It was very dark now, had been for some time. The pony, quivering with exhaustion, held its head down. Marcher knew that a man lost in a blizzard is like a man lost in an icy nightmare, only there's no awakening and he knew it. Indians in a similar fix would often kill a dying or even a surviving animal, cut open its belly, and dig their hands and arms in it for some temporary warmth. He could not bring himself to do this to the gallant pony as long as it lived . . . but the cold was beyond enduring and in his mind he knew the moment it died . . .

They started moving again, Marcher now staying at the pony's head trying to keep it from stopping, floundering, dying. He hoped it would last till dawn; then he would make one last effort on his own. But it was not to be. After a torturous hour the pony sank down. Marcher looked at it knowing his fate would probably be the same. It was time to take what little warmth was left in the dying animal. Slowly he drew his knife and came around to the now protruding belly of the sprawling animal. He closed his eyes, struggling to remember it was only an animal and inches from death. But nothing could stop a distant nagging in his mind that he would have made a poor Indian. His grip tightened on the knife but suddenly the pony was struggling to its feet again. It stood bracing itself unsteadily, its head going slowly upward, its nostrils to the wind.

Then it began to move, almost staggering into the wind. Dazed, Marcher followed it. There was something ghostlike in this procession, a man following a horse in a howling storm not knowing why except that the horse was fighting against its own death and perhaps his. Marcher had no way of knowing the pony had picked up the scent of the camp, the faint smell of cooked meat and grease still drifting from the lodge tops, the gamy smell of other ponies gathered behind their wind screens, nibbling long strips of cottonwood bark cut and left for them. Marcher did not know the pony he had almost slain was now about to give him back his life.

• • •

Black Feather waited until the camp had been dark and quiet for some time. If there were any sounds the storm had smothered them. It was well. He saw the storm as a strange ally, one that would make his approach difficult to detect and would then quickly cover his tracks when he left. He had two mounts ready, one carrying provisions, the other his gun and bow. He took only his knife with him as he stepped from his lodge. He kept a blanket around his head so that he could not be recognized in any chance encounter. It would not seem strange to see a blanket-wrapped brave in this storm. There was nothing to fear. Yellow Hatchet was dead. No white could have survived such a blizzard in this land. They would find his bones scattered by scavengers in the spring. As he came to White Bead's lodge, he paused a moment to peer toward White River's. He saw nothing.

The pounding of the wind against the lodge skins concealed his movements as he cut through the length of sinew that tied the lodge flaps together and slipped inside. The fire was very low, but he could see the soft mound in the robes that he knew would be White Bead. In two bounds he was on her, pulling away her robe, pinning her on her back, her eyes blinking open in the near darkness to see the leer of his menacing face above her and feel the freezing edge of a knife at her throat.

As Marcher struggled behind the swaying, stumbling pony he began to sense a hideous delirium rising about him. He began to feel the pony knew he was bringing it its death and was trying a fruitless escape. As he stopped to gasp for breath the faint musk of burned wood and grease-scented smoke assailed his nostrils. Camp! By God he had found the camp! He started forward with renewed strength knowing now what was miraculously keeping the pony going. Within minutes he stumbled into a snow-laden rack that had been used for drying skins. He shouted but he found his voice was hoarse and almost inaudible against the wind. He had lost track of the pony but now he could see lodges, their dark conical shapes, blown free of snow, standing out against the whiteness of the night. Within moments he had determined which one was his. White Bead would be waiting. White Bead would bring the warmth to restore him to life. "White Bead, I'm coming," he half sobbed to himself. "White Bead, I'm back!"

• • •

White Bead had to breathe in his stale whiskey breath as she stared into the wild, lustful face inches from hers. His hands began to move down her body. Above her head within arm's length lay her skinning knife, but in her desperation she made the fatal mistake of letting her eyes flick in its direction and immediately the free hand left her body, grabbed for the knife and threw it beyond reach.

She lay pinned down like a trapped animal, Black Feather clearly enjoying his power over her. Now the hand was back at her body pulling down her slim dress. First his rough fingers felt her breasts, which were beginning to swell with her pregnancy. He made some animal-like sounds which told her his lust was increasing, then the hand went lower feeling her belly. Its roundness made him grunt. "So White Bead carries the calf of the dead Yellow Hatchet." She could not control a tight squeal of disgust. Black Feather was the first to know she was with child. If anything, it seemed to excite him more. Now his hand was between her legs and he was preparing to mount her, the knife still at her throat. She could not keep him from forcing her legs open.

How it happened was almost impossible to recall, but a bulky white form in a staggering lunge came through the lodge flaps. "White Bead," it cried hoarsely. Black Feather was swift to his feet, his knife in his hand. White Bead, sensing rather than knowing it was Marcher, screamed, "Look out—he will kill!"

Marcher opened his eyes and saw a form coming at him with a knife. He had only one advantage, low as the fire was in the lodge. Coming in from the night he was able to see better than the other. Yet it was instinct that saved him. His pistol was under his tightly bound coat, his rifle still with the pony, but his hatchet was looped in the outer belt and came up freely in his hand. He had no time to aim; he merely swung it at the head that bore down on him. The flat side of the hatchet cracked against Black Feather's jaw, sending him down on one knee with a sickening whine. But the effort made Marcher crumple to the ground, his hatchet falling from his hand. Black Feather seemed to be choking, his jaw had been broken, and in a moment he was spitting forth mouthfuls of blood and shattered teeth. But he was slowly coming to his feet again and White Bead was scrambling for her knife. She saw Marcher helpless on the ground and Black Feather picking up his hatchet. She never would have made it. The hatchet rose in the air, but almost ghostlike, a hand from behind closed over it. Black Feather tried to turn but a knee in his back forced him down and twisted the hatchet from his hand. White Bead, a gasp still in her mouth, her knife poised in her hand, stood frozen, unaware of her nakedness, and saw the silent, determined face of White River as he pulled Black Feather across the lodge floor and dragged him out through the hanging flaps into the night.

PART TEN

WHITE RIVER

53

There is a golden day in May when spring rises full flood upon the northern plains and the lusty breath of life seems everywhere. It was on such a day that White Bead gave birth to a howling baby boy and André Marcher entered their lodge to gaze upon his newborn son.

Inevitably, in view of its heritage, there was no lack of names for the infant. His father wanted to call him Ethan, but White Bead, hearing a cricket chirping as she first smiled at the tiny form, called him Little Cricket. That name, at Marcher's urging, failed to stick. In time he was called Little Beaver, after Big Owl's lost son, but Marcher secretly assured himself this name was temporary. In the end the tot answered to the simple title of "Beaver."

Marcher had taken to sitting in the warming sun, holding the leather cradle and gazing at his child, his mind slipping only occasionally to the long siege of winter and his memories of the night he returned in the storm. It was the following morning that White River came into the lodge with Marcher's rifle and saddle. White Bead had been rubbing his body and nursing him all night.

"Pony all right?" Marcher had asked from beneath a hill of robes.

"Pony is dead," said White River noncommittally. Marcher looked away in a surprising tinge of remorse. "Way of things, I reckon," added White River noticing the bitter look. "Pony was fixin' to die had you gotten here half a day sooner. Horses are jest like that . . . keep a-goin' for a spell even after they passed mortal limits."

"Black Feather?" Marcher's mouth had hardened perceptibly as his mind focused more rapidly on the happenings of the night before.

"Reckon he'll stay clear for a while."

"Clear?! Clear?" croaked Marcher, trying to rise. "You didn't kill him? You didn't kill the bastard?"

"Killin' around camp is bad doin's . . . raises a heap more problems than it settles."

"Shit!" moaned Marcher, his body tightening and writhing beneath its layers of robes.

White Bead, hollow-eyed from her nightlong ordeal, came in with warm broth and said calmly, "Enough foolish talk. White River is right. It is not the Absarokee way."

Later he discovered Black Feather had moved away from camp and pitched his lodge secretly in the mountains to the west. He had not returned to the River Crows. There was too much shame to be borne there. Ominously, those who saw him reported his jaw had not healed properly; his face seemed lopsided, his mouth slanted. At any attempt to shift expressions his features grew grotesque. It was said he could only chew on one side of his mouth and then in visible pain, but these few encounters left little doubt as to his deranged mind. He had become vicious as a rabid dog, gripped by what seemed to be maniacal seizures, exploding from mute sullenness to raving ferocity. On two occasions young braves tripping upon his camp while hunting barely escaped with their lives. But whatever threat he held for the camp was subtly countered by the Indian belief that insanity was the touch of the spirits. And so, beset by other problems, the tribe attempted to forget him, avoiding his name as though he were already dead. But there were those who were sure they saw him standing in the dark on the outskirts of camp by night. Big Owl, as befitted a chief, sat and smoked quietly, not acknowledging the many whisperings this worrisome thing was stirring, but in his mind he knew that had he been a younger man he would have tracked this offal down and killed him. Still, as spring rose and stretched across the land, Black Feather lived on in the vast dark coil of mountains, his unseen presence hanging in people's minds like a malevolent eye watching in hiding from some distant ridge.

That winter, over their crackling fire, Blue Lodge looked warmly at her man, admiration in her eyes. He was surely in this cruel season the greatest of hunters, showing experienced braves how to trap a large herd of deer yarding up in a shallow basin of snow in a near hidden valley. He had almost single-handedly kept the camp supplied with meat which gave strength to those now fighting the new coughing disease that some said came from white traders who had lured away and then abandoned some of the tribes' many widows. Yet he was a quiet man, his voice rarely raised to serve himself. It was surely strange to see warriors with many coups stepping aside that he might pass. At times she worried whether he really cared for her or whether she would have him long, for there was a yearning in him and she knew now it was not for White Bead. Still that season she held her head proudly, for her people were murmuring that for his prowess in war and in the hunt he should be adopted into their tribe and made a chief. Even Big Owl himself nodded at the thought. White River only smiled at these tributes, telling her in half jest that just dealing with her was work enough for any man without him taking on her whole tribe. She smiled at him wistfully, for she, with her woman's senses, could read into these words far more than he suspected. Secretly she prayed that the spirits would help her hold him, but in solitude she cried bitterly, for being a woman she had no strong medicine of her own. There were nights when they sat together in silence, each faintly sensing the other's distress.

White River was not indifferent, but he was becoming restless, even uncomfortable, with the frequent praise and open gratitude of the Crows. The need for decision weighed on his mind. This year he was going to search for Lydia. This year he would find her and know if she had lived with his memory as he had hers. Often a cold sensation gripped his heart when he thought of the stretch of time he had allowed to pass, time when she might have forgotten him, sensibly realizing the years might have changed him, perhaps opened a new and fuller life for him. Every fear he had that she might be lost to him and would best be forgotten, she could well share in return. This put urgency in his face as he studied the sky.

Two things alone were keeping him from saddling up in the predawn darkness and heading south. The tribe would need one early spring hunt to leave meat enough in the camp to ward off sickness till the game appeared in plenty. And he could not shake the secret feeling that Black Feather was an evil of his own making. It was he who had driven that now half-mad Crow, with his fearfully distorted face, into the winter storm, not knowing he had hidden horses and gear ready to slip away. It was he who should have taken him out of camp and disposed of him. Big Owl and many of the Crows knew Black Feather was no threat to them if they kept their distance. It was Marcher, White Bead, and himself who could expect to be stalked and murdered if their vigilance slipped. On his many lonely hunts he had kept a sharp eye out for this crazy menace, but as was his way, he mentioned it to no one. Only Blue Lodge, whose sensitivity to him was increasing, knew her man was hunting more than game. She also began to understand why he constantly studied the sky these days, judging the weather.

Marcher, though he joined in the hunting and shared the work, had kept much to himself that spring. He was not only thinking of that remote life in Washington, which no longer seemed even real, much less important, but lately had been wondering at a recurring vision he had had of three little valleys he had glimpsed far below him while standing on the ledge that held Paul's star. It was just before the storm and there had been something unreal about that momentary vista, something that stayed with him and then came back as though it were a message that patiently waited entry into his consciousness. The message ultimately revealed itself but it left him strangely unmoved, unexcited, as though it were a trivial matter, a passage in a book he had found with small effort and read with little interest. Yet, curiously, it stayed with him, for he knew now the years of anguish, struggle, and despair were over; his long ordeal had not been in vain. However little it mattered anymore, he was certain now that at last he had found Paul's mine.

The camp was alive with suppressed excitement and a quickening bustle of activity. A small herd of buffalo had been sighted several miles to the east, grazing northward. The chosen hunters were gathering, sharpening their arrows, tightening the sinew about their bows, while squaws and intent young women were fetching their butchering knives. Everywhere young boys shouted as they brought in additional ponies to carry the meat. A great feast was a high point in an Indian's life and one was now in the making. Neighbors smiled or called words of encouragement to each other as the special buffalo ponies were brought forward to receive their painted medicine symbols or have good-luck amulets tied into their free-flowing manes.

White River knew this hunt would fill the long sparse racks with meat and he could leave. Parting words and gifts for Big Owl and Blue Lodge had long been forming in his mind, but knowing what his going would mean to Blue Lodge he thought it best to save all talk until the end. He looked for Marcher, who was strangely missing.

Big Owl and others were staying behind to guard the camp, but the braves grunted happily to see White River, that hunter among hunters, going along. None needed reminding that his repeating rifle was worth many buffalo. In their jubilation several braves insistently shouted for Big Owl's repeater as well, but he waved them away, saying the camp needed guarding too. A repeating rifle by itself could keep a marauding party at bay. Few knew that behind his words lay the shadow of Black Feather.

White River was remotely surprised by the quietude surrounding Marcher's lodge, but he called out until he heard White Bead bid him enter. "You ain't a-comin'?" he said, clearly mystified and faintly irritated by the relaxed atmosphere he found inside.

"No. Not go," said White Bead simply.

"Got other business," added Marcher, taking little Beaver in his arms.

White River unbelievingly looked around and saw their packs readied with the picks and pans tied on. He drew a hand over his mouth as though to block his words. "That God damned mine again," he muttered.

"Yes. But believe me, it's going to be different this time," responded Marcher quickly.

" 'Taint never different when it comes to gold—there be fools and dead fools—and you be smack somewhere in between, I'm thinkin'." He turned to White Bead, looking for some semblance of sanity.

Her face became expressionless. No one could have guessed what emotions had surged within her in a short time. Since the night Marcher had returned in the storm and she had rubbed his limbs with snow and nursed him back to health, he had become a different creature. With his own hatchet he had smashed the remaining jugs of whiskey. He had pushed himself, long before his health made it wise, to help take care of her, and above all he had stood proudly beside this baby that was theirs. She knew now for the first time that she had his love. There seemed nothing he would not do for her. He had promised her he would not seek revenge on Black Feather and had kept his word. Their lovemaking had been inhibited by her pregnancy, but it now had the firm, reassuring bite of desire and she felt herself wanted more and more. It made the woman in her sing. Yellow Hatchet was her man now and no matter what befell them she would be his woman. At first the dangers of the trip had appalled her, but she believed him when he said it was not the gold that he wanted but the satisfaction of knowing his quest had ended, that he had solved the mystery of Paul's mine. What finally won her over was something only a woman in love could understand. He had said if she and little Beaver did not go with him he would never go at all. It was not the way of the Absarokees for a man to talk so to his squaw, but at his words she fell into his arms and sobbed with joy. It was not a thing a proud Absarokee woman would have wanted her neighbors to see.

"We will not be long," she said defensively.

Though his eyes clouded, White River was never one to interfere with the will of others. He wanted to leave and say nothing, but the words seemed forced from his lips. "Sure you ain't forgettin' somethin'?"

"Black Feather," added Marcher, his tone now more serious but quiet, confident. "He'll think we left with your hunting party. We figure to leave tonight, follow your tracks for a while, then head north. Don't fret on it. I know this country every bit as well as that filthy bastard."

The sun was warm and the winds gusted gently as Marcher and White Bead, little Beaver on her back, made their way to the valleys that lay beyond the ridge.

There seemed no need to press their ponies as they rode across the land. Game was plentiful and it seemed good just to be alone looking at each other across their evening fire with their baby boy, who had spent his day staring up at lazy clouds making their way across a high cobalt sky.

Now, when it no longer seemed to count, Marcher somehow knew he had solved the riddle of Paul's star, for the map did not say the mine was behind the mirror but behind the star. Now, what was behind that star but those three little valleys? Besides, if he had ever stopped to think about it, gold was rarely if ever found on mountain-tops but almost always appeared in the depression of valleys, washouts, or streams.

Occasionally they thought about Sioux raiding parties but there had been rumors all winter that the whites were determinedly harassing the defiant Lakota, destroying their winter camps, burning their vital supplies, allowing hunger and cold to kill their women and children. Some chiefs, in order to survive, had allowed their people to be forced onto reservations in poor land to the south. There was little feeling the Sioux would be a serious threat anytime soon.

Finally arriving at the little valleys, they unhurriedly built a wickiup between the two to the west. Marcher leisurely panned his first stream with little luck. He was not discouraged. There was something pleasant and clean about things here, something that made a man feel he had at last found life and that it was enjoyable just to live it.

Suddenly he heard a pistol shot coming from the direction of their camp and raced back to find White Bead standing in her half dress, her face frozen with fear, her hand gripping his pistol and pointing with it to a rise in the land behind them. In moments he knew her cooking fire had attracted a large bear; its tracks, when Marcher reached them with his rifle, were immense. "Did you wound him?" he asked, his momentary panic starting to dissipate.

"No!" she looked at him in amazement, heightened by coming shock. "I did not try. Only to scare him—to bring you." White Bead continued to stare at him, her eyes painfully asking if he knew a wounded grizzly could be a death machine. A pistol against a thousand-pound bear was an insanity that made any talk pointless.

"I'll have to teach you to use the rifle and leave it with you," he said awkwardly in a hurried attempt to be comforting.

"No!" she practically screamed.

He looked at her, puzzlement visibly spreading on his face. "Would it not be best?"

She raised her hands to her face. With all his knowing he knew so little. Patiently he waited for her to speak. "What does Yellow Hatchet do if the great bear attacks him or his horse and his rifle is here? Besides, I cannot shoot. Even with the white man's medicine gun one must aim with the eye of an eagle to kill a grizzly."

He turned around, his features in open confusion, quietly studying their little camping grounds. "What then?" he asked himself as much as her.

"We go together," she answered at once. "Little Beaver and I go with you each morning and return each night. The bear has smelled our cooking things, our curing meat. It will be back."

"You think that's best?"

"Yes." She turned her back pointedly, her face tightening as she reached for little Beaver. "It is very lonely here. I have a bad feeling. You promised we do not stay long."

Waiting till she turned to him again, he nodded in silent agreement. The next day all three rose at dawn and headed for the second stream.

The increased throbbing of drums in the Crow camp soon had the people swaying and singing in rhythm, the young ones particularly, jumping and stepping up to the fire, their bodies glistening with buffalo grease, their faces alive with the long days of excitement that had just ended in a succulent, riotous feast. Ah-badt-deadt-deah had been good to his children, and though no one mentioned his name, for it was sacred, He was in the hearts of many.

Big Owl squatted contentedly before his lodge, warmed by the thought that joy had returned to his people, that the Sioux and Blackfeet seemed far away and perhaps weary of war, that game was filling the land in a spring of abundance that even in his memory could have few equals. And all this after a long, bitter winter. Ah, were not the ways of the spirits strange. He sat before his tipi with his favorite pipe and smoked, an old man feeling the mounting years in his limbs, cherishing that ancient balm of the aged, peace.

White River watched him, knowing he could not disturb these rare and rewarding moments for the old chief with talk of leaving. He waited till the pensive Blue Lodge went off to dance the women's dance, then joined Big Owl. They smoked in silence till White River nodded in the direction of Marcher's lodge, absently murmuring, " 'Pears they still be out."

Big Owl nodded his head faintly as though it were a matter too alien to his present mood to bring to words. White River sensed his resistance and let it go. But Big Owl knew and understood White River's concern, and in the end he could not forget that White River had been a long and loyal friend. The Absarokees owed him a debt beyond redeeming. After many seemingly endless moments of thought he uttered with only the slightest tinge of warning in his words, "The wolf still watches."

As the dancing and singing began to lessen and clouds cloaked the evening sky, White River went into Marcher's lodge and built a fire. The deception would not last long but might buy a little time—after all, had they not said they would need but "a little time"?

• • •

Marcher shook the pan one more time, then held it up to the sun. Three little specks glittered at him with a faint golden hue. He looked at them long and hard, then lowered the pan. His heart swelled strangely with the realization he had won. Slowly he turned and looked behind him upstream. He was near the right bank where the current seemed strongest. Back there somewhere was the mother lode. He moved several yards upstream and began to pan again. On his second try more specks glittered back at him. He sorted them out and, taking a leather pouch from his belt, dropped them in. On the bank White Bead saw him do this and motioned for his attention. He saw her, smiled, made a clear victory sign with his hand and started upstream again.

By evening he was gathering gold dust at every pan. When he came ashore his body moved like one finishing a long journey, his face fixed in a strange calm. White Bead looked at him in anticipation. "You have found the white man's medicine metal?"

He nodded.

"Then we will go. I have already fixed food. It is still light. We have time to travel."

He looked at her, his face still transfixed by some inchoate emotion. He took a moment to look into the leather pouch, its bottom now completely covered with gold dust. Then he moved toward her, his arm embracing her shoulders, his lips against her hairline. "Tomorrow," he whispered, and then, walking slowly, they fell into a strange and, for her, frightening and forbidding silence.

54

Like many old men, Big Owl often had to rise in the middle of the night to relieve himself. It was on one such occasion that he arose, his eyes still shut, from his robes. He stumbled behind his lodge and let the long stream go outward with a deep internal groan of satisfaction. Ah, such a relief from the familiar pain in the lower belly. If only all pain could be so relieved. By now his eyes were open and he looked up at the stars, seeing the familiar ones far to the west. It was only an hour or two till dawn. Moving back to his lodge, his breathing lighter now, his eye caught a furtive movement across the camp circle. A figure was emerging from Marcher's lodge. So they were back. But no, it was not Marcher he saw nor White Bead. The furtive figure moved silently along the curving line of sleeping lodges and the old chief's eyes peered into the darkness, his heart quickening and now fully awake, knowing suddenly it was Black Feather. Hurrying his step he brushed through his own lodge flap and rushed toward his rifle. He, Big Owl, would put an end to this evil for all time. He would be killing an Absarokee in camp, but in the darkness the figure could easily be mistaken for a Sioux scout. It was a rendering of things the tribe would be eager to accept. Yet it took awkward moments before he grasped the rifle in the darkness, rammed a cartridge home, and emerged again into the night. The camp circle was quiet now, empty. The furtive figure had disappeared. He stood there for many minutes slowly grasping what now must be done, the lines about his mouth hardening. It was pointless to stand there wishing against the cruel way of matters, knowing the spirits were watching, knowing he was a chief and a chief must protect his people from every danger that threatened them.

Lowering the gun, he settled on the ground to think, to remember that he, Big Owl, had led Marcher to the ridge where he had found that strange star. This thing he had done for the rifle that now lay across his lap. Ah, is it not the quest for power that destroys men! He for the rifle, Marcher for the gold. Time drifted by until a whisper of crimson touched the eastern sky. Only then did he rise and make his way to White River's lodge. White River and Blue Lodge both sat up as he announced himself in a tone that carried its own apology. "The wolf has cast his shadow upon the lair," he said quietly. "He has found it empty. Only the spirits know now what his sharp nose will find in the wind."

With that he pulled his robe close about him and quietly left.

Blue Lodge, her face still in the morning shadows, watched White River hurriedly packing his mount. "Is Yellow Hatchet not a strong enough warrior to handle but a single enemy?"

"Mebbe," he mumbled, his mind so occupied he was only half listening.

She grasped her own body, struggling with words that lay like a cold lump in her chest. "Then why must this badness among others bring trouble to our lodge?"

White River checked his guns, fixed the rifle in the saddle and climbed aboard. "There's a woman and a young 'un out there," he said, now more aware of the growing anguish in her voice. " 'Taint many critters can poke around for gold, watch their brood, and keep an eye out for trouble all t'once."

She looked at him, the desperation that was claiming her bringing a feverish brightness to her eyes. "I am with child," she gasped, her gaze falling to the ground as though the council had pronounced a death sentence on her.

He gazed back at her in the young dawn, hearing and yet not hearing her words. Somewhere in his mind he knew what he had heard had meanings he could not measure at the moment; somewhere in his mind he knew whatever it presaged was impossible to deal with now. Now he must hurry. Now he needed the pound of hoofs beneath him, the sweep of morning wind against his face. Still staring at her as he turned his mount to go, he murmured in a near whisper, "Reckon I'll be gettin' back soon as I kin." His voice was low but unexpectedly soft, and Blue Lodge looked up slowly to watch him galloping at full speed into the tall dark pines that rose beyond the camp.

White River followed the hunting party's tracks east, staying on the north side until he came upon the weathered tracks of two ponies turning northward and then quickly brought his mount around to follow them.

He was relieved as the sun rose in the sky to find no fresh tracks of a single pony joining them. Damn these two! He could tell as he covered the ground, pushing his mount as hard as he dared, that they had moved leisurely. In mid-afternoon he came upon their first campsite. Shaking his head, he pressed on. It was almost dark when he came to a stream where they had made their second camp, and here he knew he must rest his pony, warm some coffee, and get some grub before full darkness gave the cooking fire away.

It was hard and now even pointless to try and track at night. The hard day's ride had left his body demanding the rest that could only come from sleep. He tethered his horse in a swale and, rolling in his blanket, lay down beside it. A horse was a better sentinel than most people ever gave thought to. They had senses beyond his and he had learned to use them. With the hot food in his stomach and his hard body against the ground he started to think about Blue Lodge, but his mind seemed unready to dwell on her and he fell off into a deep slumber that lasted until just before dawn.

He came awake with a strange feeling something was wrong. His mount was standing still, looking southward, occasionally neighing and shaking its head. He rose with a stealth that only the frequent presence of death can breed in a man. Silently and staying close to the lush grass, he crawled to the ridge of the swale. He peered for long moments, his eyes adjusting to the darkness, but saw nothing. Yet there he remained, mute, motionless, until light from the east lifted the mantle of darkness from the reaches beyond. Nothing. The rolling terrain lay in its great gray emptiness without even a wisp of wind to play across the grassy mounds. He looked back at his mount. It was quietly relaxed now, its head down, softly munching grass. Perhaps it had caught the faint scent of a mountain lion or even a hunting wolf. They were surely out there somewhere. Perhaps he was making too much of a common enough alertness shown by all hoofed animals in the wild, yet something kept nagging at him, and indifferent as he tried to be about this edgy feeling, it would not settle down.

He left at once and rode hard for an hour before he stopped to eat. The bothersome feeling, one of distant unease, had not yet been shaken off. Even in the wilderness certain things had to fit. Logic and even cold reasoning were no help. The fitting took place in the deep of a man and he could feel it without knowing why. Finally, giving in to it, he led his pony back into a deep swale and then cautiously positioned himself where he could watch his back trail without exposing himself. Over an hour went by. He had almost given up, for the sun was steadily mounting the sky and time was passing. But then suddenly he saw it. It was only a black speck, but it appeared, then disappeared and then after long moments appeared again.

Now that quietly nagging feeling burst into a realization that stiffened his body. What a fool he had been! If Big Owl's aging eyes saw Black Feather in the darkness, surely Black Feather saw the startled chief. That devil knew someone would quickly ride out to warn Marcher and all he had to do was lie and wait. The rider sent to carry the warning would lead him to them. Marcher's ruse would have worked. White River was the one who betrayed their trail. And now White River had to face the chilling knowledge that he himself had had a close call. Luckily he had ridden hard the day before and Black Feather had had to stay well back to keep from being seen. But now that Black Feather had Marcher's tracks to follow, he no longer needed guides. Perhaps he had tried to pass White River in the darkness, but White River's mount smelled the pony Black Feather was likely leading by hand, since to track in the darkness a man had to travel on foot, staying close to the ground. White River's pony's neighing had alerted Black Feather, who was probably holding his own mount's muzzle to conceal his approach. Another thought now darkened his mind. Black Feather could well have passed him had he known where his camp was simply by swinging wide downwind and picking up the trail beyond. No, Black Feather knew he could not afford to leave a ready gun behind him, not if, when he found Marcher and White Bead, his approach required waiting and stealth. Besides, leaving him behind meant that White River would soon find Black Feather's own tracks pursuing the others and ride all out to overtake him. No, Black Feather had no choice. He had meant to kill him, and had White River slept a minute or two longer his body could well now be torn apart by scavengers, with the vermin eagerly awaiting their turn. Strangely and without any reason for it, the face of Blue Lodge flashed before his eyes. He turned and rolled on his back, rubbing his stomach, his eyes slowly growing harder, his jaw firming up to bring dark lines to his face. Whatever the future held, and now somehow he knew it held the unknown, Black Feather was surely not one to get careless around. He would have needed the senses of a demon to know White River had awakened in the dark and was ready that dawning.

He decided for the moment it would be wisdom to move on. This was not a place to do what he knew must be done. The wilderness had its own harsh rules of survival. Ahead he could see he was entering a valley. It was the same valley in which Coyote-Singing had followed Marcher's tracks so many worlds ago.

White Bead stared at Marcher across the fading coals of the fire. He managed to avoid her eyes, but her words, low as they were, assailed his ears. "The white man's medicine metal is an evil spirit in the mind of Yellow Hatchet."

"Another day will not matter."

"Those were your foolish words of yesterday."

Marcher looked down at the leather pouch. It was more than half full already. He'd begun to find nuggets, some resembling the one Paul had bound to the crucifix. He looked upward, his face revealing that he himself was partly mystified by his actions. The night wind overhead whispered like some lonely siren to the distant stars, making Marcher wonder how he came to this time, this place, this turning in his life. Gold he reckoned was surely the subtlest and most incomprehensible of drugs to distort the mind of man. "Tomorrow the leather pouch will be filled," he said, as though these words would ensure conviction. "We will go. It is a promise."

White Bead, opening her deerskin blouse and hugging her infant, gave it one of her breasts. "Let Yellow Hatchet remember his words. There is great danger here. My heart beats with every cracking of a twig. Spirits have come to me in the night, one had the face of Black Feather. This is a place of death. If Yellow Hatchet does not leave tomorrow White Bead and little Beaver must go without him."

He found the spot he was quietly looking for when the slope on the right of the valley rose swiftly and a split at its base left some boulders jutting out onto the valley floor. Their tracks led by the outside point of the boulders and he rode over them. It would not do to have Black Feather see his own tracks swing away. But after a few hundred yards he turned into the cut and rode quickly back to the protruding boulders. He tethered his pony as far from the point as he could, and taking his rifle, slipped back, balancing himself between the first two immense rocks. He knew it would not be long. Black Feather would surely try to reach him before he reached Marcher, and now, as the valley twisted about he could draw much closer without being seen.

As White River waited, the ancient struggle of man with his conscience began to burden him, trouble his thinking, making him wary of even sensible reasoning. Common sense shouted he should kill this renegade whose warped mind was bent on murder, kill him as any animal would kill another to preserve its own life. But he was not an animal, he was a man, and a man had to live with himself and hold his head up among other men. White River had killed his share of men, this he knew, but he had never sunk to murder. It was not that anybody would know or care, but as he reckoned things his knowing was all that mattered.

The soft clicking of pony hoofs soon reached his ears and he leveled his rifle, knowing there was a moment coming upon him from which there would be no retreat. He tightened his stomach, deciding there was only one way to play his hand. He waited until Black Feather had passed him before he called out in Absarokee, "Black Feather will go no farther!"

The Indian stopped and turned his pony slowly, staring at White River, his broken face hideous even under the dark war paint he had smeared upon it. No words were spoken until Black Feather, seeming to sum up this new and dangerous turning, finally decided White River's rifle for the moment presented him with impossible odds. "I hunt in the land of my fathers," he said sullenly, spittle spraying from his mouth. "Does the white hunter, who pretends to be a friend to the Absarokees, say Black Feather cannot do this?"

White River regarded him resignedly, knowing any words would be pointless. "The white hunter says Black Feather will soon join his fathers if he does not find another stretch to hunt." He pointed with his rifle across the valley. "Ride to that slope," he said, his breath shortening. "Then turn and keep going south. His medicine spirit must tell Black Feather that great wisdom lies in these words."

The Indian gazed across the valley. Then after a long moment his mount began to move, but White River saw the horse was coming closer to him as it made its turn. He was not surprised. Black Feather had made his decision and both now knew there was no turning back. As the pony completed its turn and Black Feather's back was toward him, White River suddenly saw the mount spin and start toward him, its hoofs digging hard into the ground for speed. Still he had been more than ready, in truth even expecting it, and the rifle flashed to his shoulder. Although Black Feather was hunched behind his horse's head, a tomahawk at the ready, White River had no trouble smashing his kneecap and tumbling him off his mount. Black Feather sprawled on the ground with a scream of pain but came up quickly on his other knee, his tomahawk already back, his arm ready to throw. White River's second shot took him between the eyes and his body was flung backward awkwardly like a wooden doll accidentally knocked aside.

He buried Black Feather in a shallow grave, not only the body but the saddle and the bridle, then covered the grave with a wide blanket of rocks. With a slap on its flank, he turned the Indian pony loose. It would soon find and join up with one of the many bands of mustangs that ran wild in these parts.

By the time he was back across the valley, the day was fast disappearing. After a sprint over their recovered tracks he found himself climbing a frontal slope that ran up until it broke and leveled back into a small valley. A sudden rustling in the underbrush made him look up abruptly and loosen his rifle. Half believing his ordeal with Black Feather was making him jumpy, he watched as two little bear cubs came out on a nearby rise and sniffed the wind. At once he put the rifle back in its saddle scabbard and pushed his mount forward. Somewhere close he knew there would be a female grizzly, probably in a bad mood, and he was not interested in tangling with her now. Sow grizzlies were especially dangerous this time of year, and an experienced hunter left them alone. Killing them—at best no job for greenhorns—was hardly the answer, for their cubs would not survive and the number of bears for coming years would be lessened that much. No, wild game would keep on supplying a man with life-giving meat once he got it through his gizzard there was a time to let animals be.

It was almost dark when he crossed the stream in the middle of the valley and ascended the other side, but there he sighted some faint glowing coals and sensed at last he had found Marcher's and White Bead's camp.

His greeting was a mixture of open surprise and almost tangible warmth, particularly from White Bead, whose eyes glowed as she saw him approaching her in the faint light. The two had already eaten, but immediately she was busy at the fire preparing him warm food. Within minutes they had settled down to talk.

"Jesus—what brings you way the hell out here?" began Marcher, his tone friendly but slightly anxious as though he was chary of his guest's answer.

"Gold," returned White River dryly. "Suddenly got an itch for it in mah palm." But his tone belied his words and the inflection was not wasted on White Bead.

"You bring warning? There is trouble?" she asked, the nervous restraint in her voice clear to the ear.

"Somethin' like that," he mumbled between gulps of coffee that was helping to wash down the iron-hard bread and slices of venison he had been served. "Figured you two would be back afore this."

"We go tomorrow," snapped White Bead, throwing a quick, defiant glance at Marcher. White River lowered his eyes to the fire. He had his first hint of something strained between them. Yet the air smacked of Marcher's success.

"So you found it, eh?" White River said, his eyes taking command of Marcher's.

"Gold!" said Marcher as though the word carried some occult power that reduced all other matters in importance. "Gold, nuggets sitting on the ground over yonder, waiting like friendly genies to be picked up."

"About what I figured," responded White River, savoring the last of his coffee and acting as though Marcher's words demanded little else in response.

"You could be rich, White River. A few days here . . . why, you could buy yourself a trading fort."

White River did not miss White Bead's irritation at these words. Her gaze turned heavily upon Marcher, and White River, knowing if an angry scene were to be avoided he must speak before she did, said, "Don't have any cravin' to be rich."

"Why?" exploded Marcher.

"Might make me forget how to take care of myself. Money a man ain't worked for sooner or later makes him look smaller."

"Well, Christ! I worked hard enough to find this damn mine."

"Then the gold's yours. Figure you know better how to handle it than me."

White Bead could not be silenced any longer. "Tomorrow we must go! We were to be but a short time. I made medicine to the spirits to protect us for a short time. But it has been many days now and the spirits are angry."

There was a long silence. Marcher looked into the already reddening coals. Something had happened to him, but he was helpless to decipher it. Surely he had known a deep and satisfying contentment before he found the gold. Surely this arcane metal placed a strange and persistent claim on his senses, devoured his will, made a mockery of his resolve. And there was White River, sitting across the fire from him, untouched by the fatal magnetism it seemed to hold for other men, indifferent to its promises of power, a man who felt himself graced if he could tackle the toils of a freighting business but who refused to carry the burden of riches his instincts told him would in no way enrich his life.

"We will go," he said at last. Then, remembering he had some unexplainable commitment to fill the pouch, a thing he could do now in a few hours, he added lamely, "We leave at noon."

55

Marcher was up at first light, having slept very little, but he found White Bead already starting a fire. She made him coffee while he pulled his few familiar mining tools together. In fact, he needed little more now than his pick. After watching him make his way to the stream, she began stripping things from the camp. He had told her to get ready to leave, he would not be long. Her answer was as unhesitating as it was unvarnished. "White Bead has long been ready!"

White River, awake at their first stirrings, had kept to his blanket idly studying his hosts. When Marcher left, he rose and came to the fire. White Bead smiled at his long form coming toward her in the young dawn and turned to make him breakfast. They did not speak much but they were comfortable together. In spite of this, the question that had troubled her eyes since White River's arrival finally made its way to her lips. "What brings White River to us? There is danger, no?"

He picked up a twig and worked it between his teeth. "Always danger when folks go traipsin' around lonely country like this."

"Black Feather?" Her eyes were glued to his. "You have seen him?"

He shifted his body as he bit down hard on the twig. "Not lately."

"But he will come. He will seek for us. No?"

" 'Taint likely, I'm thinkin'," he said evenly as he rose. Wanting the subject changed and knowing the way of women, he looked with sudden interest toward the wickiup. "Let's see that young 'un of yours."

White Bead rose and moved quickly to the wickiup, returning, her face beaming, with little Beaver. The baby was asleep. White River had to draw in his breath as he looked at the child. It did not resemble any Indian papoose he had ever laid eyes on. White Bead's half blood and Marcher's full blood had produced a baby that could pass for pure white in any settlement in the east. Its smooth, creamy cheeks were touched with a faint rosy hue, and its eyes, when it suddenly awoke with a gurgle, were blue as a June sky. As White Bead rocked it gently, a few strands of bright corn-colored hair were visible on its head.

"Sure is a right handsome little fellow," he half whispered, his mind experiencing a strange turning. "Probably he'll be pretty lookin' like his ma and have a heap more savvy than his pa."

White Bead, like women the world over, glowed at his words, her eyes drinking in this miracle she had brought to life. Soon she had her breast out to feed him and with that White River turned away, going to his mount, bringing it closer to the camp, preparing to leave.

"White River will not travel with us?" She looked up at him, betraying a surprise that could not conceal its bite of disappointment.

"Reckon not. Figure I best be moseyin' along." White River had been thinking ahead. If he traveled with them, likely they would be backtracking on themselves. His own pony's hoof marks they would expect and ignore but Black Feather's would raise questions, questions he had no hankering at the moment to answer. No, better he travel alone. Back in camp, there would be time to think of answers. Besides, there was Blue Lodge. He could no longer avoid thinking of her and what her desperate revelation meant. Likely she'd be anxiously watching the trails for him, or listening by night for the sound of hoofbeats approaching her lodge.

But White Bead held him as long as she could, weaving together questions about the hunt, the feast that followed it, the doings of the camp, the health of Blue Lodge. His drawled answers were brief enough to betray a growing impatience which finally became too awkward for her to ignore. Aware that the sun was now well up in the sky, he mounted his pony and looked once again at the figure of Marcher down near the stream, saying, "Might be best in the end . . . you know, your comin' thisaway . . . maybe now that critter will stay put."

He left sensing the gold lying in Marcher's pouch might be only the beginning of their troubles, and as he rode his eyes narrowed slowly. He was still summing up the parting look in White Bead's eyes, his instincts nudging him, telling him finally that she knew it too.

He hadn't traveled very far before he heard a great uproar coming from the tall stretch of brush that covered the slopes to his right. His experienced ears warned him unhesitatingly it was grizzlies, big ones, fighting among themselves. His horse began to shy and only a firm and ready hand on the reins kept it from bolting. He swung further to his left, deciding to give the area a wide berth. This was bear country, sure enough. A fellow on foot would need a sharp eye and a fast gun, not to mention the devil's own luck, to keep his bones from being smashed to kindling by these dangerous carnivores. He lost some time circling about, but once back on the trail of his own tracks, he stopped. Perhaps he should go back and warn Marcher and White Bead. But was there really any need? Marcher had his rifle and was a dead shot. White Bead had been born to this land and had the instincts that spelled survival. Taking a little hitch in the saddle, he decided he was fussing too much. Surely they could take care of themselves. He glanced once more toward the ridge that rose between himself and the valley that held their camp, then, pulling the rim of his hat down against the glare of the strengthening sun, he started clucking gently to his horse and continued on.

The huge bear White Bead had seen near their camp a few days before was an eleven-hundred-pound boar whose hunt for food in this season was a frantic daylong activity. It had been the smell of gunpowder from her pistol shot that turned it away. Somewhere in its past that smell had become one with danger. Almost effortlessly it had rolled over an enormous rotting log and was now licking up fat white grubs with a speed that would have surprised those looking only at its massive, hunkering body. It was only this morning that this bear, standing quietly in the brush, managed to catch sight of a small bear cub, tumbling along a short distance away. The wind was coming from its direction so there was little likelihood that the cub's sow, which the bear's instinct told it would be close by, would pick up his scent and growl in alarm. This sow had two cubs and was trailing behind them leisurely, listening to their yips and squeals as she growled and huffed occasionally to bring them closer to her. But life and death in the wild are often decided by split seconds, and in the moment the wary sow turned her head to sniff the wind behind her, one of her cubs struggled and tumbled its way forward to its death. The on-rushing boar was too swift for the cub. It died with a high, aborted squeal, its tiny skull smashed, its little ribcage collapsed and its small body held firmly between the boar's jaws.

The big sow, breaking into a savage roar, charged with incredible fury at the attacker, her more than eight hundred pounds coming at him full speed. The boar dropped the cub and met her head on, his jaws set to grip her outthrust neck. She swerved and, hammering a macelike claw against his snout, drove him back. But he came on again, the taste of the cub's blood in his mouth igniting his own fury. Finally his greater weight forced her away from the cub's body. But she was not finished, she came at him again and again in desperate repetitions, ripping one of his ears, leaving an open cut across his shoulder. But her other cub had wandered away in another direction, and suddenly two coyotes appeared in the brush and began circling it, their yellow eyes measuring it for a quick kill. They could hear the ruckus beyond and knew it for what it was. The cub yipped in primitive panic, and the mother's ears, in spite of the titanic struggle, picked it up. Instinct told her the cub beneath the boar was already dead. She swung around and raced like a driven demon to the other. The coyotes could only bolt, giving up their hope of an easy meal, but even so her swiftness was such that one was not quite agile enough and her claws caught its hind quarters as it jumped aside, breaking its back.

After licking her cub and finding it still whole and healthy—her memory of the other cub was already fading—the heaving sow settled down to devour the coyote, but her mood was still one of restless agitation and dangerous ill temper. She would be that way, on the edge of fury, for several hours.

• • •

Marcher had finished sooner than he had expected, a growing field of nuggets beginning to appear as soon as he worked his pick. Before three hours had gone by the pouch was filled. He knew it held a small fortune. Strangely, his find was not filling him with elation, the tingle of victory, the intense feeling of power and satisfaction it had so long promised. White River's words still hung in his mind like a burden he was helpless to put down. The quietude and peace he had known before he found the gold were fragmented now. He knew White Bead scorned him for his weak attempts to conceal his avarice at the first sight of gold.

Perhaps it was the depression claiming him, but coming up to the campsite now he found a curious stillness in the air, as though the surrounding hills were holding their breath. The wind had stopped and the lonely stands of conifers seemed frozen by some secret they could not share. With a sudden dread he began to realize the enormous risk he had blindly and unthinkingly laid upon White Bead and little Beaver.

Well, they were going now. He would find some way to make it up to her. Somehow he'd get his reasoning back and with it, God willing, his peace of mind. Things would be well again. He would bury the gold safely outside the main camp and forget it, aware only it was there should time and need arise.

She watched him come up to her, her face set, her eyes drawing his up to the sun which was now well up in the sky. He could see the horses were already packed. There was only one thing left to do, help her fix little Beaver, who was sleeping in his tiny cradle board hung from a nearby tree, on her back, and they would be off. He came up to her, still avoiding her eyes. "Let me tie this pick on first," he said quietly, "and I'll get the baby."

But as he turned and started toward little Beaver, whose cradle board hung barely fifty feet away, a small, seemingly frolicking, brownish bear cub tumbled out of the underbrush and placed its little paws on the tree holding the cradle board, its inquisitive nose sniffing upward. There was no danger, it could never have reached the child or harmed it if it did, but Marcher's depressed and distraught mind flashed into panic. As though there were not a moment for thought, his hatchet was out and even as White Bead, catching this deadly scene from the corner of her eye, screamed "No!" the weapon was spinning through the air with one swift downward motion of his arm. The hatchet caught the cub on the side of its head and it managed only a frenzied yip before the shock rolled it on its back, its tiny paws working weakly against the air. Without thinking, and not catching the terrifying inflection of White Bead's screams, Marcher ran forward for little Beaver. Behind him White Bead clawed desperately for the rifle hanging in the saddle scabbard screaming, "Here! Here! The rifle! The rifle!" but it was too late. Even as Marcher reached little Beaver, a thunderous roar to his left swung him around to find an enormous grizzly, its head extended, its jaws open, its long, whitish teeth standing out against the fresh bloodlike scarlet of its mouth, closing on him at incredible speed. In the fraction he had to think he knew it was hopeless, but he drew his pistol and got off a single shot. It struck the bear low in the chest but had no visible effect. The shot was still ringing out as he went down under more than eight hundred pounds of savage carnivore. With the first swing of its immense claw it smashed his shoulder and almost tore off his arm. With the second it broke his neck. It would have savaged and mauled his lifeless body further had not White Bead uncovered the rifle and, though shaking with fear, brought it into play.

Marcher had taught her to use the rifle, but it was a weapon she knew she was unfit for, her slim body unable to firm itself against its wicked recoil. Her first shot caught the animal in the hind quarters and immediately it turned to her, already into its charge. She fired again. This one smashed into the giant bear's front leg and it crumpled a moment before charging again. Her last shot came when it was almost upon her, this penetrating into its open mouth. This one would kill it, but not before its immense body landed upon her, its great claw reaching for her throat and with its last strength opening her body from breastbone to pelvis, making a dozen little geysers of arterial blood rise momentarily into the air. With a gasp that ended in the tiny echo of a moan, her smooth limbs collapsed until they were level with the ground and her soft green eyes rolled upward in death.

Now there was nothing to draw the living but the weak cry of little Beaver, which was almost inaudible in this vast emptiness. Now the land could recapture its silence as new odors arose in the wind to summon its scavengers and vermin to their appointed task.

White River was wiping his brow and eyeing the sky, curious about the unusual absence of wind. He had already entered the mouth of the little valley and was contemplating taking some precious time to rub out the tracks he had made crossing the valley to bury Black Feather.

Then he thought he heard a distant snap. It was almost as though someone had broken a tiny twig a few feet from his ear. He pulled his mount about, a disquieting premonition distantly stirring in him. Now there were three more snaps, these a trifle louder but still distant and on the edge of his senses. He sat quietly, looking back in the direction from which he had come. Slowly a disturbing tentacle of unease began to cast its lengthening shadow over his mind. Long moments passed. No matter how he weighed these distant sounds, they would not sit comfortably in his reckoning. The first snap was likely a light gun, but the second three, his experienced ears said, were reports from a rifle. That there were three of them, for reasons beyond his ken, bothered him. Why three? Marcher was a dead shot. Unless . . . yes . . . unless.

Long before he accepted it, he knew he had to turn back. The specter of going on to the Crow camp, waiting there for Marcher and White Bead to appear, while time passed and tensions grew, was something his common sense refused to allow. Better to know now. He could well be wrong, chances were he was, but the thought failed to lighten the growing heaviness in his gut.

56

The first harbinger of disaster appeared when he spotted White Bead's horse, fully packed for travel but standing with its head down in a swale, as though it had winded itself in a run and was waiting for its breath to level off and strength to return to its legs. He had some trouble rounding it up, but as he tied its reins to his saddle he drew his rifle out of its scabbard. All doubt and hope had vanished. There was only the knowledge now that some tragic, perhaps still dangerous, scene lay ahead. A quarter of a mile further on he heard what turned out to be Marcher's mount rearing and kicking about in a thicket where its free dragging reins had become ensnared on a brush-covered log. Speaking quietly to the horse, White River dismounted and freed it. This mount was also carrying a full pack, but he immediately saw Marcher's rifle was missing.

He swung into the scrub pines on the west slope to avoid appearing on the skyline as he approached the camp. But it was too quiet. Even as he peered between the squat trees and saw the distant figures on the ground he knew it was too late. He rode the final stretch slowly enough to give his mind time to grapple with the shock. Still, at the campsite his gorge rose bitterly. White Bead beside the immense body of the bear looked like a doll that had been ripped apart by some petulant maniacal ogre. Her body was red with her own blood, her once beautiful eyes stared upward with that grotesque indifference of the dead. He knelt and closed them. Then he stood choked with mute anger, his mind struggling with the sickening vacuum that was soon filling with his own unbearable guilt. Why hadn't he waited for them? Why hadn't he come back to warn them that the grizzlies were close and in an ugly mood?

It was a tiny cry coming from above Marcher's body that brought him out of his stunned state. He turned to see little Beaver hanging in his cradle board, mouthing the air and giving a gurgling cry from time to time. He moved toward the baby, the sight of it forcing him to come back to the realities that bore upon the living. Stepping around Marcher's body, he lifted the cradle board and looked closely at little Beaver, once again amazed at the clear light features and blue eyes. The baby seemed to want to be held. In his arms it soon quieted down, but its mouth kept sucking the air till a cold realization began to creep into White River's consciousness. This infant needed a wet nurse to stay alive, and he was almost two days from camp. Perhaps if he forced the pace he could cut that some, but horses had their limits. He put the baby back in its cradle and, removing his hat, ran his hand through his hair. He stared up at the sky, his way of judging time. He would have to leave at once. He could strip the other two mounts and by riding relays be back in camp in a day and a night. The baby should be able to hold out. But his eye caught something that punched like a blacksmith's white hot iron into his thoughts. Buzzards. Those damn ugly birds. He could not leave White Bead or even Marcher to them. The thought of it brought his gorge up again. He knew every minute he delayed might put little Beaver in greater jeopardy, but some things a man can't leave behind him to see in his mind's eye for the rest of his life.

He had the pick tied to Marcher's pack out and swinging at the earth as fast as his arms could work. Luckily there seemed to be a thickness of loam in these hills he had not found digging on the valley floor. In a short time he was down almost two feet. He would need more, for he had come to a quiet conviction that had been building in him as he worked. He would bury them together in a common grave. In spite of all, White Bead would have wanted it that way.

Frantically he deepened the hole, with little Beaver crying out from time to time, reminding him that the hunger pains were sharpening, until finally he reckoned it was deep enough and went to drag Marcher's body into it. He had to straighten the body in the hole, noticing as he did the leather pouch tied to the waist. At first he decided to bury it with the remains—for in truth it was the real agent of death—but then a sudden cry from little Beaver made something turn in his mind, and whipping out his knife, he cut the leather tie cord and, surprised at the weight of it, placed the pouch behind him beyond the heaped earth. Then he went to White Bead. This was harder. Her torn body seemed so light next to Marcher's. He closed his eyes as he carried her to her grave, trying to remember her as she was, not wanting this sight of her to forever sicken his memory.

He placed her in the grave almost face down, almost one with Marcher, pulling down her dress, which had ridden up over her smooth limbs. He reached for the pan he was going to use as a shovel. Then on impulse he set it aside again, noticing the trim of her dress along the shoulder and arm was decorated with white buttons. He settled on a large one that ended the sequence just above her elbow. With his knife he reached in and snipped it off, rubbing it gently with his hand as he placed it in his shirt pocket. "Never you worry, White Bead, we'll be a-watchin' over yer young 'un," he said as though that were the only thing her dead body would want to hear. His very words brought back the urgency in their message and he turned quickly to filling in the grave.

He was already tired when they left. Rocks were plentiful along the stream bed nearby but had to be carried up and placed far enough beyond the grave's edge to keep digging rodents from uncovering the bodies. It was a sizable chore, with its own demands; the heavier the stone, the more protection it gave. He did not spare himself, but his arms were like lead and they trembled a little as he fixed little Beaver's cradle board on one of the mounts. He left everything except the guns, the canteen, the pouch, and a few handfuls of food. He did not let himself think of how played out he was, for in truth the real test was still ahead.

By evening he was out of the valley and onto the rolling plains. Even though he changed mounts regularly, the horses were beginning to wear out. He would have to stop for an hour or two, aware that the baby's crying was now rising intermittently, with each new outbreak carrying more of its helpless agony.

Lifting the baby's cradle board to rock it and speak quietly to it, as he brought his canteen gently to its lips, his nose told him another problem was added to its discomfort. No one he could think of was more ill-fitted for this task, but he forced himself to undo the leather lacing on the cradle and lift out the baby, cleaning it as best he could. Whether it was the way it sucked feebly but desperately at the water spreading on its lips or the feel of its tiny body as he cleaned it he was not sure, but he began to suspect the baby felt warmer than it should. Back in the cradle board he watched it as the horses milled about, heads down, nibbling slowly on the deep spring grass, one of them shuddering and settling to the ground, betraying its near exhaustion. He would leave that one behind—it would only slow him up, and in any case he would have to abandon it after an hour or two. By then it might be too spent to protect itself against passing wolves or a wandering mountain lion.

Long before the horses were even remotely rested he saw in the final light of day the baby's face flushing, its eyes hanging shut and its tiny gurgling sounds all it could manage now after the day's crying had made it hoarse. Looking closer, he saw it was succumbing to what seemed a feverish sleep. He readied the two horses, removing the bridle and saddle from the one to be left and then fastening the cradle board and guns on the one he judged the weaker of the two to be kept. He mounted the other. Pressing ahead in the dark, particularly at a gallop, added the danger of the horses stepping into a gopher hole and breaking a leg, but in White River's mind there were few risks that could outweigh the risk of not getting this baby to camp before it sickened on him and died.

Shortly before midnight a coppery moon lifted its oval face above the horizon and the plains became bathed in a reddish light. It was a welcome sight to White River, but his mind was grimly engaged in a formula for survival. The horses were failing, their heads noticeably lower as they moved. He was still several hours from camp, but afoot it could not be less than a day. He stopped and dismounted. One quick feel of the baby's head told him it was burning with fever. He had to lift the cradle board to listen to its quick and uneven breathing, but it did not awaken even though he shook it gently and spoke to it, his mouth inches from its ear. There was only one thing left to do, and that would have to be done quickly.

The two horses left were his and Marcher's, both sturdy ponies, but the long day's ordeal had melted their muscles and nearly drained them of the energy needed to live. He would have to give them one more short rest and then his desperate gamble must begin.

As he watched for the moon to cover a short space in the sky, he cached the guns, the pouch, and the second saddle. When he figured a half hour had passed he placed the cradle board on Marcher's horse and mounted it. On his own pony he left only the bridle and reins to lead it. He moved out, his stomach tightening against an inner dread that the deadly race against death for little Beaver could well be over.

He could feel the horse dying beneath him, but with his long skill at handling ponies he kept it going. The game pony lasted almost an hour, but finally its heart gave out and with a sickening choking sound its legs tightened to bring a momentary arch to its back and it collapsed. White River, lifting the cradle board with one hand, leaped from its back.

Within moments he was on the other mount, the cradle board tied to his rawhide belt. The pony began moving forward against its own agonizing fatigue as his heel dug deeply into its flanks.

It was not yet dawn when his mind registered the fact that his final mount was only minutes from lethal exhaustion. The pony had been stumbling for some time, fighting the reins as its head became heavier, its heart straining grimly on when every cell in its body must have been wailing against this torturous flight to extinction. He was off it before it fell and its deep, sonorous gasping quickly slipped into silence as its body stiffened, relaxed, one leg moving spastically forward then settling as it quietly accepted death.

Holding the cradle board against his chest, White River began to walk, but after a quarter of a mile his own long suppressed exhaustion could no longer be denied. His body felt leaden, his hands, grasped around the cradle board, were growing numb. He was afraid to look closely at little Beaver, but the heat of the tiny body told him it was still alive. Was he ever going to make camp? Something told him he must, but after a mile or two of the uneven terrain he struck an upgrade where clearly his body and mind lost contact with each other and he found himself helplessly settling on the ground, his muscles clumsily locking together, his coordination failing as though he were drugged. With an effort he vaguely realized couldn't be repeated he drove himself forward again. He started muttering to himself as he struggled with the undulating terrain. It could only be a few miles now, he could, would, must make it. He would save little Beaver if the baby could be saved. Somehow the thought of water came into his mind and with this the realization he was suffering from an overpowering thirst. Tragically the canteen had disappeared, lost in the rapid change of mounts or during the wild ride. His body had slowly become seriously dehydrated with his day- and nightlong effort, and were it not for the high, dry air that swept past him as he traveled his clothes would have been soaked in sweat.

It was almost dawn when he was gripped with the eerie realization that though he thought he was still moving forward, in reality he was on the ground. His legs were splayed out in utter exhaustion, the cradle board lay against his thigh at an awkward angle, his face was sunk helplessly against the crook of his arm. So it was ended, he could go no farther. He must rest. When sleep came surely it would be for many hours, little Beaver would likely be dead before he awoke. A throbbing in his head became unbearable; it seemed to reach out and reverberate through his entire body, finally spreading beyond his body and entering the earth. It was a throbbing that in some ominous and inexplicable way was transforming itself into a beat. He knew that beat, he knew what it implied, a horse was coming, coming directly at him. He tried to reach for his pistol but it was gone, left somewhere behind him as one more desperate concession to speed. Dawn was coming and a ghostly light filtering over the land. A host of probable enemies spiked their way into his consciousness, even Black Feather, as his strained mind lapsed momentarily, forgetting he had put the Crow in his grave.

There was nothing he could do. The horse was almost upon him now, removing all hope that he had not been seen. He could hear the change of beat as the mount was reined up and came to a stop, its four legs only a few feet from his head. He managed to turn so he could look at the rider, and as his eyes came into focus he saw a familiar figure outlined against the dull gray sky, its gaze fixed upon the cradle board holding little Beaver. Something in a distant part of his mind told him he was saved. It was Blue Lodge.

Dismounting and hastily pulling things from her saddlepack, she knelt beside him, frantically urging him not to talk. He gestured feebly toward the baby, but it was only minutes before he had finished her canteen of water, mouthed a bite or two of food, and, wrapping himself in her blanket, helplessly surrendered to sleep. In his last moments of consciousness he realized she had taken little Beaver and ridden off, the beat of her pony's hoofs and the snap of her quirt creasing its flanks dying out quickly in his ears. It was but an hour or two before she returned. Finding him still fast asleep, she settled down to await his awakening, her broad face a tension-ridden mask of both dread and relief.

In early afternoon he stirred, shifted his body, and, suddenly recalling he had collapsed into sleep in the midst of a grave crisis, sat up. Blue Lodge tried to smile at him.

"The young 'un?" he muttered, his eyes seeking hers in answer.

"Little Beaver is with Wapiti Hawk, a medicine woman. She is from our people who live on the river. She visits her uncle, Big Owl. Her medicine is very strong."

White River sat up rubbing his legs slowly. He remembered Wapiti Hawk moving among the wounded after the costly battle with the Sioux. He tried to draw some comfort from her respected name but little came. Most of the wounded, he remembered bitterly, had died. With a grimace he fought to move his mind elsewhere, and inevitably it settled on Blue Lodge. Grateful as he was, there was something too mysterious, something that found no place in his reasoning, about her showing up that dawn. There were those who would call it a miracle, for so it seemed, but White River didn't believe in miracles.

"Fer a fact yer comin' by was sure handy," he started, "but how come Blue Lodge rides thisaway in the middle of the night?"

She reached for his hand. "I come with words of warning in my mouth. There are two whites in the village. One carries the metal star of those bringing the white man's law. They have smoked much with Big Owl. They wait now for Yellow Hatchet to return. Some say they wait for you. I waited long into the night for them to sleep. I left while still dark, walking my pony till its hoofbeats could not reach their ears. Blue Lodge is frightened." White River shook his head slowly at the mention of Marcher's name. She knew his meaning. She had known from the moment she had laid eyes on little Beaver. Poor, poor White Bead. "They are beyond the stars?" she whispered quietly.

He nodded.

When they arrived in camp the people watched them drawing up to their lodge. Some looked at them with sympathetic eyes, others held hands over parts of their face in the grieving sign. The arrival of the deathly sick little Beaver in camp and no sign of his parents told its own story.

Across the little village two white strangers were watching too. One was Marshal Peters from faraway Denver, the other a young deputy being broken in to the rigors of enforcing law in a near lawless land.

"Who might that gent be?" queried the young deputy.

Marshal Peters had spent his life trailing across this rough country. He had talked to lawmen of all stripes and knew most of the unlawful who for one reason or another had to be approached with caution. He had seen White River before, years ago on the Missouri, and knew he had been taken in by old Buzz Matlock, had become an army scout, had coolly and single-handedly climbed Independence's Whiskey Hill one night to leave Chicasaw Kane and two of his henchmen for the undertaker. That did not make him an outlaw. There were plenty of decent men with fast guns in the territories who felt there wasn't enough law enforcement to go around and just naturally filled in. But then again he was not one to trifle with either, particularly since the old chief he had just smoked with seemed pretty high on him, not an insignificant tribute coming from the hard-pressed and hard-fighting Crows. To Peters' knowledge, and to his secret relief, no lawman had ever had real reason to tangle with this man. Yet in the catechism of every U.S. marshal hoping to lay eyes on his grandchildren, there was always a first time.

"Name is White River," he half muttered to his companion, his mind already ahead of his words. "Reckon we'll just mosey over and pay our respects."

The young deputy took a hitch on his gun belt. "Could be he might be troublesome?"

The old marshal smothered a brief smile. The young ones in this business always seemed to have an itch to start shooting. He himself had long since accepted the fact that men of White River's cut usually considered his kind of law an unnecessary intrusion into the affairs of men, but as long as they weren't acting unlawfully any show of force was foolishly asking for trouble—trouble of a sort he suspected White River could handle rather better than his young assistant. "Keep your hands off your gun, this here is a social visit—lessen you make it otherwise."

White River, hearing the marshal's deep, masculine voice asking for him, stepped slowly out of his lodge.

"Howdy," began the marhsal, relieved to see White River was unarmed.

White River looked at them a few moments, taking in the marshal's star, before he replied, "Howdy. Somethin' maybe I can do for you gents?"

"Figure you could. Looking for a fellow. Easterner by his lingo. Tall like yourself, keeps his hair tied back Injun style, carries a hatchet. Most folks allow he's mighty handy with it too."

White River's face was expressionless as he heard this blunt but unmistakable description of Marcher. "What'd you want with him?"

"Seems he left a parcel of new tenants for Boot Hill back in Denver, but we didn't ride this distance just to jaw about that. This Crow village sure wasn't easy to find."

White River stood staring at the marshal without commenting. Long moments passed before it was clear he didn't intend to.

The growing set of the marshal's mouth revealed he felt it was time for some quiet but straight questioning. "You know a fellow from back east fitting that description?"

"Did," said White River whose casualness caused the boyish deputy irritation that plainly showed on his face.

The marshal hadn't missed the past tense in White River's response. "What brought him out here?"

White River's mind flashed back to the scene on the Innyan Kara which now seemed ages away. "Lookin' for a grave, as I recollect."

The marshal didn't intend for another long silence to ensue. "And . . . ?"

"Reckon he found one," allowed White River, as though there were little more to be said.

"What we 'uns want to know is where is he now?" rasped the young deputy, his agitation at White River's manner mounting until red patches appeared around his temples.

"I buried him yesterday."

"You mean he's dead?"

"Most folks in the ground are."

The old marshal raised his hand to silence his young partner. "And just how did he die?" he said with genuine interest.

"Got too close to a grizzly. Grizzlies ain't much on sociableness this time of year."

There was now another long silence broken only when the marshal, pushing his hat back, dug the gold nugget lost by Marcher in the fire from his vest pocket. He held it up for White River to see. "There's been some talk about a gold mine. Did he find one?"

White River's mind raced forward to the army of miners, claim jumpers and trash of all kinds that with any mention of gold would come to desecrate the country like a swarm of ants to fresh-spilled honey. He would have to handle this trouble-laden question with more guile than he was used to. "Not to my reckonin'," he replied with the air of a man dealing with an issue he considered sheer fantasy.

"We know for a fact he was looking for one," shouted the young deputy, "and likely found it!"

"Every critter that comes upriver is looking for a gold mine," replied White River coolly. "Sooner or later a parcel of shiftless galoots like yourself get to thinkin' he found one."

The marshal threw a warning glance at his deputy, then turned back to White River. "What about this nugget?" he asked, his tone quieting, reasonable, just short of placating.

"I rightly recollect he brought it out to these parts with him. Could have come from anywhere."

It seemed the encounter was over, but the marshal licked his lips, put the nugget away, and looked about him like a man wanting to know the terrain before he spoke. The Crows were now standing at a respectful distance but in a complete circle around him. "One more thing," he said slowly, "and I guess it's the real reason we're visiting with you. This fellow you say is dead bought a slew of cartridges in Denver, several hundred, we understand. We'd be obliged to know where they are now or where they went."

White River felt relief spreading through his veins. So this is what brought the law to this lonely mountain camp, a fear that Marcher had somehow been trading ammunition to the hostiles. His tone was measurably warmer when he spoke. "Figure you'll find most of them in his lodge. He used to trade them to Big Owl and me whenever we had need."

"You don't mind if'n we look," asked the marshal, his tone still amiable.

"Nary a bit," responded White River, pointing out Marcher's and White Bead's empty lodge.

As the two lawmen started toward the empty lodge White River called out, "Oh, Marshal, I take it those bullets were rightly paid for."

The marshal turned, a trace of confusion at the question on his face. "Oh, they were paid for all right"—then, remembering the many skins and prime pelts he had examined—"well paid for, I'm thinkin'."

"Good," answered White River. "Being as they're rightly bought goods, be sure'n leave 'em there."

The two lawmen looked at the stacks of cartridges in Marcher's lodge, realizing they'd been on a fool's errand. The young one was still fighting his anger at White River's manner. U.S. marshals deserved to be treated with respect. His mouth was twisted with resentment. "How do we know that critter with the hatchet we've been looking for is sure enough dead," he half challenged.

"He's dead," replied the marshal.

"How come you're so sure?"

"Something about the way he told it—I don't rightly know."

"I'm asking are you rock bottom sure?"

The marshal stared at him for a moment, his face faintly stained with impatience. "Yep. Just about as sure as I am you ain't going to have to worry about growing gray hair if you don't watch your mouth when talking to the likes of White River, 'specially when he's surrounded by a parcel of Indians who set a heap of store by him."

"Marshal, we're the law, ain't we? You're telling me we have to walk small for a squaw man like him?"

The old marshal shook his head slowly. "The law's business is with those who have broken it. He hasn't. Let's get moving before he gets wind of the fact you called him 'squaw man.' "

"What about that mine?"

"What about it?"

"You don't really believe that bastard is telling the truth, do you? Can't you see he's keeping it all for hisself?"

The marshal shrugged. Secretly he suspected there was a mine somewhere, but he had seen enough of mining towns and the lawlessness they gave birth to not to ever want to see another. "Get this thinking about gold mines out of your gut, son," he said without rancor. "Every time gold is discovered fifty varmints end up dead and a few hundred more figure their guns can get what digging couldn't. If you figure to follow the law, you'd better get that matter straightened out before you go much further. This hankering after gold is the surest ticket to trouble I've ever heard of, wouldn't be surprised if somehow or other it didn't do in the very folks that lived in this lodge."

In the lodge of Wapiti Hawk, little Beaver lay stripped and silent on a neatly folded buffalo robe while the long-faced medicine woman knelt to wet the baby's lips over and over again with an herbal potion she had kept brewing and lukewarm for hours. There were damp doeskins across little Beaver's forehead and long slivers of it wrapped carefully around his limbs. Wapiti Hawk chanted as she worked, but it was a low chant and did not reach beyond the lodge where she and three other squaws, two of them wet nurses, had huddled around the baby, watching the shallow breathing in grave silence since the break of dawn. The medicine woman reached in the gourd of cool water she kept beside her and with her left hand shook a few more drops onto the doeskins, keeping them moist and soothing to the feverishly tight and reddened skin.

Finally Wapiti Hawk stood up. Something would have to happen soon. Shocked at the baby's alarming signs of dehydration when it arrived, she did not need to be told the infant needed moisture and food in its body soon if it was to live. But this was impossible till the baby could be awakened from its fever-induced sleep. She had kept its limbs wet with the light herbal brew, aware errant drops were slipping into its tiny mouth, which she knew was dangerous in its comatose state, but most of the excess streaked down its tiny chin and flushed cheeks. None of the women spoke or glanced at each other. All eyes were on Wapiti Hawk and the baby.

Perhaps an hour later, perhaps less, Wapiti Hawk was making one of her endless attempts to bring the baby back to consciousness. In her heart hope was fast draining away. She began to whine at her own helplessness. She knew too much time was passing. The spirit she had called upon in her chants had seemed to abandon her. The baby's eyes were already on the stars. Then, suddenly, hearing the faintest gurgling noise, her wet finger came in contact with the tiny protruding tip of its tongue. Hurriedly but carefully she let a few drops fall upon the pink tip and saw it withdraw inward in what was the beginning of a swallow. The baby was becoming conscious although clearly too weak to cry. Slowly she urged drop after drop of the fluid into its mouth, working patiently until its eyes opened to half slits and its breathing began to become just perceptibly softer and deeper.

The many female hearts in the lodge relaxed almost audibly. They knew the crisis had passed. Wapiti Hawk motioned that the tiny body seemed cooler. Still silent, they smiled and nodded at each other knowingly. A half hour later, little Beaver was lifted to the breast of one of the wet nurses. Gently she placed the nipple of her bosom in his mouth and slowly began massaging herself, letting her milk fall in very tiny measures into his upturned mouth.

Wapiti Hawk, stepping from the lodge, stood and raised her arms to the sky, a strange chant rising from her old woman's throat. The Absarokees saw this, and as though on command began to sing with her, their voices sounding discordant, for many sang only as the heart directed, but collectively it was a primal hymn of life, a song about those who have looked upon the stars and returned. It was a song for the unnamed sacred one, Ah-badt-deadt-deah. The people were one with him again and uttering their thanks.

After the marshals left, White River, still exhausted, stretched out on his robes as Blue Lodge, hearing the camp singing and knowing the infant had been saved, put her hand out to him. "It is well. Little Beaver will be as another sun to brighten our lodge." He closed his eyes in silence and lay so still she thought he slept.

She would never know the growing turmoil of misgiving, vexation, and confusion that was besetting him. Somehow he had seemed too stunned by events in these past few days to think clearly, but now his situation was hitting him full force.

Blue Lodge had conceived his child. He had thought she was barren, as she had been a widow without children. But fate had stepped in and now his desire to leave no longer seemed clean and free of consequences. Not that he couldn't go. Indian women had no lawful hold on men who fathered their children as did their white sisters. Indifference to native girls made pregnant by drifters or other unsavory frontier types was commonplace. As a child he had seen an endless stream of crude itinerant trappers and traders, stopping in the Arikara village, leaving Indian females pregnant and departing in gruff silence. He had grown up holding these depraved and degenerate men in contempt. But now . . .

Lying there, he groped for the dimensions of his quandary, for suddenly he realized it was not only the unborn child he must think of. He and Blue Lodge had saved Beaver's life, and under Indian customs, as Blue Lodge had softly reminded him, Beaver was now their child.

It was hours before he could bring himself to think again of Lydia, but when at last he did he knew if life ever brought her back, one day he would have to tell her, one day she would have to know he had a child by Blue Lodge. For him there could be no other way.

It was the feel of White Bead's button in his pocket that made him slip off at sundown to the outskirts of camp. He had not had time to deal with the full impact of her gruesome death. That lissome, proud, and devoted girl who had kept Lydia alive in his mind was gone, her trim, gracefully rounding body sprawled beneath a cluster of rocks in that lonely valley. The weight of Marcher's pouch had forced him to bury it at his first stop. By then he was furious because he had pieced together how and why White Bead died. He had seen that bear cub with the hatchet wound. Marcher with his greed and stupidity had wiped out the life of that pretty, ill-used, but plucky young girl, who had surely brought to him his only measure of love. The thought of the price paid by others for Marcher's stubborn and selfish ways appalled him, but he was startled at how deeply White Bead's death was rocking him and filling him with foreboding. Unaccountably a macabre thought pierced his mind. What if Lydia was also dead? He stood there paralyzed for a moment. Oh, but that couldn't be. Surely he would know, something in the weakening of the sunlight and the low moaning of the wind would tell him.

Still, the frightening intimation of her death sobered him, reminded him of how uncertain were the things that made life count, how a man ought to cling to the few that came his way.

He thought of White Bead holding little Beaver on that morning before her death, her face suffused with happiness, her soft green eyes glowing with pride.

Taking the soft button from his pocket he held it up to the setting sun. "Needn't to worry, White Bead," he said, his voice almost breaking with emotion, "needn't to worry, we'll remember."

57

Blue Lodge knew that nothing burdens the heart like a loneliness that cannot be expressed. The months following Marcher's and White Bead's death were a troubled, even despairing time for White River. He spent long days in the mountains, dwelling on the many faces now missing from his life, racked by questions their seemingly meaningless deaths left unanswered. Often he returned in moods that frightened Blue Lodge, but she was helpless to change them.

With the sky sunny and clouds like islands of cotton passing overhead, Big Owl, watching her slowly trudging by, heavy with her coming child, said quietly, "There is always another day in life, Blue Lodge. One day wounds the spirit but those behind it come to heal. Open your heart, let the Great Spirit speak, for He alone sees what awaits us behind the next dawning." Blue Lodge nodded, seeking some comfort in these words, but quietly she labored on.

White River could find no escape from the lingering despondency he had fallen into. He still carried out his duties about the camp, but he moved more slowly now and with less resolve. Suddenly the world seemed older, that sense of morning in his life he had often felt in the early dawn was slipping away. In time he reckoned it was himself that was getting older, for he had heard it was in others, his woman, his children, that a man could watch himself age. Did dreams age too? Did a man one day grow too old for dreams?

One quiet afternoon, just before Blue Lodge's baby came to term, he smoked with Big Owl and let slip some of his troubled thoughts. The old chief looked at him, his aquiline face softening with understanding. "Do not worry about aging, my son. The mountains are very, very old, but are they not majestic and beautiful? In life all things are first young and then old, but he who walks with the Great Spirit finds all the days he has put into our lives are beautiful. It is only the eyes of angry and discontented men that make them otherwise."

The night Blue Lodge went to Wapiti Hawk's tipi to have her child, White River was left alone with Beaver. He heard the child waking in the middle of the night and begin its tiny crying. He took it from its leather crib and gently rocked it, his muted voice reassuring it its mother would be back at dawn. Slowly the baby quieted down and in time fell asleep. He sat with it, his strange new feeling of protectiveness keeping him from returning it to its crib. He sat there the remainder of that night with little Beaver in his arms. That night, though not yet conscious of it, his decision had been made.

The following day his own son, who would soon be named Chipmunk, came to his lodge, and Blue Lodge, seeing he had laid out their best robes for her, knew in her unerring female way that more than a son had just come into her life. She looked down, as was her way, and her face slowly softened and grew damp in relief.

With growing sons to watch and the past slowly fading, White River felt the years begin to roll over him, their passing measured only by some vague calendar carried secretly in the dim reaches of his mind. The Absarokees now looked upon him as one of their own. Blue Lodge, with her busy and talented hands, kept a clean, comfortable, happy lodge, and he, finally accepting his obvious rank in the tribe, sat beside Big Owl in the camp's ruling council. It was a life many would have thought complete. But in his heart he knew the world beyond the world of Absaroka was changing, its ominous signs becoming more and more impossible to ignore. Heavily stocked trading wagons, government agents, prospectors, even surveyors began to become common sights in long stretches of country that had known only an occasional moccasin track or the seasonal drift of game. Big Owl, hearing of these things, would sit each evening, lost in thought, watching the sun's scarlet-and-mauve plumage fade away as the day surrendered itself to night.

Looking back, White River knew he would always remember with some warmth those fleeting years with these struggling but carefree people, even though he saw the whites filling the land and grimly realized the tragic fate of the eastern tribes would soon overtake them. They lived for the moment, trusting in their spirits, singing and dancing to their drums, as they wandered about their beloved hills and clear-flowing streams. And time seemed to ride the wind in this vagabond life. Little Beaver was already almost four, and his and Blue Lodge's sturdy little son, Chipmunk, well past three. There was a contagious joy in these children. Little Beaver would strut around, and little Chipmunk, waiting only to see where he was going, would strut after him. White River didn't know why it made him smile, but he could watch these two tiny men for hours. Both were going to have strong and firm bodies, both were going to have good appetites and maybe determined ways. When White River had first lifted little Beaver to his saddle, Chipmunk sat up and howled until he too had his chubby legs clamped awkwardly around the saddle horn. If there was a difference between his two little men it was Beaver's nature to go first, even when they climbed over White River as he learned to tumble and tussle with them on the lodge floor. Beaver would be on his shoulders before he knew the game was on, while Chipmunk would stand, his wide, lustrous eyes staring up, waiting his turn, his tiny hand clutching one of his father's fingers. Blue Lodge would smile as Chipmunk murmured contentedly whenever his father picked him up so he could look down at Beaver, but adventuresome Beaver paid these tiny victories of Chipmunk's little heed.

Still White River could see they held to and liked each other, and even more in their innocent ways were beginning to show their love for him. Absarokee fathers would never have played with their children so, considering it beneath their dignity, but White River could only shrug at such dignity. He knew he was helpless before their expectant little eyes, which had a way of trapping his. Not since Buzz and Lydia had he known such a comforting life. Peace seemed to have come to the land. There were few signs of trouble. Many times they were able to raise their villages among bushes heavy with black chokeberries or red plums ripe upon the trees. The growing pony herds thrived in an almost pastoral setting and much feasting and dancing followed every hunt. Their only but growing problem was the young men. Restless and anxious for the cherished horse-stealing raids and exciting surprise attacks, where coups could be counted, they now found the white man's hand rising everywhere and were beginning to learn of infuriating treaties which no one understood but all knew were unfair. Many rode out to find soldiers traveling across their sacred hunting grounds or bivouacked alongside their secret war camps. They could only return to their lodges sickened with the knowledge that the proud life of the warrior's way was ending. For the first time whiskey began to replace the wild, daring, perilous yet man-making exploits of the Absarokee youths.

There was little soothing counsel to help meet this mounting crisis. White River listened to Big Owl tell his people their great hope lay in abiding by the laws of the whites, for their numbers were already forbidding, their power beyond matching. At reports that the buffalo were dwindling under the senseless slaughter of hide hunters he smiled wistfully and spoke of their long friendship with the whites that would soon be rewarded. The people would always have plenty he said, the white men would see it so. White River turned away. The abandoned and starving Arikara would have wept at these words.

But the uneasy Crows could only sense that, in spite of the old chief's renowned wisdom, there was melancholy in his voice, that Big Owl was living in the past, that he chose not to look beyond this sunset of his life. Some even whispered that he knew the white man's memory would be short and that in the end their long standing at his side would count for little. Some warily hinted he was praying for death before these terrible words must be spoken.

Wapiti Hawk, returning to the River Crows, pondered the calm and bounty surrounding them and sighed, thinking perhaps of her dream that the Great Spirit was giving the Absarokees a momentary rest before their next great trial began. Still, most of the tribe, knowing how little could be done about their fate, as the spirits alone controlled it, watched the meat sizzling on the fire and the young playing before the lodge, resignedly lighted their pipes and turned to dreaming or living for the day alone.

It was early spring, after a long, cold, damp spell, when White River awoke in the night to hear Blue Lodge coughing under her robes. It was not yet dawn as he lay there in the darkness, holding his breath, listening to her body-racking seizures till they ceased. Then he swore under his breath. Damnation. The coughing sickness, the one dying Crow women had been carrying back from wintering with ill and infected traders, had brought its spore of death to his lodge. Patient, hard working Blue Lodge, who asked so little for herself, lay now in the silence, aware he was awake, listening, realizing now, as she did when the coughing pains came to her chest and she gasped at the taste of blood in her mouth, that before many moons could pass her eyes would be fixed on the stars.

That morning she looked up from her cooking fire, her face strangely at peace, her hand coming over to gently smooth his troubled face. "It has been good," she said softly. "The Great Spirit has given us much."

He took her hand in his and pulled her down beside him. "We'll head for Laramie. Could be white doctors there who can cure you."

She smiled again wistfully, moving away and putting her hands lightly over her chest. "No. This badness came from the whites. If they had medicine to kill its evil spirit, it would not have traveled here. Others have gone to their big medicine lodge before and never returned. I will stay with my people."

And so the heartsick days worked their way toward summer, neither mentioning again this unseen evil that slowly corrupted her lungs and speckled her sputum with blood. He knew she was right, there was no cure. He had seen strong, vigorous whites wasting away and dying from this malady. Indians, far more vulnerable to the ills of the whites, faced a swifter and more agonizing death. Helplessly he listened to her hacking in the dead of night and watched her firm body growing lank and weak, her broad face thinning and stretching against its bone.

When not racked by coughing she cried under her robe, her tears the tears of anticipation, for their children were too young to lose their mother. But, ah, herein lay an even greater burden to laden the heart, one that time and even the gift of life would not have spared her. Little Beaver, particularly during the winter months, was too fair and had too cream-white a skin not to draw the growingly critical eyes of other children. He was afflicted with that incurable malady among children of being different. "Pale face" was a nickname hung on him early by other boys, some holding him down once in a prank and painting his face red. Chipmunk's screeching finally brought help, but in the end there is no help for a child finding itself different from its peers.

Other signs appeared like remote and ephemeral mists, but they lingered on for the mind to measure. Passing missionaries became a regular nuisance and on occasion a vague menace. "Suspect this one will be yours?" proclaimed Reverend Petigrew, his fingers lightly passing over little Beaver's fair hair.

"Nephew," mumbled White River.

"Nephew, eh?" Petigrew was rubbing the reddish fringe of hair that rimmed his bald pate. "Well, brother, just so you're here to see that he be raised as a proper Christian is all God asks."

Deciding that Reverend Petigrew and God had all the information they needed for the moment, White River started to move away.

"What happened to the parents?" called out Petigrew. It was clear he kept pretty good track of passing souls and there was no limit to his ministry.

"Died a while back," offered White River over his shoulder. "Happens a lot out here. Might be that preachin' can help some." He disappeared into his lodge, where he knew it was not likely he'd be followed.

But the lodge cover could not protect White River or Blue Lodge from a mounting truth of which the Petigrews were only a minuscule part. The country was no longer theirs. The whites were moving in, eyeing the bottomlands, driving game from the waterways. The great tribes of the plains, weakened by whiskey and disease, were being slowly herded into reservations. White River could see it would not be long before the Crows themselves would be forced to cede vast areas of their hunting grounds to the whites, and though their long friendship and service to their despoilers would bring them better treatment than the Sioux, still, any reservation, and one was already being "purposed," would be a prison not of their own making and in time would drain the pride of the people.

Though they did not discuss it, the same presentiment was in both their hearts. Children make parents look ahead, and White River and the dying Blue Lodge, could see little Beaver as a young man faced with life in a world of the whites with nothing but the way of the Indian—a way of life that lay on its deathbed—to prepare him for it. Chipmunk was another story. With his broader face, darker skin, and slightly almond eyes, he would need the people. There would be no concealing his Indian blood. The whites would turn away from him as they did from all those they decreed to be a lesser breed.

Blue Lodge, studying White River across the fire, found she could not bring herself to think of her remaining time without little Beaver, for he was now her child as much as little Chipmunk. Though tears streaked her face as she divined her man's thoughts she knew he was right. Haltingly they exchanged the few unnecessary words that merely circled and in the end made even more painful this desperate decision from which there was no decent escape. If this final agonizing sacrifice must be endured the time to do it was at hand. To wait longer would only make it more difficult for little Beaver to withstand the shock of change. One never knew about children; even another season might make it too late.

The crucial parting was planned with that grimness mankind reserves for its loftier deeds. White River prepared the night before, packing one pony with grub and bedding, his rifle, and a change of clothes for little Beaver and himself. After much thought he had ridden out to the spot where he had buried Marcher's gold and, digging in with an old spade, found the leather pouch beginning to decay. He exchanged it for another made from buffalo hide, his face once again registering surprise at the weight of it all. Nearest he could figure, the gold by rights belonged to little Beaver, but then a quandary rose to beset and burden his mind. What did a four-year-old know about gold? What would he do with it? How long would it stay his? Particularly among strangers and especially white strangers. He would have to think that predicament through, but for the moment there seemed no ready answers.

Often on sleepless nights, as Blue Lodge muffled her tortured breathing in her robes, other matters rose to gnaw at him. He could read and write a little, but he suspected it was a far cry from what the task before him might demand. Here he had taken to calling Beaver his nephew, but Easterners were God Almighty taken with birth and baptismal papers and such. He had no proof of his own name, let alone Beaver's, or even where he himself was born. Talk of Marcher and White Bead would only reveal the child was born out of wedlock, a stigma the whites would be sure to faithfully record. It was not until the day before he left that he recalled the yellow sheet Ben Amiel had written out for him to insure his payment as a guide. Tattered but legible, it was among Ben's few remaining possessions. With Big Owl's help, he found it in an old parfleche where without much reason odd pieces of belongings left by the dead were often stowed. Big Owl did not say it, but White River knew Indians had a strange regard for the white man's sign writing. Over a pipe with the chief he decided he would take it with him. It was little enough, but at least it carried his name and maybe, just maybe . . .

Blue Lodge and he, sitting by their last fire the night before, had long known the role each would have to play. There would be no wrenching parting scenes to scar the hearts of their children and echo sadly down the years. The burdens to be borne would be heavy enough without that. White River would rise well before dawn, awakening little Beaver with the pretense that they were going to hunt. They would be well away from the camp before the others awoke.

He looked at her across the fire, sensing how close death was to the bloodless face and the dark, exhausted eyes. But she was smiling, her expression a brave mixture of gratitude and resolve. "White River must promise never to come back," she said. "There is only the darkness of another life for the Absarokees. We are praying to our spirits to help us stay together as a people. Big Owl will take Chipmunk into his lodge. All Absarokees will be as parents to our son." She stopped to rest and gather her breath. "Blue Lodge has walked proud to be the woman of White River, he has made her spirit happy, her heart sing." She looked away. "I am feeling weak again. I have no more words. Blue Lodge will keep her memories of our happy days together. They will lie with her beneath many snows for many years."

Once he was awakened, little Beaver's eyes glowed with excitement in the dim firelight nursed from the coals, but White River kept his head angled into the shadows, the cool breeze, still burdened with night air, seeming as nothing compared to the chill that was working around his heart.

They moved quietly, soon becoming one with the night, leaving behind them a silence that seemed complete if one could not sense or feel in the darkness the heavily quaking body of Blue Lodge, her head buried so deeply in her robes that only the slightest murmur of her sobbing arose to join and be lost in the faint but now rising whine of the wind.

58

The journey south was an ordeal of the heart, for little Beaver soon sensed they were not hunting but traveling steadily and with intent. He began to look at White River, his eyes wide and apprehensive as he saw in the shaved but weathered face the deep caring and poorly suppressed sorrow that was burdening it.

"Where we go?" he asked at one stopping, looking down, his hands behind him.

"Visitin'," said White River, hearing his own unsubstantial voice rising hollow and unconvincing. He strove to busy himself preparing grub.

"Beaver go home now," said the little boy, still looking down but clearly on the verge of tears.

"Fixin' to right soon—hey there! Look yonder! Ain't that a sure enough eagle a-comin' over that ridge!"

Neither could swallow more than a bite or two before moving on.

Evenings were to prove most difficult of all. The least gifted of storytellers, White River had to struggle with tales of river pirates and mountain men he had picked up along the way, many without much plot or even much point. But the long day's traveling and listening to the halting drawl made little Beaver sleepy and he dozed off with a child's faith that no matter how grim the circumstances or dire the threats, somehow brave but kindly faces would emerge and set matters right.

White River often watched him as he slept, his mind roaming over the rightness of this soul-wrenching decision. Who knew what awaited this little one in the long years ahead? Would he find someone to love him, someone to care? He was going to have Marcher's good looks and White Bead's suppleness of body. He would be easy to love. But the internal agonizing and conflicting dialogue went on. Always it ended with the conviction that whatever awaited Beaver, it had to be better than what he knew would be life in a dying Indian village or the slow rotting on the whiskey-soaked, grimly hoveled, and overwrought soil of a reservation.

Sometimes when sleep overcame him White River dreamed disturbing dreams that hung in his mind the following day. One night he awoke from a startling dream about Chipmunk. In the dream he saw Chipmunk looking back at him as he moved away, going toward some far-distant mountain. The boy grew larger in the distance, until finally he stood there a tall powerful figure, smiling back at him from beyond a range of wild, craggy peaks.

Yet his most disturbing dreams were about Lydia. He had tried hard to keep his mind from dwelling on her for years, accepting the foolishness, even absurdity of his long-nurtured hopes. She would be twenty or twenty-one by now, surely a married woman with a growing family and a life too full to be burdened by distant memories. But in his dream he saw her, her body still that of an adolescent girl, her motions still graceful but her features indistinct as she moved through a great emptiness. A cold dread seized him, slowly awakening him, as he watched her disappear into a dark and endless void.

There were few restful nights.

Down on the Platte there were whites every few miles, some riding, some walking, but all of them heading west. There was talk of a railroad coming through, though wagon trains were still rolling by as if from some inexhaustible source in the east. But these were not the hunger-fighting or hazardous parties of a decade ago. Most were large trains with elected officers and their own vigilante laws, some packing equipment for bridging streams or winching wagons mired in mud. Many had hired experienced guides to get them through the mountains where the trail broke into two—south for California and north for Oregon, where there was still talk of trouble with the Utes.

Most trains he approached welcomed him, as his rough and formidable appearance was quickly rendered harmless by the presence of little Beaver. "Now if that ain't the handsomest little fellow I ever see'd. Yours?"

"Nephew. His folks got themselves ambushed up by the Yellowstone. Aim on takin' him back east to be raised up." His habitual ruse was slipping into a kind of reality.

Many invited him and little Beaver to eat with them or join in dances or hymn-singing sessions held at night, but White River kindly refused all efforts at cordiality that could lead to closer questioning. He turned instead to the weathered, usually hard-drinking guides, who proved to be former bush traders or aging mountain men. They were more his breed and took to his palaver with little effort. Some squatted and talked with him about the situation in Independence, where he had decided to head, but other than cursing the quality and price of whiskey to be found there, none could supply him with the information he sought.

On the third day his luck changed. Old Teel, the trapper turned mountain guide, spitting a stream of tobacco juice several feet from his rawhide boots, appeared one night. He came over from the wagon camp about dusk, nodding excitedly at them in recognition. "White River, by golly! Can't hardly believe muh eyes!" He seemed genuinely glad at the encounter, shaking White River's hand vigorously. "Mind the time you gunned down Sam Gome upriver here a ways, recollect it to be the night that lonesome Crow hit the island." His mood suddenly seemed to soften for a moment. "Calculate it's been a while now, ain't it." He glanced at little Beaver in friendly surmise. "Reckon you've come a ways since."

White River realized if he tried telling Teel he was taking little Beaver, a nephew, back east Teel would clearly remember him from his years on the Missouri, remember him as a loner, taken in by Buzz, remember he had no family anyone had ever heard of, no brothers or sisters and therefore, as any sheep herder could reason, no "nephews." Beyond that it was hard to believe some word of Marcher's life and death had not reached beyond the Crow camp, and Teel with his knowledge of the Crow tongue was a likely gent to have heard it. It was that kind of world. Besides, he was getting more and more annoyed with this awkward sham.

After listening to the real facts as though they were hardly a matter of deep concern, Teel eyed little Beaver with a new and openly amiable interest. "Who's a-gonna raise him up? Kinfolk?"

White River sensed what old Teel was hinting at and decided it was time to admit how helpless he felt. "Nary a one I'd know where to fetch."

Old Teel shook his head knowingly. "Had the same problem once't. Comanches did for this young 'un's whole family down on the Cimarron and left him nigh dead. But we nursed him around, we did. Soon he was as spry as a squirrel hankerin' to rut. Couldn't keep him though, too young. Trouble wuz, with us rushin' to get clear of them parts us selves, we never got no proper name for the pup." White River leaned forward across the fire, firmly fixed on Teel's words. Teel spit again. "Now back in Independence," he said casually, "there be a mission, full of fine folks . . . 'course, none that would be worth a hog's turd in a fight, but they look out for young 'uns till they can manage for themselves. Reckon the Lord set it up that way."

"Mission?" said White River uncertainly.

"Yep. Got mostly white walls around it just south of town nearby the river."

"Obliged," said White River quietly.

Teel's face showed something was puzzling him. "Yuh got a different feel to yuh somehow, White River," he said cautiously. "What's happened? Missionaries been bedevilin' yuh?"

"Missionaries! Missionaries are gopher spit compared to what's bin bedevilin' me," muttered White River.

Teel chuckled heartily. "Goes against nature, I always say, to set around a-stewin' over miseries when there's whiskey to be drunk. Got me a jug in the wagon if yer a mind to wet down some trail dust."

White River looked at little Beaver, who was rolling in his blankets, ready for sleep, not knowing these few words uttered at this chance meeting might have decided his future. Silently White River weighed Teel's invitation. Thoughts of the mission seemed to have lightened some of his burden. "Can't say I ain't sufferin' from a mighty dry," he mumbled. Then, after waiting a few minutes while Beaver dozed off and Teel replaced his chaw of tobacco, they rose and moved casually toward the wagons that loosely rimmed a fire in the center of the camp.

• • •

The mission was larger and more rambling than he expected. It was clear the long, low building had been added to recently, for building materials were still lying around, but for all that its white-washed adobe walls shone with the brightness of snow in the sun. At the far end three robed figures were looking up at a bell tower as though they found the elevated symmetry of the wall a peaceful sight. It was.

One, noticing him standing uncertainly with little Beaver, approached in slow measured steps, his hands held together beneath his robe, a rough wooden crucifix hanging loosely before him. His thin face was alert but kind, and his eyes followed little Beaver as the child moved to hide behind White River. "Morning, brother," said the robed man. "God has brought you here; in what manner can we serve Him and you?"

"Don't rightly know," replied White River, feeling awkward as he knew he would. "Might be we could talk some."

The other gestured toward the gate. "Come in then and rest. There will be something cool for you and the child to drink. Perhaps some toys for the little one. All are welcome here. Consider our mission your home."

"Be obliged er . . . er . . ."

"Arnold. Brother Arnold. Brother Clement is head of our order, he will be with us presently."

Seated in the shade of an inner courtyard, White River watched little Beaver play tentatively with a strangely proportioned rocking horse. Too much hay had been tied inside its head piece and it sat leaning forward like a pony that had been frozen in the first stage of its buck. Little Beaver soon lost interest. He was too used to the real thing.

Brother Clement turned out to be portly but not soft-looking. His voice had that distant ring of spiritual authority and his face a clean if not angelic cast to it. Mostly there was something frank and outgoing about him. White River felt himself relaxing a little. His instincts told him he had just encountered a sure enough man.

"God be with us," said Brother Clement, settling down. His eyes only once speedily took in White River's garb, then his gaze fixed itself permanently on his face. "In what way can we serve you and your fine little boy?"

"Not mine," said White River.

"Oh. Forgive me. A relative perhaps? A nephew?"

White River sensed the futility and now even stupidity of this growing lie. "No, just a little fella whose mummy and daddy got themselves kilt back yonder."

"Mercy," said Brother Clement, folding his hands before him. "However, we must always believe and trust that the Lord works in strange ways."

White River, far from understanding this remark, let it pass. Later he would have to study how Brother Clement, a gent who seemed slick about these things, could blame the Lord for what he felt was greed and stupidity.

It was clear now to Brother Clement why White River had come. He looked at little Beaver contemplatively. "It's always a difficult decision," he said as though he felt once again the responsibility that guiding other people's lives involved.

"He's a good little fella," urged White River, the words somehow gagging in his mouth. He could not quite look into little Beaver's big blue eyes following the conversation with that trepidation a child feels when it knows it is being seriously discussed by adults.

"We have a few women who help with the children," began Brother Clement, "but they are already sinfully overworked and there is, of course, the question of proper and adequate food."

White River watched him in silence for a moment. "Schoolin'?" he asked as though other matters mentioned could be dealt with.

"Oh, that's certainly no problem. Many, many of our brothers are highly educated and even experienced, having found God late in life. No, that is not our concern. I do not believe there is a school in these parts that compares with our mission's."

White River shifted his long body like one who is taking a new tack on things. "This young 'un has got some money," he said with just a touch of caution. "It rightly belongs to them who raises him."

Brother Clement seemed to come out of his deep thought. "Money?" he muttered as though he did not see how such a word made its way into the conversation.

"For a fact."

White River had noticed that neither brother had chosen to ask his name. Now Brother Clement seemed constrained to do so. "You must forgive me, sir, I've neglected to inquire as to your name. It is a common oversight here, we tend to think of all men as brothers."

"River . . . er . . . White River."

Brother Clement discreetly contained his uncertain reaction to this identity and drew some sheets of paper from a large pocket in his cloak. "And the child?"

White River took a deep breath. The moment he had worried and fretted about for weeks was suddenly upon him. "Ben," he uttered with unexpected effort, his voice seeming to have acquired a fringe of hoarseness.

Brother Clement began to write and speak at the same time. "Benjamin . . . yes?"

White River looked down into his cupped hands, still appearing to have trouble with his breathing. "Amiel—like his Pa, I reckon."

Brother Clement stopped and looked up as though he sensed the rising tension behind this strange manner of expressing a child's name. His brow knitted slightly but his voice remained soft as he asked, "You knew the father then?"

"Some. Hired out to him for a spell a while back."

Awkwardly and self-consciously he drew out the yellow sheet he had been carrying carefully in his breast pocket, unfolding its fraying parts and gently passing it over.

Brother Clement studied it for a moment, then said aloud but with markedly less confidence, "Amiel, Benjamin Amiel. Well . . ." He could not help but notice that the date on the document made it clearly older than the child. Somehow his instincts urged him to seek further explanations, but his faith assured him God would make His workings understandable to all in His service in His own good time. "Well, Mr. River, you mentioned some matter having to do with little Benjamin. Perhaps you will be good enough to help us with your point."

"Be obliged," said White River, unable to conceal his momentary relief. "This young 'un has money left by his folks when they went under. Reckon it belongs to them that rightly raises him."

"I see," uttered Brother Clement. It was clear he was trying to evaluate the full import of White River's words. "I do not mean to probe, Mr. River, but I find it unavoidable to ask how much money?"

"Don't for certain know."

"You don't?"

"No, it's in gold nuggets and sech, but I reckon it comes to a heap." White River took the heavy poke from his waist and laid it before the still puzzling Brother Clement.

There was a long moment of silence. Finally Brother Clement looked at the poke awkwardly and with only a summary inspection put it down. "I'm afraid I know very little about gold."

"Likewise."

"Then perhaps we shall need help." Brother Clement produced a small bell from somewhere and rang it, its tinkling sound carrying strangely into the air.

Within moments Brother Arnold was at his side.

"Have Pedro take the burro and seek Mr. Cobler," said Brother Clement in his still soft voice. "If he is busy we shall be patient, but let him know we less wordly souls have need of him."

Brother Arnold bowed and turned away.

Brother Clement now steepled his fingers and leaned toward White River and little Beaver. "Mr. Cobler is a just and uprighteous man. He does not seem very devout, but he is God's servant nonetheless. We have great faith in him."

"He a preacher?" inquired White River, already wary of the answer.

"No, Mr. River, a banker."

Mr. Cobler was nothing if not businesslike. Small and perched behind thin glasses, he examined the situation before him as any black-sleeved clerk might lick his pen and attack a ledger awash with overdue bills.

White River watched him in a state approaching amazement. He had never seen a more energetic or more knowledgeable machine. Cobler rustled some papers he had taken from his case. "Need some signatures, of course," he rattled away. "Now where are those scales?" An old-fashioned balance scale had been brought to him and after testing it with some silver dollars he apparently kept for just such a purpose he began to weigh the gold ore. He took a deep breath at the total, but his hands never stopped moving. He recorded the weight of the gold on the papers, signed them with a quick sweep of his hand and offered the pen to White River. Signing his name was one thing White River could do but he had to do it slowly and his embarrassment, which the brothers overlooked, and Cobler, with the skill of an experienced banker, merely kept his eyes down and his back noticeably stiff.

Brothers Clement and Arnold were asked to sign as witnesses, and after distributing copies as though they were napkins for a hurried meal, Mr. Cobler was on his way again. Without requesting help, he lugged the heavy pouch to his surrey and climbed in after it. "Back tomorrow," he said matter-of-factly and, tipping his hat perfunctorily, hurried off.

"A fine man," said Brother Clement in quiet admiration.

"Reckon," responded White River, slowly folding the paper he had been handed and which he was sure would be only the first of an endless line of papers that seemed to mount as you approached citified folks. It fitted his notion of civilization, though. Everything went on paper till a man had to read about what he was worth without ever having a chance to touch it.

White River spent the remainder of that day watching Beaver slowly mingling with the other children of the mission. They were all sizes and shadings but seemed remarkably quiet for children. Still Beaver clearly had little trouble making friends, for soon they were playing some kind of game and Beaver was running for a beanbag that had been thrown swiftly back and forth. The little boy seemed to be enjoying this chance to be with youngsters again in a youngster's world, yet every so often he would look up to catch White River watching and would hold on to his gaze, the wide eyes gravely questioning what these new surroundings really meant.

Finally he came over. "When we go home?" he asked in Absarokee, for like Chipmunk he was quickly mastering both languages.

White River knelt down and replied in English, "Maybe we'll just set here for a spell." He glanced over to where the children were still at their game. "Seems like there's a heap of funnin' for a little fella hereabouts."

Beaver turned to look back at the play area. He moved closer to White River, taking his hand. "Man calling me Ben," he whispered.

White River tried to laugh and look unaffected. "Oh, that's just a way these folks down here have of meanin' Beaver. Likely you'll hear it heaps of times."

Beaver looked at him and then, putting his head down, hugged him tightly. "You stay with Beaver," he murmured, his face hard against White River's shoulder.

White River was grateful the child could not see his face. "Sure enough . . . lessen, of course, I got me a mite of travelin' to do."

He could feel the boy's body stiffening.

"You go away?"

"Maybe jest for a spell—nothin' to take on about."

"Come back?"

"Reckon so."

"You bring Chipmunk?"

"Mebbe one of these days, but betcha every little fellow in camp would if he knew be jest a-rarin' to get on down here 'n play with all these new friends of yours."

Beaver pulled back, his eyes fixed again on White River's. "Tell Chipmunk Beaver have new name, Ben."

"Tell him first chance."

Beaver's eyes held to his for a moment longer. In them lay the faith that little children carry unaware of the burden such faith can place upon those that love them.

"Seven thousand dollars," said Cobler as though he were reading a railroad timetable, "possibly a few dollars more or less when certain smelting, legal, and assaying costs are dealt with. But the bank will accept the ore as collateral for that amount, barring of course your opting for another disposition."

At a time when a sizable spread, even with stock on it and within a day's ride from the mission, could be bought for under twenty-five hundred dollars, seven thousand dollars seemed a fortune.

Brother Clement looked reassuringly at White River before he replied, "I believe that will be quite satisfactory, Mr. Cobler. Mr. River, though, may want time to consider its final disposition."

"No trouble," said Cobler, grabbing his hat. "You'll find me at the bank as usual. Good morning to you gentlemen." Cobler was off.

It was the following day before White River, irritated and feeling low at his ignorance of such matters, hit upon a plan he decided made the most sense. He went to visit Cobler. Inside the iron-gated door of the bank a middle-aged woman, her eyes passing an open and uncharitable judgment on his attire, ushered him, in a businesslike manner, into a small office where he found Cobler's bespectacled face framed by two steeples of ledgers.

"Morning," said Cobler as he continued to fill out some forms spread before him.

"Mornin'," uttered White River, sitting in the only chair available and finding it predictably uncomfortable and ludicrously small for his body.

"Business?" said Cobler, continuing to write.

"Just a question or two, I reckon."

"Shoot. Should be finished with this in a moment."

White River haltingly outlined his predicament. He knew nothing about money matters, but he was concerned about little Ben and wanted to do right by the mission. He cautiously tested his opinion of Brother Clement on the diminutive banker. "Seems a fine gent, that Brother Clement, 'pears to be dependable and sech."

"Right as rain," Cobler shot back. "Don't make them any better." Uncharacteristically, he sat back. "Don't hold much to religion myself, for a fact, always figured hard work was the best way to serve the Lord. Had a brother-in-law back a ways, used to be a whiskey drummer out of St. Louis. After the law fried his oysters he got religion and set up a miserable stir, rocking the county with his moaning and groaning and plenty of 'Come to Jesus' kind of talk. Even got folks to giving him money to fight sin, though I always figured the money was going to the enemy. Got himself shot up and killed in a whorehouse a while back. Never saw an account so neatly balanced."

White River smiled. One couldn't help liking this little bespectacled man and trusting him too. "As likely you know I'd be beholdin' to you for any advice, Mr. Cobler."

"Advice is the best bargain we got to offer today."

"It's about the boy. . . ." White River seemed to run out of words.

"Correct. I imagined as much. Mr. River, split the money in half, less of course what you're likely to need for yourself. The mission will be more than happy with close to four thousand dollars. It will lift the mortgage on them new buildings and property and fetch them fifty acres of tillable river bottom land to boot. Hard cash goes a long way out here. As to the boy, I'll put his share into a trust, manage it myself, by the time he's ready to go east for some first-class schooling he'll likely own half the county."

White River looked at him with a new curiosity that almost eclipsed his sudden expression of relief. "East?" he said as though the word were new to him.

"Of course," continued Cobler as though the matter was pointless to discuss. "Oh, over to the mission they'll teach him reading, writing, arithmetic, and plenty of Bible, which they wisely get in before the kids get a whiff of history. But for real education he's got to go east. I did." He tapped his head puckishly. "It's given me a sizable edge over these muscle-headed farmers. I've enjoyed the hell out of it ever since I set up in this bank. Intend to go on enjoying it."

So it was decided. Brother Clement gave the arrangement his blessing, mentioning with evident satisfaction how the Lord took care of those who with faith and charity labored to do His bidding.

Cobler, having seen the yellow paper, insisted White River take the two hundred dollars owed him and two hundred more for what he called his "guardianship." White River, listening, looked perplexed.

Cobler rambled on. "Best thing to do with it, friend, is put it into land. Man can't hardly go wrong owning space folks need to live on."

White River looked at the gold coins that almost covered the palm of his hand. It was clear he was undecided whether or not to take them. "Makes it kind of legal," continued Cobler, straightening out a mess of papers Brother Clement had been instructed to sign. He moved over to White River and closed his fingers over the coins. "You earned them right and proper, friend. See you spend them that way."

"You say land," White River finally muttered.

"Right. And steer clear of those rascally speculators, they'd sell creek bottoms to blind orphans."

White River looked at him long and hard. It was clear his mind was grappling with a thought. "Wonder could I ask you a favor, Mr. Cobler?"

"Be my pleasure, Mr. River."

"Used to be a spread of land outside of Laramie, fellow name of Buzz Matlock owned it. Know it's been deserted for a spell but figure I'd like to buy it if some folks ain't already claimed it."

Cobler stroked his chin studiously. "Well now, we could sure enough run a search. Luckily there's a land office right here in Independence, keeps records on most transactions in this territory. Fellow name of O'Shaughnessy runs it. Wouldn't think he could run an empty stable to see him after his noon jug, but he knows that Laramie country pretty well, claims he's thrown his best drunks in that sutler's hole outside the fort. Might possibly have some information for you by tomorrow. If so I'll send it out."

"Be obliged."

"No trouble," said Cobler, taking his hat. "Well, it's been real pleasant, Mr. River. Just remember banks charge interest for money but advice is always free. Probably explains why nobody wants it." They shook.

Then Cobler was gone. White River watched his little surrey bump its way down the road, knowing he would never see him again but that one day little Beaver would discover that he had over him the hand of a kindly and conscientious man.

The following day the sun lay in an autumnal haze upon the courtyard as Brother Clement's soft brown eyes rose from the papers he had been diligently studying and resolutely signing for almost half an hour. White River's eyes met his and both knew the final moments had come. Clement's voice was made almost husky by the sentiments he was sure his remaining remarks would be stirring in the other. He had not missed some of the scenes passing between White River and little Benjamin and sensed their meaning. "Circumstances in the wilderness must surely have made baptism difficult," he said, his voice consciously held even, "so we will presently baptize Benjamin and provide him with proper papers."

"Obliged," murmured White River.

Brother Clement, his voice now struggling with some rising inner emotion, continued. "In the eyes of our Savior, Mr. River, your apparent love for this boy makes you in some way his father, just as He who loves us all is Father to us all."

"Reckon," White River half whispered.

Brother Clement folded his hands before him. "In this life we must all carry our cross, endure the trials set upon us and do right as He has given us the power to see right."

White River tried to answer, but a choking sensation stopped him.

Brother Clement's voice remained steady but it was now lined with compassion. "Would you care to see little Benjamin again?"

White River looked down at a few stray leaves that had fallen early, their dusty yellow seeming to hint at the coming change of season. "Best not," he finally murmured, "best he jest gets to figurin' I'll be along again someday."

Brother Clement bent his head in acquiescence. He could not bring himself to look into White River's eyes. "The Lord is our Shepherd. We shall find our everlasting comfort in Him who takes from us our burdens so that we may rest."

For a long moment they sat together in silence, the day seeming to take on a peculiar hue. Somehow there seemed more amber in the sunlight upon the courtyard, more stillness in the leaves above, and a rising sense in both of them that this shining and tragic moment could never be erased from time.

He was over a quarter of a mile from the mission when something impelled him to look back. In the distance he could see a tiny figure standing against the white adobe wall. He stared at it for a moment, then raised his arm in a gesture that only carried the whisper of a farewell. He wasn't really sure, for rising moisture was distorting his sight, but somehow he knew the tiny figure beyond had raised an arm in return. When he moved on he found his cheeks were damp and growing even damper with tears. Surprised at how long it was before they stopped, he wiped them away with a strange awareness that there were times when maybe a fellow had to cry for two.

Riding slowly, he circled the town, keeping his mind on little things to hold out the big ones, passing broad earth-scented areas of freshly cleared and plowed ground, studded in the distance with tiny wood-framed shacks, some with pale feathers of smoke bending over them that disappeared into the wind. When they finally ran out he hit heavy stands of tall hardwood trees, their leafy crowns throwing cool peninsulas of shade across the heated land.

That evening he made camp beside the river, hearing for the first time, as he lowered gear from his mount, a rustle of paper in his shirt pocket. It was a moment before he remembered Brother Arnold handing him a note when he arrived at the mission. It was a message from Cobler, which the brother's hushed blessing hinted was likely bad news.

He waited till he had warmed and eaten a little grub before he built up the fire and took out the banker's neatly penned sheet, reading it slowly, but suddenly holding his breath as he did.

> Dear Mr. River,
>
> Regret to inform you land you inquired about already claimed. O'Shaughnessy reports young lady from Oregon showed up last year, took title and has built a small pine shack on Matlock's old spread. No reason given but doesn't believe she'll sell. Also reports officers from the fort trying to court her say the place now looks much the way it did years ago when Matlock was alive. New owner appears to be quite a young lady. O'Shaughnessy claims if she stuck a foreign flag over her shack half the garrison would desert. Maybe there's more to all this than an old banker can figure out. Advise you to make further inquiries on your own. Ask for Lydia.
>
> Yours truly,
> J. P. Cobler

He read the trembling note several times before he could shift his eyes from it and glance into the fire. She was back. She was there, knowing sooner or later he'd return, knowing the little ranch and its memories would call him back. Oregon? The remote poorly mapped end of the northern trail! He would never have found her. She had to come back to where she knew he would look. He lay there staring into the dying flames for an hour, listening to the river murmur as it swept by in the darkness, the dancing firelight bringing to his mood the quality of a dream. But he was slowly embracing the reality that Lydia—his Lydia—had raised a new pine shack where Buzz's old one had stood. It was a message she knew would be carried over the trailways telling him she was home. The young sylphlike girl of his dreams was suddenly a flesh-and-blood woman with the courage and beauty to make her way from Oregon to a lonely and deserted piece of ground and there stir the emotions of a fortress full of men. That nagging fear he had carried over the years that life might be cruel to her, that others would not appear to love and protect her as did he and Buzz, was wrong. His instincts told him whatever trials she had endured, and surely there were some, Lydia had come forth from these years smiling and unafraid.

He settled back and gazed up at the stars, suddenly aware other thoughts were waiting to claim his mind. Dreams could become realities but they could not hold their place in time. Great and fateful happenings had swept the earth in the years they had been apart; great changes had come over that mighty stretch of country that lay beyond the night murmurings of the river, beyond the guardian bluffs and the endlessly rising grassy plains, that raw and lordly land that ran to high white mountain peaks, looming like massive sentinels against the sky. Nor would this awesome land change alone. Its great tribes with their braves singing and stark primitive colorings were fading; the medicine spirits that spoke to their hearts were slipping away, vanishing like the lonely throb of their hide drums upon the wind. Mighty warriors that had smiled and scoffed at death were asleep in their beloved hunting grounds, their burnished bodies turning to dust, their spirits on that long journey beyond the stars.

And what of him? Had these years with their strange happenings wrought in him a different and perhaps deeper man? Of all those who awoke one morning in what now seemed another age to gaze upon the dark lonely hump of Innyan Kara, he alone remained. Amiel, Marcher, Ironfoot had gone back to the earth, those they loved, White Bead and Blue Lodge, joining them, time already erasing all but his memory of them. Was there some reason why they had come together? Was it part of a plan as inscrutable as the reason for life itself? After long moments, his eyes set hard upon the stars, he knew in his heart there was. Big Owl said all things in life had meaning, but like the beauty of a morning such meanings were grasped by the heart alone.

As he lay there, sleep slowly claiming him, his mind began to drift away and with his last drowsy glimpse of the heavens he caught a meteorite streaking brightly in its long arc to the east. In a second it was gone, but in his mind as he surrendered to sleep it glowed on, a tiny spark in the cavernous bowl of night. Then it was not just a spark but a distant flame, a flame that grew as it came toward him, becoming as it did a consuming fire whose halo of light drove back the darkness. And now he could see there were figures around it, many figures, and they were moving, dancing, the chant of their voices acting as a drum to the rhythm of their feet. The conflagration drew closer and now he could see their faces, faces from out of the past, Ironfoot and Snow Runner and Crows long since lost in battle; and as the light spread he could see that beyond them danced the Sioux with rattles in the air, the Cheyennes in their buffalo headpieces, the Blackfeet, the Shoshones, and suddenly he made out the figures of White Buffalo Horse and Red Legs, those long dead Pawnees, all dancing together. And suddenly he could see White Bead as she led Marcher out to the fire, their bodies taking up and joining the rhythm of the dance. To the side, bathed in the golden light of the flames, Ben Amiel's face was looking on, his body swaying gently as the rhythm claimed it too. And there before him danced those who had made up the mosaic of that strange life, dancing in a world now vanishing, dancing still in the memories they and their days had left him. But then as suddenly as it had come the great glowing canvas began to disappear, the light that had been the fire began to recede, drifting further and further away till it became no more than a speck of light that hung beyond him as he slowly opened his eyes. It was just before dawn and as he raised his head he could see the speck of light still glowing in the distance. It was the morning star.